Louis the
Well-B...

Jean Plaidy, one of the pre-eminent authors of historical fiction for most of the twentieth century, is the pen name of the prolific English author Eleanor Hibbert, also known as Victoria Holt. Jean Plaidy's novels had sold more than 14 million copies worldwide by the time of her death in 1993.

For further information about Arrow's Jean Plaidy reissues and mailing list, please visit
www.randomhouse.co.uk/minisites/jeanplaidy

Praise for Jean Plaidy

'A vivid impression of life at the Tudor Court'
Daily Telegraph

'One of the country's most widely read novelists'
Sunday Times

'Plaidy excels at blending history with romance and drama'
New York Times

'It is hard to better Jean Plaidy . . . both elegant and exciting'
Daily Mirror

'Jean Plaidy conveys the texture of various patches of the past with such rich complexity'
Guardian

Louis the Well-Beloved

JEAN PLAIDY

arrow books

Published by Arrow Books in 2007

1 3 5 7 9 10 8 6 4 2

First published in the United Kingdom in 1959 by Robert Hale and Company
Published in paperback in 1972 by Pan Books Ltd

Arrow Books
The Random House Group Limited
20 Vauxhall Bridge Road, London SW1V 2SA

www.rbooks.co.uk

Addresses for companies within The Random House Group Limited can be found at:
www.randomhouse.co.uk/offices.htm

The Random House Group Limited Reg. No. 954009

A CIP catalogue record for this book is available from the British Library

ISBN 9780099493365

The Random House Group Limited makes every effort to ensure that the papers
used in its books are made from trees that have been legally sourced from well-managed
and credibly certified forests. Our paper procurement policy can be found at:
www.randomhouse.co.uk/paper.htm

Typeset by SX Composing DTP, Rayleigh, Essex
Printed and bound in Great Britain by
CPI Cox & Wyman Ltd, Reading, RG1 8EX

❖ Contents ❖

⚜ Chapter I ⚜

THE OLD KING

The woman at the window was staring along the Avenue de Paris; she could survey the Grande Écurie and the Petite Écurie; and there was much coming and going. She was trembling, and anxious that the child should not notice her agitation.

But he was pulling at her skirt. 'Maman Ventadour, you are looking out there and not at me.'

She turned from the window and as she glanced at him her expression grew soft, as it always did for this beautiful and beloved child.

'Watch,' he commanded.

As the Duchesse de Ventadour nodded to imply that he had her attention, he put his hands on the carpet and his feet swung into the air. His face, upside-down, scarlet with the exertion, laughed at her, demanding her approbation.

'That, my darling,' she said, 'was very good. But you have shown me how clever you are. Let that suffice.'

He was on his feet, his head on one side, his thick auburn hair falling about his animated face. 'I would like to show you again, *Maman*,' he said.

I

'No more now, my dearest.'

'But just once more, *Maman*.'

'Just once,' she agreed.

She watched him turn his somersault, while he shrieked with delight as he bounded to his feet once more; and she smiled saying to herself: Who would harm him? Who could be anything but moved by his charm and his beauty?

He was contented now; he came to stand by her knee and leaned his head against her breast while she let her fingers caress those masses of auburn hair.

She was unable to resist the impulse to hold him tightly against her for she feared that, with one of those sudden movements of his, he might look quickly into her face and sense her apprehension.

'You're hurting me, *Maman*,' he said; but she did not hear him, for she was recalling how she had saved his life three years before, when she had entered the sickroom where the doctor, Fagon, had she not interfered, would have carried out his drastic 'cures' on this precious body as he had on the boy's mother, father and brother.

'I shall nurse the child,' she had said then, fiercely determined: 'I . . . and I alone.'

There had been no protest, which was strange, for Madame de Maintenon believed Fagon to be the foremost doctor in France. But perhaps three deaths in one year had shaken even her faith. Perhaps there had been something so fiercely maternal about the Duchesse de Ventadour that it had been deemed wise to try her nursing in place of Fagon's disastrous treatment.

So out of the sickroom – the two-year-old child in her arms, wrapped in blankets which she had brought with her – had marched Madame de Ventadour; and night and day she had nursed the sick child, brought him out of danger and cared for him since, so that he would allow no other to look after him, to be his governess and companion, to take the place of the mother who had died six days before his father.

Now he wriggled out of her arms and two dimpled hands were placed on her lap while he stared up at her.

'Great-grandfather is going away,' he told her.

She caught her breath but said nothing.

'He will not be King then,' he went on. 'There must be a King of France. Do you know who, *Maman*?'

She put her hand to her breast; he was so observant that he might notice how her fluttering heart disturbed her corsage.

He had sprung back; he was standing on his hands, his legs waving in the air, his face flushed and impish.

'I'll tell you, *Maman*,' he said. 'When my great-grandfather goes away, I shall be King of France.'

⚜ ⚜ ⚜

In the great state bedroom Le Roi Soleil lay dying, as he had lived, with the utmost dignity. He lay back in the great bed which was as high as the cornice, and the corners of which were decorated with ostrich feathers. The hangings were of damask – gold and silver – because it was late August and the heavier ones of crimson velvet had not yet replaced them.

He had in life strictly observed the stern Etiquette of Versailles, and it was characteristic that he should continue to observe it with death close at hand. The calmest person in the death chamber was Louis Quatorze.

He had made his confession; he had received Extreme Unction, a ceremony which had taken place under the eyes of

3

those of his subjects who had come to the palace to see him die, as in the past they had come to watch him dance in the state apartments and walk in the exquisite gardens about the château. He accepted them now as always. He was their King and, while he demanded complete obedience from them, he would not shirk what he believed to be his duty towards his subjects.

He had sent away Madame de Maintenon, his children's governess whom he had secretly married thirty years before. She had wept so sorrowfully and he could not bear to see her tears.

'You are grieved to see that there is little time left to me,' he had said to her. 'You must not grieve for I am an old man and have lived long enough. Did you think that I was immortal? I have made my confession. I put my trust in God's mercy. I could wish, now that I have come to my death-bed, that I had lived a saintly life.'

She had nodded; she had ever been ready to remind him of his sins; and when she had left him it was easier for him to forget them.

The pain in his leg was at times so acute that he could think of nothing else. The herb baths and the asses' milk had failed to cure that leg, and it was no use their trying to hide from him the fact that gangrene had set in; he himself had suggested amputation but it was too late. He was living through his last hours.

It was all over; the long reign had come to an end. For seventy-two years he had been King of France – he had grown from the petted to the adored; and perhaps because he had never during the whole of his life completely forgotten the humiliation his family had suffered when he was a child during the war of the Fronde, he had acquired that supreme dignity, that determination that he alone should be the head of his state. *'L'état, c'est moi!'* he had said; and that was never forgotten.

When one was nearing the end, one remembered incidents which at the time they had happened seemed insignificant but which were, when recalled, seen to be revealing. There had been an occasion when he had paid a call on Condé at Chantilly and the fish ordered for the banquet had failed to arrive. The cook, so overcome by what must have seemed to him a major tragedy – the god-like King having to sit down to a banquet which was not quite perfect – had committed suicide, being unable to face the shame.

And at the time, thought Louis, it had not seemed incongruous.

He looked back now and saw himself passing majestically through life. The ceremonies of the Court in which he played the central part were performed as though his person were sacred; and indeed he had come to think it was so. He had stood at the head of the state; and unlike other Kings of France he had never allowed his mistresses to take a hand in the government of the kingdom. *He* was the state – *he* and he alone.

Here in this bed, which he knew he would never leave, he had time to look back over his life and to some extent assess his actions. There had always been those to tell him that he was a god and he had no wish to contradict this. But gods did not lie a-bed with an evil limb which was destroying them. He was mortal; he was full of human weaknesses; and because there had never been any to point these out to him he had never sought to suppress them.

He knew that every day in France there were people who died of starvation, and that it was he who had wasted the substance of France on wars. Ah, but had that not been for the glory of France, for the enrichment of his people? No, for the glory of Louis, for the enrichment of Louis! War had excited him. He had had dreams of a French colonial Empire, the greatest in the world. And all over the country there were examples of his love of ostentation.

There was this château itself, Versailles, which he had determined should be the most splendid in the world; and it was by no accident that symbolism had crept into the decorations. Le Vau's columns had been intended to represent the months of the year; the masks on the keystones over the ground-floor windows showed the progress of man through life, for Versailles was meant to represent a solar system which revolved about one great sun – and that sun was Le Roi Soleil.

And because of this passion for building great châteaux, because of his determination to go to war, many of his people had suffered.

If I could begin again, thought the dying King, I would act differently. I would make the people my first consideration and they would love me now as they loved me in the days when they first proclaimed me – a four-year-old boy – their King.

Four years old! he ruminated. It was too young to become the King of France.

And now in a nursery close to this room there was another little boy who in a day or so – perhaps two, but no more – would wear the crown of France.

Contemplating the accession of Louis XV, Louis XIV became so alarmed for the future that he forgot to regret the past.

He lifted his hand and immediately a man of about forty came to his bedside.

6

'Your wishes, Sire?' he asked.

Louis looked searchingly into the face of his nephew, Philippe, Duc d'Orléans, who reminded the King so strongly of his own brother, the mincing, often vicious Monsieur, who had always been dissatisfied with a fate which had brought him into the world two years after Louis.

Orléans had a somewhat evil reputation. His affairs with women − for in this respect he was unlike his father − were notorious; he was ambitious in the extreme; he scorned religion and took volumes of Rabelais into church to read during Mass; it was said that he was interested in black magic, had a vast knowledge of poisons (he had been suspected of having poisoned the little Dauphin's parents, the Duc and Duchesse de Bourgogne); he drank to excess. Yet Louis knew that he was not as evil as rumour made him out to be, and that he even found a certain pleasure in his notoriety and sought to exaggerate it. Perhaps he wished to inspire fear in those about him.

He was good-natured and kind-hearted; he was clever; he was fully aware of the dangers which could befall a country without a leader; and he had a strong family feeling. His love for his mother bore witness to that. He would be kind and tender to the Dauphin. Louis knew the rumour that he had poisoned the little boy's parents was false. He was a strong man, and a country governed by a Regency had need of strong men.

'Nephew,' said the King, 'have the child brought to me. I would speak to him before I die.'

Orléans bowed. He called to one of his men who were stationed at the door of the bedchamber: 'His Majesty asks for the Dauphin. Have him brought here at once.'

✤ ✤ ✤

Little Louis, his hand in that of Madame de Ventadour, allowed himself to be led to the King's bedchamber. He was momentarily aware of the solemnity of the occasion, for all visits to his great-grandfather were solemn. He was not sure that he wanted to go; he would have preferred to call to one of the younger pages and play turning somersaults or hopscotch with him.

That one, thought Louis, smiling at a boy as he passed. The boy bowed low but Madame de Ventadour was pulling the Dauphin onwards.

Louis' attention was inconsequently directed to the frieze of boys at play which the King had had designed for the apartment. The sculptures seemed real to him.

'*Maman*,' he said, 'I will climb the walls and play with them.'

But Madame de Ventadour was not listening, and one look at her tightly compressed lips reminded him that he was going to visit his great-grandfather; but only momentarily, for his attention was quickly caught by the *œil-de-bœuf* window which gave the name to this chamber and, snatching his hand from that of Madame de Ventadour, he ran to it.

But she was quickly beside him. 'Not now, my darling,' she said. 'We have had a summons from the King, and when the King commands all must obey him.'

Louis stood still, his brows drawn together, a question on his lips; but he did not ask it, for he knew that if he did Madame de Ventadour would not answer; she was not thinking of him; she was thinking of the great state bedroom beyond this *œil-de-bœuf* to which he and she had been commanded to go, and which they were about to enter.

8

The silence in that room alarmed the child; he was aware that all there were conscious of him. He saw weeping men and women and his great-grandfather propped up in the magnificent bed. A priest was praying at the balustrade which was some few feet from the bed, and the purpose of which was to prevent people from coming too near. But what was most apparent to the child was a sickly smell which was new to him and which filled him with repulsion.

Madame de Ventadour had taken him to edge of the bed. There she fell on her knees, not relinquishing her grip upon him. Little Louis watched his great-grandfather's trembling hand stretch out to touch the governess' shoulder.

'I thank you, Madame,' said the King. 'Set the Dauphin in that armchair that I may look at him.'

She obeyed. Little Louis' attention strayed momentarily from the bed to the armchair which was vast and seemed as though it would swallow him; his legs stuck straight out and he looked at his own feet as though they belonged to a stranger; but then he was conscious of that sickly smell of death which reminded him that this was an occasion different from all others.

He did not want to be here. He looked for the informality of his own apartments, or the fascination of the *œil-de-bœuf*; he wanted to wander in the gardens, mischievously hiding from Madame de Ventadour. He thought of letting his fingers dabble in the cool waters of the fountains; playing in the Grotte de Thétis or the Orangerie. He hunched his shoulders, forgetting again the odour of this apartment, overlaid with a tension which was recognizable even to his childish mind.

But his great-grandfather was speaking to him, and everyone was listening and looked solemn as they stared at the boy.

9

'My dearest child,' his great-grandfather began, and Louis gave him that disarming smile which Madame de Ventadour thought the most charming in the world. 'Very soon now you will be a King.'

The Dauphin continued to smile. He would have a crown. Could he turn somersaults in a crown? He longed to try.

'The greatest King in the world,' went on Great-grandfather, 'and you must never forget your duty to God. I hope you will not do as I have done. Avoid wars, my dear child. Remain at peace with your neighbours. There is happiness in peace. Serve the people. Work hard to lighten their sufferings. Listen to the advice of good counsellors . . .'

Little Louis was watching his great-grandfather's mouth; he continued to smile. But his attention quickly wandered to the picture of David playing the harp, which hung on one side of the bed and of John the Baptist on the other. He knew who they were, because Madame de Ventadour had once told him. Could he play the harp? He was going to be a King . . . the greatest King in the world, so he would play the harp if he wished to. He wondered if John the Baptist could turn somersaults.

'I wish to thank you, Madame,' the King was saying, 'for the care you have bestowed on this child. Continue to do so, I beg of you.'

Madame de Ventadour answered, in a voice high with emotion, that it would be her greatest joy to obey the command of His Majesty.

'My child,' said the King, 'you must love Madame de Ventadour. You must never forget what she has done for you.'

He had caught the boy's attention with those words. This was something he could understand. He began to wriggle out of the chair; he was going to take Madame de Ventadour by the hand and drag her away. He was tired of this room; he did not like it any more. Neither David nor John the Baptist had any charm for him.

'Madame,' said the King, 'bring the child close to me. My eyes are failing and I cannot see him clearly.'

As Madame de Ventadour lifted him in her arms, he whispered: 'No.' But Madame de Ventadour took no heed; he was seated on the bed and was so close to the old man that he could see the deep lines on his face and the sweat on his brow. The lines were like furrows in the fields. Louis imagined that he was running along them across those fields, away . . . far away from Versailles and the death-bed of his great-grandfather.

The old hands had seized the child; he was caught in a close embrace — an embrace with death, it seemed to him. He was suffocating; the old face, the all-pervading odour, nauseated him; he wanted to cry out to be rescued, but he was afraid. He held his breath. Maman Ventadour had said that all bad things were quickly over. Like taking medicine. Be a good boy; take it and there was a sweetmeat to remove the taste.

'Lord,' said the King, 'I offer Thee this child. I pray Thee to give him grace. May he honour Thee as a true Christian King and a King of France.'

'I cannot breathe,' said the Dauphin under his breath. 'I do not like you, Great-grandfather; you are too hot and your hands burn me.'

The worst was yet to come. The old lips were on the young ones. This was a bad thing which could not be endured.

Loud sobs broke from the Dauphin. '*Maman . . . Maman . . .*' he cried.

Madame de Ventadour had come to stand by the bed, ready to face the majesty of Kings, the dignity of death, for the sake of her beloved child.

As she lifted him he turned to her eagerly, his arms were tight about her neck, his face buried against her – dear, sweet-smelling *Maman,* the safe refuge in a frightening world.

Her eyes pleaded with the King.

'Madame,' said the dying Louis, 'you should take the Dauphin to his own apartments.'

As calmly the King sat in his bed, there was no one in the château who did not marvel at the manner in which he prepared himself to die.

Deeply repentant of past misdeeds he was eager to leave his state in proper order; he had realised that, although in the first half of his reign he had made his country great and had brought a prosperous era to France, the country was now steeped in debt, the population decreased and poverty widespread. These were the results of war and he had learned too late that wars brought more disaster than glory. Taxes were higher and new ones, such as the *capitation,* had been imposed. When he had ridden about the country and admired the magnificent buildings he should have seen them, not only as monuments to art and the good taste of the King, but as the outward sign of a great extravagance which his long-suffering people could not afford.

Too late he saw his mistakes, but he would do his best to rectify them now. France needed a King as strong as he had been in the days of his prime, and what had France? A little boy of five.

What calamity had befallen this country! His son, the Grand

Dauphin, had died of smallpox. The Grand Dauphin's son, the Duc de Bourgogne, had died – six days after his wife had fatally fallen victim to the purple measles – of a broken heart, it was said; for the devotion of the Duc to his Duchesse was known throughout the country. Their eldest son, the five-year-old Duc de Bretagne, had died in the same year, leaving his younger brother to be Dauphin of France. It was as though some evil curse was at work to rob France of her rulers.

A little boy of five to be the King of France! When he thought of that he knew there was no time for remorse; he must act quickly. Yet he could do no more than advise his ministers, for although his word had been law during his lifetime, who could say that it would remain so after his death?

He put aside the dispatch boxes and summoned the most important men in France to his bedside.

He surveyed them in silence, his thoughts resting on those two with whom he intended to entrust the most important tasks of the Kingdom: the Duc d'Orléans and the Duc du Maine. Orléans was shrewd; he was, until little Louis came of age, at the head of the royal family; he should be Regent. Du Maine, the King's son by Madame de Montespan, had been legitimised; he was an admirable man, religious, living a virtuous life; he would be the man to take charge of the new King's education.

The eyes of the old King were growing dim now, but he raised himself slightly and spoke to those about his bed; 'My friends, I am well content with your services to me, and I regret I have not rewarded you as you deserve. I pray you, serve the Dauphin as you have served me. Remember, he is young yet – but five years old. I vividly recall all the trials that beset my childhood when I, almost at the same age, inherited the throne of France. Let there be harmony between you all; therein rests the security of the State. I appoint my nephew, the Duc d'Orléans, Regent of France. I pray that he will govern well and that you will obey him and sometimes think of me.'

Many of those who stood about the bed were weeping.

'I cannot live many more hours,' went on Louis. 'I feel death close to me. Nephew, I appoint you Regent. And you, du Maine, my son, I ask you to care for the education of this child. I would beg you to remember that he is young yet – oh so young; and I would have him continue in the life he has so far led with his governess, to whom, as we have seen, he is so deeply attached, until he is seven years old. Then he must be taken from Madame de Ventadour and learn to become a King. Gentlemen, I bid you farewell. You see one King close to the grave and another scarcely out of the cradle. Do your duty to your country. Long live France!'

There was nothing more that he could do. The night was at hand and he was not sure that he would see another day. He sent for his priests, and all night they remained by his bedside.

He prayed with them. He was ready to leave. 'Oh, God,' he murmured, 'make haste to help me.'

When the dawn light penetrated that gilded chamber on the morning of the 1st of September, those about the bed heard the rattling in his throat. The glances they exchanged were significant. 'An hour . . . perhaps two . . .' they whispered.

They were right. At a quarter past eight that morning Louis XIV relinquished the splendour of Versailles which he had created and handed it down to his heirs.

The Grand Chamberlain was summoned to the bed-chamber. He knew for what purpose.

Very soon he stepped on to the balcony, and the crowds

below, who had gathered in expectation of this event, gasped as they saw the black plume in his hat.

'*Le Roi est mort!*' he cried.

Then he stepped back and appeared again, this time wearing a hat with a white plume. '*Vive le Roi!*' he cried.

Young Louis had been taken to the Galerie des Glaces by Madame de Ventadour. The Galerie completely absorbed him. It seemed to him of enormous proportions, a world in itself. He stood still to stare at the allegorical figures which decorated the ceiling and imagined himself up there among them; it was fascinating to see himself reflected in the mirrors with that fairytale background of silver flower-tubs and tables and enormous chandeliers.

He felt happy to be there because he had seen so many people from the window of his apartments that day. They were all watching the château, and they had seemed to him unbearably ugly. Here in the great Galerie he was alone with Madame de Ventadour, and everything he could see (for miles and miles, he told himself), was bright and beautiful. He felt a great desire to run from one length of the Galerie to the other, and was about to do so when he felt his governess' restraining hand on his shoulder, and was aware that several people were coming towards him.

At their head was his uncle Orléans; Louis liked his uncle, who was always ready for a joke and excited him because he was supposed to be very wicked. There were also the Duc du Maine and the Comte de Toulouse, the Duc de Bourbon and the Duc de Villeroi. This was indeed an important occasion.

As always Louis turned to *Maman* Ventadour to see what

her reaction was to this intrusion. She was standing very still, almost at attention like a soldier and, as her eyes met his, Louis knew she was very anxious that he should behave in such a way that she would be proud of him. And because he loved her so much and always wanted to please her, provided it was not too difficult, he also stood still, waiting.

His uncle of Orléans came to him first and, instead of lifting him high and placing him on his shoulder as he usually did, he knelt and taking the boy's hand kissed it.

'As the first of your subjects, Sire,' he said, 'I come to offer my homage and my services to Your Majesty.'

Louis understood. His great-grandfather had gone away, as he had heard it whispered that he would, and he himself was King. His fluttering thoughts were halted; he did not attempt to seize his uncle's sword or to pull at the gold tassels of his coat; he was absorbed by one thought only: He was the King. From now on he would be called 'Sire' and 'Your Majesty'; men would bow before him and he would one day sleep in the great state bed.

Thus, as one by one these men came and knelt before him and swore their allegiance, he stood erect, his eyes shining, so that those who saw him asked themselves: Is it possible that one so young can understand so much? And Madame de Ventadour stood by, her pride in her loved one apparent.

In the next few days young Louis discovered that there were disadvantages in being a King. He wanted to say: 'That's enough. No more kings!' as he did when playing. It was disconcerting to discover that this was not a game but would go on all his life.

He must attend certain solemn occasions, be still for long at a time and say what he was told to say. It could be wearying.

Madame de Ventadour was dressing him in new clothes which he did not like. They were black and violet, and he must wear a hideous black *crêpe* cap.

'I do not like them, *Maman*,' he protested.

'But just once we will wear them.'

'But I do not want to wear them even once.'

'You must be obedient, my darling.'

'Am I not the King, *Maman*? Must Kings wear ugly clothes? Great-grandfather did not.'

'He would have done so if the people had expected him to. Kings must do what the people expect them to.'

'Then what is the good of being King?' demanded Louis.

'That you will discover,' answered Madame de Ventadour beguilingly. And he was silent, eager to make that discovery.

But the waiting was so long and tedious. He was to go to Paris and there attend a *lit de justice* at which the Duc d'Orléans would be formally proclaimed Regent.

It was an exciting moment when he was taken into the Grande Chambre. There were crowds of people everywhere, it seemed, and as he entered all stood up and took off their hats. He looked at them with shy curiosity, and someone cried *'Vive le Roi!'* That meant himself, and he would have run towards the man who had shouted that, had he not felt a restraining hand upon him. Madame de Ventadour was close beside him. He would go nowhere without her, he had declared, and although she shook her head and said he would have to grow up quickly and learn to be without her, he knew she was pleased; so it was safe to insist; he would stamp his foot if necessary and tell them all . . . every one of them . . . that he would go nowhere without his dear *Maman*.

He was lifted in a pair of strong arms which he knew belonged to the Duc de Tresmes who was the Grand Chamberlain. All was well, though, because *Maman* walked very close to the side of the Duc.

At one end of the Grande Chambre was a throne, and on this had been placed a velvet cushion. The Duc de Tresmes set Louis on the cushion, and Madame de Ventadour said in loud ringing tones: '*Messieurs*, the King has called you here to make his wishes known. His Chamberlain will explain them to you.'

Louis looked intently at his governess. His wishes? He wondered what they were. Was it a surprise? Something he had told her he had wanted . . . as he did on fête days?

But he could not understand what they were talking about and he was so tired of sitting on the velvet cushion, so he tried to catch his governess' eye. 'Let us go now,' he wanted to whisper. But when he was about to speak she looked away quickly and he was afraid to shout.

He stared at the blue velvet with the golden lilies embroidered on it. Then he noticed the wonderful red hat which was worn by the Archbishop of Paris. He had never before seen such a hat. He knew now what he wanted. He wanted that red hat because he hated his own black *crêpe* cap so much. He was the King and he could have what he wanted, for what was the use of being King if he could not?

The Archbishop knelt at his feet and the hat was very near. Louis' little hands darted out to seize it; and he would have had it had not the ever watchful Madame de Ventadour restrained him in time.

'I want the red hat,' he whispered urgently.

'Hush, my darling.'

Monsieur de Villeroi bent over him. 'Sire, it is necessary that you attend to what is being said,' he murmured.

'I want the red hat,' whispered Louis.

Monsieur de Villeroi looked helpless and there was a faint ripple of laughter among those who stood near the throne.

'You cannot have the red hat . . . now,' said Madame de Ventadour out of the corner of her mouth.

Louis was amused; 'I am the King,' he said out of the corner of his.

'You must attend,' hissed Monsieur de Villeroi, looking very fierce.

Louis scowled at him. Under his breath he said: 'You go away.'

Immediately he was tired and feeling fretful, but he kept his eyes on the Archbishop's hat.

He was asked if he approved of the ceremony which had just taken place appointing the Duc d'Orléans Regent of the Kingdom. Louis stared blankly at the Duc de Villeroi.

'Say yes,' he was told.

He put his lips tightly together and continued to stare at Monsieur de Villeroi, who looked helplessly at Madame de Ventadour.

'Say yes,' she urged. 'Say it loudly; shout it . . . so that all may hear.'

But no, thought Louis. He had been refused the red hat; he would refuse to say yes. On either side of him Madame de Ventadour and the Duc de Villeroi continued to urge him; he stared at them with those beautiful dark blue eyes with their fringe of long lashes, his lips pressed tightly together; he would not speak.

'Take off your hat,' said Madame de Ventadour.

Louis smiled then. He was ready to take off the black *crêpe* thing; and still keeping his eyes on the red one of the Archbishop, he did so.

'The King has given us the sign of his assent,' said Villeroi; and the meeting was over.

But outside the people were calling for him. They wished to have a sight of their little King. On the steps of the Sainte-Chapelle he was held high in the arms of the Grand Chamberlain, and the people shouted his name.

He stared at them. Many of them were as ugly as those whom he had seen from his windows. He did not like them very much; they shouted too loudly and every eye in the crowd was fixed upon him.

'He is tired,' said Madame de Ventadour. 'It would be well to go on our way.'

So he was soon in the carriage, beside her, and when she was holding his hand he did not feel so disturbed by the faces of the people who lined the route and peered at him through the carriage windows.

He heard the booming of guns.

'They are firing from the Bastille because you are the King and they love you,' Madame de Ventadour told him; and he saw some of the birds which were sent out from the four corners of Paris. 'They mean that liberty is reborn,' she told him. And when he asked: 'What is liberty, *Maman?* And what is reborn?' she answered: 'It means that they are glad that you are the King.'

'Where are we going?' he asked.

'To Vincennes,' she answered him, 'and there we shall be by ourselves again as we used to be.'

'Even though I am the King?' he wanted to know.

'Even though you are the King you are but a little boy yet. We shall play our old games and do our lessons together. There will be no more sitting on velvet cushions wearing a *crêpe* hat for a while.'

'Oh,' said Louis reflectively. Then he laughed. Being a King was not what he had thought. He had believed Kings had all they wanted, but that was false, for the red hats of Archbishops were denied to them.

✤ Chapter II ✤

THE YOUNG KING

*J*t was a late September morning a year or so after the
death of Louis XIV, and the mother of Philippe of
Orléans, the aged Madame of the Court, had come to call
upon her son at Palais Royal.

When Madame de Ventadour had taken the little King to
Vincennes the Court had moved from Versailles and had its
being in the Palais Royal, the home of the Regent.

The Duc d'Orléans was not displeased with life. He visited
his little nephew frequently and assured himself that Madame
de Ventadour was the best possible guardian for the boy at the
moment; but he made sure that young Louis lost none of his
affection for his uncle. Meanwhile it was very pleasant to take
on the role of King in the boy's place.

Madame embraced him warmly and he immediately dismissed all his attendants that they might be entirely alone; and
when they were, he looked at her with affection and said: 'You
have come to remonstrate with your wicked son, Madame. Is
that not so?'

She laughed lightly. 'My dear Philippe,' she said, 'your
reputation grows worse every day.'

'I know it,' he admitted gleefully.

'My dear, it was all very well when you were merely Duc d'Orléans, but do you not think that now you have attained the dignity of Regent of France you should mend your ways?'

'It is too late, *Maman*. I am set in my ways.'

'Is it necessary to hold a supper party at the Palais Royal every night and a masked ball at the Opéra once a week?'

'Very necessary to my pleasure and that of my friends.'

'They are calling them your band of roués.'

'The description is adequate.'

Madame clicked her tongue, but the look of reproach which she gave her son only thinly disguised the great affection she had for him. It was no use, she thought, feigning to disapprove of him; he was much less wicked than he pretended to be; he was so affectionate to her, and their daily visits meant as much to him as they did to her. Any mother would have been proud of such a son, and a woman would be unnatural not to adore him. He was so amusing – no one made her laugh as he did; moreover he really cared about the country and worked very hard to improve conditions. But he had been brought up to a life of debauchery. She should never have approved of his father's choice of a tutor. The Abbé Dubois, who was his evil genius, had introduced him to lechery at an early age and Philippe was soon on such terms with it as could only mean a lifelong devotion. He was *méchant*, this son of hers, but how dearly she loved him!

'Nevertheless, my dear,' she said, 'it is time you employed a little moderation.'

'But *Maman*, moderation and I could never agree . . . particularly in this matter which you are pleased to call "morals".'

'You have so many mistresses.'

He snapped his fingers. 'What matters that, so long as I keep faithful to one doctrine? You know I remain adamant in this: I never allow them to interfere with politics. While I am wise enough for that, what matters it how many mistresses I have?'

'True enough,' she said. 'But what of your daughter?'

Philippe turned on her almost angrily. 'My daughter!' he repeated.

'You must face the truth,' said Madame. 'It is said that you visit the Duchesse de Berry frequently and that your affection for her goes beyond the paternal.'

Philippe murmured: 'My God! Cannot a man have an affection for his daughter?'

'Not such a man, with such a daughter and such an affection.'

Philippe stood very still fighting his anger; then he turned to his mother and putting his arm about her shoulders began to walk up and down the apartment. 'Has it ever occurred to you, *Maman*, that these marriages which are made for us should be sufficient excuses for the sins we commit? Myself, I must marry because the King my uncle wished to find a husband for his daughter, who was also the daughter of his mistress. And my little girl at fourteen is married to her cousin, the Duc de Berry, because he is the youngest grandson of the King. There is often no affection, no friendship even, between us ... but marriage there must be because the King ... the State ... so wills it. We must have compensations.'

'I know it well, my son,' said Madame. 'I do not blame; I only counsel.'

'My poor little girl,' he went on, 'married at fourteen, a widow at eighteen! She finds herself rich and free. I know ... I know ... she has made herself as notorious as her father. She makes love every night with a different lover . . . she drinks herself insensible. Careless of public opinion, she has named her friends her "roués". She has inherited every one of her father's sins, so she provides scandal for the Court and the whole of Paris. She has done all that — so there must be a scandal to outweigh all other scandals; therefore, says the Court, there is an incestuous union between her and her father! *Maman*, do you not know that I have my enemies?'

'It would be remarkable if a man in your position had not.'

'And some,' said Philippe, 'are very close to me.'

She caught his arm in sudden fear. 'Take care, my Philippe.' He kissed her cheek lightly. 'Do not concern your dear head with my dangers. I am a wicked man, heading for hell fire, but I can defend myself from my enemies.'

Madame had lost her usual lighthearted mood. 'I remember the time when the Duc de Bourgogne was buried . . .'

'I remember too, *Maman*. Shall I ever forget? The mob shouted insults after me. There were cold and suspicious looks at Court. It was believed that I had murdered my kinsman to clear my way to the throne.'

'If anything happened to Louis they would blame you.'

'Nothing shall happen to Louis. King of France! It is a great title. One would be proud to aspire to it. *Maman*, suspect me of any form of lechery that your mind can conceive; call me drunkard, gambler — even accuse me of an incestuous relationship with my daughter, but never . . . never let it enter your head for a moment that I am a murderer.'

She turned to him, her eyes flashing. 'There is no need to ask me that. What I fear is that others might slander you.'

He drew her to him and held her against him. 'Dear *Maman*,' he said. 'My dearest, why should we feel this anger?

Louis is at Vincennes, well guarded. A tigress could not guard her cub as old Ventadour does her little King. No harm can come to him with old *Maman* Ventadour. Louis is safe . . . and so am I. I shall remain at the head of affairs until my little nephew is of age. Have no fear, *Maman*. All is well.'

She laughed. 'You are right of course. You understand, my son, I have your well-being so much at heart.'

'I know it well. Come, let us talk of other matters.'

She put her head on one side and regarded him. 'It is no use asking you to take fewer mistresses, but could you not be more selective? There are few of them real beauties. They only have to be good-tempered and indelicate to satisfy you.'

'I will tell you a secret, *Maman*,' he said gaily. 'It is this: In the night all cats are grey.'

Shortly afterwards, when she left him, she felt less disturbed because she was sure she had put him on guard against his enemies. Meanwhile one of them was paying a visit to the Palais Royal.

Philippe received the Maréchal Duc de Villeroi with much less pleasure than he had his mother.

He knew what Villeroi wanted He was an old man and he was afraid that he might die before he had an opportunity of performing the task which had been allotted to him. Let him wait, thought Philippe. Young Louis shall continue a baby for a little longer. Indeed, as far as Philippe was concerned, the longer Louis remained a baby, the better.

'Ah, Monsieur de Villeroi,' he murmured falsely, 'this is indeed a pleasure.'

His smile as he regarded the old nobleman was slightly cynical. The fellow belonged to the old school, and no doubt that was why Louis Quatorze had selected him to be the young

King's governor when the boy should be released from the Ventadour apron strings. Villeroi had many qualities which old Louis would have wished to see passed on to his great-grandson; and how impatient Villeroi was to pass them on!

'You are disturbed by something?' asked the Regent.

'Disturbed? Yes, I confess it. Since the King's death it would seem a new age of debauchery has come to France. The young people nowadays appear to be entirely devoid of morals.'

Philippe smiled insolently. He knew that the old fellow was implying that the Regent set a bad example which the youth of the country followed.

'The King grew pious in his old age,' he murmured languidly. 'Doubtless you have heard the adage: "When the Devil was sick, the Devil a monk would be".' Philippe's fingers caressed the gold embroidery on his coat. 'It is a state of mind which could affect any of us. Let the young enjoy themselves. Youth is brief.'

Villeroi stared at the ceiling. 'As you know, Monsieur le Duc, I have not lived the life of a saint, but the orgies of which one hears . . .'

'Ah, you have made many conquests, I know,' interrupted Philippe. 'I remember what you have told us about them. They were worthy to be boasted of: I grant you that. Conquests in love are of greater consequence to some than conquests in war. I suspect you to be one of these.'

Villeroi flinched before this sly reference to his tendency to boast of his love affairs and to his scarcely glorious military career.

He changed the subject abruptly. 'It would seem that a woman is not the person to bring up the King of France.'

27

'I agree in that,' said Philippe. 'But even Kings must first be babies. As yet His Majesty is too young to leave his governess' care.'

'I maintain that it is time he was in that of his governor.'

Philippe smiled. 'We might ask His Majesty with whom he prefers to live – *Maman* Ventadour or Papa Villeroi.'

'He is too young to make such decisions.'

'I doubt not he will make them. He has a will of his own.'

'But the King would soon grow accustomed to the change. He must learn to be a man, not the pet of the ladies.'

'Why should he not be both?' asked Philippe. 'Many of us aspire to be.'

'I fear, Monsieur le Duc, that you have misunderstood my meaning.'

'Your meaning is perfectly clear to me, Monsieur le Maréchal. It is this: The King should be taken from the care of his governess and put into yours. Not yet, Monsieur. Not yet. He is but six. When he is seven that will be time enough.'

'Another year!'

'It will soon pass. Be patient. Your time will come.'

Villeroi bit his lip in anger. His fingers were trembling to take his sword and drive it through the heart of the smiling Regent. Lecher, gambler, drunkard, Villeroi felt sure he was capable of anything. He was one of those who believed the stories concerning Orléans and his daughter – worse still he believed that this man was responsible for the three deaths which had taken place in one year – those of the King's father, mother and elder brother.

And if, thought Villeroi, Orléans had hastened those three to the grave, what were the chances of little Louis with no one but a foolish woman — albeit she was devoted to the child — to stand between him and his murderer?

But he saw there was nothing he could do. He must wait for another year before he could devote his life to the preservation of the King.

Life was pleasant for Louis. He had been delighted when he and Madame de Ventadour had left Vincennes for Paris. His new home was the Tuileries and, although it could not have the same charm for him as Versailles, he was interested in the great city where he was allowed to drive, sitting in his carriage with Madame de Ventadour beside him.

The people fascinated him while they filled him with a slight alarm. He could never grow accustomed to their stares; he would have liked to have driven among them unnoticed, but it appeared that could not be, for everywhere he went they seemed to congregate to stare and shout at him. Even when he played on the terraces of the Tuileries they would stand about and come as close as they could; they would point and say: 'Look, there he is.'

Nothing could be enjoyed without their presence. They were in the Champs Elysées when he drove there, and they congregated outside the Palais Royal when he paid a visit to his uncle. He was for ever being held up in the arms of some official to wave to the people, or taken out onto some balcony that they might shout at him.

'Ugh!' cried Louis. 'I do not think I like the people.'

That was something he must never say, *Maman* Ventadour told him. He belonged to the people and they belonged to him. He must never forget that he was King of France.

Yet he did forget – for days at a time he forgot. When he played games with his good friend, one of the pages, they would fly kites, play hopscotch, dress up, fight each other, shriek at each other and both forget that he was the King. Those were the happy times.

It had not occurred to him that life could not go on as he lived it under the indulgent care of *Maman* Ventadour, but one day when he was seven years old he noticed that she was looking sad and very solemn.

He was immediately alarmed, for although he often plagued her he loved her dearly and, when he saw her truly sad – not pretending to be sad because of his naughtiness – he was genuinely sorry.

'*Maman*,' he demanded, 'what ails you?'

'My dearest,' she said, 'there will come a time when you will pass from my care.'

His face darkened and he said: 'It shall not be.'

'It must be. I am only a woman, and careful plans have been made by your great-grandfather for your education and upbringing.'

'But he is dead, *Maman*, and I am the King now,' said Louis slyly.

Madame de Ventadour did not pursue the subject. There was no point in making him unhappy before she need – even if it meant only another day or so in which they could live the old life.

But she could not ward off time, and the day came when the startled child was taken to an ante-room where he was stripped of all his clothes. He was then led into a great chamber where were gathered all the highest officials of the Court together with the leading doctors of France.

Louis stood aghast, staring at them all, but his uncle took him by the hand and led him into the room.

'It is an old custom,' whispered Philippe. 'Merely to show them what a fine man you are.'

'But I do not wish to be here without my clothes,' said Louis shamefacedly.

'It is nothing,' said his uncle. 'We men think nothing of it.'

Then he was prodded and patted and tapped and turned this way and that. His physique was a subject for admiration, as was his beauty. All the same he felt humiliated and angry, yet he knew that this was merely another of the burdens which must be borne by kings. One of the men then spoke: 'Are all agreed that our King Louis XV is sound in all his members, well nourished and healthy?'

There was a chorus of 'Agreed.'

His hand was then taken by Madame de Ventadour who led him back to the small chamber where he was dressed.

He quickly forgot the incident; he did not realise that it was but a preliminary to a more significant event.

Two weeks later Madame de Ventadour sought Philippe of Orléans, in accordance with the formal ceremony which the occasion demanded, and she said to him: 'Is it your wish, *Monseigneur*, that I should relinquish the King's person to you?'

And to this Orléans replied: 'That is my wish, Madame.'

'Then I pray you follow me.'

When Louis saw his uncle he was ready to leap into his arms, but Philippe held up his hand to warn the boy that this was one of those occasions when ceremony must be observed.

Then Madame de Ventadour said in a voice broken with emotion: '*Monseigneur*, here is my charge who was entrusted to me by King Louis XIV. I have cared for him to the very best of my ability and I now give him to you in perfect health.'

Philippe sank to his knees then, while Louis looked in bewilderment from his uncle to his dear *Maman* Ventadour.

'Sire,' said Philippe. 'I hope you will never forget all that this lady has done for you. When you were very little she saved your life, and since then she has cared for you as devotedly as though she were your mother.'

Louis nodded. He was searching for words to ask what this meant, but he could not find them. A strange feeling in the pit of his stomach warned him that he was very frightened.

At that moment three men entered the room; one was the Duc du Maine whom he called uncle and of whom he was fond; the others were the Duc de Villeroi and André Hercule de Fleury.

'Sire,' said Philippe, 'you are no longer a child and must devote yourself to serious matters; you must begin to prepare yourself for your great destiny. To help you in this, here are the Duc de Maine who will superintend your education, Monsieur de Fleury, Bishop of Fréjus, who will be your tutor, and the Duc de Villeroi who will be your Governor.'

Louis looked at the three men stonily. 'And *Maman* Ventadour?' he asked.

'Sire, she will always be your friend, but you will cease to live with her and will have your own household.'

Louis stamped his foot. 'I want *Maman* Ventadour,' he cried.

Madame de Ventadour knelt beside him and embraced him; she felt herself held in a firm, hot clasp. 'Listen, my dearest,' she said, 'it is merely that you will have your own household. I shall come to see you.'

'But I do not want them,' he whispered. 'I want you, *Maman*.'

The three men were trying not to look at him; Philippe went on as though the King had not spoken. '*Messieurs*, this is a sacred charge. I trust you will consider it before aught else. It will be necessary for you to bestow every care and all the affection of which you are capable upon our King.'

'We swear to do this,' said the three together, as the King turned his face away from Madame de Ventadour momentarily to scowl at them.

Madame de Ventadour rose. She took Louis by the hand and pulled him towards the men. Villeroi put out a hand to take the King's but Louis had gripped Madame de Ventadour's skirt and had nothing but frowns for his new Governor.

Madame de Ventadour said: 'Now, my dearest, I must go and leave you with your new guardians.'

She withdrew her skirt from his grip, but with a loud sob he flung himself into her arms and cried: 'Do not go, *Maman*. Do not let them take me away from you.'

Over his head, she looked at the three men. 'In time he will understand,' she said.

So they nodded and left her alone with the sobbing child.

He would not eat. Every now and then a sob shook the small body. Madame de Ventadour tried to soothe him but there was no real comfort to offer, since all he asked was to stay with her, and that could not be. At last exhausted he slept, and when he awoke he found that, instead of Madame de Ventadour, his Governor, the Duc de Villeroi, was sitting by his bed. He started up in dismay but the Duc said: 'There is nothing to fear, Sire. In a short while you will find your Governor as much to your liking as your Governess was.'

'Go away,' said Louis.

'Sire, it is the wish of the people . . .'

'I am the King,' said Louis. 'I have wishes too.'

'They shall be granted, but . . .'

'I want my *Maman*,' said Louis. 'Bring her to me.'

Villeroi said: 'There are many things you will learn, Sire, and they will be of great interest. You shall learn to fence and dance and sing. You shall hunt. You will find life much more interesting when you live among men.'

'I want *Maman* Ventadour,' said Louis stonily.

'You shall see her now and then.'

'Now!' commanded Louis.

'First you will eat, Sire?'

Louis hesitated. He was hungry, but his fear of the future was greater than his hunger.

'Bring my *Maman* first,' he said.

And after much attempted persuasion it was at length realised that Madame de Ventadour must be brought back.

She comforted him; she explained that he was the King and must do, not what he wanted, but what was right. If he did that, she said, he would be a very happy man.

He clung to her, and cried until he was exhausted; and then suddenly the understanding came to him that there was nothing he could do but accept this life which was thrust upon him.

Bravely he kissed Madame de Ventadour and allowed himself to be led into the new life which would be dominated by his guardian, the Duc de Villeroi.

❀ ❀ ❀

It was less miserable than he had believed it could be. Indeed, he began to realise that what they had told him was true; living with men was more interesting than life with Madame de Ventadour. Moreover he saw her frequently and that was always a pleasure. He was realising that he had not only Madame de Ventadour but a new and exciting existence.

In the first place the Duc de Villeroi sought to please him in every way; he flattered him and lost no opportunity of calling everyone's attention to the beauty and the outstanding intelligence of his charge. That was pleasant. He saw more of his amusing Uncle Philippe, who always made him laugh and whose coming always put Monsieur de Villeroi into a bad mood which he unsuccessfully attempted to hide from Louis. But Uncle Philippe laughed slyly at the ill humour of Monsieur de Villeroi, and Louis joined in the laughter.

His tutor made the deepest impression upon the boy. Fleury was not outwardly sycophantish, and perhaps for this reason won the boy's respect. He had a quiet dignity and, because he rarely gave an order as such, he extracted the utmost obedience from his charge.

Being determined that the King's education should be as perfect as he could make it, he had called in assistants. There was a fellow-historian, Alary, to add his wisdom to that of Fleury for the King's benefit, since it was of the utmost importance that the King should have an understanding of history; there was the mathematician, Chevalier, and the geographer, Guillaume Delisle. And if Fleury felt further experts were needed he did not hesitate to call in professors from the Lycée Louis-le-Grand.

Fleury had arranged that there should be lessons in the mornings and evenings, so that there would be an interval when the boy might amuse himself with his favourite games and pastimes. Important subjects, such as writing, Latin and history, appeared on the curriculum every day; others were spread over the week. Fleury planned to have a printing press set up so that Louis might be taught typography; military science was not forgotten and, as it was Fleury's wish that this should be of a practical nature, he planned to have the Musketeers and the King's Own Regiment perform manoeuvres in which the King could take part.

Thus being educated became a matter of absorbing interest to the boy, who proved to be of more than average intelligence.

There were other matters to interest him. He formed a friendship with one of his pages, the Marquis de Calvière, and these two spent many happy hours playing games and taking their toys to pieces and putting them together again. Louis developed an interest in cooking, and he enjoyed making sweetmeats and presenting them to Madame de Ventadour, Uncle Philippe, Villeroi, Fleury – any with whom he felt particularly pleased.

It was impossible to be bored with so much of interest happening and it was not long before Louis discovered the intrigue which was going on.

Monsieur de Villeroi feared and hated someone. Louis wondered whom.

One day as they were making sweetmeats while the Duc de Villeroi was enjoying a siesta, Louis asked young Calvière if he had noticed it.

'Look,' said the King. 'This is to be an Easter egg. For whom shall it be? My Governor? Uncle Philippe? Or Maman Ventadour? Or Monsieur de Fleury?'

'That,' said Calvière, 'is for you to decide.'

'Monsieur de Villeroi locks up my bread and butter,' Louis announced.

The page nodded.

'And my handkerchiefs,' went on Louis. 'They are kept in a box with a triple lock.'

'He is afraid,' said Calvière.

'Of what?'

'He is afraid of poisoners.'

'He is afraid someone will poison *me*!' said the King. 'Who?'

Calvière lifted his shoulders. 'That egg is not the right shape,' he said.

'It is,' said Louis.

'It is not.'

'It is.'

Louis picked up a wooden spoon and would have brought it down on the page's head but Calvière jerked up his hand and the spoon hit Louis in the face. In a moment the two boys were wrestling on the floor.

Suddenly they stopped and went back to the bench. 'I shall make fondants,' said Calvière.

'My egg shall be for Uncle Philippe. I love him best today.'

'I know why,' said Calvière laughing. 'It is because Monsieur de Villeroi made you dance before the ambassadors.'

Louis stood still, remembering. It was true. The Maréchal had made him strut before the foreign ambassadors. 'What do you think of the King's beauty?' he had asked. 'Look at his beautifully proportioned figure and his beautiful hair.' Then Villeroi had asked the King to run round the room, that the ambassadors should see how fleet he was; and to dance for them that they might see how graceful. 'See! It might be his great-grandfather dancing before you. It is said that none danced as gracefully as Louis XIV. That is because they had not seen Louis XV.'

'I like making sweetmeats better than dancing,' said Louis. 'Uncle Philippe does not ask me to dance. He laughs at old Villeroi. Yes, my egg shall be for Uncle Philippe.'

And as the two boys continued their sweet-making the page said: 'I wonder who Villeroi thinks is trying to poison you.'

They began enumerating all the people of the Court until they tired of it; and when the egg was completed and was being tied about with a blue riband Uncle Philippe entered the room. As Louis leaped into his arms and was carried shoulder-high about the apartment he called to the page that Uncle Philippe should certainly have the Easter egg, for he was his favourite person today.

Uncle Philippe had brought Easter eggs for Louis who immediately shared one of them with Calvière, while the Duc d'Orléans listened with amusement to their comparisons of other people's sweetmeats with their own.

Later, when Uncle Philippe had left, Louis showed the eggs to Villeroi, who seized them at once and said they must be examined.

'We have already eaten one,' Louis told him; and Villeroi's face turned white with fear.

Louis did not notice anything strange in this, at the time, but later when he was writing in his book in Latin his mind wandered from the sentiments he was expressing.

'The King,' he wrote, 'and his people are bound together by ties of mutual obligation. The people undertake to render to the King respect, obedience, succour, service and to speak that which is true. The King promises his people vigilance, protection, peace, justice and the maintenance of an equable and unclouded disposition.'

It was all very boring, and it was small wonder that his attention strayed.

Suddenly he began to chuckle. Papa Villeroi thinks Uncle Philippe is trying to poison me! he told himself.

It seemed indescribably funny; one of those wild adventures which took place in the imagination and which he and Calvière liked to construct; it was like a game; it must be a game. He wondered if Uncle Philippe knew.

It was impossible not to be aware of the awe which he, a ten-year-old boy, was able to inspire in those about him. There was not one of these dignified men of his household or of the Regency Council who did not take great pains to propitiate him. This afforded the King secret amusement, but he was intelligent enough not to overestimate his power. He knew that in small matters he might have his way, but in the larger issues – as he had seen at the time of his parting with Madame de Ventadour – these important men about him would make the final decision.

He had enjoyed watching, with Calvière, the feud between his uncle Philippe and his governor Villeroi. The two boys entered into the game. When they were alone, Calvière would leap forward whenever Louis was about to eat anything, snatch it from him, eat a piece, and either pretend to drop dead at the King's feet or declare: 'All is well. We have foiled the poisoners this time, Sire.'

Sometimes Louis played the page. It added variety to the game.

The Duc d'Orléans noticed the secret amusement of the boys, the looks which passed between them, and he knew that he and Villeroi were the cause of them.

Orléans wondered then what Villeroi had hinted to Louis. It could have been nothing blatantly detrimental, for Louis was as affectionate as ever towards him. But Villeroi had conveyed something, and Orléans was doubly on the alert, and was determined to take the little King out of the care of Villeroi as much as possible. Villeroi in his turn was aware of the additional alertness in the attitude of Orléans, so he increased his watchfulness.

Villeroi was determined to make another *Grand Monarque* of his charge. Often, instead of the handsome little boy, he saw the handsome King. He wanted young Louis to follow slavishly in his great-grandfather's footsteps.

The boy must perform a ballet, for Louis Quatorze had excelled at the ballet. Everyone declared that the child's dancing reminded them so much of great Louis that it was as though he lived again in his great-grandson. That delighted Villeroi.

The child must meet the people on every possible occasion. When the cheers and cries of '*Vive notre petit Roi*' echoed in his ears, Villeroi declared he was supremely happy. He insisted that his little charge ride with him through the streets of Paris and appear frequently on the balconies.

Often in his dreams Louis heard the shouts of the people and saw faces which took on a nightmare quality. The shouts grew raucous and threatening; the faces savage and inhuman.

He would protest that there were so many public displays. 'But you must love the people as they love you,' Villeroi told him. He loved some people – *Maman* Ventadour, Uncle

Philippe, Papa Villeroi, and many others; but *they* did not stare and shout at him.

'Papa Villeroi,' he said, 'let us go to Versailles. I do not like Paris. There are so many people.'

'Some day . . . some day . . .' Villeroi told him.

And Louis would grow wistful thinking of Versailles, that fairytale château which had seemed to him full of a hundred delights, and in which he could shut himself away from the shouting people.

Philippe, eager to wean the King from the overwhelming devotion of Villeroi, took him to the Council of Regency. Louis was a little bored by the long speeches and the interminable discussions but he liked to sit there among these men and feel that he was their King.

He asked that whenever the Council sat he should attend.

Villeroi beamed with pleasure. 'You see,' he said to the Duc d'Orléans, 'how intelligent is His Majesty. I am not the only one who finds it difficult to remember he is but ten years old.'

'Ah,' said Orléans, 'he grows apace in mind and body. He longs to escape from his Governor's leading strings.'

There was a threat in the words. Soon, implied Orléans, he will not need your services, Papa Villeroi.

When that time comes, thought Villeroi, I will expose you, Monsieur d'Orléans, in all your infamy, before you have an opportunity to do to that innocent child what you did to his parents.

Villeroi was certain that only his watchfulness and care had preserved Louis' life so far. The King should continue in his care.

I believe, thought Orléans, that the old fool's brain is softening.

On one occasion, while the Regency Council was conducting its business and Louis sat in a chair of state, his legs not reaching the floor, fighting a desire to go to sleep, he heard a slight scratching on the legs of his chair and as he looked to see what it was, a black and white kitten sprang onto his lap.

Louis caught the furry little body and held it. A pair of wide green eyes surveyed him calmly and the kitten mewed. The gentlemen of the Council stopped their talk to look at the King and the kitten.

The Duc de Noailles, who could not bear to be in the same room as cats, sprang to his feet.

'Sire,' he said, 'I will order it to be removed at once.'

Uncle Philippe reached to take the kitten from Louis, but the King held the little creature against him. He loved the kitten which already sensed his sympathy and began purring contentedly.

Louis then decided to exert his authority, to show these men that he was the King.

He stroked the kitten and, without looking at Monsieur de Noailles or Uncle Philippe, he said: 'The kitten shall remain.'

There was a brief silence, then Orléans turned his smiles on Noailles and murmured: 'The King has spoken.'

It amused Louis to see the horror on the face of de Noailles. He felt very happy that day; he had a new companion and he had realised that in small matters he could have his way.

After that occasion the kitten joined in the frolics he shared with Calvière; and Louis was watchful that no harm should come to it; he was ready to fly into a rage with anyone whom he suspected of ill-treating it, so very quickly all learned to pay proper respect to the little 'Blanc et Noir'.

Louis took it everywhere he went and, if he did not take it, it followed him.

The Court declared that there was a new member of the Regency Council: His Majesty's kitten.

✤ ✤ ✤

It was hot in the church and Louis longed for Mass to be over.

The air inside the building was stifling for the place was thronged with people who had come to celebrate the feast of Saint Germain l'Auxerrois.

The droning of voices seemed to be receding; he was only vaguely aware of the Duc d'Orléans standing close to him, and when he clasped his hands together discovered that they were burning.

Orléans laid his hand on the King's shoulder and whispered: 'You are feeling ill?'

Louis lifted a pair of glassy eyes to the Duc, and as he did so he would have fallen had not Orléans stooped swiftly and gathered him into his arms.

There were too many witnesses for the news to be kept secret. All over Paris the word was spreading: The King has been taken ill.

Many spoke of the dreaded smallpox; but there were many others who were already whispering the word: poison.

✤ ✤ ✤

Villeroi wrung his hands; he stormed up and down the apartment.

'That this should have happened,' he cried to all those who had assembled to listen to him, 'after all the precautions I took. It is cruel. It is too wicked to be contemplated without fury.

Those who have done this deserve to die the most cruel death which can be inflicted. This innocent child, this sacred child . . . so young, so full of health one day, struck down the next!'

Fleury did his utmost to calm the old man.

'Monsieur le Maréchal, you go too far,' he remonstrated. 'You should not make such accusations without proof. It is said that the King suffers from the smallpox. That is an act of God, not of man.'

'Smallpox!' cried the old man, wild with grief. 'They are devils, these poisoners. They can brew their wicked potions to make their victims appear to be suffering from any disease they wish. What have we heard, I ask you? The Duchesse de Bourgogne died of purple measles. Purple measles! Measles administered by a fatal dose of poison. The little five-year-old Duc de Bretagne died of the same. Indeed it was the same! The same fiends brought about his death as they did that of his mother . . . and father. Ay, his father also. He died of a broken heart, we were told. It is all one to these wicked men who seek to remove those who stand in their way. They can administer purple measles or break a heart. They are fiends . . . fiends, I tell you. And now they have begun their evil tricks on my beloved King.'

'You should calm yourself,' said Fleury. 'There will be some to report what you say to those who might take it amiss.'

'Take it amiss!' shouted the old man. 'Let them. Let them. If any harm comes to my King . . .'

Fleury tried to soothe him, but his hints were so obviously directed at the Duc d'Orléans that Fleury was certain Villeroi would not long remain Governor of the King.

Fleury was not altogether displeased. He himself was an ambitious man, and the removal of the King's Governor could bring the tutor closer to his pupil. He had won the affection of the boy King; and if Louis recovered from his illness, who could say what good might not come to his dear Fleury? As for Villeroi, the old fellow was a fool. He should know by now that it is wiser to show friendship to your enemies whatever you feel about them. Orléans might laugh at the old man's antagonism, but on occasions like this he must see how dangerous it could be.

Villeroi's vituperations were not long-lived for, on the third day after Louis had been taken ill, it became apparent that he would recover.

✤ ✤ ✤

'*Vive le Roi!*' The words had been echoing thorugh the streets all day.

Louis shuddered to hear them, and planned to shut himself in a cupboard with his kitten until the shouting was over. That was not possible, for they would hunt until they found him; they would remind him that all the shouting was for love of him.

For days the celebrations had been in progress. A special Te Deum had been sung at the Sainte Chapelle, processions had paraded the streets, and deputations to the Louvre had followed one another. The women from Les Halles had marched there in triumph to the sound of drums, bringing presents which represented their trades. There, to be presented to the King, was a sturgeon eight feet long, oxen, sheep and baskets of vegetable produce.

'Give thanks to God,' they cried, 'for He has preserved our beloved little King. God bless the King. Long life to our beloved Louis!'

45

There was dancing in the streets; and the heart of the revelry was the Tuileries, the home of the King.

Villeroi went about embracing everyone – except the Duc d'Orléans and his faction – declaring that he would give all the rest of his life willingly to have witnessed this moment.

The people of Paris, having such a good excuse for revelry, could not be induced to stop. Violins joined the drums and the dancing grew wilder. There were free performances at the Comédie Française and at the Opéra, and firework displays on the River, when enormous sea serpents, with fire coming from their mouths, were sent out amongst the boats. This was revelry such as all Paris loved, but there was scarcely a man or woman in the crowd who would not have declared that the sight which gave them the most pleasure was that of the small velvet-clad King who watched them with such charming restraint and Bourbon dignity, so that it might have been a miniature Louis Quatorze who stood there acknowledging their applause – Louis Quatorze in the days of his glory, of course, for the old King had not been so popular towards the end of his life. But here was a King who was going to lead France to prosperity. Here was a King whom his people would love as they had not loved a King since great Henri Quatre.

The excitement reached its climax on the day when the King emerged from the Tuileries to attend the thanksgiving at Notre Dame. In his blue velvet coat and white plumed hat he was an enchanting figure; his auburn hair flowed over his shoulders and his big, dark blue eyes surveyed the crowd with an outward calm, although in his heart he hated these scenes. He could not like the people *en masse*, even when they cheered him and called out blessings on their darling.

Without emotion he watched the flags fluttering from the

buildings, the people dancing in the streets, the women who threw him kisses and wiped their eyes because they were so happy that he was alive and well.

'See,' cried Villeroi, always beside him, always urging him to display his charm and his handsome looks, 'the people love their King.'

Villeroi's eyes were aflame with pride, but Louis, standing beside him, bowing gravely to the crowd, only wished to escape. His demeanour served to make the people more wildly enthusiastic.

He raised his hat and bowed to his people, but seized the first opportunity to turn from the balcony and step into the room.

There he stood among the curtains, wrapping them round him as though he would hide himself from those who sought to send him out once more onto the balcony. They would do so, he knew, because the people were still shouting his name.

Villeroi was pulling at the curtains. 'Come, Sire, the people cannot have enough of you.'

Louis put his head out of the folds of heavy damask, keeping the rest of his body hidden. '*I* have had enough of *them*,' he announced.

'You joke, dear Master.'

'It is no joke,' said the King. 'I shall now go to find Blanc et Noir. It is time he was fed, and I trust no other to do that.'

'Sire, you would play with a kitten when your people are calling for you?'

'Yes,' said Louis, 'I would. I love my kitten.'

'And your people?'

Louis shook his head.

Villeroi pretended to consider that a joke. 'All these people are yours, Sire . . . yours, all yours . . .' He knelt down by Louis and the child saw the glitter in the eyes of the man. 'Think of this: France and all her people are yours to command.'

Mine to command, pondered Louis. So when I say 'Go away' they should go away. Mine to command? But that is later of course, when I am grown up. Now I am only a child, though King, and must do as they say. But one day there will be no one to deny my wishes. All will be mine . . . mine to command.

He was resigned. He must wait. Childhood did not last for ever.

'Sire, you will step once more on to the balcony. Listen! How they call for you!'

But Louis shook his head. Villeroi saw that stubborn set of the lips and as usual he gave way.

'Then,' he ventured. 'I pray you walk with me before the windows. I will draw back the curtains. Then they will see you. I fear they will never go home until they have caught one more glimpse of you. They love you so.'

Louis considered. He wanted to escape from the sound of their shouting. He nodded slowly, and Villeroi drew back the curtains.

Now the people could see their King at the windows and the cry went up from thousands of throats: 'Long live the King! Long live Louis!'

Villeroi was wiping his eyes, unable to control his emotion. Louis was thinking: One day I shall do as I wish. Then they may shout themselves hoarse, and I shall not listen to them.

✤ ✤ ✤

Further plans were being concocted for the King's future. His illness had made many members of the Court very thoughtful. Death was ever lurking in the streets of Paris and not all the splendour of Versailles nor France's doctors could stand against it.

The Duc de Bourbon, grandson of Louis Quatorze, though not free from the bar sinister, was very eager that a match should be made for the King, for if the boy should die without heirs the crown would pass to Orléans, and that would be very hard for the rival House of Bourbon to tolerate.

'The King should be married,' he announced to the Council.

'At his age!' cried Orléans.

'Even if the consummation of the marriage were postponed for a while, a marriage should be arranged. In three years' time His Majesty will be fourteen. Old enough for marriage. It is a King's duty to beget heirs for France, and he cannot start too early.'

'He is but eleven!' cried Villeroi.

Bourbon and Orléans looked at the old man quizzically. It was clear what was going on in his mind. A wife for his little darling! Someone who might have greater influence over him than his doddering old Governor!

The two dukes avoided each other's gaze. They were the real rivals. Villeroi did not count. The reason Orléans had allowed him to continue in office was because he knew that he could at any moment dismiss him. Bourbon was another matter.

But the shrewd Orléans saw how he could turn this situation to advantage.

Philip V, the first Bourbon King of Spain, had taken over that crown twenty-one years before on the death of Philip IV. He was a grandson of Louis Quatorze and therefore closely related to the royal house of France. He had a young daughter, Maria Anna; she was only five years old, six years younger than the King, but if she were brought to France for betrothal that should satisfy those who demanded that the King should marry, and at the same time it would be some years before that marriage could take place and be consummated.

Moreover, the son of Philip V, Luis, Prince of the Asturias, could be married to Mademoiselle de Montpensier, who was a daughter of the Regent.

An excellent arrangement, thought Orléans, for then, should the King die without heirs, his close ties with Spain would surely bring their help to win the throne for himself.

He smiled disarmingly at the Council. '*Messieurs*,' he said, 'we are all then agreed that it would be well for His Majesty to contemplate marriage. It would delight the people. What more charming than to see not only their handsome darling in the streets of their capital but by his side a pretty little girl! My friends, there is one country to which we are bound more closely than to any other. Our kinsman sits on the throne of Spain. He has a daughter. Let us bring Maria Anna, Infanta of Spain, to Paris. She will be brought up with the King, and when these two children are of an age to marry, the ceremony and consummation shall take place.'

Eventually Orléans won the Council to his support, for all were aware of the advantages of strengthening relations with Spain. There was no need at this point to state his intentions with regard to Mademoiselle de Montpensier and the Infante Luis.

Orléans was well pleased with the arrangement. He turned to Villeroi. 'You will acquaint His Majesty with our counsel?'

Villeroi nodded grimly. 'I will acquaint His Majesty, but whether His Majesty will agree . . . that is another matter.'

Orléans gave Villeroi his insolent smile. 'As His Majesty's

Governor you have no doubt taught him that the good of his people comes before his own wishes.'

Villeroi lifted his shoulders. 'I can do my best,' he said.

✦ ✦ ✦

Louis received the news blankly. A wife? He wanted no wife. He did not like women overmuch – except of course his dear *Maman* Ventadour.

He much preferred the society of men and boys with whom he could hunt and play cards, two pastimes for which he was developing a passion.

'I shall not have this girl brought to my country,' he declared.

'Sire, it is the will of the Council that she shall come.'

'I am the King.'

'It is the wish of the people.'

'Do the wishes of the King never prevail?'

'A King must consider his people.'

'But you have always said that I am the King and the people are mine to command. No, Papa Villeroi, I will not have this girl brought to France.'

Villeroi returned, not without some elation, to the Regent.

'His Majesty will have none of the marriage,' he told him.

'His Majesty must be persuaded,' answered Orléans.

Villeroi put his head on one side and smiled his knowing smile. 'I know His Majesty as well as any, and there is a streak of obstinacy in his character.'

Old fool, thought Orléans. It is certainly time you went.

He dismissed Villeroi and sent for Fleury. Here was a man worth four of the old Maréchal.

'The King must be made to agree to this marriage,' said Orléans.

Fleury nodded. Orléans was right. It was Fleury who in his lucid manner showed the King how foolish it would be to offend the King of Spain, not to trust his Regency who had decided that the marriage would be a good thing, not to accept this young girl who need make no difference to His Majesty's life for many years to come.

It was Fleury who led a somewhat sullen boy into the Council Chamber.

He came without Blanc et Noir, and his eyes were red from crying. When he was asked if he would agree to the match with Spain he gave them a quiet 'yes'.

He had lost his kitten, who had strayed out of his life as casually as he had come into it. He could not be found, and the necessity to accept a wife seemed of small consequence compared with the loss of his dear Blanc et Noir.

❖ ❖ ❖

The pretty five-year-old Infanta had arrived in Paris. She was a charming child and the Parisians were immediately enchanted. To see those two together – handsome auburn-haired Louis and his little pink and white Infanta – would soften the hardest heart, and the people expected them to be seen often together.

So much, thought Louis, was expected of a King. He must have this silly little girl at his side every day; he must hold her hand in his while the people applauded them.

He would let her see though that it was merely because he was forced to do so that he appeared friendly to her. He had not spoken to her since her arrival.

But it was quite impossible to snub the child. She had been told that she was to make a brilliant marriage with the most desirable monarch in the world. She thought he was quite handsome and everything she had heard of him was true. It seemed natural to her then that such a god-like creature should not deign to speak to her.

She herself was delighted with all things French. She would jump and skip about the palace for very joy because, as she would confide in anyone from highest official to humblest lackey, one day she was to marry Louis and be Queen of France.

The arrival of the Infanta was followed by a period of celebrations, and always at the centre of these Louis must be seen, the five-year-old girl at his side.

When she gazed at him in adoration he wanted to tell her that it was due to her that he could no longer hunt as he wished or play cards with his favourite page; every day there must be this endless round of so-called gaiety.

He did not want that. He did not want a wife.

Meekly Maria Anna waited for his favour. It would come to her, she was assured, because she was going to be Queen of France and Louis' wife. All husbands loved their wives, so Louis must love her one day.

In the meantime she was happy to bask in the caresses of the Court which could not do anything else but pet such a charming little creature – especially as she was destined for the throne.

She and Louis were together at the revelries which were given in honour of the Spanish ambassador, and one day there was a special firework display which Louis and Maria Anna watched together.

Maria Anna squealed with pleasure and bounded up and down in her seat. She looked so young, so excited, that for a moment she reminded Louis of his lost kitten.

'Louis,' she cried, 'Look at the fireworks. Oh . . . so lovely! Do you like them, Louis?'

She was accustomed to chattering to him and receiving no answer, so when he looked at her, smiled and said 'Yes', she was startled.

She turned to him, her eyes wide with excitement, as a smile of the utmost pleasure spread across her face. She got up, she ran to the nearest official, caught his knee and tried to shake him. She then jumped up and down in great excitement.

'Did you hear?' she demanded. 'Louis spoke to me . . . At last he has smiled and spoken to me.'

✦ ✦ ✦

Soon after the arrival of the Infanta, one of Louis' dearest wishes was granted. He was allowed to leave Paris for Versailles.

This afforded him great pleasure. It meant, to some degree, an escape from the people. Versailles was a little too far from the capital for them to come each day to the château. Perhaps this was one of the reasons why he loved the place so much.

But it was not the only one. The beauty of Versailles had enchanted him from the moment he had seen it. He had inherited from Louis Quatorze his interest in and love of architecture. He was delighted therefore to see again that most magnificent of all his châteaux rising before him with its façades in that delightful stone which was the colour of honey; the fountain playing in the sunshine, the exquisite statuary, the beauty of the avenues, the charm of the gardens – every flower, every stone of this palace delighted him as it had the great-grandfather who had created it.

It did not matter that beside him rode the five-year-old girl whose exuberance and hero-worship he found so annoying. Let her bounce on her seat, let her chatter away. He would not look at her; he would not answer her. He would only think: I have come home . . . home to Versailles. And never again, if he could have his way, would he leave it.

Louis occupied the state bedroom of his great-grandfather, with the council chamber on one side and the *œil-de-bœuf* on the other. He did not greatly like this bedroom, for it was big and draughty; moreover he would always remember being brought here by Madame de Ventadour when he had seen the old King for the last time. But it was good enough to be here. He was learning to be philosophical. He would not ask for too much. Later he would choose his own bedroom, his own suite of rooms. But that would be when he had grown out of this restricting childhood.

Now there was a Court once more at Versailles and, because the King was too young to lead it, it must be led by the Regent. Philippe was growing older and less inclined for adventure. The gay happenings assigned to him were rather of the imagination than actual, but he did not mind this. He had no wish to lose his reputation as one of the foremost rakes in France.

This meant however that the young people of the Court took their cue from what they believed the Regent to be, and promiscuity became the order of the day.

This state of affairs came to its zenith when an orgy which had taken place in the park of Versailles itself came to the notice of the public.

Here many of the young men from the noblest houses in France appeared dressed as women; but the orgy was not confined to the practice of perversion; men and women sported on the grass and made love in the shadow of the trees – while many did not even look for shadow.

Madame, the Regent's mother, called on him the day following that on which these scenes had taken place.

'They have gone too far,' she told him. 'In Paris people are talking of nothing else. You are the Regent, my son, and it is under your rule that this has happened. There will be many to say that Louis is in hands unfit to have charge of him. Take care.'

Orléans saw the point of this. As for himself, he was too old for such revelries now, and that made it easier to believe that this time they had gone too far.

Villeroi was stumping through the Palace. He would not have his beloved King exposed to such dangers. He was going to ask the Council what they thought of a Regent under whose rule such things were possible.

It gave Orléans great joy to discover that two of Villeroi's grandsons had participated in the adventure.

'Such scandal,' he said slyly. 'Grandsons of the King's own Governor! It will not do, Maréchal. It will not do.'

'If they have done wrong, they should be punished,' said the Maréchal. 'They were not the ringleaders, however, and they are young.'

'In a matter such as this, Maréchal,' said the Regent, 'we should favour none. Do you not agree with me?'

'Is is the ringleaders who should be punished . . .' muttered Villeroi.

'We will send *them* to the Bastille, but all' – Orléans paused and smiled into the old man's face – 'all who took part in this disgraceful display shall be banished.'

It was no use pleading for them, the Maréchal knew. Better by far to let the matter pass off as quietly as possible. But it was not in the nature of the Maréchal to show tact. He continued to storm about the Palace.

'All very well to blame these young people. But who sets the pace, eh? Tell me that – who sets the pace?'

* ✦ *

'I would speak with the King,' said the Regent to the Maréchal when he called on Louis who was, as always, in the company of his Governor. 'And I would see him alone.'

'But Monsieur le Duc!' Villeroi's smile was bland. 'It is the duty of His Majesty's Governor to attend him on all occasions.'

'His Majesty is no longer a child.'

'But twelve!'

'Old enough to take counsel of his ministers without the attendance of his . . . nurse.'

Villeroi was scarlet with rage. 'I shall not allow it,' he cried.

Louis looked from one to the other and realised that he had been mistaken in thinking that this enmity between them was a game.

Orléans had recovered himself first. He bowed his head and proceeded to speak to Louis while Villeroi stood by, his wig tilted a little too far over his forehead, his rage subsiding to give place to triumph.

But afterwards the Maréchal felt uneasy. The most important man in the country was Orléans and it had been somewhat foolish to oppose his wishes so openly.

Villeroi knew that Orléans would not let the slight pass

without some retaliation, and after a great deal of consideration he had come to the conclusion that his wisest plan would be to humble himself and apologise to the Regent. He decided to do this without delay, and called upon him.

As he entered the Regent's apartments, the Captain of the Musketeers, the Comte d'Artagnan, intercepted him.

Villeroi looked at the man haughtily. 'Conduct me at once to the Duc d'Orléans,' he commanded.

'Sir, he is engaged at this moment.'

Villeroi did not like the insolence of this man and he made as though to pass him.

'Sir,' said the Comte d'Artagnan, 'you are under arrest. I must ask you to give me your sword.'

'You forget, sir, to whom you speak.'

'Sir, I am fully aware to whom I speak, and my orders are to take your sword.'

'That you shall not do,' blustered Villeroi; but when d'Artagnan lifted his hand several of his musketeers came forward and surrounded the old man. In a few moments they had seized him and dragged him out of the Palace.

There a carriage was waiting, and d'Artagnan forced him to enter it.

'Whip up the horses,' cried d'Artagnan.

'This is monstrous,' spluttered Villeroi. 'I have my work at the Palace. Where are you taking me?'

'To your estates at Brie,' d'Artagnan answered him. 'There, on the orders of the Duc d'Orléans, you will remain.'

'I . . . I . . . Governor of the King!'

'You no longer hold that post, sir.'

'I'll not endure this.'

'There is one other alternative, sir.'

'And that? . . .'

'The Bastille,' said the musketeer.

Villeroi sank back against the upholstery. He realised suddenly that he was an old man who had been foolish; and old men could not afford to be foolish. The long battle between the Regent and the King's Governor was over.

✤ ✤ ✤

'Where is Papa Villeroi?' asked Louis. 'I have not seen him all day.'

No one knew. They had seen him preparing to call on the Regent that morning, and none had seen him since.

Louis sent for Orléans.

'The Maréchal is missing,' he said. 'I am alarmed for him.'

The Regent smiled suavely. 'Sire, there is no cause for alarm. Old Papa Villeroi is an old man. He yearns for the peace of the countryside – where he belongs.'

'He has gone on a holiday! But he did not ask if he might go.'

'He has gone for a long, long holiday, Sire. And I thought it best that you should not be grieved by sad farewells.'

Louis, looking into his uncle's face, understood.

Tears came to his eyes; he had loved the old man who had flattered him so blatantly.

But Orléans was embracing him. 'Dearest Majesty,' he said, 'you grow too old for such companionship; you will find the greatest pleasure in life awaiting you.'

Louis turned away. He wept all that night for the loss of poor Papa Villeroi. But he knew it was useless to demand his return. He must wait for that glorious day when it would be his prerogative to command.

＊ ❖ ＊

There was little time for grief. Life had changed abruptly. Louis had a new Governor, the Duc de Charost; life at Versailles became staid, as it had been during the last years of Louis Quatorze. But the King passed from one ceremony to another.

In the autumn he was crowned at Rheims, and immediately after the coronation there was another ordeal to pass through which was very distasteful to him.

Many had come into Rheims to see the twelve-year-old boy crowned King of France; and among them were the maimed and the suffering. They were encamped in the fields close to the Abbey of Rheims awaiting the arrival of the King. Louis, seeming almost supernaturally beautiful in his coronation robe of cloth of gold, his dark-blue eyes enormous in his rather delicate face, his auburn hair hanging in natural curls over his shoulders, must walk among those sick people; he must stop before each, and no matter if their bodies were covered with sores, he must place the back of his hand on their cheeks and murmur that as the King touched them so might God heal them.

Watching him, the hearts of the sick were uplifted, and emotion ran high in the fields of Rheims. This boy with his glowing health and his beautiful countenance was chosen by Providence, they were sure, to lead France to greatness.

Louis longed to be at peace in Versailles, but before returning there he must be entertained at Villers-Cotterets by the Duc d'Orléans and, because the Bourbon-Condés could never be outshone by the rival house of Orléans, he must be similarly and as lavishly entertained at Chantilly.

Next February the King embarked upon his fourteenth year and he was considered to have reached his majority. More festivities there must be to celebrate his coming of age; and in honour of this was held the *lit de justice* in the Grande Chambre where he solemnly received the Great Seal from the Regent.

❧ ❧ ❧

Orléans remained the most important minister in France. It was not forgotten that should the King die without an heir he was next in the line of succession. His greatest rival was the Duc de Bourbon, who yearned to step into his shoes.

Bourbon was far from brilliant. He was thirty-one and his mother was one of the bastards of Louis Quatorze; he could therefore claim to be grandson of the old King, which he never forgot nor allowed anyone else to forget. He was possessed of great wealth and Chantilly was one of the most luxurious houses in France. He devoted much of his time to eating and making love; the rest he spent in asking himself why he should not one day oust Orléans from the post he held and occupy it himself.

He was in continual fear that the King would die and Orléans take the throne, thus frustrating his own ambitions.

Extremely ugly, he had little to attract women but wealth and his titles; and it was largely due to his mistress, Madame de Prie, that ambition had been born in him. Tall and gaunt, his legs were so long and fleshless that he looked as though he were walking on stilts. Being so tall he had formed a habit of stooping, which had made him round-shouldered and, as though he were not unprepossessing enough, when he was young he had had an accident while riding, and this had resulted in his losing an eye.

Yet Madame de Prie, one of the loveliest women at Court, had become his mistress, and it was Madame de Prie's ambition to be the power behind the throne.

Louis she did not consider – he was but a child. She determined that her lover should take the place of Orléans as first minister of France; and as the King was not yet fourteen that would mean that the Duc de Bourbon would be, in all that mattered, ruler of the country.

Bourbon, recently widowed, allowed Madame de Prie to dominate him. This woman, wife of the Marquis de Prie and daughter of a very rich financier, was a born schemer; and although Bourbon would have preferred to feast with her and to make love, he allowed himself to listen to her schemes and to agree with them.

Orléans knew what they planned. He was as determined to foil the schemes of Madame de Prie as she was to carry them out. The possible death of the King held no such qualms for him; for if Louis died, he would take the throne, and when he himself died there was his son, the present Duc de Chartres, to succeed him.

It was true that the Duc de Chartres was more interested in religion than in politics. What did that matter? The Duc d'Orléans did not see how his family could fail to remain in power to the detriment of the Bourbons.

One evening, reviewing this situation and enjoying a great deal of satisfaction from it, he sat in his room in the lower part of the château – for he occupied those apartments which had been used by the Dauphins. Very soon he would go to the King's apartments and present him with certain papers to sign, but it was not yet time to do so and he grew drowsy.

He was vaguely depressed. It was so quiet in his quarters

that he seemed to slip into a dream of the past. He was thinking of his daughter, the Duchesse de Berry, who had recently died – he had loved her passionately and her death had overwhelmed him with grief – when a page came to tell him that the Duchesse de Falari had called to see him.

The Duchesse was one of his mistresses, who had lodging in the Palace. He had kept but a few at Versailles since the orgy in the park, after which life at the château had been so staid.

He had asked that she be brought to him, for it seemed that, in his present mood, she, who was noted for her vivacity, was the sort of companion he needed.

'Come, my dear,' he said. 'Sit down awhile with me. I was feeling a little depressed. I am sure you will cheer me.'

'Depressed!' cried the Duchesse. 'But why so? What is there to depress you, Monsieur le Duc . . . you, who are said to be next to the King in all but name?'

'Ah,' replied Orléans, 'such a remark would at one time have pleased me greatly. Alas, I must be growing old, for my thoughts tonight have strayed beyond affairs on Earth.'

The Duchesse looked at him in alarm and he went on: 'Do you believe that there is a life after death?'

The Duchesse was now quite startled. This was the man who had taken Rabelais to church that he might amuse himself during Mass!

'You are ill?,' she said.

'I asked a question.'

'Do I believe in a life after death?' she mused. 'Yes, I do.'

'Then why do you live as you do here on Earth?'

'Before I die,' she answered, 'I shall repent. That is the way of the world. Were I to repent now, I must reform my ways. Oh, what a dismal prospect! Do you not agree?'

He did not answer. 'Do you not agree with me?' she repeated.

Then she saw that he had slipped sideways in his chair.

She bent over him in alarm and understood. She rushed out of the apartment calling for help; but by the time it arrived the Duc d'Orléans was dead.

Louis wept bitterly. His genial Uncle Philippe . . . dead! Life was too cruel. He had been taken from Madame de Ventadour; Papa Villeroi had been torn from him, and now Uncle Philippe was dead. There was only one to whom he could turn: Fleury. His tutor now occupied first place in his affections; and Fleury was there to comfort and advise.

The shrewd Bishop of Fréjus was determined one day to be France's Premier Minister, but he was clever enough to see that the time had not yet come. He would wait until an occasion arose when he would have the King solidly behind him, and when the King's support would count for something.

At the present time he would have too many against him if he stepped forward into the position he coveted. He summed up the qualities of the Duc de Bourbon who, he guessed, would immediately do his utmost to step into the place vacated by Orléans, and decided Bourbon was no very formidable rival.

Let Bourbon take the place he coveted; let him hold it . . . for a while, until the time was ripe for Fleury, Bishop of Fréjus, to become the power behind the throne.

Bourbon lost no time in coming forward, prodded as he was by his indefatigable and most ambitious mistress. The Duc de Chartres (now Orléans), but twenty years of age and devoted to theology, was not a suitable person for the post, he declared;

therefore, as Prince of the Blood Royal who had, he was always ready to point out, family connexion with great Henri Quatre, it was for him to step into the breach.

Would the King accept him?

The King, mourning his beloved Uncle Philippe and prompted by Fleury, gave the required answer.

The most important lady of the Court was now Madame de Prie. Gaily she gave herself to the task of governing France.

She realised however that her favours came from her lover, and was determined that he should not marry a lady who was as eager for power as herself; so her first task was to find a suitable wife for him. She should be the most insignificant woman in the world.

She confided her plans to her lover, who was so besottedly enamoured of her that he agreed with all she suggested.

'Will you marry the lady I have found for you?' she asked him.

'If you command it,' he told her.

'Then prepare yourself – for I have found her.'

'Pray tell me her name.'

'It is Marie Leczinska, daughter of Stanislas.'

'What! The exiled King of Poland?'

'Exactly. Why should you not have a King's daughter? As an exile he will be glad of any match. She is very plain, but I shall be there to compensate you for that.'

'You have enough beauty to satisfy any man,' he told her.

'That is why you shall have the plainest wife in the world.' Bourbon grimaced.

'Plain, homely, humble, she will be delighted to marry a

royal Bourbon. She is exactly the wife I have been seeking for you. She will never interfere with us. Is that not what we seek?'

'It is.'

'You may leave it to me,' Madame de Prie told him. 'I shall see that a marriage is arranged.'

♣ ♣ ♣

In the scandal which ended in the dismissal of the Duc de la Tremouille, Bourbon forgot his suggested marriage with the King of Poland's daughter. The Duc de la Tremouille was the leader of a little group of young men which included the Duc d'Epernon, son of the Comtesse de Toulouse, the young Duc de Gesvres, and another boy who, although only fifteen, was already a secretary of state. This last was de Maurepas – far more clever than any of the others but, because he was not of such high birth, less prominent.

Fleury, anxious that Louis should not become interested in women, had encouraged the King's friendship with these young men, not at first realising that in their languorous habits, their fondness for lying about on cushions, doing a little fine embroidery, talking scandal and eating innumerable sweetmeats, lay danger.

The Court was horrified. Was Louis to become another Henri Trois to be ruled by his *mignons*? Louis was fourteen – strong and healthy, apart from those occasional bouts of fever which seemed to attack him from time to time; he was capable of begetting children. What was the Duc de Bourbon thinking of, what was Fleury thinking of, to allow such dangers to come within the range of the King?

Bourbon acted promptly. He ordered de la Tremouille's

guardian to get the young man married and remove him from Court; so the little coterie was scattered.

Louis allowed them to go without comment. He was now becoming accustomed to losing his friends.

Shortly after the dismissal of de la Tremouille Louis became ill with fever, and once more alarm spread through Paris.

When Madame de Prie heard the news she hurried to her lover.

'What will happen to us if the King dies?' she demanded.

Bourbon regarded her in perplexity.

'I will explain,' said the strong-minded woman. 'Young Orléans will take the throne. Then, Monsieur le Duc, you will be dismissed from your office.'

Bourbon nodded. 'The King must not die,' he declared.

'Indeed not! And there must be no more shocks such as this.'

'How can we prevent his taking these fevers?'

'We cannot. Therefore he must produce an heir to the throne. If he died then, you would still continue in your position.'

'But the Infanta is only a child. There can be no heir for years.'

'Not if he is going to wait for the Infanta.'

'But indeed he must wait for the Infanta. How else?'

'By taking another wife, of course.'

'He is betrothed to the Infanta.'

'A child of eight! It is quite ridiculous. That boy has become a man, I tell you. What is going to happen if you keep him unmarried? There will be a mistress before long. A mistress! Imagine that. How many ambitious women do you think there are in this Court simply waiting to leap into his bed? And then, what of us? Or what if he should have a friend . . . a *mignon* like

67

de la Tremouille? The position would be the same. We are here, my dear friend, at the head of affairs. We must not be so foolish as to allow others to push us aside.'

'But an heir . . . it is impossible!'

'Nothing is impossible if we decide otherwise. The King must be provided with a wife, and that silly little child sent back where she belongs – to her own country.'

'You would make war with Spain!'

'Bah! Does Spain want war with France? France and Spain . . . are they not both ruled by Bourbon Kings? No! A little coolness perhaps. But what of that? It will be forgotten, and we shall make our little King a husband and get the heir we need.'

'But . . .' stammered Bourbon . . . 'how can we do this?'

She smiled and, putting her hands on his shoulders, drew him to her and kissed him. 'First,' she said, 'we will have the people talking. That is always the way to get delicate matters started. Oh, the people of Paris! How they love their little King! You will see, in a very short time you will hear them saying that our King is a man, that were he married to a woman of his age there would be a Dauphin of France by now. Wait, my darling. You have but to leave this little matter in my hands.'

'You are not only the most desirable woman in France,' murmured the Duc, 'you are possessed of genius.'

Tears streamed down the fat pink cheeks of Maria Anna as her carriage rolled southwards.

Louis had not said goodbye to her. She had not known at first that she was being sent away. She had merely thought that she was going on a visit.

Now she had been told. 'You are going home. Will that not be delightful? You will see your dear family; and how much more pleasant it will be to live in your own country!'

'Is Louis coming?' she had asked.

'No. Louis must stay in France. You see, he is the King.'

'But I am to be the Queen.'

'Perhaps of some other country, eh, my little one?'

Then she had understood, and she could not speak for crying. Ever since that day at the firework display, when he had spoken to her, she had always believed that one day he would love her. He had spoken to her several times since then – not much, but when she had said to him it was a fine day he had agreed, and she adored him.

But it was all over. She was no longer the affianced bride of the beautiful King of France.

So, though she stared at the French countryside, the little Infanta was aware of nothing but her own grief.

✣　✤　✣

Madame de Prie laughed when she heard of the reactions of Philip V.

'He is so furious,' declared Bourbon, 'that he is ready to go to war. He declares that he will not allow his daughter to be so insulted.'

'Let us not concern ourselves with him.'

'He is sending back the Regent's daughter, widow of Luis.'

Madame de Prie snapped her fingers. 'That for the Regent's daughter! Let her come back. We will accept her in exchange for their silly little Infanta. Come, we must find Louis a wife quickly.'

The persistent Madame de Prie had already made a list of

ninety-nine names; among these were the fifteen- and thirteen-year-old daughters of the Prince of Wales – Anne and Amelia Sophia Eleanor.

Bourbon hesitated over these two before he said: 'But they are Protestants! The French would never accept a Protestant Queen.'

Even Madame de Prie was ready to concede that he was right on that point.

'There is young Elizabeth of Russia . . .' she began; then she stopped.

She must be very careful in this choice of a bride for the King. If a dominating woman were chosen, all her efforts would be in vain. Who knew what influence a wife might not wield over one as young and impressionable as the King.

Then she turned to her lover, her eyes shining.

She said slowly: 'When I was searching for a bride for you I selected the most humble woman I could find.'

'Marie Leczinska,' said Bourbon.

'My friend,' cried Madame de Prie, 'I am going to ask you to relinquish your bride. The King shall have her instead.'

'Impossible!' murmured Bourbon; but a light of excitement had begun to shine in his eyes.

'Have I not told you that nothing shall be impossible?'

'The people will never accept her.'

She threw herself into his arms. She was laughing so much that he believed she was on the verge of hysteria.

'I have decided,' she said. 'I swear that in a very short time Marie Leczinska shall be Queen of France.'

❧ Chapter III ❧

MARIE LECZINSKA – QUEEN OF FRANCE

*J*t was quiet in the sewing-room of the Wissembourg house. Mother and daughter stitched diligently; they were both working on a gown of the daughter's, which caused them many a grimace, for the gown should by now have been consigned to the rag-bag or at least to a lower servant.

How tired I am, thought the ex-Queen of Poland, of living in such poverty!

The younger woman had not the same regrets, for she could not remember anything but a life of exile and poverty. She had been mending her clothes and getting the last weeks of wear out of them for the greater part of her life.

'Perhaps,' sighed the Queen, 'our luck will change one day.'

'Do you think my father will be recalled to Poland?'

Queen Catherine laughed bitterly. 'I see no reason whatsoever why he should be.'

'Then,' said Marie Leczinska, 'how could it change?'

'Your father hopes you will make a good marriage.'

'I?' Marie laughed and, as she stared at the garment in her hand, a flush touched her cheeks. 'What chance of making a brilliant marriage has a penniless Princess, daughter of an exiled King, without dowry, without grace, without beauty?'

'Marie Leczinska, do not say such things.'

Marie knew that her mother was really angry when she called her Marie Leczinska; for in the heart of the family she was affectionately called by her nickname Maruchna.

'Should not one say what is true?' she asked quietly.

'Many less beautiful than you have made grand marriages.'

'What use to delude ourselves?' demanded Marie. 'I have not forgotten the words of Anne of Bavaria when she heard that there were plans to marry me to the Duc de Bourbon.'

'These Bourbons!' cried Queen Catherine. 'They have too grand an opinion of themselves. Anne of Bavaria, Princess Palatine, does not forget that she was the widow of a Condé – and, so, thought her grandson too good for you. She forgets that the Condés are not what they were in France since the death of the *great* Condé.'

'Oh, Mother, let us not talk of greatness and marriages for me which can only take place in our imagination. We are here in this house and we are together. We love each other; why cannot we content ourselves with being a little family of no importance?'

'Because the throne of Poland belongs to your father, not to Augustus Elector of Saxony; and he will never be resigned. He will always hope to regain it. Maruchna, each night he prays that his greatest desire may be granted. Kings can never be reconciled to living in poverty, dependent on the help of friends. It is too humiliating to be borne.'

'Yet to me,' said Marie, taking her needle and beginning to work on the worn-out garment, 'it seems even more humiliating to be hawked round Europe as a prospective bride – and rejected.'

'It has happened to Princesses more fortunate than you are.'

'All the same I would prefer it not to happen to me. I would rather stay here, living as we do, turning old dresses to give them a new lease of life. I hope I shall be offered to no one else. I felt sick with shame when Father tried so hard to marry me to Ludwig Georg of Baden. *He* would have none of me; and now you see I am not considered good enough for the Duc de Bourbon.'

Catherine smiled secretly. 'There has been much correspondence going on between Bourbon and your father. Madame de Prie sends letters regularly.'

'Madame de Prie?'

'Yes. She acts on behalf of the Duc de Bourbon. She is a lady of some influence at the Court.'

Marie did not answer; she was certain that the arrangements for the Bourbon marriage would end as had all others. She was thinking that she would probably marry Le Tellier de Courtenvaux, who was merely in charge of a regiment of cavalry in Wissembourg. He had asked for her hand but her father had indignantly refused it. His daughter to marry with a man who was not a peer of France! Yet, thought Marie, Father should forget his grand illusions; he should realise our position and accept it.

She pictured herself never marrying at all, remaining in this house – if they were allowed to remain here – all the days of her life.

Her mother read her thoughts. 'Your father will never consent to a marriage which he considers it beneath your dignity to make.'

'Then, Mother, let us cease to think of marriage.'

'If you married the Duc de Bourbon,' mused Queen Catherine, 'we should at least be lifted from this wretched poverty. How your father has suffered! To be dispossessed of his crown and his country and to live on charity! It is more than his proud spirit can endure.'

'He has long endured it and, if perforce he must continue to do so, he will.'

'You should not be so resigned, Maruchna. How do we live here – in a house borrowed from a Councillor of the Elector Palatine, on an income from the Duc d'Orléans which is not always regularly paid . . . from moneys sent by friends in Lorraine, Sweden and Spain. We are never quite sure that we shall receive our remittances. When I think of the old days I could weep, I tell you.'

'Tears will avail us little. Look, Mother, I do not think there will be more than a month's wear in this gown even when it is turned. Is it worth the effort?'

The Queen shook her head impatiently. 'I have great hopes of Madame de Prie.'

'If I leave Alsace I shall take you and Father with me.'

The Queen smiled. The result of exile, she supposed, had bound the family close together. Her husband Stanislas loved his Maruchna with a love that was surely blind, for he saw her – penniless and plain as she was – as one of the most desirable *parties* in Europe.

'I should be sorry to leave Alsace, though,' murmured Marie. 'We have our friends here.'

The Queen smiled sadly. Poor Maruchna! She had never known what it meant to live the life of a King's daughter. She thought it was wonderful to visit Saverne, the home of the Cardinal de Rohan in Strasbourg, or that of the Comte du

Bourg in the same town. It was significant of the depth to which they had fallen that the daughter of the King could be overwhelmed by the hospitality of friends such as these.

There must be a marriage with Bourbon. She and Stanislas fervently hoped for it, for the Duc was connected with the French royal house, and such a marriage would mean the end of poverty.

'Listen,' said the Queen, 'I hear someone riding to the house.' She dropped her needlework and went to the window, then turned quickly and smiled at her daughter. 'It is!' she cried. 'More letters from the Duc de Bourbon or Madame de Prie. I recognise the man's livery.'

'Mother, do not excite yourself. It may be that the letters contain more reasons why I am not a fit bride for the Duke.'

Catherine came back to the table. 'Oh, Maruchna, you give way too easily. One day our luck must change.'

'Let us finish the dress, Mother. We have spent so much time on it already and if it is not going to be worth the effort, let us not waste much more.'

They were working when Stanislas, the ex-King of Poland, burst into the room.

Marie had never seen her father so excited. It was strange also that he should come upon them thus unceremoniously for, although he lived in exile on the charity of his friends, he had always endeavoured to preserve the atmosphere of a court in his household. It was true it consisted of a few, very few, noblemen who had followed him into exile and now bore the grand-sounding names of Chamberlain, Secretary and Grand Marshal; there were but two Polish priests to the household, and as there were no state affairs to be discussed, the time was spent in attending church and reading, although he had always made sure that Marie should be taught to dance, sing and play the harpsichord.

'Wife! Daughter!' cried Stanislas. 'I have news. First let us go down on our knees and give thanks to God for the greatest good fortune which could come our way.'

Marie obeyed her father; Catherine looked at him questioningly, but he would say nothing until they had finished the prayer.

Marie thought, as she joined in the thanksgiving: It is strange to be thankful when one does not know for what. Is it Bourbon? No. It must be something greater than that. The greatest good fortune, he had said. That could mean only one thing.

The prayer over she looked at her father, affection shining in her eyes.

'So, Father,' she said, 'you have been recalled to your throne?'

Stanislas smiled at his daughter and shook his head. 'Better news than that. Yes, even better than that.'

'But what could be better?' demanded the Queen.

'Madame,' said Stanislas, looking from his wife to his daughter. 'Look at our little Maruchna. Then thank Heaven for our good fortune. Our daughter is to be the Queen of France.'

✤ ✤ ✤

The young King was not displeased to hear of the proposed marriage. He was now fifteen and eager for a wife. He had so far shown no interest in women, which was largely due to the influence of Fleury who was determined that he should not be dominated by anyone but himself.

76

The proposed Queen seemed as ideal from Fleury's point of view as she did from that of the Duc de Bourbon and Madame de Prie. A girl humbly brought up, plain and meek – what could be better? Fleury was as eager to promote this marriage as were the Duc and his mistress.

The girl was twenty-one – only about seven years older than the King; and they need only wait until the little Infanta had been received by her outraged family in Spain before announcing the proposed marriage.

On a Sunday in May, Louis himself told the members of the Council: 'Gentlemen, I am going to marry the Princess of Poland. She was born on June 23rd, 1703, and she is the only daughter of Stanislas Leczinska who was elected King of Poland in July 1704. He and Queen Catherine will come to France with their daughter and I have put the Château of Saint-Germain-en-Laye at their disposal. The mother of King Stanislas will accompany them.'

The news soon spread through Paris. The King to marry the daughter of an exile! It was incredible when any of the most important Princesses of Europe would have been ready to marry Louis, for not only was he the monarch of the greatest country in Europe, but he was young, and as handsome as a god. And he was to marry this woman, of whom so many of them had never heard, the daughter of an exile, penniless, of no account and some seven years older than himself.

Rumour grew throughout Paris. One day, the proposed Queen was said to be not only plain, but downright ugly. By the next day she was deformed; by the next web-footed. The marriage, it was decided, could only have been arranged by Madame de Prie because she wished to remain the power behind the throne.

Paris murmured angrily. Songs were sung in which the appearance of Marie was described as hideous. 'The Polish woman', she was called – the woman whose name ended in ska.

They called her the *Demoiselle* Leczinska and waited in rising indignation for her arrival.

❧ ❧ ❧

Everything was changed now in the house at Wissembourg. Those who had followed Stanislas into exile wore expressions of sly content; when the Cardinal de Rohan and the Maréchal du Bourg visited the family there was a subtle change in their manner, particularly towards Marie.

Queen Catherine ceased to regret the past; she even ceased to mourn the recent death of one of her daughters; she had Marie left to her, and Marie was going to make a great change in the lives of her parents.

Stanislas was jovial, and it delighted Marie to see him thus, for the affection between her father and herself was greater than that they had for any other. They were alike inasmuch as they could accept good fortune with pleasure and bad with resignation – unlike the Queen, who had been unable to hide her grief and dissatisfaction during the long years of exile.

'My dear,' he told Catherine gaily, 'now is the time to redeem your jewels.'

'The Frankfurt Jews will never relinquish them unless paid in full,' declared Catherine.

'Ha, they shall be paid,' laughed Stanislas. 'I have lost no time in raising the necessary loans.'

'You have done this!'

'You forget, wife! I am no longer merely the exiled King of Poland; I am the father of the future Queen of France.'

Preparations went on at great speed. Everyone worked feverishly, beset by one great fear. What if the King of France should change his mind? It was unbearable to contemplate and it seemed hardly likely that this was to be, for news was brought to the house that Madame de Prie herself had arrived in Strasbourg and was on her way to visit Marie and her father.

Madame de Prie! How could they do enough for this woman to whom they owed everything? Stanislas had quickly made himself aware of the state of affairs in France and he realised the importance of this woman.

A banquet must be prepared for her – at least a banquet such as they could afford and could be served in such a small house.

Madame de Prie arrived, gracious and charming, yet determined that they should not for one moment lose sight of her importance.

She took in each detail of Marie's appearance. It was true, thought Madame de Prie with pleasure, that she was no beauty. She was without elegance; by no means the sort of woman to rule through her personal charms. She seemed overwhelmed by her good fortune and fully aware that she owed it in a large measure to Madame de Prie.

The scheming woman could not have found anyone more to her taste.

She embraced Marie, not with the respect due to the Queen of France, but with a certain benevolent affection which she might have shown to a protégée.

'I have brought presents from the Duc de Bourbon for you and your parents,' she told Marie. 'I could not resist bringing something for you myself, and I believe I know what will appeal to you most and what you doubtless need. Allow me to show you.'

Imperiously Madame de Prie ordered the cases to be brought into the room, and when they were opened she took out gossamer undergarments and silk stockings so fine that Marie gasped in astonishment.

'They are for you,' said Madame de Prie, taking Marie in her arms and kissing her.

'I thank you with all my heart!' cried Marie. 'I have never before seen such beautiful things.'

Madame de Prie laughed with pleasure. She was thinking of the future – with herself supreme – for the Queen of France would remember to whom she owed her position and be for ever grateful to the all-powerful Madame de Prie.

Stanislas, no less than Madame de Prie, the Duc de Bourbon and Fleury, was eager that there should be no delay. Delays could be dangerous, particularly in view of the mood of the Parisians towards the *'Demoiselle'* whom they did not think good enough for their handsome little King.

On the 15th of August the marriage was celebrated at Strasbourg by the Cardinal de Rohan, Bishop of Strasbourg, with the young Duc d'Orléans, as first Prince of the Blood Royal, to stand proxy for Louis.

The delight of Stanislas was not unmixed with apprehension. It had not been easy for him to muster a court worthy of the occasion, although now that arrangements had gone so far he found new friends to rally to his side. But the energetic Madame de Prie was at hand and, since she was determined that the marriage should take place without a hitch, it did so. All the nobility of Alsace came to the rescue, sending their sons as pages or to fill any role for which they were needed. The

Duc d'Antin gave dignity to the exiled court by appearing as Ambassador Extraordinary and Minister Plenipotentiary of France, and Stanislas gave similar rank to a member of his household, so that diplomatic dignity was preserved.

Marie, dressed as she had never been dressed before, in a gown of green brocade beautifully embroidered and trimmed with silver lace, looked pleasant and certainly not in the least like the deformed creature whom the people of Paris believed her to be.

She felt dazed with the wonder of all this as she entered the church, her father and mother on either side of her, the Duc d'Orléans, her bridegroom by proxy, going on ahead with the two ambassadors.

It was difficult for her to believe, when that ceremony was over, when the Te Deum had been sung and the cannons had roared, that she was the Queen of France.

She dined in public, served by the King's officers at the Hôtel de Ville, and there was dancing in the streets, where free bread and wine were provided for all.

She felt bewildered and very apprehensive, for although all these great noblemen and the people of Strasbourg acclaimed her and called her Queen, she had yet to face the people of Paris and her husband.

There was little time for contemplation, as two days after the ceremony in Strasbourg the journey to Fontainebleau began.

As soon as the procession set out the rain began to fall. Marie sat in the royal coach looking out on the fields in which the precious corn was being ruined, while the Duc d'Orléans with his entourage rode ahead that he might receive her in the towns through which they passed. The carriage of the Duc de

Noailles went before her followed by the pages on horseback, and the Guards rode beside the royal coach; behind them came the carriages of noble men and women who had come to Strasbourg to attend the wedding. The procession was two miles long, including the service waggons.

The people of the countryside came out to cheer the Queen as she passed through it. They threw flowers at her carriage, and she saw that they had hung out flags even in the smallest villages. In spite of the evil weather they determined to give her a good welcome.

It seemed to her that the people at least were glad to see her, but she herself was horrified by the signs of poverty which she glimpsed in those villages. When she noticed how thin and poorly clad the people were, she was glad the King had sent her fifteen thousand livres that she might distribute *largesse* on her passage through the country.

The progress was slow on account of the weather, and often the Queen's carriage became bogged down in the mud. There were constant delays and often she heards news that disturbed her.

There was a shortage of bread and there had been riots, not only in Paris, but in the provinces, when the people had stormed the bakers' shops for bread.

The names of the Duc de Bourbon and his mistress, Madame de Prie, were mentioned. It was said that they had taken advantage of the situation and become even richer by their speculations in grain to the detriment of the people.

Marie however, sympathetic as she was, could do no more than distribute her *largesse*, and before her journey was over she found her purse empty. But there was little room in her thoughts for anything else but her meeting with the King, for at last the procession was nearing Moret where Louis had arranged to meet her.

Louis was uneasy. He had been so eager to have a wife that perhaps he had consented too readily to accept this one. The words of the Parisians rang in his ears, for he had heard some of the songs which were being sung in the Paris streets.

The incessant rain was depressing. He had heard that the citizens were rioting in Paris. They did not blame him for their poverty; they blamed him for nothing, and wherever he went they cheered him. But they blamed the Duc de Bourbon and Madame de Prie, particularly the latter, who they declared was the First Minister's evil genius.

Louis did not want to think of the people's plight; he did not want to think of the people. Ever since Papa Villeroi had forced him to undergo so many public appearances he had fought shy of them.

Now he would think of his wife. If he did not like her he would ignore her, as he had heard de la Tremouille ignored his wife. He would let her know that he was the King and that if he was not pleased with his marriage it should be as though no marriage had taken place.

Humpbacked! Web-footed! It was alarming.

But there was no help for it now. He must go to Moret and meet her.

She was late arriving. News was brought to him that her carriage was stuck in the mud and that thirty horses had had to be attached to it to drag it out.

They were putting a carpet over the mud where her carriage would stop and he was waiting to greet her. And here was the carriage, and here was she.

His eager eyes took in every detail of her appearance as she stepped out of the carriage.

She was wearing the dress in which she had been married, and green and silver became her; over it she wore a purple velvet cloak and her big hat was trimmed with ostrich feathers.

The rain had stopped and even the wind was still. Trumpets sounded a fanfare and drums were beaten; all those who had gathered to see this historic meeting cheered wildly and Louis, looking at his bride, felt a tremor of emotion pass through him. She was certainly not deformed; she was not even ugly; and with the ostrich feathers dropping over her face he thought her beautiful.

He, who had never been interested in women until this moment, found an excitement, a great delight, take possession of him.

He was a King and he was a husband. He felt pleased with what life had given him.

She would have knelt, but he would not allow her to; he put his arms about her and embraced her.

Then they stood for a few seconds smiling at each other. Louis, in his awakening manhood, thought her the most beautiful woman he had ever seen.

As for Marie, she found that reports of him had not been exaggerated. She could truly say that she had never before seen such a handsome young man. And when he smiled at her tenderly, as he was doing now, welcoming her to his country, so content that he, the greatest monarch in the world, should share his throne with one who was little more than a beggar maid, she felt that she had won happiness such as she had never dreamed could come to her.

The second marriage ceremony was performed on the following day in the chapel of the Palace of Fontainebleau. This was a far more impressive occasion than the first. All the great nobles of the Court were present, precious stones glittering on their robes of state. The chapel had been decorated for the occasion and the hangings were bright with the golden lilies of France.

Louis led the procession which passed from the King's great Chamber to the Gallery of François Premier and the Staircase on either side of which were stationed the Swiss Guards.

The beauty of Louis aroused admiration in all who beheld him, as he walked among the Princes of the royal blood. He was so graceful; those manners, reminiscent of his great-grandfather, which had been insisted on by Papa Villeroi, were so gracious, so regal, that it was difficult to believe he was but fifteen and a half.

The Queen followed, the Duc de Bourbon on one side, the Duc d'Orléans on the other, while the Princesse de Conti, the Dowager Duchesse de Bourbon and Mademoiselle de Charolais held up the train of purple velvet lined with ermine.

These Princesses were a little piqued. They – royal ladies – to hold the train of the daughter of the King of Poland who, even had he not been an *exiled* King, would have seemed far below their rank!

They had been warned that they must remember that Marie Leczinska was no longer merely the daughter of Stanislas; she was Queen of France. They were trying to remember it now, but their difficulty in doing so was apparent in their expressions.

Cardinal de Rohan, Grand Almoner, officiated at Fontainebleau as he had at Strasbourg. He called attention to the greatness of France's beloved King and to the renown of his forbears. He declared that it was with great joy that he presented to His Majesty a virtuous and prudent woman.

Thanksgiving hymns echoed through the chapel, and Louis, shyly taking his bride's hand, led the way to the royal apartments.

There a banquet was held and, as the King and Queen sat side by side, the Duc de Mortemart knelt before Marie to present her with a casket covered with velvet and gold embroidery; this contained jewels which were called the *corbeille* – wedding gifts for the Queen to present to the members of her household.

Marie looked at them in delight. She turned her flushed face to that of her husband and cried in simple pleasure: 'Never before in the whole of my life have I been able to give presents.'

Louis, deeply touched by those words, took her hand and pressed it firmly.

She was by no means ugly, and she was good. He was contented; and in that moment he told himself that he would rather have Marie Leczinska for his wife than anyone else in the world.

After the banquet a play of Molière's was performed before the King and Queen to the satisfaction of everyone except Voltaire who, having been brought to Court by Madame de Prie, had written an entertainment of his own and was acutely disappointed that preference should be shown to a dead writer when a living one had his reputation to establish.

The next day all noticed the change in the King. He was ecstatically happy, completely contented. The courtiers smiled fondly at him and knowledgeably at each other. The marriage was a success.

Exuberantly, and with the Queen smiling beside him, Louis called for his barbers.

'Cut off these curls,' he said. 'I am no longer a child.' So the lovely hair was shorn, and Louis gave no regretful glance at the soft auburn curls lying on the floor by his chair. They set the wig on his head. It had the desired effect. He might have been eighteen or nineteen – nearer the age of his bride.

✤ ✤ ✤

The next days were given to celebrating the marriage. There were firework displays, illuminations, dancing in those streets which but a short while ago had been the scene of bread riots. There was free wine, which meant that the people could forget their miseries for a while.

'Our little Louis is a husband,' they said to one another. 'Soon he will dispense with his ministers and rule alone. God bless him! That will be a happy day for France.'

Louis was their hero; it was the First Minister and his mistress, and also their creature, Pâris-Duverney, whom they had made Minister of Finance, who were the villains.

Even Voltaire was happy. Madame de Prie had presented him to the Queen, and one of his entertainments had been played; moreover a pension had been granted him; so all his dissatisfaction with the proceedings was over and he had nothing but praise for all.

There were deputations to be received from the merchants; as usual on such occasions the women from Les Halles were prominent. It was they who, in their best clothes, sent a deputation carrying a basket of truffles. 'Eat a great many of them, Your Majesty,' said their spokeswoman; 'and implore his Majesty to do likewise, for they will help you to get children.'

Marie graciously accepted the truffles and assured the women that she would do her duty, and that she prayed, as earnestly as they did, that before long she and the King would give them a Dauphin.

Meanwhile Louis, exploring the road of conjugal adventure, was becoming more and more pleased with Marie. This was his first experience with a woman, and he was finding in himself a hitherto unsuspected sensuality. Unlike many young men of his Court he had in the care of Fleury been kept innocent and almost ignorant of love-making. Now he was exulting because he had discovered an avenue which seemed to him to offer even greater excitement than hunting or gambling.

He felt deeply grateful to the Queen – his partner in this bliss; their mutual ecstasy clothed her with a beauty which seemed dazzling to him. Beside her, all other women seemed dull, lacking perfection.

If any of his courtiers referred to the beauty of another woman, he would say sharply: 'She is well enough, but compared with the Queen she seems almost unattractive.'

Fleury was delighted with this state of affairs. He could congratulate himself that he had been wise in not allowing the King to indulge in love affairs before his marriage. The de la Tremouille affair had presented a danger, he was ready to admit, but that had been safely overcome; and now here was

Louis, passionately in love with his Queen – the very best way in which to ensure a fertile union.

It was not necessary to wait for his spies to tell him how often the King spent the night with the Queen, because this happened every night.

Villeroi had instilled in the King his respect for Etiquette and this was not forgotten even in the first heat of passion. The ceremonies of the *lever* and *coucher* were conducted as carefully as they had been in the days of Louis Quatorze. The Queen would be helped to her bed first, and the King's *coucher* would take place in his own bedroom. When he was installed in his bed and those privileged noblemen who had assisted at the *coucher* had been dismissed, the King would make his way across the Galerie des Glaces to the Queen's bedroom, accompanied only by his *valet de chambre*.

His sword would be set beside the Queen's bed, and the Queen's lady-in-waiting would draw the curtains about the bed, shutting her in with her husband, before she retired.

In the morning the King must leave the Queen's bed and return to the great state bed in the Louis Quatorze bedroom for the ceremonial *lever*. This was an occasion when rivalry ran high for the privilege of handing him his garments which were passed from hand to hand – in order of the status of those present – until they reached the King himself.

It was a delightful existence. The King and Queen were never seen without each other those days. The Queen rode out hunting with him, and sat beside him when they picnicked in the woods all through the summer. The idyll went on into the winter when sledging parties took the place of picnics. The people gathered to see the King and Queen, gliding over the ice in a sledge made to look like a great sea-shell decorated with Cupids, their arms about each other – a charming enough pair of lovers to delight Gallic eyes.

'Good days are coming,' the people told each other. 'Give him a little time to be young and in love, let him prolong his honeymoon a little longer; then it will be for him to cast off his mercenary ministers and govern us himself. He is good and kind, and he will understand our sufferings. Long live our little Louis!'

Louis was not aware of the people; he was only conscious of the charms of his Marie and the delights of requited love.

Marie's pleasure was complete when her father came to Fontainebleau for, gay as he had outwardly been, she had always before been conscious of the cloud over his happiness. He would constantly yearn for the throne he had lost. But now, he assured her, nothing on Earth could give him greater joy than to see her the beloved wife of the King.

He and her mother stayed with Marie for three days at Fontainebleau. Even Catherine was contented. There need no longer be the depressing business of fighting poverty. Were they not father- and mother-in-law to the greatest King in Europe? The splendour of the French Court dazzled them; and to see Marie in the centre of it – not only Queen of France but so loved by the King – made them feel as though they were dreaming and so much sudden good fortune could not possibly be theirs.

Louis was gracious to them; artlessly he seemed to thank them for having produced one so perfect as his Queen. Instead of the Château de Saint-Germain they were to have the Château de Chambord which he was having refurnished and made ready for them. Meanwhile they would take up their residence at the Château de Bourron.

Before he left for Bourron, Stanislas and Catherine embraced their daughter with great fervour.

'Do not forget,' Stanislas said, 'that it is the Duc de Bourbon who rules France. In no way antagonise him. Remember too all that you owe to Madame de Prie.'

'I can never forget it,' murmured Marie.

'They are your friends; the King loves you. There is only one thing I need to make my contentment complete. That is a Dauphin for France.'

And Marie, as astonished by her sudden good fortune as her parents were, had no doubt that, as so much had been granted her, this would not be denied.

❧ Chapter IV ❧

MADAME DE PRIE
AND THE DUC DE BOURBON

*J*t was during the winter that Louis first took Marie to
Marly, that delightful château which Louis XIV had built
between Versailles and Saint Germain.

Marie was delighted with Marly, perhaps because it was so
beautiful, set among the woods with its view of the river,
perhaps because at that time she was in love with life.

There was good hunting to be had in the surrounding
country and each day the King and his bride rode forth,
returning in the evening to cards and other entertainments.

Always in attendance were the Duc de Bourbon and
Madame de Prie. The latter had been installed as the chief of
Marie's ladies-in-waiting; and it became a regular routine that
whoever wished to approach the King or Queen could only do
so through the good graces of Madame de Prie.

Had Louis and Marie not been so absorbed in each other
they would have noticed that the Queen of the Court was not
Marie, but Madame de Prie, who, while she insisted on
everyone's observing the strictest Etiquette, did no such thing
herself.

She would go in and out of the Queen's apartment without being announced. She advised the Queen not only on what to do but what to wear; and remembering her father's advice and her own gratitude, Marie willingly accepted these suggestions.

Recklessly, during those weeks at Marly, Marie gambled at the instigation of the King. It seemed a great joke to him when counting their debts they discovered them to be 200,000 livres.

'200,000 livres!' cried Marie. 'Why, it is a fortune. In the days at Wissembourg we could have lived on that for a very long time.'

That delighted Louis. He proudly told her that she need not now feel the least concerned about losing 200,000 livres. They would play as recklessly tomorrow night just to prove it.

One day she came upon three of her ladies – the Duchesses d'Epernon, de Beuiune and de Tallard – gossiping together, and noticed that when she approached they grew silent. She was naturally eager to learn all she could about the Court, and these ladies, she believed, could tell her a great deal.

'You must not fall silent when I appear,' she told them. 'I like to join in the fun.'

The ladies tried to look innocent but they failed somehow and, when she insisted on hearing what they had been talking about, they told her that they had discussed the affairs of the Duc de Richelieu who was said to be one of the biggest rakes of all time. He was so very handsome.

Marie, whose upbringing at Wissembourg had been a very strict one, did not immediately grasp the nature of those adventures in which the Duc de Richelieu had apparently indulged to such a great extent.

'We were talking about the duel which the Marquise de

Nesle fought with Madame de Polignac,' Madame de Tallard eventually explained.

'A duel between ladies!'

'Oh, yes. It was with pistols. You see, they were both desperately in love with the Duc de Richelieu and decided on a duel.'

'How . . . immodest!' said the Queen.

The Duchesse d'Epernon murmured. 'But, Your Majesty, such things happen.'

'I hope we shall never have anything so disgraceful happening at our Court. I shall expect all my ladies to live virtuously and in a way to be an example to all. Tell me, does this immorality exist today . . . here?' Marie pursed her lips so that she looked very prim. 'I must speak to Madame de Prie about it.'

The Duchesse de Bethune tried hard not to smile but did not quite achieve her intentions, and Marie was shocked into sudden suspicion. Madame de Prie and the Duc de Bourbon *were* very friendly. They were frequently seen in each other's company and they did appear to be on terms of the utmost affection.

Marie said tensely: 'What is the relationship between the Duc de Bourbon and Madame de Prie?'

'Why, Madame, it is common knowledge that she is his mistress.'

'But . . . Madame de Prie has a husband . . .'

Her ladies looked at her blankly.

Marie realised that there were doubtless a great many things going on at this brilliant Court of which she was in ignorance.

She was deeply shocked. Her first impulse was to send for Madame de Prie, to tell her that this disgraceful association must cease. But this concerned the Duc de Bourbon, First Minister of France, and Madamce de Prie whose power had put Marie where she was.

Marie understood then that it was necessary to adjust her principles. The relationship between those two powerful people was something she must accept, disapprove of it though she so heartily did.

✤ ✤ ✤

Those were fateful days for Louis and Marie. Their lives lay before them and to each Fate offered at the time a choice of two ways. To each was given the opportunity to mould the destiny of France; each was too young, too inexperienced – in Louis' case too lazy, in Marie's case too unimaginative – to choose the path which would have led to glory.

Louis was beloved by his people. His handsome looks had won their hearts: his perfect manners enchanted them. His people looked to him to bring prosperity to the country and, because he was young and had won their affection, they did not ask of him impossibilities. They were ready to be patient. All they asked of him was that, when he was old enough to rule, he would rule them well. They asked for his consideration of their sufferings; they asked that he should use his undoubted talents to serve them.

Louis, enthralled by being a husband, eager to indulge his pleasures such as hunting and gambling, and having always relied on his governors and tutors to do the serious business of the State, was eager to escape from the people and enjoy his life. This they would forgive while he was young, but already he was growing towards an age of responsibility.

As for Marie, Louis was in love with her and ready to be

guided by her. At this time, when she could give him the sexual satisfaction he desired, she could have established herself as his confidante and adviser for all time. It was true that a man of such insatiable desire as Louis was already showing signs of becoming, could not be content with one woman; an experienced woman of the world would have realised this and consolidated her position while she had an opportunity of doing so.

Marie, being ill-advised by her parents, misjudged not only her husband's character and her own possibilities but the true quality of the men who sought to govern the King.

She believed in the shrewd cleverness of the Duc de Bourbon and bowed to his wishes and those of his mistress in every way; while she completely ignored the man for whom Louis had the greatest regard and affection, the man who the King, if not the Queen, was clever enough to see had a deeper grasp of affairs and a more altruistic attitude towards the state: Fleury the Bishop of Fréjus.

Marie knew that the Duc de Bourbon and his henchman, Pâris-Duverney, together with Madame de Prie, were seeking an opportunity to oust Fleury from his position because it was clear that he was endeavouring more and more to influence the King. For instance, it was impossible to speak to Louis alone on state matters for Fleury always made it his duty to be present.

Madame de Prie pointed out to the Queen that the King was now a husband and old enough to do without the continual attendance of his tutor. Marie declared that she believed Louis had a great affection as well as respect for Monsieur de Fleury.

Madame de Prie said: 'His Majesty will form a habit. Monsieur de Fleury belongs to the days of his boyhood. And out of the kindness of his heart he lets him remain.'

'The King has a kind and loyal heart,' mused Marie complacently, for such a quality in the King gave her great contentment.

When she was next alone with the King, she discussed his Ministers with him and suddenly said: 'Louis, how do you like Monsieur de Fleury?'

'Very much,' answered the King.

'And the Duc de Bourbon?'

'Oh . . .' Louis shrugged his shoulders. 'Enough.'

His tones when he spoke of the two men were so different that Marie should have recognised the wisdom of strengthening her friendship with the tutor, even if this did mean irritating the Duc de Bourbon and his mistress. But Marie had learned no diplomacy in the home of her exiled father and had little understanding of the importance of insinuation and innuendo such as that which flourished at the stylised Court of France.

✦ ✦ ✦

Madame de Prie conceived a plan which was to result in the expulsion of Fleury from Court.

'For,' she said to her lover, 'he obstructs you in every way and it is clear what that fellow is after. He is quite cunning. He plans to take your place. I shall not feel happy until Monsieur de Fleury receives his *lettre de cachet*.'

'How do you plan to remove him? He has the King's confidence, remember.'

'By means of the Queen.'

Bourbon smiled. The schemes of his mistress never failed to astonish him.

'You have that letter from the Cardinal de Polignac,' went

on Madame de Prie. 'which is a direct attack against Fleury. It shows him in a very unflattering light, does it not? And there's truth in it. The man seeks two things; to get his Cardinal's hat and rule France. He wants to be another Cardinal Richelieu or Mazarin. That letter should be shown to the King when Fleury is not present to defend himself. You could then discuss Fleury's ambitions with Louis, make him realise exactly what Fleury is after.'

'But how to see Louis alone without Fleury – that's the problem.'

'I think,' said Madame de Prie, 'that our dear Queen might help us in this. After all, she owes us everything.'

'What do you propose?'

'That the Queen shall ask Louis to come to her apartments, and when he arrives you will be there with the letter. You will hand it to him.'

'What if Fleury should hear of this and attempt to join us? You know he is Louis' shadow.'

'He will simply be refused admittance to the Queen's apartment. She is not very fond of him, you know. She will agree readily. Does she not owe it to us?'

'You have genius, my dear.'

'One needs it, *mon ami*, first to reach a high place at this Court – then to keep it.'

✦ ✦ ✦

Louis, having been asked by the Queen to join her in her apartments, was astonished to find the Duc de Bourbon there, and displeasure tinged his astonishment when the Duc brought a paper from his pocket which, he said, he thought the King should read.

Louis read the accusations against Fleury; they angered him for he believed them to be false, and he felt irritated because he had been lured to accept and read such a document in private. If the Duc de Bourbon had wished to present such a letter to him it should have been in the Council Chamber, when Fleury would have been present to answer any accusations against himself.

Louis rarely showed anger and he restrained that which he now felt, so he merely folded the paper and handed it back to the Duc de Bourbon.

'Sire,' said the Duc, 'may I ask what you think of the sentiments expressed in the letter?'

'Nothing,' said the King shortly.

'But . . . Sire . . . if these accusations are correct would you not have certain orders to give?'

Had Madame de Prie been present she would have flashed a warning glance at her lover. The Duc was suggesting that Louis was incapable of making his own decisions and should accept the advice of his ministers, as he had before his coming of age.

'My orders are that matters remain as they are,' retorted the King.

Bourbon's face expressed his concern. Marie's heart had begun to beat fast with apprehension, for the King had included her in his cold looks.

'Your . . . Your Majesty is displeased . . . and with me?' murmured Bourbon, unable to prevent himself from learning the worst.

'I am,' retorted the King.

'Your . . . Your Majesty continues to have the greatest confidence in Monsieur de Fleury?'

'That is so.'

The Duc was now apprehensive.

'Sire,' he said, 'I would give my life to serve you. If I have done aught that is wrong I crave your pardon.'

Louis hated scenes. They distressed him. He rarely reprimanded anybody; if reprimand there had to be, he arranged that others should give it. He was annoyed that the Queen should have placed him in such a position. But rather than display his irritation with them both he walked quickly towards the door.

Marie, trembling with fear, put out a hand to touch his arm as he passed her. He pretended not to see it.

❖ ⚜ ❖

Fleury had friends at Court. There were some shrewd people who realised the affection and respect which this man had aroused in his pupil. The Duc de Bourbon and his flamboyant mistress could not, it was believed, reign supreme for ever; their reign could only last while the King was too young, too inexperienced to recognise their worthlessness.

Therefore, when Bourbon visited the Queen, and the Queen asked the King to join them, this was immediately made known to Fleury who, knowing the existence of the Polignac letter and guessing Bourbon's project, made haste to the Queen's apartment and demanded of her attendants to be taken to her presence.

'Monsieur de Fleury,' was the answer, 'the King is with the Queen, and Monsieur le Duc is with them. Orders have been given that no one – not even yourself – is to be admitted.'

This was an insult which could not be tolerated. If the King had given such orders it was significant that Fleury would never achieve his ambition and become chief minister of France. If on the other hand – which was more likely – this was the result of one of Bourbon's schemes to undermine the King's friendship for his tutor behind the latter's back, then prompt action was necessary.

Fleury, showing greater astuteness than Bourbon, reckoned that if Bourbon won, he, Fleury, would be sent from Court; therefore he could lose nothing and retain his dignity if he left of his own accord.

If on the other hand the King refused to listen to Bourbon's slander, he would be more infuriated than ever with the Duke should Fleury go away.

So Fleury went hastily to his apartments and wrote a letter to the King in which he said that as he was locked out of His Majesty's counsels, there appeared to be no further need for his services. He would therefore retire from Court in order to live in peace with the Sulpicians of Issy. He was leaving immediately to avoid the pain of farewell.

When this letter was brought to Louis he was dumbfounded. Fleury gone! But how could he conduct his affairs without Fleury? In all matters of importance he had relied upon the tutor.

He was alarmed. He shut himself into his apartments and wept bitterly. He raged against the Duc de Bourbon and his scheming mistress against the Queen whose folly had made this possible.

This was the first time he had felt critical towards Marie. Angrily he blamed her now. But for her foolish action in ignoring Court Etiquette, he would not have been lured into this controversy with which he did not know how to deal. He was sixteen years old, lacking in the experience which was so necessary in a situation such as this, and he feared Marie had not only allowed Bourbon to use her in his intrigues but had involved him also.

'Stupid woman!' he murmured; and he marvelled that he could see her as such – Marie, his Queen who, but a short while ago, had seemed perfect in his eyes.

The King could not remain locked in his apartments for long. He must make up his mind how to act and, because he was uncertain, he sent for a man whom he had come to trust; this was Monsieur de Mortemart who was First Gentleman of the bedchamber.

Louis commanded Monsieur de Mortemart to shut the door and send all attendants away as he wished to speak to him concerning a private matter.

He explained his predicament. 'The Queen is involved,' he said. 'Monsieur le Duc is First Minister. Monsieur de Fleury is merely my tutor.'

'But, Sire,' cried Mortemart, 'it would seem unimportant that Monsieur le Duc is First Minister and Monsieur de Fleury merely your tutor. You are the King.'

Mortemart was one of those astute courtiers who recognised the superior powers of Fleury, and was therefore ready to back the tutor against the First Minister.

'Were you in my place, what would you do?' asked Louis.

'I should order Monsieur de Fleury to return at once. I should . . . I think I should, Sire, command Monsieur le Duc to write to him asking him to return.'

Louis smiled slowly. 'And I think,' he said, 'that I like your advice.'

Marie was frightened. Fleury was now back at Court, and the King outwardly showed his affection for the old man while the coldness of his manner towards the Duc and his mistress was apparent.

That was not all. The King's attitude had changed towards Marie. Often she would find him looking at her critically, as though he were discovering certain facts about her which he had not noticed before.

Marie knew that she was not beautiful; she had always understood that she was somewhat plain, before Louis had assured her to the contrary.

He still spent his nights with her, leaving the state bedroom after the ceremonial *coucher*, his *valet de chambre* carrying his sword and setting it beside the bed before he helped Louis discard dressing gown and slippers. But a change had crept into their lovemaking. Louis was still overwhelmed by the act of love; yet it was as though he had made a further discovery. It was the act itself which appealed to him; his excitement had little to do with the woman who shared in it. It was his youth, his inexperience, his sudden awakening to manhood which had deluded him.

A coldness had crept into his passion. It terrified the Queen.

Fleury would not be satisfied until he had rid the Court of his enemies. He did not wish to include the Queen among these for naturally he could not rid the Court of her. He thought her a foolish woman to cling so stupidly to the Duc de Bourbon's faction when any sensible person would have known that it was in decline.

It was not that they had any affection for her. They were using her now as they had used her from the beginning; and she, poor fool, seemed unable to see it.

There was no need, Fleury decided, to try to ingratiate himself with the Queen. At one time he had thought she might be an influence at the Court; now it was clear that she never would be. Louis was turning from her; very shortly there would be a mistress. Fleury hoped there would not be one only. A necessary evil, he decided, but less dangerous in the plural than in the singular.

He was exerting all his efforts to oust Bourbon from Court. The time had come for him to take the helm, now that he had proof that the King was loyal to him. The sooner Bourbon, Pâris-Duverney and Madame de Prie were relegated to obscurity the better.

Marie asked the advice of the old Maréchal Villars whom she believed she could trust.

'The king once loved me,' she said, her voice breaking in a sob. 'I fear he no longer does.'

The old Maréchal looked at her sadly. 'It is clear, Madame,' he said, 'that the King's feelings towards you have changed. You should not appear sullen because of this, but remember that there are many watchful women of the Court who are looking for an opportunity which could well arise out of such a situation.'

The frightened Queen could not resist the temptation to appeal to Fleury himself.

'Madame,' the Bishop reproved her, 'you so clearly support those who do not please the King.'

'You mean Monsieur le Duc and Madame de Prie?'

'Those two and Monsieur Pâris-Duverney.'

'But what have they done? Why should I suddenly cease to feel affection for my friends?' wailed Marie.

'Pâris-Duverney has lowered the value of money. His laws

have made chaos in the factories. The Duc and his mistress are completely egotistical. They do not seek to bring prosperity to France but to themselves.'

'How could I turn against them when they have been my friends?'

Fleury smiled wanly. 'They may have been friends to you once, Madame,' he said; 'but they are so no longer.'

He was implying that, but for them and their selfish policy, the Queen of France would not now be Marie Leczinska. It was true, thought Marie. Her fairytale marriage had been the result of the determination of two ambitious people to seize power.

Marie laid her hand appealingly on Fleury's arm.

'I . . . I find the King grown cold towards me,' she said.

Fleury looked at her, and there was a mild pity in his eyes. 'That, Madame.' he said, 'I cannot change.'

There was no help from any quarter. Marie could not tell her parents what was happening to her marriage. They believed that the fairytale was going on; they believed in the 'happy ever after' ending. It did them no harm and much good to go on believing – for, as in the case of Fleury, they could not make Louis fall in love with her again.

The Court was waiting. They knew it could not be long delayed, for Fleury was impatient, and Louis was leaning more and more on his counsel.

The people were restive; they showed very plainly that they were dissatisfied with the rule of Monsieur le Duc and his mistress. Every day there were demonstrations in Paris. The heavy taxes must be abolished. Bread must be cheaper. On every occasion the Duc de Bourbon, his mistress, or the Minister of Finance were blamed for this state of affairs.

Suddenly the King seemed to have forgotten his enmity towards the Duc de Bourbon; he took to receiving him more frequently and in the most friendly fashion.

One summer's day Louis decided to visit Rambouillet that he might hunt for a few days.

The carriage, which was to take him there, arrived and, as he was about to step into it, he saw the Duc de Bourbon among the courtiers.

'You will join me at Rambouillet,' he said to Bourbon, smiling affably. 'Do not be late. We will expect you to supper.'

Bourbon's face flushed with pleasure; his eyes glinted as he met those of Fleury and his other enemies. See, he seemed to be saying, you thought this was the end of me. You forget I am a Prince of the Royal House — ties of blood bind me to the King. I am not so easily dismissed.

The King's carriage had rumbled away and Bourbon was preparing to enter his when the Duc de Charost came towards him.

'Monsieur le Duc,' he said, 'I have been commanded by His Majesty to give you this.'

Bourbon stared at the paper in the other's hand. A terrible suspicion came to him as he took it; that his suspicion was correct was clear to see when his face paled for a second before the blood rushed back into it as he read:

'I command you, if you will avoid punishment for disobedience, to retire to Chantilly. There you must remain until I give further orders. Louis.'

This was his *lettre de cachet*, the dismissal from Court.

It was the first indication of Louis' methods, of his determination to avoid unpleasantness.

Those who had seen the friendly smile he had bestowed on Bourbon before he stepped into his carriage were astonished that he could have behaved so, knowing that the worst blow which could befall an ambitious man was about to be dealt to the Duc de Bourbon.

The Queen was distressed.

Her friends dismissed from Court! She felt it would have been disloyal not to plead for them.

The King listened to her coldly. 'Madame,' he said, 'you waste your time.'

'But Louis . . . these were my friends!'

'You have acted foolishly in giving your friendship to such people.'

'But . . . they have been so good to me. When I first came to Court . . .'

'When you first came to Court you were the Queen. If you had shown that dignity which your rank demanded, you would not have allowed such people to dominate you. You must understand that the Duc de Bourbon is no longer First Minister. I do not think Madame de Prie will be long at Court. And you, Marie, will listen to what Monsieur de Fréjus tells you, for he will make my wishes known to you.'

'But Louis, surely *you* will make your wishes known to me.'

He smiled at her, almost tenderly, not because he felt tender towards her but because he could sense her growing hysteria.

He patted her arm. 'All is well,' he said. 'We have rid the

Court of those who did harm to the State. The people will be pleased that we have acted firmly.'

Marie controlled her feelings and bowed her head.

Was there no way back to that ecstatic honeymoon?

Although Fleury was not named First Minister he assumed power. His first acts were to assign Pâris-Duverney to the Bastille and banish Madame de Prie to her castle of Courbépine which was in Normandy. She went, raging against Fleury and her fate.

A Cardinal's hat arrived from Rome for the Bishop of Fréjus – an additional honour. Fleury had proved that his waiting game had been a successful one.

The people applauded his accession to power, since the first law he made revoked the unpopular tax known as the *Cinquantième*. They believed that, with the dismissal of Bourbon and his mistress, prosperity would return to France; and the day on which the Duc's retinue left for Chantilly was one of rejoicing throughout the capital.

Marie soothed the distress caused by the loss of her husband's love, with her passion for food. Her appetite astonished everyone; she would sit at table calmly eating, for she let nothing disturb her at meals, and the amount of food she consumed was phenomenal.

There was an occasion when, after having eaten a hundred and eighty oysters and drinking a great quantity of beer, Marie suffered such acute indigestion that it was believed she had contracted a fever.

Louis had been hunting, and had reached the Palace very fatigued and hungry. After consuming a large quantity of figs, walnuts and milk, he too was taken ill.

The rumour spread through Paris. 'The King and Queen are ill of fever. Both ill! Can it be poison?' The King however quickly recovered; not so Marie, and her illness lasted for several days.

During that time Louis visited her and, feeling sorry to see her so wretched, he was more affectionate towards her than he had been.

Marie's spirits rose. She believed then that now the Duc de Bourbon and Madame de Prie were safely exiled and Cardinal Fleury was making the country prosperous again, Louis might forget his disappointment in her.

While Louis was with her it was easy to believe this. Later that year the good news was spread throughout the country; the Queen was pregnant.

✢ ✤ ✢

Fleury's two great desires were to maintain peace and to curb the country's expenditure. Although he was seventy-two when he came to office his vitality was amazing and he appeared to assume that he had a clear twenty years of good work before him. In the Court he was nicknamed His Eternity.

Having dismissed certain of the Duc de Bourbon's supporters he chose his own ministers with care, the two chief of whom were Chauvelin, whom he made Keeper of the Seals and Secretary of State for Foreign Affairs, and Orry, who was created Controller General of Finance. These two men stood firmly behind Fleury, and they made a formidable trio – Fleury shrewd and cautious, Chauvelin possessed of a brilliant wit and a satirical tongue, and Orry a pompous man who could subdue all but the most brave by his frowns.

Fleury knew that he could not have better men to serve him than Maurepas and Saint Florentin, and he retained these two in their respective posts.

Fleury had his enemies who, behind his back, cynically compared him with two other great Cardinals who had ruled France – Richelieu and Mazarin. What a difference! they sneered.

They recalled the magnificence of these Cardinals of the past and the manner in which Fleury lived. It was said that his *petit-coucher* was the most ridiculous ceremony ever witnessed at Versailles. He would enter his cabinet, about which assembled all those who hoped for favours from the most powerful man in France, and take off his clothes himself; he then folded them as though he must take the utmost care of these simple garments; then he put on his old dressing gown and slowly combed his white hair (he did not possess more than four hairs, said the courtiers) while he chatted with those who had come to see him.

He kept a free table, which was necessary to his position, but the same dish was always served at it, and often there was not enough for all those who assembled there. When he was diffidently reproached for this he answered: 'Silver and gold do not drop from trees as do the leaves in autumn.'

His great plan was to restore good relations between France and Spain, for these had naturally deteriorated greatly since the little Infanta had been sent home in such an insulting manner to make way for Marie Leczinska. He quickly made the Spanish aware that he, Fleury, had had no hand in that disgraceful business.

Louis looked on at the actions of the man who, although he did not the bear the title of First Minister of France, was so in all but name. He felt happy to be able to assure himself that the management of affairs was in such capable hands. With a good conscience he could give himself up to hunting and playing cards.

❧ ❧ ❧

It was hot in the bedchamber. Outside the August sun shone down on the people who were waiting for the news. Many had crowded into the Palace, into the Queen's bedchamber; it was the privilege of the people to witness the birth of royal children.

Louis was deeply moved. This was another new experience. He was about to become a father and he was full of exultation.

He forgot his annoyance with the Queen. Poor Marie, she had been led astray by that scheming woman, Madame de Prie. He should not blame her; she had come to the Court quite inexperienced of such women. Dear Marie! And now she was going to give him and France the heir.

In her bed Marie, suffering the pains of childbirth though she was, felt intensely happy. She was about to prove that she could do her duty by the King and France. His manner had been changing towards her. Eagerly he would talk of the child who was soon to make its appearance.

He referred to the baby as 'He'.

'Let the child be a Dauphin,' she prayed.

She knew that her father and mother, all those who loved her, would be thinking of her at this time. If she could produce a Dauphin she believed she could regain all that ecstasy which had been hers when she first came to France.

'A Dauphin,' she whispered, as her women wiped the sweat from her brow. 'Give me a Dauphin.'

✤ ✤ ✤

All over Paris there were celebrations. The fireworks were magnificent; the churches were filled with those who had come to join in the thanksgiving; from the churches the people crowded to the Comédie Française and the Opéra, for on such occasions of rejoicing the actors and management gave the traditional free performances.

The Parisians were ready to take any opportunity for celebration; but the joy was not as wild as it would have been for a Dauphin.

'Ah, well,' said the philosophical citizens, 'they are young yet. Time is before them; and at least she has shown that she is fertile.'

They crowded about the Palace and called for their King. When he appeared on the balcony, a baby on each arm, the crowd roared.

Two baby girls! It was almost as good as a Dauphin; and a Dauphin would come in time.

'Long live the King!' cried the people. 'Long live Mesdames Première et Seconde!'

The cry was taken up all over Paris. Louis, walking up and down the apartment, a little girl on each arm, heard it and smiled at his wife.

'I think,' he said to her, 'that the people are well pleased with Madame Louise-Elisabeth and Madame Anne-Henriette. Did you hear them, Marie? They are calling for another glimpse of Madame Première and Madame Seconde.'

'You . . . are pleased?' asked Marie anxiously.

Louis laid one of the babies in her arms and gently touched the cheek of the other.

'When I look at these two little creatures,' he said, 'I would not wish to change them . . . even for a Dauphin. Besides! . . .' His smile was affectionate. 'The next *will* be a Dauphin.'

So Marie was able to close her eyes, to slip into a sleep of exhaustion, utterly contented, believing that the life which lay before her would be made good by her children and her loving husband.

✣ ✣ ✣

The Duc de Bourbon was making frantic efforts to return to Court. His punishment had been very severe. The Court had been his life, and to be forced to live in the country without the company of Madame de Prie was hard to bear indeed; but an additional torment had been inflicted. He, whose great delight it had been to hunt, was forbidden to do so.

Bourbon was desolate, ready to humble himself to regain something of his old position. This was what Fleury and the King desired for him; it was gratifying to see the once arrogant Duke made humble.

Bourbon was constantly pleading with nobles of the Court to use their influence to have at least the ban on hunting rescinded, while in Chantilly he raged against his fate and spent his time planning how he could possibly escape this deprivation of all that had given him the greatest pleasure in life.

Eventually he achieved his desires, attaining them through his marriage with Charlotte of Hesse-Rheinfels – which, pleasing the King and Fleury, resulted in his recall to Court.

Madame de Prie was possessed of greater dignity than her lover.

In her Normandy château she attempted to gather about her a circle of wits and writers, and as many courtiers as she could lure from Versailles. She wanted to make her circle renowned and even feared at Court.

Despising the weakness of her lover Bourbon, and realising that he had escaped her, she took a new lover – a young country gentleman of great personal charm.

She was gay and appeared to be in high spirits, but she was thinking only of the Court and yearning to be once more its most brilliant member. She spent her days in planning entertainments, writing letters to her friend, that rake, the Duc de Richelieu, who was away on an embassy in Vienna.

Determined to attract attention to herself she pretended to be a prophetess and foretold her own death, but no one believed her, for she was extremely beautiful, full of vitality and only twenty-seven years old.

'Nevertheless,' she declared, 'my end is near. I sense these things, and I know it.'

She continued to live gaily, adored by her lover, writing her verses and letters, giving one brilliant entertainment after another.

When the day drew near on which she had prophesied she would die, she saw sceptical looks in the eyes of her friends, and decided to give a great banquet three days before the appointed one. It was the most brilliant of all her entertainments. She read her newest verses to her guests and told them that this was a farewell banquet.

Her lover implored her not to joke about such a serious matter, but her answer was to take a diamond ring from her finger and give it to him.

'It is worth a small fortune,' she said. 'It is yours to

remember me by. I have other gifts for you, *mon ami*. Diamonds and other precious stones. They will be of no use to me where I am going.'

Her guests joked with her.

'Enough of this talk of death,' they said. 'You will give many more parties such as this one.'

Her lover tried to give her back the ring, but she would not take it, and two days later she pressed more jewels on him.

'Now,' she said, 'I want you to go away, for I would be alone.'

He had always obeyed her, and he did so now. She smiled at him fondly, as he said: '*Au revoir*, my dearest.' But she answered '*Adieu!*'

The next day – that which she had named as her last on Earth – she shut herself in her rooms alone and thought of the past: of all the ambition and the glory which was hers no longer and which she knew she could never regain.

She poured herself a glass of wine and slipped into it a dose of poison.

When her servants came into her room they found her, dead.

✣ ✣ ✣

Stanislas and his wife came to Versailles from Chambord.

The ex-King of Poland embraced his daughter with tears in his eyes. Queen Catherine watched them with restraint; she had never given way to displays of affection as these two had. She believed herself to be more of a realist than her husband and daughter.

Stanislas, his arm about his daughter, had led her to a window seat, and with arms still entwined they sat down.

'And how is the King feeling towards you now, dearest daughter?'

'So loving, Father. It is like a second honeymoon.'

The relief of Stanislas was obvious. 'How glad I am! I have had some anxious moments. At the time of the dismissal of the Duc de Bourbon . . .'

'I know, Father,' said Marie. 'Louis was very angry then.'

'The whole Court expected him to take a mistress. Yet he did not.'

'I could not have borne that,' said Marie sharply.

Her father put his head close to hers and said: 'Yet, my child, should it come, you must meet it with fortitude.'

His brow was slightly wrinkled; he was aware of his wife; he did not wish her to be reminded of his own peccadilloes, for he himself had found it impossible to live without women. His wife was a prim woman and he feared that Marie – much as he loved her – might be the same.

'Louis is young and virile,' murmured Stanislas. 'Such matters could be unavoidable.'

Marie laughed. 'I have something to tell you, Father.'

Stanislas took both her hands in his and kissed them. 'Again?' he said.

'Yes, Father, I am already pregnant.'

'It is excellent news. We will pray that this time it will be a Dauphin.'

'Louis is enchanted!' cried Marie.

'Keep him so, my child. And remember, the more children a Queen bears, the stronger is her position. There must be many children, for children fall an easy prey to sickness. One son . . . two . . . three . . . You cannot have too many.'

Marie nodded. 'It shall be so,' she said. 'It is what we both wish.'

The babies were brought in, and Madame Première and Madame Seconde kicked their fat little legs and gurgled and screamed to the delight of all who beheld them.

The King joined them, and his pride in his daughters was obvious.

Stanislas, watching Louis and Marie together, prayed that Marie would take the right course when the mistresses appeared – as it seemed inevitable they would.

There he stood, the handsome King of France – his features so beautiful as to be almost feminine; yet there was a certain sensuality beginning to dawn on that handsome face. How graceful he was, how perfect his poise and manners! Even Stanislas could see that Marie seemed rather stocky beside him, lacking his grace, rather like the daughter of a prosperous tradesman than the daughter of a King.

Yet, thought Stanislas, my darling girl has the most important of all qualities a Queen should possess. Already she has produced twins and there is another child on the way.

Let her find content in her children, thought Stanislas, and resignation to accept whatever must come to her. That is the way for Marie Leczinska to remain firmly on the throne of France.

♣ Chapter V ♣

MADAME DE MAILLY

All through France there was rejoicing, for on a September day in the year 1729 the Queen gave birth to the Dauphin.

The child was doubly welcome for the baby who had been born in the year following the arrival of the twins, had been a girl – Louise-Marie, Madame Troisième.

The Queen had come triumphantly through the ordeal. She had shown the people that she could bear children – in 1727, the twins, 1728 Madame Troisième, and now in 1729 the Dauphin. Who could ask more than that?

The bells were ringing throughout Paris and the people were determined to make these celebrations excel those which had taken place in honour of the girls. The fireworks were more dazzling, the illuminations brighter. As soon as darkness fell boats bearing lights passed along the river, and the people danced and sang in the streets.

When the King went to Notre Dame for the thanksgiving service the crowds cheered him as even he had never been cheered before. They were delighted with their King – handsome and gracious, he had again proved his virility. They had not been pleased when such a godlike creature married a plain woman of little importance, yet even the marriage was proving successful. Four children in three years! It was as though Providence had sent the twins as a sign of the fertility of the Queen.

Louis insisted that the little boy should have for his governess the person whom he considered most suited to the task, one whom he had loved all his life: Madame de Ventadour.

And as she took the child in her arms immediately after his baptism by the Cardinal de Rohan, she looked at the little figure with the ribbon of Saint-Esprit wrapped about him, and tears came into her eyes for, as she said, it was as though her dearest one was once more a baby.

❖ ❖ ❖

The next few years passed pleasantly for the King, and slightly less so for the Queen.

She was being more and more deprived of the King's society. She realised that she could not mix happily with his friends; Marie found much at Court to shock her.

The King was a faithful husband – though a demanding one. Yet in spite of this, morals at the Court were in the Queen's eyes outrageous.

One of the leading lights was Louis Armand du Plessis, the Duc de Richelieu, who was notorious for his love affairs and who had papered the walls of his apartments with pictures of the nude female form in attitudes which he considered amusing. The Queen remembered that before she had seen this man – he had been away from the Court on a mission to Vienna – she had heard that two women had fought a duel for his favours. It was said that he had begun his rakish career in his very early youth at the Court of Louis Quatorze, and his first mistress had been the Duchesse de Bourgogne, the King's mother.

Matching him in vice was Mademoiselle de Charolais who made a point of taking a new lover once a year. Love affairs to be complete should be fruitful, she declared; and to prove how successful she was, had a child every year by a different lover.

The Comte de Clermont kept numerous mistresses and made no secret of this.

As these were typical of the people who frequented the King's hunting parties, it was small wonder that the Queen was not encouraged to attend them. In fact during those years it seemed to Marie that she had either just borne a child or was about to do so. The little Duc d'Anjou had been born in 1730, the year following the birth of the Dauphin. 1731 was surprisingly a barren year, but in 1732 Adelaide made her appearance; and already Marie was pregnant again.

Each night, with occasional exceptions, the King visited her; she found herself exhausted by her nights with him and her frequent pregnancies, and made excuses for sleeping alone.

'I believe it to be sinful to gratify the lusts of the flesh at certain times,' she told Louis.

He was indulgent and as long as the saints' days were not too frequent made little protest.

The courtiers were watching this state of affairs between the Queen and the King with some amusement; secret wagers were laid as to how long it would be before the King took a mistress.

Richelieu and that rake, the Comte de Clermont, would have advised the King of all the pleasures he was missing by remaining faithful to his far from attractive wife, but they were not unmindful of Fleury who, in his cautious way, was watching Louis no less closely than they.

Fleury had no desire for the King to select a mistress. He knew, from the records of the past, what havoc a mistress could play in state affairs. At present the King was faithful to the Queen and the Queen was producing children. That was satisfactory. Fleury was eager that this state of affairs should be preserved as long as possible; and remembering the astute conduct of Fleury in the case of the Duc de Bourbon, those courtiers who might have induced the King to satisfy the lusts of the flesh outside the marriage bed refrained from doing so.

That year 1733 was a significant one in Marie's life. One event which seemed of overwhelming importance to her was the sudden death of Augustus II, who had usurped the throne from her father.

Marie trembled with excitement when she heard the news, and she asked herself, now that Stanislas was Louis' father-in-law, why he should not regain his throne with the help of France.

His greatest rival for power was the son of Augustus, whom Austria and Russia favoured; but Stanislas with France behind him, thought Marie, had as good a chance of aspiring to the crown of Poland as any.

Fleury was not anxious to give that support. Both Portugal and Prussia had candidates and, with Austria and Russia supporting the son of Augustus, he feared war. He was also uncertain what effect her father's regaining his throne would have on the Queen. She would naturally become more influential, and he and she never been good friends.

There were many in France who were ready to go to Poland to defend the cause of Stanislas. England, Fleury knew, would be watching affairs closely. Fleury was eager for good relations with England and had formed a friendship with the Prime Minister, Robert Walpole, Earl of Orford.

Walpole's advice to Fleury was that the electors of Poland should be bribed to elect Stanislas, and that the ex-king should go to Poland in person to conduct the campaign. Fleury decided to accept this advice, and the Queen took a fond farewell of her father who, embracing her warmly, told her that he loved her beyond all others and that he was happy to think that it was she who had wrought this change in their fortunes.

He left France disguised as a merchant, taking only one friend with him who in his turn hid his identity in the guise of a merchant's clerk. At the same time a French noble, the Comte de Thianges, who bore a faint resemblance to Stanislas, sailed from Brest with all the pomp of a King. This somewhat unnecessary and farcical project, it was said, originated in England and Fleury had adopted Walpole's suggestions.

Stanislas had some initial success, for the bribes were effective and he was elected King of Poland.

The news was taken first to Louis who read the dispatch and hurried to the Queen's bedroom to explain to her what had happened.

They embraced and, when Marie wept, the King was moved to see her do so; that night they were very tender to each other and it was like a return of the honeymoon days.

But that was not a happy year.

The little Duc d'Anjou, who from birth had not been as sturdy as his brother the Dauphin, became weaker as the year progressed and, before its end, he died.

The Queen's grief was as great as that of Louis. They had

only one son now and they were alarmed for the health of the other children. All, with the exception of the five-year-old Louise-Marie, were healthy, but death struck suddenly and unexpectedly and there was fear in the royal household.

Nor was it groundless. Shortly after the death of the Duc d'Anjou, litde Madame Troisième fell sick, and none of the doctors could save her.

To lose two children so suddenly, and with a short interval of time between the two deaths, threw Marie into a frenzy of superstitious fear.

'It is as though God seeks to punish us for something,' she told her ladies.

She thought of the extreme sensuality of the King, in which she was forced to join, and she shuddered.

There was bad news from Poland. The Russians and Austrians were not prepared to see Stanislas oust their candidate for the throne.

They threatened invasion, and Stanislas, finding himself deserted by those friends who had accompanied him to his country, realised that there was nothing he could do but abdicate.

The son of Augustus II, Augustus III, was elected King of Poland.

Stanislas appealed to France; and Fleury, realising the strategic position of the country, decided on war.

'Disaster!' mourned the Queen. 'There is disaster threatening on all sides.'

Then she thought of her dead son and daughter, and wept afresh.

'It would seem that those I love are doomed,' she cried. 'What will become of my dear father?'

When Louis came to her that night she told him that it was a saint's day and that as she was already pregnant there could be no reason for their indulging in sexual relations, except sheer carnality.

The King was annoyed.

'We are married,' he pointed out. 'Now if I were like some members of my Court you might have reason to complain.'

'As it is a saint's day . . .' she began.

'A very obscure saint's day,' he grumbled.

'Louis,' she said earnestly, 'these tragedies have made me consider. I think we should abstain on *all* saints' days.'

Louis stared at her in horror. 'You have forgotten how many saints' days there are in the calendar,' he said curtly.

'No, I do not forget,' she said; 'and we must always remember them in future.'

Louis disliked scenes, so he did not insist on sharing her bed.

He left her. On his way back to his own apartments he met the incorrigible Richelieu who, seeing the King returning from the Queen's bedchamber, hastily veiled his expression; but Louis had seen the cynical smile, the puzzled look which indicated that Richelieu was trying to remember what saint's day it was.

Louis felt angry; the Queen was putting him into a ridiculous position. He considered Richelieu and his innumerable amorous adventures; he recalled some of the exploits of the Comte de Clermont. It seemed that in the whole Court only the King behaved like a respectable married man – and the Queen had the temerity to decline his attentions.

Yet she had suffered greatly over the loss of the children,

and the anxiety regarding her father's position. Louis was not easily aroused to anger; he was a patient man.

Give her time, he thought. She will recover from these griefs. But when he began to consider all the saints' days which occurred in a year, he was uneasy.

The following night he sat with his friends at a small supper party. Richelieu on his right hand was as usual boasting of his affairs with women. The King drank more than usual and after the solemn *coucher* in the state bedroom made his way to the Queen's bedchamber.

When his dressing gown and slippers had been taken from him by his *valet de chambre* the Queen started up in her bed. In horror she stared at his flushed face.

'But Louis,' she cried, 'you are not sober.'

He signed for the curtains to be drawn about the bed, and this was immediately done. Marie however set her mouth in prim lines. This was more to be deplored than usual. This was drunken lechery.

'No,' she protested. 'You must leave me at once.'

'Do not be so foolish,' said Louis, the wine having heated his blood, destroying his usual calm.

'Is it foolish to hate . . . lechery?' cried Marie, her arms folded across her breasts.

Louis looked at her and suddenly he knew that he disliked her. He remembered that when he had married her she had been the daughter of a penniless exile.

'Madame,' he said, his voice slurred, 'you forget to whom you speak.'

'I am in full possession of my senses. *I* am not drunk,' she retorted.

'You will be sorry for this night's work,' said Louis.

'Sorry! If I can send you back to your apartments I shall be sorry for nothing.'

'I repeat,' said Louis, 'that you will be sorry, Madame.' He left the bed and stood looking at her through its curtains, inclining his head unsteadily. 'I pray you,' he said, 'no longer take such pains to protect that which is not desired.'

Then he left her and went back to the state bedroom.

His valet looked astonished to see him – not only returned, but obviously in a state of unusual anger.

Looking at the man, Louis knew that even if no one had overheard that quarrel in his wife's bedroom, what had taken place would soon be conjectured and rumours spread.

'Go out,' he said to his valet, 'and bring me a woman . . . Find a beautiful woman and bring her to me . . . without delay.'

The valet ran from the King's apartment. It had happened at last. Now the fun would start. This would be but the beginning. Tomorrow the whole Court would be seething with the news.

Who? pondered the valet. That was important.

He wanted advice – the advice of Cardinal Fleury or Monsieur de Richelieu. But there was no time. The King was in no mood for delay. The King had changed; never had he been as he was tonight. He was angry, and the valet must act with speed.

The first likely woman he saw was one of the waiting-women of the Princesse de Rohan.

He stopped her. He said: 'Will you spend the night with the King?'

She stared at him. 'Are you quite well?' she asked.

'Quite, and there is no time to waste. The King is furious with the Queen. He wants you to take her place . . .'

'Only for tonight?' she said; and her eyes glistened. The King was handsome; and the possibilities were endless.

'That rests with you,' said the valet.

She threw back her head and laughed suddenly.

'Take me to him.'

The valet wondered what he would find when he returned to the royal bedchamber. Would Louis have become more sober? Would he have to get himself and the young woman out of a delicate situation?

He need not have worried. When he returned, the King was impatiently waiting – a strange new King full of fire and passion, a King who was weary of playing the faithful husband to a woman who was too concerned with saints' days.

✦ ✦ ✦

The next day there was great excitement throughout the Court. The old era was over; a new one was about to begin. Richelieu, Clermont, Mademoiselle de Charolais might be amused; the King's ministers – Fleury at the head of them – were deeply concerned.

This was no time to stand quietly by, letting matters take their course.

The young lady of last night's adventure was unlikely to be of any importance. She was not exceptionally beautiful or clever, and the very manner of her coming to the King's bedchamber would make it difficult for her to be the participant in anything but the lightest love affair.

She gave no concern. But it was quite clear that very soon there would be someone who could have a great influence on the King.

There were two rival circles of the Court, one of them, known as the Chantilly circle which had its headquarters at the home of the Bourbons and of which Mademoiselle de Charolais, the Duc de Bourbon's daughter, was the leading spirit, and the other, that of Rambouillet which was presided over by the Comte and Comtesse de Toulouse.

The more respectable of these two groups was that of Rambouillet, and it was in this circle that Fleury proposed to look for the woman who should be the King's new mistress.

The Comte de Toulouse was the illegitimate son of Louis Quatorze and Madame de Montespan, and therefore a kinsman of the King; and it was with his Comtesse that Fleury decided to discuss this matter of providing a mistress for the King. He therefore asked the Comtesse to visit him, which she promptly did, guessing the nature of the matter he had to discuss with her.

Madame de Toulouse was only too glad to be of assistance. For if the King's mistress were a friend of hers, she would lose nothing by the connexion.

Fleury bowed over her hand and begged her to be seated. He then came straight to the point.

'You are aware, Madame,' he said, 'of this rift between their Majesties?'

'Yes, Monsieur le Cardinal. Who is not?'

'It was inevitable. The Queen has many good qualities but she lacks some of those which are necessary to a man such as the King.'

'It is true,' said the Comtesse. 'In the first place she is six or seven years his senior. That is not good. Some women might have seemed nearer his age, but she, who is always wrapped round with shawls and has no sense of elegance . . .' The

Comtesse lifted her shoulders. 'Poor lady – she is for ever pregnant, and that is not conducive to elegance, I fear.'

Fleury went on: 'Her good deeds are numerous. Her friends are virtuous.'

'But so dull,' murmured the Comtesse.

She smiled, thinking of the Queen's efforts to attain culture – her singing, her playing on the harpsichord, her painting. She excelled in none of these pursuits and the courtiers inwardly groaned when asked to hear her sing and play or were given one of her pictures which they must praise enthusiastically and place in a prominent position in their apartments lest it should come to the Queen's ears that they did not appreciate her efforts.

'It is natural,' added Fleury.

'And I marvel that it did not happen before.'

'The King will shortly settle his affections on some woman other than his wife, I fear,' said Fleury. 'And when that happens it will be well for us all that she should be the right woman.'

'Indeed yes,' agreed the Comtesse.

'I would wish,' went on the Cardinal, 'that she should be modest. It would be painful if she sought great favours for herself and her family. For that reason I would not wish her to be a member of a house of high nobility.'

The Comtesse's eyebrows were raised in surprise. 'Your Eminence would not introduce a woman of the lower classes to the King's bed!'

'Oh, no, that would be unthinkable. What we need is a woman who has charm, is of the nobility but not the *haute noblesse*, you understand. She must be discreet, glad to serve the King in this capacity and not ask too much in return.'

'I will be frank,' said the Comtesse. 'I anticipated this call and I have already given the matter much thought.'

'You have a suggestion?'

'I have. I am thinking of the eldest daughter of the Nesle family, Louise-Julie. She is married to the Comte de Mailly. He is very poor and could be persuaded to stand aside, I doubt not. Louise-Julie is a pleasant creature. I would not call her beautiful, but she has great charm.'

'The Nesle family,' interrupted the Cardinal, his eyes sparkling. 'I see that you have understood perfectly, Madame. But is not Madame de Mailly one of the Queen's own ladies?'

'It is true, but is that important? Kings have chosen their mistresses from their wives' circles before this; and in any case, if she were not already one of the Queen's ladies-in-waiting, she would very soon wish to be so.'

The Cardinal nodded. 'We will see what happens with Madame de Mailly. First we must bring the King to a receptive mood. I do not think it will be difficult. He is incensed with the Queen's rebuffs, and his pride is hurt. I think at this stage we should call in the help of one of his close friends. I am sure the Duc de Richelieu would be only too delighted to help. I know he has long been trying to lure the King to unfaithfulness. I will send for him now, and we will put this project before him.'

When the Duc de Richelieu heard the plans of the Cardinal and the Comtesse he was much amused.

'I approve,' he said. 'I approve with all my heart. If we do not do something for our beloved Louis he will become as dull as his Queen. We shall have him walking about the Court muffled in shawls, painting – Oh, God, preserve us from that! – playing the harpsichord and telling us that Madame Adelaide has taken three tottering steps, or has learned to say "Your Majesty". No, something must be done.'

He gave them the benefit of his sardonic grin.

'Madame de Mailly? H'm. Charming. She has such delightful legs. One of those women who have been given subtler gifts than beauty. Madame de Mailly would be ideal . . . for a start.'

'Then I pray you,' said the Cardinal, 'prepare His Majesty to meet the lady. You could explain better than most . . .'

'The delights of love!' cried Richelieu. 'But it is natural, is it not, that I, a sinner, should give a better account of them than a man of Holy Church.'

The Cardinal was too pleased with the plan to be irritated. Madame de Mailly would be an ideal mistress. He was certain that she would not only keep her fingers out of the great state pie, but prevent the King from dipping his into it also.

Richelieu winked lewdly at the Cardinal. 'Leave His Majesty to me,' he said. 'The task of luring him from the virtuous paths of matrimony shall begin without delay.'

✤ ✤ ✤

The King's three principal *valets de chambre*, Bachelier, Le Bel and Barjac, were excited. Life had been a little dull. It was not very amusing to conduct the King to the Queen's bedchamber every night, place the sword close to the bed, take the King's dressing gown and slippers and come quietly back to the royal bedchamber to wait the return journey next morning and the conducting of the King back to the state bedroom for the ceremonial *lever*.

Now there would be more exciting times ahead; and if the King were going to develop a taste for women other than the

Queen, the duties of the *valets de chambre* could become not only more interesting but more profitable.

Madame de Mailly, when approached by the Comtesse de Toulouse, was excited.

She had no love for her husband, her cousin, the mercenary Comte de Mailly who was continuously bewailing his poverty; moreover she had always greatly admired the King. She and Louis were both in their twenty-third year and she, in common with most, had always considered the King the most handsome man at Court.

A meeting was arranged between them, and Bachelier took Madame de Mailly to the King's apartment; but when they were alone together they were both overcome by shyness.

Louis had up to this time never been at ease with women. The efforts, first of Villeroi and later of Fleury, to keep him innocent had had this effect on him which, even though he was a deeply sensual man, made it difficult for him to deal with a situation such as he now faced.

Madame de Mailly, who was by no means inexperienced, was half in love with the King, and for this reason found herself embarrassed. She could have wished that they had met at one of the gatherings at Rambouillet and become attracted to each other. That she had been brought to the King's apartments by his valet added to her embarrassment.

She, who was noted for her vivacity and kindly wit, found herself tongue-tied. The King, unable to banish from his mind the erotic images which the conversation of the rake, Richelieu, had put there, was equally unable to make adequate conversation.

They were cool and polite with each other and the meeting was a failure.

She left the King, certain that she would never be sent for again.

Louis was not eager to grant her another private interview, and those who had planned for him were afraid that soon he would be the prey of any scheming woman who sought to rule France through him.

Madame de Mailly was severely talked to by her promoters. Doubtless she had behaved like a prim young virgin. Did she not realise that the King was in revolt against the primness of the Queen? She must greet him with voluptuous looks. She must not enter and curtsey. Let her be lying on a couch, say *en déshabillé;* her most attractive feature was her legs, which all admitted were the best at Court. Let her make the most of her charms. Would she try again?

She was eager to do so. All that remained was to persuade Louis to meet her once more. This was difficult but, when it was pointed out to the good-natured young man that if he did not see her, poor Madame de Mailly would be brokenhearted, he gave way.

His surprise was intense when he entered the intimate apartment to find her already there. He could only stand and stare at the half-nude young woman who was smiling at him seductively from the couch.

For a moment he was prepared to turn and escape; but Bachelier was behind him, and he did not want the valet to witness his embarrassment.

'The lady awaits Your Majesty,' said Bachelier, and in the excitement of the moment gave Louis a push which sent him reeling forward.

Madame de Mailly held out her arms and caught Louis in them, while Bachelier gently closed the door.

The seduction of the King was thus effected, and Fleury sighed with relief. He was now free to deal with state matters.

But first he presented the Comte de Mailly with 20,000 livres — his reward as a complaisant husband. Fleury was eager also that the affair should be conducted with as much secrecy as was possible. Versailles of course could not but be aware that the King had a mistress, but he did not wish the people of France to know of the King's lapse.

At this time he was adored by his subjects; and although the squat and rather heavy Queen did not appeal to them as did their handsome King, they were ready to concede that she was a good Queen who had done her duty to the state. The people liked to think of their Louis as a sedate young man, eager to do his duty, a worthy husband and father — for all that he was handsome and looked god-like in his robes of state.

There could not have been a better choice, thought Fleury, for Madame de Mailly was a kindly woman, one who seemed content with the King's affection, not seeking honours for herself.

✦ ✦ ✦

After the awkward beginning Louis became more and more interested in Louise-Julie de Mailly. The Queen had never joined him in his ecstasy as this woman did. It was like learning new lessons, each more delight-giving than the last.

To him his mistress was the most beautiful woman at the Court as, in the first few days of his marriage, the Queen had been. She was tall and very slender; her only beauties were her large dark eyes and the legs for which she was already famous.

Her complexion was sallow, her features irregular; but she was very charming because of a particularly sweet nature.

Louis had been fortunate. She did not seek honours. Very quickly she had fallen in love with the King and she declared that merely to be with him was reward enough for her.

The King was enchanted, for she was ready at any time to lead him into thickets of sensuality which he had never dreamed existed.

She gave herself no airs about the Court and was always extremely respectful to the Queen. The liaison was ideal and the King and Louise-Julie de Mailly believed it would go on all their lives.

Marie bore another daughter that year; this was Victoire.

The King did not altogether neglect his wife, nor forget the need to add to the royal nurseries. Almost immediately after the birth of Victoire, the Queen was once more pregnant. Marie had grown more bitter, and declared fretfully that her life was little more than going to bed and being brought to bed.

Meanwhile the King and Madame de Mailly fell deeper in love. It was she who was present at all the hunting parties and rode beside him; who sat with him at intimate suppers he gave to his friends.

It seemed now that the King would be as faithful a lover as he had been a husband.

❧ Chapter VI ❧

MADAME DE VINTIMILLE

*J*n the last four years the Queen had become resigned to the King's infatuation for Madame de Mailly; she realised that, since she must accept his having a mistress of some sort, there could not have been one who made less trouble.

She had her children. Sophie had been born in 1734, Thérèse-Félicité in 1736, and Louise-Marie had just made her appearance. Ten children in ten years; no one could ask more of a Queen than that.

There might be no more. Even for the sake of getting another boy (out of the eight surviving children seven were girls) Louis rarely visited her at night.

There were many who thought she was to blame. But she was worn out with the exhausting business of child-bearing, and her doctors had warned her that she should take a rest from it. When Louis did come she prayed by her bed-side in the hope that he would fall asleep before she had finished her prayers; which he often did. Abstention on saints' days was a great help; and the visits grew more and more rare since Madame de Mailly was always waiting for him.

Marie had now made her own way of life; and her own little court was apart from that of the King. Her day was planned to a calm and sedate pattern. In the morning she attended prayers and studied theological books; after that there would be a formal visit to the King; then she would paint, because it gave her great pleasure to present her pictures to her friends. She attended Mass and then went to dinner. This she took with her ladies, most of whom had tastes similar to her own. After that she would retire to her room to work on her tapestry or play the harpsichord. Then she would read quietly by herself until it was time for the household to assemble for cards. Sometimes she would visit the apartments of friends; but it was understood that the conversation in her presence must never include scandal. She had grown very religious and gave extensively to charities. Her great indulgence was the table; and her figure, because of this and the continual child-bearing, had grown more stocky; and as she had little interest in the fashions of the day, she did nothing to improve this. Many of the courtiers dreaded an invitation to her evening parties; their great fear was that they would be unable to hide their yawns or, worse still, fall asleep.

How different it was to be invited to join the King! Indeed it was considered a very great honour to receive such an invitation, for Louis, who had always wanted to live privately and enjoy the company of a few intimate friends, had had the *petits cabinets* constructed. They were under the roofs of the Palace, built round that small courtyard, the Cour des Cerfs, and were a series of small rooms joined together by winding staircases and small galleries.

A great deal of care had gone into the construction of these little rooms, for Louis was discovering that great passion for architecture which he had inherited from his great-grandfather.

Exquisitely carved were the panels, and the walls had been treated to look as though they were made of porcelain. Louis had greatly enjoyed planning these rooms, and they were extremely graceful, with nothing flamboyant about them. The decorations were delicate scrolls and sprays of flowers.

The *petits cabinets* were like a miniature palace, aloof from the great one. Here Louis had his bedroom, his libraries, and — the most important room of all, for this was that in which he entertained his friends — the *salle à manger*. So fascinated had he become by these little apartments that he could not resist adding to them; he now had his workshop; he was very interested in working in ivory; he had his own bakery and still rooms, for he had retained his early interest in cooking. It was his great pleasure to summon experts to these rooms and take lessons from them.

Often during one of those intimate supper parties he would prepare the coffee himself and even serve it. It was during these occasions that he was at his most charming — perhaps because he was really happy then. The ceremonies of the Court, which had been such a delight to his great-grandfather, were extremely tedious to him. Therefore to be in his beloved little apartments with Madame de Mailly beside him, and a few friends with whom he could talk, not as a King but as one of them, was his idea of pleasure.

On these occasions there were no formal bows and curtsies; some sat on the floor, the King often among them. There was complete relaxation and all were regretful when the King gave the customary *'Allons nous coucher'* and the party broke up.

Almost sadly he would make his way to the large

bedchamber where the wearisome business of the *coucher* must be carried out.

Louis had always disliked the enormous state bedroom of Louis Quatorze, and for years it had been his practice, after the *coucher*, to slip out to a smaller and more cosy room which he shared with Madame de Mailly; but at this time he had asked himself why he should not have his own state bedroom, and such a room had been prepared for him. This room, on the north side of the Cour de Marbre and on the second floor of the Palace, which was decorated by the sculptor Verberckt and in which the bed with its balustrade had been set up, was fast becoming the centre of activity in the Château.

Marie was rarely invited to be present at these gatherings to which foremost members of the Court eagerly sought to be asked. She tried therefore to be contented with her own way of life.

She longed to bring up her children but this was denied to her. The little girls had their governesses whom the King had appointed, and only visited their mother once a day, and then there were always other people present. The little girls were charming – Adelaide was quite pretty and a little headstrong – but they always stood on ceremony with their mother. How could they do otherwise?

She saw the Dauphin more frequently because his apartments were on the ground floor of the Château, immediately below her own; but, as in the case of her daughters, his education was taken out of her hands.

Louis was often in the boy's apartment, for the King was immensely proud of his nine-year-old son and repeated his clever sayings to his friends, who received them with the required awe and astonishment.

One day when the little girls were brought to the Queen for the daily visit, she saw that something troubled them. The two elder girls – the twins, Louise-Elisabeth and Anne-Henriette – did not accompany them; and six-year-old Adelaide led the group.

All were amused to see what dignity that child had and how she inspired awe in the others; Victoire and Sophie were particularly impressed by her; perhaps two-year-old Thérèse-Félicité and the baby Louise-Marie were too young to be influenced as yet.

As they came forward and curtsied to their mother, Marie noticed that Adelaide's eyes were stormy.

'Is all well with you, my daughter?' asked the Queen.

'No, *Maman*.'

Victoire had caught her breath, and Sophie, her eyes going from Victoire to Adelaide, did likewise.

'You must tell me your trouble,' said the Queen.

'*Maman*,' burst out Adelaide, 'we have heard that we are to be sent away.'

Victoire nodded, and Sophie, watching her sister, did the same.

'We do not want to go away, *Maman*,' went on Adelaide. 'We are to go to a convent. We do not want to go.'

'Ah,' said the Queen, 'there comes a time in the life of us all, my daughter, when we are forced to do that which we do not like.'

Adelaide's eyes were pleading. '*Maman*, could you not say we must stay?'

Marie felt sad. What power had she to decide the fate of her children? She knew that the young girls were to be sent away. It had been decided without consulting her. They were to go to the abbey of Fontevrault, there to live simply and be taught by the nuns. Poor little creatures, they would find the austerity of the abbey a great contrast to the splendour of Versailles. She was sorry for them, but there was nothing she could do about it.

She could not tell her children that she had not been consulted and that if she gave her opinions they would be ignored. To do so would be beneath her dignity as a Queen. Therefore she would not meet the pleading gaze of five pairs of eyes, and instead assumed her sternest expression.

'And how are you progressing with your embroidery?' she asked the two elder children.

Victoire as usual looked to Adelaide to answer their mother's question, but Adelaide burst out passionately: *'Maman,* do not let them send us away.'

Marie felt an impulse to gather them into her arms, to tell them that she would fight all those who tried to take her little girls from her; but how could she do this? There were too many watchers and the etiquette of the Château must be maintained, no matter if the little girls thought her harsh and cruel. It was quite unthinkable to cuddle them at this hour of the morning. What a bad example to them that would be!

She said stonily: 'My children, the first thing Princesses must learn is obedience.'

Adelaide looked as though she would burst into tears. Marie fervently hoped she would not, for that would be the signal for the others to start. Adelaide remembered in time where she was, and the teaching of her six years, so she swallowed her tears and held her head high; and when Marie gave her permission to leave, she curtsied faultlessly.

The others, watching Adelaide for their cue, behaved with

the same decorum.

When they had gone Marie thought to herself, why should I allow them to be taken from me? They will remain for years in Fontevrault. Why should I be separated from my children?

This was due to Fleury, she knew. It was the old Cardinal — now past eighty and as energetic as ever — who made all the decisions.

She would ask the Cardinal to call on her and see if she could help those little girls, even though he had never considered her of any importance. It was due to Fleury that her father had lost the throne of Poland. Fleury had deeply deplored France's being dragged into war on account of Stanislas. But it had not really been on his account. Fleury, of course, if he had had his way, would never have gone to war at all, but there had been a strong party in France who sought every opportunity of making war on the Austrian Empire, and Fleury had found himself overruled; so France had joined forces with Spain and Sardinia, and the attack had begun.

But it was little help that came the way of Stanislas who, on the election of Frederick Augustus had fled to Danzig, there to await the help he expected from the country of his son-in-law.

Some Frenchmen would have espoused the cause of Stanislas; Fleury was not among them. But there had been a very gallant gentleman, the Comte de Plélo, Ambassador at Copenhagen, who had determined to do so.

When the commander of the small flotilla, which Fleury had sent, realised the numbers of Russians who were massed against him, he decided that he would not fight and turned back from Danzig. Then the Ambassador, de Plélo, himself led a small force against the Russians; it was a gallant effort but Plélo was killed and Stanislas forced to leave Danzig, disguised as a peasant.

But in the Rhineland and Italy the war went on, although Fleury, whose obsession was to keep France out of war, had no heart for it, and as soon as he could he sought to make peace, and by the autumn of 1735 had begun negotiations.

Frederick Augustus was acclaimed Augustus III King of Poland, Austria took Parma and Placentia, and Spain acquired Naples and Sicily.

What of Stanislas?

It was decided that he should be given Lorraine, for François, Duke of Lorraine was to marry Maria Theresa, who was the daughter of the Emperor and his heiress. It was unthinkable that France should ever allow Lorraine to fall into Austrian hands; therefore Duke François was to take Tuscany in exchange for Lorraine, and the latter was to be given to Stanislas, although on his death it was to be returned to France.

Thus, instead of Poland, Stanislas had been given Lorraine. A poor consolation for a King, thought Marie bitterly; and she blamed Fleury, who had denied him the help he had asked in his time of need.

As he had refused to help her father, she was sure he would refuse to help her little girls.

He came to see her on her invitation and when she had asked him to be seated she said: 'I have been visited by my daughters, Monsieur le Cardinal. They are greatly distressed.'

He looked surprised that she should bother him with the affairs of children.

'It is sad to be sent from one's home,' she went on.

'Madame, children must be educated.'

'They could have a better education here in the Palace.'

'But Madame, have you considered the cost to the Exchequer?'

She gave him an impatient look. He was obsessed by economies. Only recently he had had the beautiful marble cascade at Marly removed and replaced by grass. This, he had said, would save the Exchequer a thousand crowns.

Marie had been angry when she had heard this; it was at the time when Lorraine had been awarded to her father. Fleury had told her then that the throne of Lorraine was better for her father than that of Poland, and she had retorted bitterly: 'Oh, yes, Monsieur le Cardinal, in the same way that a grass plot is better than a marble cascade!'

It was no use trying to plead with such a man. He believed he knew how to cure the ills of his country and his unpopularity with the Queen did not deter him at all, since he had the complete confidence of the King.

'They are breaking their hearts,' she went on. 'Cannot you understand? Here in Versailles they are happy. You would banish these little children to that dismal abbey!'

'Madame, the Princesses' household costs the Exchequer a great deal. In the Abbey of Fontevrault they will learn discipline with their lessons. I believe that in sending them we are doing not only the sensible thing but what is right.'

He was not in the least moved. He did not see the plight of little children torn from their homes; he saw only the saving of money for the Exchequer.

Marie sighed. She had been foolish to ask him to come to her.

Adelaide slipped away from Victoire and Sophie. This was not easy, for they followed her everywhere; and, although she looked upon this as her due and generally was pleased by their devotion, it could at times be awkward.

She smoothed down her velvet dress. It was a deep-blue colour which was called at Court *l'œil du Roi*, because it was similar to that of Louis' eyes. She had asked that she might wear this dress today; she had a special reason for it, she said; and this had not been denied her. Her nurses had felt sorry for the little girl who was to be banished from the Court and were eager to grant her small requests.

Victoire had said: 'Adelaide, what are you going to do?'

And Sophie had stood in her quiet way, looking from one sister to the other.

'It is a secret,' said Adelaide. 'Perhaps I may tell you later.'

Victoire and Sophie looked at each other and had to be content with that.

When Adelaide left them, she made her way to the second floor and to the little apartments of the King. Adelaide was in no awe of her father. She believed him to be the kindest man on Earth, because he always was kind to her. He would play with her, and she knew that when she could think of something clever to say, it pleased him; she knew too that if she cried he was ready to promise anything – not that his promises were always kept – because he could not endure the tears of little girls. There was another point: she was pretty. She had heard the Marquise de la Lande, her *sous-gouvernante*, mention it often to one of the nursery attendants. 'Madame Adelaide is the most beautiful of them all.'

If one were pretty and bold, one could perhaps ask favours. Adelaide was so desperate that she was going to try.

She saw one of the pages and, as he bowed at her approach, she said imperiously: 'I would speak with His Majesty.'

The man, trying not to smile at her grown-up manners, said with the utmost respect: 'Madame, His Majesty, as far as I know, is at Mass.'

Adelaide inclined her head and went on towards the little apartments.

Louis, returning from Mass, felt uneasy — as he always did at such times. He wanted to lead a virtuous life and, much as he enjoyed the society of Madame de Mailly, there were times when he was deeply conscious that in such pleasure was sin.

He tried to raise his spirits by reminding himself that soon he would be leaving for Choisy, that delightful château lying among beautiful wooded country watered by the Seine, which he had bought that it might provide a refuge for himself and Madame de Mailly: and having bought it he could not resist embellishing it. Now it was indeed beautiful with its blue and gold decorations and the mirrored rooms.

He longed for the peace of Choisy whither he and his mistress might go with a few chosen friends; he wished that he need not feel these stirrings of conscience. Surely he could be forgiven. Marie, his Queen, had no physical satisfaction to offer him, and he was a healthy man of twenty-eight.

'Time enough for repentance in forty years' time,' the Duc de Richelieu would say; but Louis had a conscience which from time to time could be very restless.

He was therefore thoughtful as he made his way towards his bedchamber; and as he came into the ante-room, he was astonished to see a small figure running towards him.

His knees were caught in a wild embrace and a voice, strangled with sobs, cried: 'Papa! Papa! It is your Madame Adelaide who speaks to you.'

He lifted the child in his arms. There were real tears on her cheeks. As soon as her face was on a level with his, her arms were round his neck and her wet, hot face buried against him.

'What ails my dearest daughter?' asked Louis tenderly.

'They are going to send Adelaide away from her Papa.'

'And who is doing this terrible thing?' he asked.

'They say *you* are.'

'*I?* Would I send my dearest Madame Adelaide away from me?'

'No . . . no . . . Papa. That is why you must stop them before *they* do. *They* are going to send us to the nuns for years . . . and years and years . . .'

'It is because lessons have to be learned, my darling.'

'I'll learn them here . . . quicker.'

'Oh, but this matter has been well thought out, and it is decided that the nuns will make the best teachers for you and your sisters. It will not be long before you are all home again.'

'Years and years,' she cried; and burst into loud sobs.

'Hush, my little one,' said Louis, looking about him in consternation for someone to take the sobbing child from him; but Adelaide was not going to let him escape as easily as that. She tightened her grip on him and sobbed louder than ever.

'Hush, hush, hush!' cried Louis.

'But they will send me away from my Papa . . . Stop them, please. Please . . . please . . . *please!*'

'But my dear . . .'

'You are the King. You *could!*'

'Adelaide . . .'

She began pummelling his chest with her small fists. 'Could you? Could you?' she demanded.

'You see, Adelaide . . .'

'You will send me away, and I shall die,' she wailed. 'I *will* die, because I won't live away from my Papa . . .'

Then she began to sob in earnest. This was no feigned distress. She was older than the other children and she knew that if she left Versailles for Fontevrault it would indeed be years before she returned.

The Duc de Richelieu had stepped forward and murmured: 'Shall I send for Madame's *gouvernante,* Sire?'

'No . . . no!' screamed Adelaide. 'I will not let my Papa leave me.'

'What can I do?' asked the King helplessly.

'Sire, since the lady declares she will not release you, you can only go with her to Fontevrault or keep her here with you at Versailles.'

'Or,' said the King, 'insist that she goes without me.'

'I do not think, Sire, that it is in your nature to refuse the loving request of a beautiful young lady.'

Adelaide was alert, but she continued to sob and cling to her father.

'Well,' said the King, 'one more at Versailles cannot cost the Exchequer so very much.' He kissed his daughter's hot cheek. 'Come, my child, dry your eyes. You are to stay with your Papa at Versailles.'

Adelaide's answer was a suffocating hug. 'My new dress is the colour of Your Majesty's eyes,' she said. 'That is why I love it.'

'How charming are ladies . . . when their requests are granted,' murmured Richelieu.

The King laughed; he held Adelaide high above his head so that the carvings on the ceiling seemed to rush down to meet her.

'Madame Adelaide,' he cried, 'it pleases me as much as you that you are to stay with us.'

And the next day Adelaide watched her four little sisters driven away to Fontevrault with the Marquise de la Lande. She wept a little to lose them, but she was filled with gratification because she was staying behind and because she had discovered that, if she wanted something, it was possible to get it by asking for it in a certain manner in a certain quarter.

The little Princesses had been away for a year, and Adelaide often forgot their very existence for days at a time. When she did think of them she pitied them in their grim old abbey. It was so much more fun to be at Versailles where she was often with her father. Sometimes he came to her nurseries to see her; sometimes she accompanied him to the apartments of the Dauphin – although she did not like this so much as her brother was apt to command her father's attention and divert it from herself.

Adelaide adored her father, and everyone knew of this adoration. Not that Adelaide attempted to hide it. That would have been foolish. Her father was the most important person at Court, and while he loved her Adelaide could see that she was important also.

To her mother she was almost indifferent. She had sensed the rift between the King and Queen, and gave her allegiance to her handsome, charming and all-powerful father, rather than to her fat and too pious mother.

Louis was growing more interested in his children, for as they grew away from babyhood they attracted him more strongly. Both Adelaide and the Dauphin had spirit, and he admired them for that quality.

Adelaide was a pretty little girl and therefore delightful, but Louis the Dauphin, being the heir to the throne, was the important member of the family.

News was brought to the King that someone must speak to the boy because he was growing too headstrong. There was no one who had the authority to do this but the King, for the young Dauphin had declared to his tutors that he would one day be King and therefore it was they who should take orders from him, not he from them.

When Louis visited the Dauphin in his apartments on the ground floor of the Château, the ten-year-old boy, seeing his father approach, bowed low.

The King smiled. The Dauphin usually greeted his father by leaping into his arms and asking for a ride on his shoulders. The Dauphin was feeling his dignity and growing up.

Louis tried to remember himself at the age of ten. How did he behave then? Was he as wilful as the Dauphin? He did not think so; but if he had been, there was some excuse for him, because he was then already King.

'Well, my son,' said Louis, 'I have been hearing reports of your conduct.'

The Dauphin turned to his tutor who was standing by, and said: 'You may leave us.'

The tutor looked at the King, and Louis nodded to confirm the boy's order. The Dauphin knew he was going to be reprimanded and did not want this to happen before his tutor. When he had gone, the King sat down, and drawing the boy to him said: 'Was that the man whose face you slapped?'

'Yes, Papa. He deserved it!'

'In your judgement or his own?'

The boy looked astonished. 'He is a man who will not listen to reason,' he said haughtily.

The King was secretly amused.

'*Your* reason, naturally,' he said.

'*Reason!*' said the Dauphin firmly.

Louis laughed. 'My son,' he said, 'one day you will rule this kindom. A King is unwise who does not listen to the advice of his counsellors.

'I am ready to listen, Papa.'

'Listening is not enough,' said the King. 'Advice must be also considered and, usually when one is very young, taken. When I was your age . . .'

The boy's expression had changed. He drew closer to his father. 'Tell me, Papa, about when you were a boy. Tell me about the day they carried you into the Grande Chambre and you asked for the Archbishop's hat, or when little Blanc et Noir came to the Council meetings.'

Louis told the boy, projecting himself into those days of his childhood, hoping that by so doing he was giving a boy, who was destined to be a King of France, a glimpse of the duties of kingship.

The boy's face glowed; his eyes softened.

When Louis had finished, he said: 'Papa, if you were my tutor instead of the Abbé de Saint-Cyr . . .'

'I know, my son, you would not slap my face. Is that it?'

'I would not,' said the boy gravely.

'Even though *I* would not listen to *your* reason?'

'I would love my tutor so much that reason would not matter,' said the boy.

Louis could not help boasting about his son's intelligence; he would repeat his sayings, so that the Court began to smile when they had heard them a few times. Louis was becoming a fond father, infinitely proud of his Dauphin.

A few shrewd people would approach the boy and ask him to put in a good word for them with his father. The young Dauphin, enjoying the feeling of importance, would do his utmost to have these requests granted; and as Louis wanted the Court to know in what esteem he held his son, unless they were very outrageous, he invariably concurred.

✤ ✤ ✤

It was charming to have a family about the Court. Louis often regretted the absence of the four little girls at Fontevrault. The twins delighted him, and it was sad to think that they were nearing the age when marriages should be arranged for them.

Louise-Elisabeth and Anne-Henriette were twelve years old, and Don Philip, the son of Philip V and his second wife Elisabeth Farhese, was looking for a bride.

With seven daughters for whom husbands should in time be found, the marriage problem must be tackled early. One of the twins must go to Spain.

The twins knew this and they were anxious.

They liked to walk together in the gardens of the Château, talking of the future when they would be parted.

On this day in the year 1739 they were strolling under the lime trees when Louise-Elisabeth said: 'The Spanish Ambassador has been so much with Papa lately.'

Anne-Henriette nodded. She stared at the fishpond with its porcelain tiles on which were painted birds looking so natural that they might have been real.

She did not say that he had called on their father this morning, and that he was even now closeted with him and the Cardinal and other important people. She was afraid, because Louise-Elisabeth was considered to be the elder and she felt sure that if this marriage were arranged it would be for her sister and not for her.

'I wonder what it is like in Spain,' she said.

When Louise-Elisabeth answered there was a note of hysteria in her voice: 'They say it is very solemn there.'

'That was long ago. The King is a relation of ours. I have heard that the Court of Spain is more French than Spanish since the Bourbons ruled.'

'It would be only natural that it should be.' Louise-Elisabeth looked back at the honey-coloured stones of the Château which was home to her, and a great love for it and all it contained swept over her.

'Perhaps,' went on her sister, 'it is not very much different from Versailles.'

'But you would not be there . . . our brother and mother would not be there. And Papa . . . There would be another King . . . not Papa. Imagine that! Can you? I cannot. A King who is not our father.'

'He may be very kind, all the same.'

'He could not be like our father.' There was a sob in Louise-Elisabeth's throat.

'One would grow used to him. And perhaps in time be Queen of Spain.'

'No,' said Louise-Elisabeth, 'there are too many to come

before Don Philip.' But her eyes had begun to glisten, her sister noticed; and she felt glad.

Gentle Anne-Henriette would suffer more if she were dragged away from her home. She had not Louise-Elisabeth's desire for power. The elder twin had always been the more imperious, the more ambitious, the leader. Anne-Henriette had been content to be led by those she loved.

She believed now, that as one of them had to go it would be better if Louise-Elisabeth did. She would be unhappy for a while but she would soon begin to make a place for herself in her new country; whereas if she, Anne-Henriette, were made to leave Versailles, her heart would break. She would be sad enough at parting with Louise-Elisabeth, but at least the rest of the family would be left to her. She would have her beautiful and beloved home in which to nurse her grief, and gradually grow away from it.

She prayed that if she married, it would be someone whose home was here. Perhaps that was not an impossibility.

Louise-Elisabeth continued to talk of Spain. She had been reading about that country. Elisabeth Farnese was very ambitious for her sons and she commanded the King, it was said.

Already she plans, thought Anne-Henriette.

Then she smiled, for she heard someone coming towards them and, even before she saw him, Anne-Henriette guessed it was the young Duc de Chartres, the grandson of the late Regent, the Duc d'Orléans.

He was very handsome; indeed in Anne-Henriette's eyes he was the most handsome person at the Court comparing favourably even with her father. He bowed before the Princesses.

'Madame Première, Madame Seconde!' he murmured.

'Greetings on this beautiful morning.'

Both Princesses smiled at him, but his eyes lingered on Anne-Henriette.

'I hope I do not intrude?' said the Duc. 'May I walk with you?'

Anne-Henriette looked at her sister. 'But of course,' said Louise-Elisabeth quickly; and it was clear that her thoughts were with the conference in the Palace and not on such trivial matters.

'There is great activity in the Palace this day, Monsieur de Chartres,' said Anne-Henriette.

'That is so, Madame.'

A look of anxiety had come into his eyes; he continued to gaze at her as though he were unaware of the presence of Madame Louise-Elisabeth.

When the Duc de Chartres had joined the girls, their *gouvernante* and *sous-gouvernante*, who had had them under surveillance from some short distance, approached; but before they reached the little group a breathless page came running to them.

Both Princesses and the Duc de Chartres seemed to be holding their breath, waiting for the words of the page who, they believed, could tell them a great deal.

'What do you want?' called Louise-Elisabeth before the page had reached them.

'Madame . . .' He paused, and it seemed to them all that the silence went on for a long time; but that was an illusion.

'Madame Louise-Elisabeth,' he continued, 'His Majesty would speak with you at once.'

The tension was relaxed. Louise-Elisabeth bowed her head. She began to follow the page across the grass, back to the

Palace – on her way to Spain and who knew what honour and glory.

Anne-Henriette stared after her. She did not realise that the women had now joined her. She was only aware of the exquisite beauty of Versailles and the intense joy in the eyes of the young Duc de Chartres.

✦ ✦ ✦

In the Abbaye de Port Royal a young woman sat angrily stitching at a piece of embroidery. Her needle jabbed at the work and she scowled at the stitches.

She had commanded one of the young ladies, who was also in the convent and in a similar position to herself, to come and talk to her. Pauline-Félicité de Nesle always commanded and, strangely enough, others obeyed. The conversations which took place between her and her chosen companions were usually monologues interspersed with exclamations of admiration, surprise, or monosyllabic queries. She would allow nothing more.

Now she was saying: 'Do you realise that I am twenty-four years of age? Twenty-four! And shut away in a place like this. I am expected to grow quiet and modest and contented with my lot. Contented! I, Pauline-Félicité de Nesle, to spend the rest of my days here! Is it not ridiculous?'

She paused for her companion's nod which was quickly given.

'All this . . . while my sister is at Court. And moreover not as a humble lady-in waiting. My sister could rule France if she wished. It is only because she is a fool that she does not. Louise-Julie is the King's mistress. Think of that. Imagine the time she has . . . and compare her life with mine. Anyone would be a fool to endure it. I am not a fool. Do *you* think I am a fool?'

'Oh, no, Mademoiselle de Nesle.'

'Then shall I stay here, stitching on stuff like this? Saying my prayers? Watching my youth fade away? King's mistresses should help their families. It is a duty. If I were in Louise-Julie's place . . . but I am not. Yet why am I not? I tell you it is only lack of opportunity. She married our cousin, the Comte de Mailly, and that took her to Court. Had I been the eldest daughter, had I married the Comte de Mailly and gone to Court, I tell you, it would now be Pauline-Félicité, not Louise-Julie who was the most important woman at the Court. Do you not agree?'

'Oh, yes, Mademoiselle de Nesle.'

'And if I were the King's mistress, I would not be content to remain in the background. I would rule France. I would give that old fool Fleury his *congé*, for it is he, not my sister, who rules the King. And that is not how it should be. Everyone knows that it is the King's mistress who should rule, not some stupid old minister who has too long eluded the grave. Oh, if I were in my sister's place things would be very different at Court. You believe that?'

'Oh, yes, Mademoiselle de Nesle.' Her companion looked at her and thought: Oh, no, Mademoiselle de Nesle. Pauline-Félicité did not see herself as others saw her. She was by no means beautiful. She was very tall and in fact ugly, although it was an ugliness which attracted attention. It was impossible to be in a room with Pauline-Félicité, no matter how many others were present, and not notice her. Moreover she was clever. She knew a great deal more about the affairs of the country than anyone else in the convent. She made it her business to know, as though it was all part of some great plan. Everyone was in awe of her – even the Mother Superior, because her tongue was so quick and clever and no one could escape it.

Therefore it was neccessary to go on saying: Oh, yes, or Oh, no, Mademoiselle de Nesle, whichever the fiery Pauline-Félicité demanded.

'I shall tell you what I now propose to do,' said Pauline-Félicité. 'I am going to write to my sister and remind her of her duty. I am going to tell her that she must arrange for me to go to Court without delay. Are you looking sceptical?'

'Oh, no, Mademoiselle de Nesle.'

'I am glad of that, for you would then be stupid. You would look very foolish when my invitation came, would you not? I have decided to waste no more time. I am going to write to my sister immediately. Here . . . you may finish this piece of embroidery for me.'

Pauline-Félicité threw the work into her companion's lap and stalked from the room.

⚜ ⚜ ⚜

An uneasy atmosphere prevailed in the intimate circles of the Court.

Louis was still paying occasional nightly visits to the Queen; she was still trying hard to elude him. Often at his intimate supper parties he would drink too freely and at such times his restraint would desert him.

Marie had been pregnant once more, but on account of over-exertion she had had a miscarriage; her doctors thought she had borne too many children too quickly. Marie thought so too, and on one occasion when Louis came to her room, there was a scene which was witnessed by no member of the Court because it took place in the early hours of the morning. All that the King's attendants knew was that he walked out of the Queen's bedroom and seemed to have come to a decision.

They were right. He had decided that henceforth all conjugal relations should cease, and thus little Louise-Marie would remain Madame Dernière.

From that time his liaison with Madame de Mailly was no longer kept a secret. The people would understand that, since the Queen must have no more children, the King was entitled to have a mistress. The people of France were very indulgent about such matters.

Even though she was now recognised as King's mistress, Louise-Julie was uneasy. She fancied that the King relied upon her a little less than before, and that were he not so kind-hearted he might have deserted her for someone else. She was passionately in love with him and was far happier when she could live with him in comparative seclusion at Choisy rather than in the limelight of Versailles.

All about her, she knew, were eagle-eyed men and women, watching for the least sign of the King's waning affection. The men were anxious to promote the women they favoured; the women were waiting for a chance to take her place.

But Louis remained simple-hearted. His dread of unpleasantness increased rather than diminished as he grew older. He would have to be very enamoured of another woman before he could bring himself to dispense with an existing mistress.

Strangely enough the woman she most feared was the recently widowed Comtesse de Toulouse – plump, very good-looking still, but well advanced into middle age. The Comtesse had approached Louis slyly; she did not seek to become his mistress; she felt as a mother to him. Louis was continually at Rambouillet, since the Comtesse, on the death of her husband, had begged Louis to look after her and her son.

She was a clever woman, this Comtesse, for she knew that the Condés were planning to rob her son of his status. Her husband the Comte had been the illegitimate son of Louis Quatorze and Madame de Montespan, and his father had made him legitimate. Now that he was dead, said the Condés, they did not see why the son should be considered to have legitimate connexions with the Royal Family. Madame la Comtesse was going to fight with all her cunning to preserve the state of her son, the Duc de Penthièvre, and if the mother-love which she was preparing to bestow upon the King turned into another kind of love, so much the better for the Toulouses.

She was undoubtedly successful. Not only was the young Duc named as Prince of the Blood but the Comtesse had a special apartment at Rambouillet set aside for the King – a refuge, she called it, to which he could turn when he felt harassed by state duties and needed a little motherly care.

Louis himself was feeling very sad, because it was time that his daughter Louise-Elisabeth left home for her marriage with the Infante Don Philip.

He had watched with mild regret the departure of his little daughters; they were so young that they had not yet completely captured his affections. It was a very different matter to see the twelve-year-old Princesse depart, particularly as he had to witness the grief of Anne-Henriette and little Adelaide, both of whom he was beginning to love dearly.

He himself had been ill and was feeling restive. Ennui was beginning to take possession of him. Life seemed to go on in a monotonous pattern, and even hunting, gambling, the mother-love of the Comtesse de Toulouse, and the passion of Louise-Julie de Mailly could not rouse him from this lethargy which was tinged with melancholy.

One day Louise-Julie said to him: 'Louis, I have received many letters from my younger sister. She longs to come to Court.'

Louis nodded without interest.

'She writes the most amusing letters. Pauline-Félicité was never the least bit shy. You see how she writes in this bold hand-writing. *I . . . I . . . I!* You see, all down the page.'

Louis took the letter and read it; he smiled faintly.

'She *is* eager,' he said.

'May I invite her to Court?'

'It would seem unkind to deny her something on which she has so clearly set her heart.'

'I will write to her today,' said Louise-Julie. 'I think you will find her rather outrageous . . . quite different from anyone else.'

Louis yawned slightly. 'It will be a change,' he murmured; but Louise-Julie saw that he was not really interested in her sister. Did that mean that he was no longer interested in her?

Pauline-Félicité swept through the Court like a whirlwind. Surely, said the courtiers, there was never a woman so ugly who gave herself such airs. But they had to concede that it was an ugliness which could not be ignored. It was a compelling ugliness inasmuch as when Pauline-Félicité was present she automatically became the magnet of attention.

She was undoubtedly witty, and before she had been at

Court a week her sayings were being quoted. She was no respecter of rank and had even made sly comments on the King.

'His Majesty has lived all his life in leading strings,' she declared. 'What matters it who holds the strings? He is controlled by old age, middle age and youth – by the Cardinal's ancient hands, the motherly ones of Madame de Toulouse, and the loving ones of my sister. What fun, should His Majesty escape and learn to totter along by himself!'

These remarks were recounted to the King and when she was next at one of his intimate supper parties he commanded Pauline-Félicité to sit beside him.

'You are an outspoken young woman,' he told her.

'I speak the truth,' she retorted. 'It is more stimulating than lies which can be so monotonously boring. Your Majesty must know this, for you have been constantly fed on the latter.'

Louis smiled. 'I believe,' he said, 'that there has been a faint flavour of truth in my diet on certain occasions.'

'A spicy ingredient,' she retorted, 'which has been too often lacking.'

'In order to make the meal more palatable,' murmured Louis.

'Yes . . . and the palate, knowing little but flattery and lies, has become jaded.'

'How is it that you know so much about me?'

'Despite your crown, Your Majesty is but a man. Therefore, if I use my knowledge of men, I add to my knowledge of Your Majesty.'

'There are many people here who consider you insolent, Mademoiselle de Nesle.'

'But all consider me interesting, Sire. You see how they are striving to overhear what I am saying.'

'Might it not be what *I* am saying?'

'No, Sire, it is enough that you talk to me. No effort is required to see that. But what I dare say to you is of the utmost interest.'

'So they taught you to speak truth at your convent.'

'Not they! They taught me etiquette, deportment and how to work flowers on a canvas. It was too boring to be endured.'

'So you wanted to come to see the Court?'

She lifted her eyes to his face. 'To see Your Majesty,' she said boldly.

The king was excited. She was enough like her sister to appeal to him. The fact that she was far from beautiful added piquancy to her attraction; there were so many beautiful women at Court waiting to pounce on him, that often he felt as he had when he was a little boy and had wanted to escape from the people. He did not want to escape from Mademoiselle de Nesle. She amused him, and he discovered that in her company he was no longer bored.

Now he must see her every day. Fleury was anxious, Madame de Toulouse furious, and Madame de Mailly broken-hearted; but the inevitable had happened. The King was no longer in love with his mistress; her sister had taken her place in his affections.

❖ ❖ ❖

Now Pauline-Félicité was a constant visitor to the *petits appartements,* and at the intimate suppers her place was beside the King.

Her ascendancy over him amazed everyone. It seemed

incredible that Louis, who had all his life been accustomed to flattery, should be so enthralled by a woman whose prime characteristics were her outspokenness and her caustic tongue.

When it was announced that Mademoiselle de Nesle was to be married, the whole Court understood what that implied. The young woman was to become the King's mistress and, because King's mistresses were always married women, if he should happen to fall in love with an unmarried one efforts must be made with all speed to put an end to her single state.

Felix de Vintimille, who was a son of the Comte du Luc, was selected for the honour of becoming the husband of the King's favourite, and the ceremony was performed by the Archbishop of Paris who was an uncle of the bridegroom and delighted at the turn of events, as the family would lose nothing by having obliged the King in this way.

Louis attended the wedding and took a prominent part in the hilarious ceremony of putting the couple to bed. This ceremony was even more farcical than usual, for it was the King who took the place of the bridegroom, and the Comte de Vintimille who rode off afterwards in the King's carriage.

Now Pauline-Félicité was beginning to realise her ambitions. In the short time since she had come to Court she had achieved the first. Her plans did not end there. She was now Madame de Vintimille with a husband in name only; she was beloved of the King and she was going to rid him of the influence of that doddering old Cardinal and make him take an interest in state affairs, where of course he should follow her advice.

Madame de Vintimille was following foreign affairs with a great deal of zest.

The Emperor Charles VI of Austria had died; he was the last male descendant of the great Emperor Charles V, and thus there was no son to follow him. There was however his daughter, Maria Theresa, who had been recently married to Duke François of Lorraine.

Maria Theresa was twenty-three years of age and, as she had known that she would one day inherit her father's dominions, she had prepared herself for this duty. A clever young woman, determined to make her country great, she was fully aware of the difficulties which beset her. The war of the Polish Succession had weakened the country to a great extent – the army had been reduced and the exchequer depleted.

Her Empire was large but scattered. It consisted of Austria, Hungary and Bohemia, and there were possessions in Italy and the Netherlands. She was wise enough to know that such scattered possessions could provide great difficulties for their ruler.

Moreover there were many who, believing they had a claim to the Austrian Empire, pointed out that its rule should not be placed in the hands of a woman. Augustus III, who was now not only the King of Poland but Elector of Saxony, staked a claim on the grounds that his wife was a niece of Emperor Charles VI. Charles-Albert, the Elector of Bavaria, claimed the throne through his grandmother who was also a niece of Charles VI.

Becoming aware of these claimants, others arose. There were Charles Emmanuel of Sardinia, Philip V of Spain and Frederick II of Prussia.

It was small wonder that the young woman saw trouble all about her; but she knew that her most formidable enemy was Frederick of Prussia.

Frederick was the first to act. He claimed Silesia and offered money and an alliance to Maria Theresa in exchange for the territory, but Maria Theresa, young and idealistic, retorted sharply that her duty was to defend her subjects, not to sell them.

This was what Frederick was waiting for. He gave the order for his armies to march on Silesia.

France so far had remained outside the conflict, and Fleury, now approaching ninety, wished to keep her so. But there were men in France who had other ideas, who were young and passionately eager to enhance the glory of their country. They saw the means of doing so and a strong party, led by Charles Louis Auguste Fouquet, the Comte de Belle-Isle, rose in opposition to the Cardinal, and decided to set Charles-Albert, the Elector of Bavaria, on the Imperial throne.

Under the influence of Madame de Vintimille the King was on the side of the young men who were eager for war.

Fleury wrung his hands but he could do nothing else. Frenchmen were ready to rise against the hated Austrian, and the country was in favour of the war.

The result was a treaty between Prussia, Bavaria and France, and the French army was sent to make war on Austria.

The King, now visibly changed under the influence of Madame de Vintimille, followed the progress of the war with the greatest enthusiasm. His mistress compelled his interest and he, following her lead, discovered his boredom was receding.

There was one matter on which Madame de Vintimille was eager to have her way and which she found the most difficult of all her tasks. Try as she might to have Fleury removed from Court, the King remained firm in his determination to keep the old man in office.

'Why, Madame,' he said, 'this is an old man. It would break his heart to be dismissed from Court.'

'So France must be destroyed for the sake of one old man's heart!'

'Fleury is no fool.'

'Oh, no,' she mocked. 'He is as alert and as virile as one can expect – at ninety.'

'He is not yet that,' laughed Louis. 'Oh, come, let us talk of other matters.'

'So Fleury stays?' she asked, almost challengingly.

But Louis' expression was equally challenging. 'Fleury stays,' he repeated.

Madame de Vintimille was angry. She very much disliked being crossed. Moreover Fleury's position had been strengthened if anything by the recent death of the Duc de Bourbon, that enemy whom the Cardinal had once had dismissed from Court. Fleury could never feel safe while Bourbon was at Court for he knew that Monsieur le Duc would never forget the terrible humiliation he had suffered at his hands. The Duc de Bourbon was not an old man when he died, being only forty-seven, but he had made himself rather ridiculous in his last years by his extreme jealousy of his wife. Monsieur le Duc had quite blatantly been the lover of the Comtesse d'Egmont, but had raged against his wife when she had in retaliation taken a lover, and he had created quite a scandal by locking her up in a barred room at the top of his château and keeping her a prisoner there.

Madame de Vintimille was certain of one thing; before

many months had passed, she was determined, Cardinal Fleury should receive the dreaded *lettre de cachet*.

In the meantime her attention was slightly diverted when she discovered that she was pregnant.

Delightedly she carried this news to the King.

'Our child,' she said, 'will be a boy.'

Louis was amused. 'You are sure to be right,' he said. 'Providence would not dare go against your wishes in such a matter.'

✤ ✤ ✤

So during those months Madame de Vintimille was constantly at the side of the King. Her arrogance and outspokenness endeared her to him, for he admired her alert mind and he appreciated her sincerity.

She was clever and there was no doubt that she brought a brilliant mind to the study of state affairs. Louis found that with her beside him the position of King in such times, although bringing with it its anxieties, was a very interesting one.

Although there were often quarrels, she meant more to him than had any woman he had so far known and he was very much looking forward to the birth of their child.

'You are sour and spiteful,' Louis told her on one occasion. 'There is one thing which would cure you: You should have your head cut off. You have such a long neck. It would suit you. Your blood should be drained off and lambs' blood substituted.'

'What nonsense you talk!' snapped Madame de Vintimille. 'Of what use should I be to you, headless? And if you want a woman who mildly agrees with you on all occasions, pray say so, and I will return to the Abbaye de Port Royal.'

Louis laughed at her. 'You would die rather. Ah, now I know a way of revenge: Send you back to your convent.'

'Very well, send me back and I'll send you back to boredom.' It was a good answer and it delighted him.

'I shall never send you away,' he said. 'For ever you shall remain here at my side.'

Then she smiled, thinking of the honours that should be given to this son of hers whom she could feel moving within her.

✦ ✦ ✦

It was August of the year 1741, and Madame de Vintimille had made all the necessary preparations for her confinement. She wanted the birth of her child to be of as much account as the birth of a Dauphin. That self-willed boy in the royal nursery was now twelve years old, apt to strut, full of his own importance.

A few days before the child was due to be born, while she was staying at Choisy, she felt suddenly so exhausted that she retired to her bed and when her women saw how drawn she looked, they were alarmed. Had her pains started? No, she told them, they had not. She merely felt very weary. She would rest and be quite well in the morning.

Her women noticed that she had started to shiver, and that her hands were burning.

'Madame has a fever,' said one.

'It is to be hoped not . . . at such a time.'

'Oh, she will recover. She has determined to have a healthy child – so how could it be otherwise?'

But during the night there was consternation among her

servants, for she was slightly delirious and seemed to think she was plain Mademoiselle de Nesle living in a convent.

In the morning the King called on her, and was horrified at the sight of her; she did not even know him.

'She must not stay here,' he said. 'She must be brought to Versailles. There she will have the best of attention. There her child shall be born.'

So a litter was improvised and Madame de Vintimille left Choisy for Versailles. When she was brought to the château the Cardinal de Rohan hastened to put his apartments at her disposal, and thither she was taken while the King summoned his doctors.

She lay for a week, burning with fever in this state of exhaustion, and at the end of that time her child was born.

It was a boy. Naturally, said the Court. How could it be otherwise when Madame had decided it should be so? Now she would recover.

But she continued in a state of semi-oblivion, and it was necessary for others to look after the introduction into the world of this boy for whom his mother had planned so much. Had she been conscious she would not have been pleased by that reception. The Comte de Vintimille made a protest that the child, whom they were attempting to baptise as his, was certainly not his son. Louis however commanded that he should withdraw that protest. Monsieur de Vintimille did so, somewhat sullenly, but his important relations, the Cardinal de Noailles and the Marquis de Luc were present at the baptism.

Still Madame de Vintimille did not recover; instead her fever grew worse, and less than a week after the birth of her son, she died.

Louis was bewildered. She had seemed so full of life, and their tempestuous relationship had been of such short duration. He could face no one; he wanted to be alone with his grief. He wept bitterly, reliving scenes from their life together. Mass was said in his bedroom, for he could not face his friends in the first agony of this sorrow.

The Queen came to his apartment. Gently she expressed her sympathy.

'I know,' she said, 'what regard you had for Madame de Vintimille.'

The King gazed at her with leaden eyes.

'Louis,' she went on, 'you must not give way to your grief in this way. You have your duties.'

He looked at her most angrily. 'She was young . . . She had more vitality than the rest of us. Why . . . *why*? . . .'

'God has his reasons,' said the Queen significantly.

Louis looked at her in horror. Then he said: 'I thank you for coming. I should be happier alone.'

Marie left him, but she had set him thinking. Was this God's vengeance, his punishment for the sin he and Madame de Vintimille had committed? Then he forgot his own fears in the contemplation of his mistress, struck down without time for repentance. What was happening to her now? He was left; he had time to repent. But what of her?

He felt full of remorse. I should not have made her my mistress, he told himself, forgetting her determination to fill that position. Had I not, she might have returned to her convent – innocent as she came from it. Here was an added lash with which to torment himself.

There was another visitor. It was the Comtesse de Toulouse, who embraced him with that half-sensuous, half-motherly affection which she never failed to offer on every possible occasion.

'My beloved Sire,' she murmured; 'what can I say to you? How can I comfort you?'

There was comfort in weeping in the motherly arms of Madame de Toulouse.

Madame de Mailly came to him. She stood at some distance, looking at him, and suddenly he knew that, of all the sympathy which had been offered to him, this of his discarded mistress was the most sincere.

'So,' he said shamefacedly, 'you have come back.'

'Yes, Louis,' she answered, 'as I always should if I thought I could be of use to you.'

'You are welcome,' he told her.

Madame de Toulouse was not very pleased to see Madame de Mailly welcomed back, but she was too wise to show this.

'Between us,' she said, 'we will make you happy again.'

'I cannot bear to be here . . . near her death-bed,' said Louis.

'Then we will go away,' said Madame de Toulouse. 'We will leave at once. Let us go to Saint-Léger. There we can be at peace.'

'Thank you, my dear ones,' said the King.

At Saint-Léger he continued to mourn.

He would sit for hours brooding over his brief love affair with that remarkable woman. He told himself that there could never be anyone like her; and although the motherliness of Madame de Toulouse and the unselfish devotion of Madame de Mailly comforted him they could not bring him out of his melancholy.

He felt sick with horror when he heard that, when the corpse of his beloved mistress had been taken, wrapped in its shroud, from the Palace, a mob of people in the streets had seized it and mutilated it.

The people remembered their sufferings, and they believed that the extravagances of King's mistresses added to these. They did not blame their handsome King who, in their eyes, could do no wrong; but with bread scarce and large families to be fed, there must be a scapegoat.

Louis' grief subsided into melancholy. Madame de Mailly would have given him comfort which she well knew how to give, but he denied himself this.

From now on, he had decided, he would change his mode of life. He was going to live virtuously. Her death had shown him what he must do. Had she not always influenced his actions?

'Glad I am, my dear,' he said to Madame de Mailly, 'of your friendship, but the relationship between us must not go beyond that. From now on I shall abstain from all fleshly pleasures. I hope that by so doing I may expiate her sins . . . and my own.'

Thus passed several weeks at Saint-Léger.

✦ Chapter VII ✦

DUCHESSE DE CHÂTEAUROUX

A penitent King, in the eyes of such rakes as the Duc de Richelieu, meant a dull Court. Moreover ambitious men, such as the Duc had time to be when he was not indulging in his amours, had always dreamed of promoting some woman of their choice to the position of King's mistress, thus ensuring special favours for themselves.

The celibacy of a man such as Louis could not be of long duration. Louis did not know himself if he imagined it could be. But Louis, in many ways, was taking a long time to grow up. His natural innocence was so deep-rooted that only a long life of depravity could destroy it.

Louis had a fondness for the Nesle girls. The Marquis de Nesle had had five daughters; the family was of the old nobility and, like so many in that category, had outlived its wealth. It seemed strange that these women should appeal in a sensual way to the King. Neither Madame de Mailly nor Madame de Vintimille had been beauties; yet for years the former had remained the King's only mistress, only to be displaced by her ugly sister.

There is some quality in these Nesle girls which only Louis

has discovered, thought Richelieu; and he considered the rest of the family. Of the three remaining sisters one was ugly, even more so than Madame de Vintimille had been, for she lacked her extraordinary vitality. She was Diane-Adelaide, the youngest of the family. Then there was Madame de Flavacourt who had some beauty and a great deal of charm. But the one on whom the attention of the Duc de Richelieu became fixed was the widowed Madame de la Tournelle, for she was a beauty – the only beauty among the Nesle girls. Her complexion was dazzlingly clear, her wide eyes deep blue in colour, her face perfect in its contours; and above all she had a grace and elegance which were outstanding even at Court.

Richelieu considered her. She was his cousin and he knew her to be the mistress of his nephew, the Duc d'Aiguillon, and that the two of them were passionately in love with each other; so enamoured was the Duc that he was contemplating marriage.

Marie-Anne de la Tournelle could be, thought Richelieu, an ambitious woman; she was also a clever one. At the moment her love for the weak but handsome Duc d'Aiguillon obscured her judgement, but Richelieu believed that if she made herself agreeable to the King he would be ready to desert his life of piety, and the Court would grow lively again.

Why should he not be interested in the young widow? She was beautiful and she had the mysterious quality of being a Nesle.

Walking with the King at Saint-Léger he talked of her.

'My nephew gives me some concern, Sire,' he said. 'He hopes to marry Madame de la Tournelle.'

'You do not approve of the match?' asked Louis.

Richelieu was momentarily thoughtful. 'It is good enough.'

The King's eyes filled with tears. 'Is she not the sister of . . . of . . . ?'

'Of our dear Madame de Vintimille, yes. I wonder she did not bring the young woman to your notice. But perhaps she wisely did not. Madame de Vintimille was noted for her wisdom.'

'Why was she wise not to do so?'

'Ah, Sire, one glance at this fair creature would suffice to tell you that. She is the most beautiful woman we have seen at Court for a long time.'

'Madame de Vintimille was wise enough to know there was no such reason why she should not introduce her sister,' said the King coldly.

'No, Sire – indeed no. But those who love can be jealous, even when it is ridiculous to be so. Do you not agree? And Madame de la Tournelle is . . . quite enchanting.'

'Why are you set against the match with d'Aiguillon?'

'The boy is my nephew and, rake as I am, I would prefer not to be tempted to seduce his wife!'

'I am surprised,' said the King, 'that *you* should consider such obstacles.'

'One likes to set oneself a standard, Sire. But the lady . . . oh, she is enchanting.'

Louis was thoughtful. It was long that he had lived in celibacy; and he had begun to imagine a woman who might compensate him for his loss: she would show the devotion of Madame de Mailly, the vitality of Madame de Vintimille – and if she were beautiful in addition, how fortunate he would be. But where find such a paragon? Perhaps in the Nesle family which had given him so much?

Richelieu called on Madame de la Tournelle. She was inclined to be suspicious, believing he was eager to foil her romance with his nephew.

'Salutations to the most beautiful lady at Court,' said Richelieu.

Marie-Anne de la Tournelle inclined her head in acknowledgement of the compliment.

'And my nephew is the luckiest man in France. I understand his devotion, but frankly, Madame, if you will forgive the impertinence, *your* choice is a little surprising.'

'I find it difficult to forgive your impertinence,' she said icily.

'Nevertheless you will. Aiguillon – he is a good fellow, a simple fellow at heart . . . but one would have thought that a lady of such grace and beauty would have looked beyond him.'

She was alert. She had seen her sisters installed at Versailles as King's mistresses; she had thought Louise-Julie a fool, but she had admired Pauline-Félicité. If she were ever in a similar position she would imitate the latter rather than the former.

Being ambitious, having an imagination, it was impossible not to have imagined herself in the same position as her sisters. Was Richelieu suggesting that, if she made a bid to step into her sisters' shoes, she would have his help?

'My sisters looked high,' she said; 'and what did they gain? I am not the only one who is sorry for Madame de Mailly; and Madame de Vintimille is beyond pity and envy.'

'Madame de Vintimille was unlucky. Madame de Mailly foolish. If you should find yourself in a similar position, you need be neither unlucky nor foolish.'

'Good day to you,' she said. 'I see you have determined to

separate me from the Duc d'Aiguillon. That, Monsieur, you shall not do.'

✤ ✤ ✤

Richelieu's words had impressed Louis. He could not live the life of a monk for ever. His thoughts dwelt continually on Madame de la Tournelle. Surely if anyone could make him forget his sorrow it would be the sister of his dead mistress.

He returned to Versailles and, when he saw her, he, who had abstained from feminine company so long, became obsessed by one idea: to make Madame de la Tournelle his mistress.

Marie-Anne found herself in a difficult position. She was ambitious; she saw no end to the honours which would come her way if she became the King's mistress. On the other hand she had the humiliating example of her eldest sister before her and, oddly enough, she was still deeply enamoured of the Duc d'Aiguillon.

Louis sought her company on all possible occasions. He began by talking of his devotion to Madame de Vintimille. To this she listened gravely but refused to acknowledge that he was making advances to her. She wept over her sister's death and told him how deeply she regretted it, making it quite clear to Louis that she had no wish to take that sister's place.

Louis was nonplussed. Most of the women of the Court had quite clearly shown their eagerness to comfort him.

Strangely enough she appeared to be endeavouring to ingratiate herself with the Queen, conducting herself with the utmost decorum and eagerly seeking opportunities of being in attendance on Marie. On the other hand when invitations to join supper parties in *petits appartements* came her way she found excuses to avoid doing so.

The more she appeared to elude him, the greater did Louis' passion grow.

'I fear,' he told Richelieu, 'that Madame de la Tournelle is determined to remain faithful to the Duc d'Aiguillon.'

'Does it not show, Sire, what a disinterested person she is — to choose my poor nephew when she might be the friend of Your Majesty? Such affection as she gives would be well worth winning.'

'She reminds me of Madame de Vintimille,' mused Louis.

'Ah, there is the fire of that dear lady living on in her sister.'

Louis said: 'Is there no way of tempting her?'

'She is beyond temptation, Sire. The only way would be to show her the worthlessness of Aiguillon. Alas, he is such a worthy young man. How tiresome of him!'

Richelieu looked slyly at the King, wondering how long he was prepared to wait for Madame de la Tournelle.

✦ ✦ ✦

Richelieu decided to take matters into his own hands. D'Aiguillon might be a worthy young man, but he was human. If he were sufficiendy tempted he would surely succumb.

He decided on action, and sent for a very beautiful woman who had been his own mistress and who was eager to profit from the benefit his influence could bring to her and her family.

She came, and, when she asked what he wanted, he told her quite simply: 'I wish you to tempt my nephew to write you an indiscreet letter.'

'But how?' she asked.

'He is young; he is susceptible; and you are beautiful. If you write to him — not only once but many times — telling him that you have fallen madly in love with him, you are certain to receive some response.'

'And when I do?'

'I should like you to obtain a letter from him in which he agrees to visit you. It should be in no uncertain terms of course.'

'I see,' said the Duke's ex-mistress. 'I will do my best.'

'I know my dear, that you will succeed. The young man is not a complete boor. He cannot fail to find you . . . irresistible, as I have done in the past, and as so many will in the future.'

'And what reward shall be mine – apart from the amorous attentions of Monsieur le Duc d'Aiguillon?' asked the lady.

'You shall be presented at Court. Presented by the Duc de Richelieu. There, my pretty, is that not reward enough? For if you are clever you might find yourself a very exalted lover indeed. But first, of course, you must bring me what I need.'

Richelieu was not disappointed.

It was only some weeks after his interview with his ex-mistress when he was able to take a letter to the King.

'Sire,' he said, 'I plead a private audience.'

Louis complied with his wishes and, when they were alone, the Duc produced the letter.

'It is from d'Aiguillon to . . . to whom?'

'To his latest *inamorata*.'

'Madame de la Tournelle knows of this? . . .'

'Not yet. I thought Your Majesty would enjoy the pleasure of showing it to her.'

The King read the letter. It was written in no uncertain terms. The Duc d'Aiguillon was sorry that he had ignored the lady's previous letters, but she must not despair. He was going to see her and then, he believed, he could relieve her of her sadness and wipe away her tears.

'You arranged this?' Louis accused the Duc.

Richelieu smiled his lewd smile. 'Sire, I could no longer endure to see your wretchedness. It grieved me even more than the folly of the lady. Shall I have her brought to your presence?'

Louis considered this. 'Yes,' he said. 'Send her to me.'

Madame de la Tournelle came at the King's command, looking very lovely in a gown of lilac-coloured satin; and Louis exulted at the sight of her.

When she knelt before him he raised her. 'Madame de la Tournelle,' he said, 'I have long sought your friendship . . . your affection . . . and it has been denied me.'

'Sire,' she replied. 'I am a foolish woman who cannot govern her own feelings.'

'I admire you for it, Madame.'

'And I thank Your Majesty for the indulgence you have shown me.'

Louis inclined his head. 'I fear, Madame, that you have been betrayed by one whom you trusted most.'

'Sire?'

'Read this.'

As she read it the flush which grew in her cheeks made her more beautiful than ever, and her blue eyes flamed with anger.

'You see by whom the letter is written?'

'By the Duc d'Aiguillon.'

'And not to you, Madame; although you doubtless believed that he would not write such a letter to anyone but yourself.'

She crunched the paper in her hand.

'I have made a mistake, Sire.'

He would have put his arms about her, but she withdrew and he saw that she was trembling with misery or rage – he was not sure which.

'Sire,' she pleaded, 'have I your permission to retire?'

Louis smiled tenderly. 'I would always have you do as you wish,' he told her.

✤ ✤ ✤

Marie-Anne de la Tournelle paced up and down her room. Her anger against the Duc d'Aiguillon was great but her mind was not entirely on her lover. For a long time she had been tempted by the thought of becoming the King's mistress, and had often called herself a fool for refusing such a triumph. Now it seemed that her mind had been made up for her. Her *affaire* with the Duc d'Aiguillon was over. Love had betrayed her; she was now at liberty to devote herself to ambition.

She sat down at her *toilette* table and looked at her reflection in the mirror. She could be called one of the most beautiful women at Court; at the same time the face which looked back at her was not the face of a fool.

Thinking of the future she could cease to think of d'Aiguillon. She saw herself as a figure of great power. France was at war and there was much suffering in the country. What if she, through the King, ruled France? What if her name were handed down through the years to come as the woman who made France great?

She might make of the King a great soldier, leading his armies to victory. She would rid the country of the Cardinal who should have retired from Court life years ago. The Comte de Maurepas was another who should be dismissed. He was not suitable to hold a high post in the government of the country. He was nothing more than an elegant jester; he was far too frivolous for politics. His satires and epigrams were amusing enough, but one did not ask for that sort of cleverness in a minister. The state of the country was not a matter for joking.

The more she considered what her new role might be, the more delighted she was with it. It was so soothing to contemplate this, because doing so she could feel less humiliation at the deceitfulness of d'Aiguillon. She could even become secretly pleased that he had failed her, so that now she could take the path which she felt had been ordained for her. She could dedicate herself to ambition and to France.

One of her women came to tell her that the Duc de Richelieu was asking to be brought to her.

She said: 'Do not bring him to me. I will go to him.'

She went to the room in which he waited; he was at the window looking out on the gardens, and swung round as she entered, and bowed ironically, she imagined, yet triumphantly.

'Well, Madame,' he said. 'So my nephew is exposed in all his perfidy.'

'Let us not discuss him,' she said. 'He is of the past.'

'I have always known that sound good sense lay hidden beneath your feeling for that young man. Clear away the mists of passion, and there it lies . . . with its limitless horizons.'

'Have you come to offer your advice?' she asked.

'So you would take my advice? How clever of you – you who are young and beautiful – to take the advice of one who is not young and not beautiful.'

'Is that clever?' she asked. 'I want your advice about matters which I do not understand.'

He nodded. 'You have not made the conquest very easy for

His Majesty,' he mused. 'It has made the chase longer and more exciting and – happily, owing to the disaffection of my wicked nephew – not too fatiguing. It is well to remember that that is how the chase should be. It must be exciting and of sufficient duration. But never, never must the hunter become too tired to continue. You have two examples before you. Madame de Mailly was very foolish – there was no chase at all. Why hunt the tame hart? Madame de Vintimille ... Oh, she died so soon. Who knows ... His Majesty might have begun to tire of her tantrums ... given time.'

Madame de la Tournelle nodded in agreement. 'Neither of them was possessed of physical charm.'

'Yet even beauty can pall. There is one point I would stress: Insist on recognition. Do not let this *affaire* be a secret one. That would be beneath your dignity. Insist that you are proclaimed *maîtresse-en-titre*. Your status should not be that of a light-o'-love.'

'I had thought of that.'

Richelieu nodded. 'I can see, Madame, that when you asked my advice it was not that you needed it but because you would be kind to one who adores you and wishes you all success.'

'This also I have considered,' she said: 'If there should be children, they must be legitimised. As for my financial position ...'

'It would be undignified for you to be forced to consider money. Therefore it should be placed at your disposal as is the air you breathe.'

'I should need rank ...'

'A Duchesse ... no less.'

'There are certain people whom I should not wish to remain at Court.'

'The Cardinal is very old. It is unbecoming that a non-agenarian should be at the head of affairs.'

Marie-Anne de la Tournelle smiled sagely. 'I see, Monsieur le Duc,' she said, 'that your opinion coincides with my own.'

'Then,' said Richelieu, 'you and I, Madame, are friends. There is only one relationship which could bring me more delight.'

Her glance was a cold rebuke. Inwardly Richelieu grimaced. Already, he thought, she gives herself the airs of the first lady of the Court. One must tread warily with Madame de la Tournelle, but she will not forget the friend who has made her elevation possible.

✦ ✦ ✦

Marie-Anne de la Tournelle was the accepted favourite. The King was completely entranced. She had done for him that which he had failed to do for himself: banish the memory of her ugly sister, Madame de Vintimille.

Those who remembered the days of Louis Quatorze said that here was another Madame de Montespan. Richelieu was delighted with her schemes; he proffered perpetual advice to his cousin, who now called him uncle, because, as she said, he was of an age to be an uncle and she liked to think of him in that role.

They worked together, and two of their first objectives were to be the dismissal of Fleury and the reduction of the power of Maurepas. Both Fleury and Maurepas were however aware of her intentions and determined to fight for their places.

Madame de la Tournelle had made up her mind to control the King; and while she despised her sister, Madame de Mailly, she realised that Louis, although tired of his former mistress, retained some affection for her.

Louise-Julie was a fool, but her gentle disposition and her generous nature had endeared her to many, and Louis found it painful to be harsh with such a person. But Marie-Anne had decided then that Louise-Julie must go, for *she* was not going to share the King's attention with anyone.

She made her plans. She would force the King to take an interest in state affairs, and do her best to make of him a soldier. France was engaged in war; what more suitable than that the King should appear at the head of his armies?

But that could wait. In the meantime she had battles to fight at home.

The King had promised to fulfil all the conditions she had made before her surrender. The whole Court now accepted her as King's mistress. She was rich; she was flattered at every turn; courtiers and tradesmen attended her *toilette* as though she were royal or of the utmost importance – which she believed she was.

If she were not yet a Duchesse, it was because the tricky Maurepas was doing all he could to prevent the carrying out of the necessary formalities; but he should pay for that in due course.

Fleury was doing his best to persuade the King to give her up; and for that Fleury's days were numbered.

She was no impetuous fool though. She knew how to wait for what she wanted.

The King was scratching on her door and she received him with the utmost pleasure. He came unattended and, after love-making, she believed the time had come for her to make the first of her requests.

'Louis,' she said. 'I find it humiliating that my sister remains at Court.'

Louis was taken aback. 'But . . . she does no harm.'

'To me she does. How can I endure to look at one whom you once loved?'

'There is no need for jealousy. How could I possibly give her a thought now!'

'Then,' she said, 'I pray you grant me this. Send her away.'

Louis visualised an unpleasant scene and he was embarrassed; it would be one of those which he always endeavoured to avoid.

'You do not care whether she goes or stays,' said Marie-Anne. 'You let her stay because you lack the courage to tell her to go.'

Louis looked at her in surprise, but she was sufficiently sure of herself to continue: 'One of us must leave the Court. I find it too humiliating to know that I am referred to as one of the Nesle girls.'

'But you are not. You are to be the Duchesse de Châteauroux.'

'Yes, indeed, when Monsieur de Maurepas decides that I may. Louis, you are the King, but there are times when this seems difficult to believe. Maurepas, Fleury . . . it would seem that these are the real rulers of France.'

'They are good ministers. They do what they believe to be their duty.'

'Which is to warn you against me!'

'That is not all they do. In any case,' he added quickly, 'that is something at which they would never succeed.'

They shall go, she decided, but for the moment she would not press for their dismissal.

'You must decide,' she said. 'Either I or my sister leave the Court.'

Louis looked sadly at Louise-Julie de Mailly. He could not help remembering how happy they had been during the first years of their association. She loved him still, he knew; and she loved him so sincerely that had he lost his crown and become a penniless nobody her love would not change. He was wise enough to know too that it was an affection which a King could rarely claim. Surrounded by flatterers, sycophants – place-seekers – he should have cherished this woman and kept her beside him always.

But the dominating Madame de la Tournelle, her irresistible sister, had stated her terms and they must be fulfilled.

'I . . . I do not require your presence at Versailles,' Louis told Louise-Julie.

She looked at him with such stricken eyes that he was ashamed.

He laid his hand on her shoulder, and went on: 'I am sorry, my dear, but these things must be.'

She knew who had done this, but she did not rage against her brilliant sister, she did not marvel that a member of her own family could rob her of all the joy that was left in her life. Louis remembered how, on the death of Madame de Vintimille, it was this woman who had forgotten her humiliation and had come to comfort him; he remembered how she had taken Madame de Vintimille's child and cared for him. It was a cruel thing he was doing, and he was ashamed; but he must do it, because Marie-Anne was resolved that one of them must go – and he could not allow her to be that one.

He looked helplessly at Louise-Julie, wanting her to understand that he had been forced to this measure.

She saw his embarrassment and she knew full well that he hated scenes of this sort. It was typical of her that she humbly bowed her head that he might not be further distressed by the anguish in her face.

'I will leave at once, Sire,' she said.

'Thank you,' said Louis, and his gratitude was obvious.

She turned and went away into a blank future; for she did not know how she was going to live. Dismissal from Court meant that she was no longer a *dame du palais* and she saw not only obscurity but poverty awaiting her.

But this was the decree of Madame de la Tournelle, and she no less than Louis must accept it.

Marie-Anne was triumphant. One by one her schemes were reaching fruition.

At last she was the Duchesse de Châteauroux, a title which carried with it a yearly income of 85,000 livres.

Her next task was to goad the King into action. She believed that if Louis became a King in very truth and placed himself at the head of affairs, those ministers of his, on whose downfall she had determined, would be denuded of their importance.

She would give herself to lovemaking with the required ardour, but afterwards, when the King lay sated beside her, she would lure him into a discussion of his ministers.

'My dear,' said the King, 'you concern yourself overmuch with matters of state. Why do we not give ourselves entirely to pleasure? There are others quite capable of managing state affairs.'

'I do not see, my dearest,' answered the Duchesse de Châteauroux, 'why we should not have both the pleasure of being together like this and the satisfaction of governing the kingdom.'

'You will kill me!' said Louis lightly.

She clenched her fist suddenly and said vehemently: 'So much the better. I would kill the King you have been and resuscitate you. You would be reborn a real King.'

'You are in earnest?' he asked.

'In earnest, yes.' She leaned on her elbow watching him, her beautiful hair falling about her face, her large blue eyes gleaming with enthusiasm. 'Louis, you are young as yet; you are handsome. The people love you; but if you do not give yourself to the governing of the people, they will not continue to do so.'

'They are not pleased now,' he reminded her, 'because you usurp the place of the Queen.'

'The Queen! She is unworthy of you, Louis.'

'Only you are worthy to share the throne, but the people do not see it thus.' He took her hand and would have kissed it, drawing her down beside him, putting an end to this conversation, but she would not allow him to do this.

'I would see you as France's greatest King,' she said. 'I would have you lead your armies to victory. I can picture you, returning to Paris . . . victorious. How they would love you then!'

'They would still not love you.'

'Why should they not? They would know I had had a hand in bringing about the change.'

'That you had killed me,' he murmured languidly, 'that you had resuscitated me . . . and that I was reborn.'

This time she did not resist. She remembered the warning of Uncle Richelieu: The chase must not be too fatiguing.

But she was going to have her way as she had before.

✤ ✤ ✤

This interlude took place in the delightful château at Choisy, and it was a few days later when a messenger arrived from Issy.

The King received him at once, for he knew that Fleury was resting there.

'The Cardinal is very ill, Sire,' Louis was told. 'He is asking for you.'

'Take this message to him,' said the King. 'I am leaving at once. Perhaps I shall be at Issy before you.'

Marie-Anne came to him.

'Is it dignified for a King to hurry to a subject because he is requested to do so?'

Louis said: 'This is my friend, the tutor of my boyhood. Moreover he is an old man and sick. Nothing . . . nothing would keep me from his bedside at such a time.'

She was quick to see her mistake. She should not imagine that Louis was completely malleable because he gave way so often to avoid a scene.

'I did not understand he was so sick,' she said.

Louis left and arrived at Issy almost immediately after the messenger had told the Cardinal that he was on his way.

As Louis embraced his old mentor, tears streamed from his eyes.

'Do not weep for my going, dearest Majesty,' said the Cardinal. 'I have had a long life, and I am happy that much of it has been spent in your service.'

'I shall miss you so sadly.'

'There will be others . . .' The Cardinal frowned; but this was not the time to warn the King against Madame de

Châteauroux. The Cardinal knew his King; if the Duchesse disappeared from Court there would be others to take her place. 'I go,' said the Cardinal, 'leaving France a sick country. She is now plunged in war, and I never liked war. Wars bring no prosperity. There are religious conflicts . . . parliamentary troubles . . .'

'Let them not concern you, my dear friend,' said Louis. 'You have done your best. It is for others to deal with our troubles.'

'It has been a good life,' said the Cardinal.

Louis took his hand and kissed it. 'You have brought much good to me.'

'I would say farewell to the Dauphin,' said the Cardinal.

'It would upset him,' protested Louis. 'He is but a child.'

'He will have to grow accustomed to saying goodbye for ever to old friends, Sire.'

'It shall be as you wish. I shall give orders to his governor to bring him here.'

Louis said nothing more but continued to sit by the bed.

'Of what do you think, Sire?'

'Of the early days. Of our first meeting. Of your attempts to teach me.'

'I loved you dearly,' said the Cardinal.

'I loved you too,' answered the King.

'When all my enemies were about me . . . you stood there to defend me,' said the old man. 'My blessing on you, Sire. Long life to you! Prosperity to France!'

There was silence while the tears were on the cheeks of both.

Fleury was dead. The news spread through Paris. The frosty January air seemed more invigorating, and speculation sparkled through the capital.

The Cardinal had been in power so long that the people were glad to see him go.

France was suffering from war and its twin sister, taxation. The old rule was passing; the new one could not be worse.

The King was now in his prime. He was thirty-three years of age and, said the people, he had never yet been allowed to rule. The Cardinal had kept the reins in his hands and now the Cardinal was dead.

There was a new cry in the streets of Paris and about the Château of Versailles. The Duchesse de Châteauroux heard it and exulted. Fate had performed one of her tasks for her.

'*Le Cardinal est mort*,' cried the people. '*Vive le Roi!*'

✤ ✤ ✤

Everyone was amazed at the energy displayed by the King. No sooner was the Cardinal dead than he assumed the government of affairs and placed himself in no uncertain manner at the head of state. He was so charming that he won not only the respect but the affection of all. The people ceased to grumble; they told themselves that, now they had a King to rule them instead of a Cardinal, France's troubles would soon be over.

Louis took time off from state affairs to indulge his passion for hunting, and it was his custom to do so some little distance from the capital, near the forest of Sénart.

One day he noticed a young woman following the hunt. She was elegant and very pretty indeed, and Louis made up his mind that he would discover who she was. He guessed that she was either a member of the nobility – otherwise she could not have joined the hunt – or perhaps she owned land in or near the forest, for those who lived near the King's hunting ground were granted permission to follow the royal hunt when it was in their neighbourhood.

By the end of the day, however, he had forgotten the young woman, but when he next hunted, there she was again. She was exquisitely gowned and this time not riding but driving in a carriage, a very elegant carriage.

The King turned to the equerry who was his master of hounds and said: 'Who is that beautiful creature?'

'Why, Sire,' was the answer, 'it is a lady who bears the name of Madame d'Etioles. Her home is the Château d'Etioles, although I hear she is something of a hostess in Paris also.'

'You know a great deal about the lady, Landsmath.'

'Well, Sire, she is something of a charmer. I reckon there's not many prettier in the whole of France; that's what I'd say.'

'I think I agree with you,' said Louis. 'She must be fond of the hunt. I have seen her on more than one occasion.'

'She is eager to have a glimpse of yourself, Sire. That's what I would say.'

'A crown is like a magnet, Landsmath.'

'That's so, Sire. Particularly when it is on a handsome head.'

'I wonder if she will follow the hunt tomorrow.'

Richelieu brought his horse close to the King's. 'Sire,' he said, 'if you would be in at the kill there is no time to be lost.'

During the hunt the King forgot the pretty Madame d'Etioles; but Richelieu, who had overheard Louis' inquiries, did not, and, as soon as he could he rode his horse close to that of the Duchesse de Châteauroux.

She looked over her shoulder and he signed to her to fall a little behind the King.

'Well?' she asked of him.

'Just a word of warning,' he said. 'The king is being shadowed by a very pretty woman.'

Madame de Châteauroux frowned. 'Do you think I am not capable of holding the King's attention?'

'It might prove a task of some enormity when your opponent is so charming.'

'Who is she?'

'Madame d'Etioles of the Château d'Etioles. She appears at the hunt each day . . . very attractively attired. She does not look the King's way but, depend upon it, the parade is all for him.'

'What do you know of her?'

'Little, except that she is very pretty, that she is elegant and wears clothes which in themselves would attract attention to her person. Beware, Madame. This lady might be a formidable enemy.'

'Nonsense,' snapped the Duchesse. 'I am in complete command of His Majesty's affections. You may think no more of this matter.'

Richelieu shrugged his shoulders. 'I but warn you,' he murmured, and rode away.

⚜ ⚜ ⚜

In her apartments at Versailles Marie Leczinska passed the dreary days. Louis was completely lost to her now and she knew she could not regain his affection.

She must live her lonely life, which was devoted to good works, eating, and the indulgence of that vanity which made her secretly believe that she was a good musician and a fine painter.

She had visualised it all so differently, dreaming of a happy and united family. Perhaps such dreams had been the result of inexperience. Could kings ever lead a domestically happy life?

Nevertheless she had much with which to be thankful. She had her children. There was the Dauphin whom she visited frequently and who had grown out of his wilfulness and appeared to take after her. He had become serious and studious. She was sure he would one day make a good king.

She wished she could have all her children about her, but the little ones were still at Fontevrault. Adelaide was her father's girl; and how pretty she was! And lively too. Poor Anne-Henriette! She was listless these days. There were times when Marie feared she might be going into a decline. Had she loved the Duc de Chartres so much? It seemed a pity that they could not have married. Then Marie could have been sure of keeping her daughter in France and Anne-Henriette would not have lost her gaiety. But she will grow out of it, thought the Queen. She is young yet and romantically minded. Alas, it is dangerous for the daughters of Kings to dream of romance.

The marriage of Louise-Elisabeth had not been very successful. Don Philip lacked energy, and it was all his ambitious mother could do – aided by his wife, who was proving equally ambitious – to arouse some vitality in him.

It was the hour when Marie's daughters came to visit her. When they did so she wished that she could unbend with them as Louis could so successfully; she wished she could assure them that, in spite of her prim and solemn manner, she loved them dearly.

They looked charming, she thought – her sad seventeen-year-old Anne-Henriette in her gown of pale mauve, and Adelaide in rose-coloured satin.

They curtsied and Adelaide asked to see her latest painting.

Marie Leczinska was delighted, for it did not occur to her that Adelaide had no wish to see the painting, and that as they prepared for their interview with her, her daughters planned together what they would say.

'I shall ask to see the pictures,' Adelaide had said.

'That leaves the music for me,' added Anne-Henriette. 'But I shall ask about the music almost at the end, otherwise we shall have to listen to her playing on the harpsichord for a whole hour.'

'Is it worse than merely talking?' Adelaide had asked and Anne-Henriette had replied that she was not sure. 'But perhaps it is not so difficult to listen to her playing. One can sit still and think of other things.'

'You are not still thinking of Monsieur de Chartres!' Adelaide had said, and Anne-Henriette had half-closed her eyes as though she had received a blow. Adelaide had then taken her sister's arm and pressed it, adding: 'I am sorry, I should not have reminded you.'

Reminded me! Anne-Henriette had thought. As if I shall ever forget!

'Don't say any more, please,' she had murmured.

Now they were in their mother's presence, and Adelaide was saying: 'Please *Maman*, may we see your latest picture?'

So the Queen showed her painting of a part of the gardens of Versailles, and the girls said falsely that it was more beautiful than the original. And afterwards Anne-Henriette asked for music and they sat pretending to listen to their mother's stumbling attempts at the harpsichord. Adelaide was dreaming that her father had decided to go to the war and take her with him. She saw herself riding beside him in scarlet and gold, carrying the royal standard, everyone cheering as she passed. She saw herself performing deeds of great valour and winning the war. There she was, riding in triumph through the streets of Paris at her father's side, while men and women threw garlands of flowers at her and cried out that this beautiful Princess was the saviour of France.

Anne-Henriette was thinking of all the hopes which had once been hers and now were dead. Why had they been led to believe that they might marry? It was all a matter of policy. One set of ministers pulling one way, another in the opposite direction: and on the dictates of these men depended the happiness of two people.

She had heard that it was Cardinal Fleury who had disapproved of the match because of his enmity against the House of Orléans. The Cardinal had no doubt believed that the marriage of the Duc de Chartres to a Princesse of the reigning King would have given him and his family greater ambitions than they already had. As if he was not of royal blood already! As if he thought of anything but Anne-Henriette!

She remembered the day her suitor had returned from the hunt. Until that time they had been full of hope. He had said to her: 'While he is hunting, your father is always well pleased with life. If there is an opportunity I will ask him then.' She did not see the squat and ungainly figure of her mother, with that self-satisfied smile on her face as she plucked at the strings; she saw the Duc de Chartres, returned from the hunt with that look of utter despair on his face. 'You asked him?' she had demanded. And he had answered: 'Yes. He did not speak; he merely looked at me with a great sadness in his eyes, pressed my hand and shook his head. How can they do this to us! How can he . . . he . . . who has a wife, family and *friends*! . . .' But, even in that moment of anguish, Anne-Henriette would not hear a word against her father. '*He* would not forbid us. It is in the hands of others. It is the will of the Cardinal.'

Oh, how they had hated the Cardinal; and now he was beyond hatred; but marriage was beyond *them*, for the Duc de Chartres had been married to the daughter of the Princesse de Conti, and Anne-Henriette was left with her sorrow.

While they were together thus, news was brought to the Queen from the Abbey of Fontevrault. The two girls watched their mother as she read the letter which had been handed to her. Then Adelaide went to the Queen and said: '*Maman*, is it bad news from Fontevrault?'

The Queen nodded. 'Your little sister, Thérèse-Félicité is dangerously ill.'

Adelaide and Anne-Henriette tried to remember all they knew of Thérèse-Félicité, but it was six years since they had seen her, and she had only been two years old when she had left Versailles. It was impossible to feel real grief for a sister whom they could not remember.

Marie remembered. She sat still, remembering. They had been taken from her, her little girls, six years ago, because Cardinal Fleury wished to limit expenditure.

Her eldest had been taken from her too, for Louise-Elisabeth, far away in Spain, seemed lost to her; death had taken the little Duc d'Anjou and Madame Troisième, and now it seemed she was to lose yet another. She remembered that Thérèse-Félicité, Madame Sixième, was the child who had borne the strongest resemblance to her grandfather, Stanislas.

She did not cry. To shed tears would be undignified in front of her daughters. So she sat erect, her mouth prim, and none would have guessed at the despair in her heart.

✤ ✤ ✤

News of the sickness of Thérèse-Félicité depressed the King. He wished that he had known this child as he knew Anne-Henriette and Adelaide. The others would be growing up. Soon they must return but, perhaps with France at war and himself thinking of going to join his Army, it would be well if they stayed a little longer at Fontevrault, and in any case Thérèse-Félicité must not be moved now.

Madame de Châteauroux seeking to cheer him decided that she would give an entertainment at Choisy for him. Louis was delighted, and he and a few of his intimate friends arrived at the Château.

Richelieu who as First Gentleman of the bedchamber accompanied the King everywhere, was a member of the party. He was uneasy. He had thought a great deal about the pretty young woman who had appeared at the hunt in the forest of Sénart. Madame de Châteauroux was his protégée and he intended to make sure she kept her place.

He had made inquiries about Madame d'Etioles and these had resulted in an astonishing discovery. She was the daughter of a certain François Poisson, a man who had made a fortune but had been obliged to leave Paris during a season of famine as he had been suspected of hoarding grain. His son and daughter had been well educated, and the girl, Jeanne-Antoinette, had eventually been married to a man of some wealth. This was Monsieur Charles-Guillaume Lenormant d'Etioles. In Paris they entertained lavishly and the young woman, who was clearly ambitious, had gathered together a small salon of literary people. It was said that Voltaire had become a member of the circle and was a great admirer of Madame d'Etioles.

All this was interesting enough, but there was one other matter which greatly worried the Duc, and of which he felt he should lose no time in acquainting the Duchesse de Châteauroux.

Thus he made a point of speaking privately to her. 'What is this matter of such urgent moment?' she asked him haughtily.

Already, he thought, she is forgetting who helped her to her position.

'You will do well to note it, Madame,' he told her grimly.

She was quick to see that she had offended, and at once pacified him. 'My dear Uncle, I am harassed. The King must be lifted from this melancholy he feels because that child is sick. I want you to be your wittiest tonight.'

'All in good time,' said Richelieu; 'but I do want you to understand the importance of the *affaire d'Etioles*.'

'D'Etioles! That woman from the country?'

'She is also of Paris. Such elegance could surely only be of Paris.'

'She seems to have caught your fancy.'

'Let us hope that it is mine alone. I have heard an astonishing thing about that woman. A fortune-teller told her when she was nine years old that she would be the King's mistress and the most powerful woman in France. Her family have believed this, no less than she does herself. She has been educated for this purpose.'

The Duchesse laughed loudly. 'Fortune-tellers!' she cried. 'Oh, come, *mon oncle,* do you believe the tales of dirty gipsies?'

'No. But Madame d'Etioles does. That is the point at issue.'

'Believing she will take my place can help her little.'

Richelieu caught her arm. 'But she is convinced and so does everything possible to make her dream a reality. Such determination could bring results. She is beautiful. Already she has brought herself to the King's notice. Have a care!'

'Dear Uncle,' said the Duchesse, taking his arm and pressing it against her body, 'you are my guide and counsellor. I shall never forget it. But the King adores me . . . even as he did my sister, Vintimille. Do you not see that we Nesle girls have something which he needs?'

'He tired of one Nesle girl.'

'Louise-Julie! Poor Madame de Mailly!'

'Poor indeed,' sighed Richelieu. 'I heard only yesterday that she is so poor that she is quite shabby, that her clothes are in holes and she does not know how to find the money to feed her servants.'

'What a fool she was!' cried the Duchesse. 'She could have become rich while she enjoyed Louis' favour. But this is to be a happy occasion. Do not let us even think of anything depressing.'

'All I ask you is: Remember that she was a Nesle girl, and the King replaced her.'

'By her sisters! I have two, I know, who have not yet aspired to the King's favour; but Diane-Adelaide is so ugly, and she has, as you know, recently married the Duc de Lauraguais. As for the other, her husband is so jealous that he has already declared that if Louis cast his eyes upon her he would not hesitate to shed the royal blood. Louis may have looked her way, but you know how he hates scenes of any sort. No, Louis will remain faithful to me because my two sisters are protected from him – one by a jealous man, the other by her ugliness.'

'He could look outside the Nesle family. He could look at this young woman.'

'But, my uncle, he shall not look.'

Nevertheless, when he left her, she was uneasy. She could remember the woman now, dressed in light blue with a great ostrich feather in her hat. Dressed to attract attention, riding in a carriage which would also attract attention – always putting herself in the path of the King.

The King had decided to hunt in the forest at Sénart, and the Duchesse de Châteauroux, who did not seriously believe in Richelieu's warnings, had forgotten the woman who lived close to the forest and who had caught the King's passing interest.

The party set out and, while the hunt was on, the rain started. No one minded a little rain, but this was a cloudburst, and someone – there may have been an ulterior motive in this – suggested that the party take cover, adding that not far off was a château where they could be sure of being hospitably received.

The King agreed that this was a good idea, and the Duchesse was of the same opinion, so to the château the party made their way.

The Duchesse's rage was so great that she could hardly control it when she saw that the châtelaine was the pretty young woman who had followed the hunt in her elegant garments and her attractive carriages.

'Sire,' cried this creature, curtseying in a manner which would not have shamed Versailles, 'I am overwhelmed by this great honour.'

The King's eyes glistened, for she was indeed charming.

'It is good of you to say so,' he replied. 'I fear we inconvenience you by calling upon you thus unexpectedly.'

'Your Majesty would be welcome at any time. My only regret is that we have not had the opportunity to prepare for this great honour.'

The Duchesse was regarding Madame d'Etioles coldly. 'We were not warned that there was to be such a rain-storm,' she said, implying that only such a storm could account for their presence in the home of one who was clearly not of the nobility.

The King seemed to think this ungracious, and he murmured: 'I am beginning to rejoice that the rain came when it did.'

Madame d'Etioles, retaining her dignity, ordered her servants to bring refreshment for the hunters; and while they took it she managed to remain at the side of the King; but the Duchesse on his other side would not allow the forward young woman to say very much, and continually contrived to turn the King's attention away from the hostess to herself.

As soon as the rain stopped, she declared, they must go on their way, so the King not wishing to offend her agreed.

'This,' said Madame d'Etioles, raising her glowing eyes to the King, with a look which held a certain dedicated expression, 'is the most important day in my life. I shall never forget that the King called at my humble château.'

Louis murmured gallantly: 'I, too, shall remember.'

Madame de Châteauroux was drawing him away and out to their horses. She was determined that such a contretemps should never be repeated.

That evening the King was in a mellow mood and ready to be entertained. He was extremely gracious to the Duchesse, as though to make up for his mild interest in the pretty young woman of the afternoon's adventure.

Card-playing began and, during a lull between games, one of the party, Madame de Chevreuse, said artlessly: 'What a pretty creature that woman was! I mean the one who gave us shelter this afternoon.'

There was silence about the table but the King smiled reminiscently.

'Madame d'Etioles,' went on Madame de Chevreuse, 'was so exquisitely gowned that one would have thought she was a lady of the Court.'

The Duchesse suddenly realised that the King was more than a little interested in this woman who was placing herself in his path at every opportunity. She felt very angry with Madame d'Etioles who, not content with intruding on the hunt and luring the King into her château, had succeeded in forcing her way into this party.

She brushed past Madame de Chevreuse and, having heard that lady complain bitterly of a diabolical corn on her right foot, the Duchesse brought her own foot down heavily on the spot where she knew that corn to be. With all her weight she pressed upon Madame de Chevreuse's foot.

There was an agonised scream, and Madame de Chevreuse lay fainting in her chair.

'I must have trodden on her foot,' said the Duchesse. 'We will call her attendants and have her taken to her bed. She will recover there.'

Madame de Chevreuse was taken to her room, but everyone present had seen the light of battle in the eyes of the Duchesse.

The name of Madame d'Etioles was not to be mentioned in the King's presence again.

Shortly afterwards notice was conveyed to the lady that she must not appear in the forest when the King was hunting. If she did so she would incur the extreme displeasure of the Duchesse de Châteauroux, and steps would be taken to make that displeasure felt.

Chapter VIII

THE KING AT METZ

*L*ouis had decided to join his armies and take an active part in the war of the Austrian Succession.

On the death of Fleury he had chosen the Maréchal Duc de Noailles as his mentor for, determined though he was to rule himself, Louis could not easily cast off the influence of his upbringing. Since he had become King of France at the age of five, he had been surrounded by men older than himself on whose wisdom he had been taught to rely. So he had to find a substitute for the Cardinal.

De Noailles, who had had the confidence of Louis Quatorze, advised Louis on policies similar to those which had been carried out under his predecessor; Noailles reminded the King that his great-grandfather and Henri Quatre had never allowed themselves to be ruled by favourites to the disadvantage of the state. Louis decided to follow this rule.

His subjects were delighted to see the King in the lead, and they marvelled that one possessed of such intelligence should have allowed himself to be governed by the Cardinal for so long. They did not at that time understand the inherent indolence of Louis' nature, and that fatalism which was beginning to grow within him. At this time, when he was learning to understand the glory and stimulation of being a King in more than name, Louis was unaware of these qualities which unless kept in check could destroy him or France – perhaps both.

The English had entered the war on the side of France's enemy, and Noailles was alarmed at the fight put up by the infantry of George II.

France at this time had a considerable number of men in the field and was engaged in activities on three fronts – in Alsace, on the Rhine and in West Flanders. Noailles was in charge of the Flanders army, and it was to this front that the King decided to go.

This decision was widely discussed at Versailles and the Queen longed to accompany her husband. It was not, she believed, an unnatural request. Queens had followed their husbands into battle before, and there was useful work which she and her ladies could do.

She longed to ask Louis to take her, but since his friendship with Madame de Châteauroux the relationship between them had deteriorated rapidly. They had come as close to quarrelling as was possible to such a man as Louis. She had objected fiercely to the position which the Duchesse occupied as *maîtresse-en-titre* and which seemed to put her above the Queen. Louis had retorted that she must accept Madame de Châteauroux.

Marie had been unable to control her temper; she was more fiercely jealous than anyone would have believed possible. As for the King, he could not forgive her for having so continuously refused his uxorious attentions. He pointed out that she had no right to prevent others accepting what she had declined.

Thus they were not on speaking terms, except of course in public.

But now that he was going to the war she was afraid for his safety and, made anxious as she was by the bad news of little Thérèse-Félicité from Fontevrault, she was determined to do all in her power to accompany him. So she suppressed her pride and wrote a note to him asking him to allow her to go with him in any capacity which he thought fit. She begged him not to ignore her note.

Louis did not ignore it, but he replied that her place was at Court, and she could serve no useful purpose by following him to war. Moreover the Exchequer could not stand the expense of her journey.

❦ ❦ ❦

It was during the month of May that the King left Versailles. His going was one of those Court 'secrets' of which everyone was aware.

After supper on the 3rd, his *coucher* took place at half past one with all the usual formality. It was arranged that as soon as those who attended had been dismissed, the King should rise again and prepare himself for his journey.

It was all over; the night gown had been put on, his nightcap had replaced his wig, the handkerchief handed to him from its velvet cushion, and the curtains had been drawn about the bed.

For a few minutes the King lay still, waiting; then the curtains about his bed were quietly drawn back again and he got out of bed.

He was excited. He was asking himself why he had not before this taken an active part in affairs. This was living the life of a King.

Those few, headed by Richelieu, who were helping him dress, handed him his garments, even at such a time not forgetting that they should be passed through various hands until they reached the King.

There was silence as the King was dressed, and so, when there was a scratching at the door, everyone heard it.

All looked at the King, who hesitated for a second and then nodded slowly.

'See who is there.'

The door was opened and a small figure in slippers and dressing gown came into the bedchamber. It was the Dauphin.

He ran to his father and threw himself into his arms.

'But my son,' cried the King, 'what is the meaning of this?'

'I want to go with you. I want to be a soldier,' said the boy.

'How did you know I was leaving for the front?' the King demanded.

'I make it my duty to know,' said the boy with dignity.

The King embraced him. 'Oh, my dear son,' he said, 'what pleasure it would give me to take you with me!'

'I am fifteen,' said Dauphin Louis. 'That is old enough, Father.'

'Not quite,' said the King. 'Moreover you are the Dauphin, and my only son. You must consider how important it is that one of us must stay behind.'

'My mother can look after affairs.'

The King smiled. 'No, my son. Your desire to go to war does you credit, but, much as it would please me to have you with me, we must both remember our duty to France. You must not be put into danger – not at least until you have a wife and son of your own. Then, you see, you would have given an heir to France.'

The boy nodded gravely. 'Father,' he said, 'I must marry soon and have an heir. Then I shall be ready to make war on France's enemies.'

'Well spoken,' said the King. 'And now . . . go back to your bed . . . go quickly that none may see you, because, my boy, in coming to me thus you have behaved without that decorum which should always be observed by the Dauphin of France.'

The boy looked at his father solemnly and then, suddenly realising that he was going away and into danger, he threw his arms about him and was so reluctant to let him go that it was the King who had to withdraw himself.

The Dauphin then fell on his knees, kissed his father's hand and, rising without a word, sped from the room lest those watching should see that he was crying.

Louis smiled sadly, then he said briskly: 'Come, there is much to do if we are to leave by three o'clock.'

He then asked to be alone that he might write some letters. He wrote to the Queen, to the two Princesses and to Madame de Ventadour. Then he spent some time with his confessor before, in the freshness of that early May morning, he left Versailles for the front.

✤ ✤ ✤

As soon as Louis arrived at Lille his presence made a deep impression.

There was nothing so inspiring to the soldiers as the sight of their King at their head, joining in the fight with them, leading them into battle – which, they declared, was what a King should do.

Many of the men from the provincial towns and villages and from the poor of Paris had never seen him before; and when he appeared among them he seemed god-like to them, for not only was he an extraordinarily handsome man, but there was in his face a gentleness, a kindliness which, since he was proving himself to be brave, made a deep impression on those men.

Because he avoided all unpleasantness, his manner was affable in the extreme; yet because he had been well drilled in perfect manners he never for one moment lost his dignity.

Thus, as soon as he appeared, he brought with him a new spirit to the army.

Enthusiastically Louis gave himself to his task and planned the campaign with Noailles. As a result Menin fell to France, and this was quickly followed by the capture of Ypres.

At home in Paris there was wild rejoicing. The people had been right; their King only needed to be free of his Ministers and he would lead his people to victory and prosperity.

'Long live Louis!' cried the people of Paris.

❖ ❖ ❖

The Duchesse of Châteauroux who had been living in the country at Plaisance with her sister – the ugly one who had become the Duchesse de Lauraguais – heard of the King's victories.

'Why,' she said, 'Lille must be as safe as Paris now. And how weary Louis must be with only the company of soldiers!'

Her sister looked at her in astonishment. 'You are suggesting that you join him at the front?'

'Why not? I am sure he will be pleased to see me.'

'He has refused to allow the *Queen* to go with the army.'

'The Queen! Of course he has refused the Queen.'

'So . . . you have decided to go?'

'Yes, and to take you with me. You should begin to prepare

'at once.' The Duchesse's eyes began to gleam as they did when she was eager to put some project into motion. 'I see no reason why we should not set out without delay.'

'Marie-Anne,' said her sister, 'has it occurred to you that although the King is very popular wih his soldiers, *you* might not be?'

'Soldiers! Who cares for the soldiers!'

'Louis might.'

'My foolish girl, he cares far, far more for me than all the soldiers in his army.'

'You are very sure of yourself, sister.'

'I know Louis. You do not. We shall make ourselves useful, of course. We will become . . . *vivandières,* shall we say?'

Madame de Lauraguais looked scornful, but she knew from experience that it was no use trying to stop her sister from carrying out a plan she had set her heart on.

The Duchesse de Châteauroux began working with all her well-known energy. The first thing that was needed was the consent of the King. That was not difficult to get. Then they must call on the Queen to ask her permission. Not that Marie-Anne would take much notice of that; but Louis would prefer everything to be done with as little controversy as possible.

Strangely enough the Queen put nothing in the way of the expedition. She shrugged her shoulders. 'Let the women go if they wish it,' she said. But when she returned to her needle-work and her painting there was a great bitterness in her heart that she should have been refused and they allowed to go.

The Duchesse and her sister with a few other ladies set out for Lille without delay. It was something of a shock to find that her beauty made no impression on the army – unless it was a bad one.

All the glittering jewels, the elegant gowns, only aroused irritation in the soldiery. Aren't there women enough in Flanders? they asked each other; if the King wants one of that sort, he wouldn't have much difficulty in finding her.

Ribald songs were sung about her. She ignored them.

'What do I care!' she said to Louis. 'My joy in seeing your success in war overwhelms everything else. Louis, it is what I always wanted for you: To see you free of doddering old men, King in your own right, bringing back glory to France. I am the happiest woman in the world.'

Louis arrived at Metz at the beginning of August. Here he was preparing more campaigns.

Frederick of Prussia had been watching the King's triumphs in the Netherlands with great interest, and he felt that while the forces of Maria Theresa were occupied in other regions, here was an excellent opportunity for him to attack the Empress on the Bohemian front. He felt the time was ripe for an alliance with Louis and negotiations were afoot.

When Madame de Châteauroux and her sister arrived in Metz shortly after the King, the people jeered at them as they rode through the streets; but neither Louis nor his mistress greatly cared for the people, and because they could not be housed together, the King caused a closed-in gallery to be made from the apartments which he occupied to those in the Abbey of Saint-Arnould where the sisters were lodged.

It was announced that the closed-in gallery was to be used by the King when he went from his apartments to Mass; but the people knew very well for what purpose it had been built, and their anger against the favourite was increased. They continued however to make excuses for Louis. He was their beloved King, but he was young, and he was so kind that it was easy for a scheming woman to rule him.

It was while the King was at Metz that the envoy of Frederick of Prussia arrived, and a banquet was given in his honour. The Duchesse, who fully approved of the suggested alliance with Prussia, and whose importance Frederick realised (he had written flattering letters to her), sat on the King's right hand and there was a great deal of revelry.

It may have been that the King ate and drank too freely, or that all the excitement and fatigue of the last months were beginning to make themselves felt, but on the morning following that of the banquet, those who came to rouse him found that his temperature was high, his skin clammy and that he was delirious.

Alarm spread throughout the French camp. The King, it was said, was dying.

The Duchesse de Châteauroux came quickly to his bedside and, taking her sister with her, installed herself in the sickroom. She it was who decided who should be allowed to see the King. She was determined to keep him alive, realising that if he died he would take all her hopes with him to the grave.

Reluctantly she allowed the Princes of the Royal Blood, the young Duc de Chartres and the Comte de Clermont, to see the King. They insisted on the presence of the Bishop of Soissons, the King's chaplain, who declared that, in view of the King's condition, his confessor, Père Pérusseau, should be sent for.

The Duchesse protested. 'The King will think that he is dying, if you bring his confessor here.'

'Madame,' answered the Bishop of Soissons, 'the King *is* dying.'

'No!' cried the Duchesse; but it was a protest rather than a statement in which she believed. She covered her face with her hands, for she saw the empire which she had built up crumbling before her eyes.

✦ ✦ ✦

Père Pérusseau arrived at the King's bedside. He was a man in a quandary. When he looked at the King he was shocked to see how ill he was, yet he remembered that Louis was subject to fevers and had on other occasions been close to death.

If he were to absolve the King it would be necessary to send Madame de Châteauroux from Metz, since he could not promise redemption if Louis continued to keep his mistress at his side. It was all very well to send her away if the King should die, as the Dauphin would not hold it against him if he did so; and there was scarcely a man at Court who would not be pleased to know she had been humiliated.

On the other hand, the King might not die – and what of his position then if he irritated her by sending her away? She was a woman who would not readily forgive her enemies.

Meanwhile the Duchesse was in anxious conversation with her adviser, Uncle Richelieu who, as first gentleman of the bedchamber, was naturally present.

'What is going to happen?' she demanded of the Duc.

'That none can say,' was the answer. 'If he is really dying, you will have to leave. The question is, how can you do so in secret? You will not have very gentle treatment from the crowd if the King can no longer use his authority to protect you.'

She was afraid, and Richelieu, who had often been irritated by her arrogance, could not help feeling a slight triumph even though he had allied his cause with hers.

They were talking in a small ante-room which led to the King's bedchamber. 'Call the priest in here,' she commanded.

Richelieu did so.

The harassed Père Pérusseau looked as though he would rather face Medusa than the Duchesse de Châteauroux.

'Is the King to be confessed?' she demanded.

'I cannot answer you, Madame. That depends on the King's wishes.'

'If he is, will it be necessary for me to leave?'

'I find it difficult to answer that, Madame.'

'You must know!' she retorted. 'I do not wish to be sent off openly. If I have to go, I will travel secretly.'

'It . . . it may be that the King will not wish to be confessed.' murmured the priest.

'I feel sure His Majesty *will* wish to be confessed,' put in Richelieu gloomily.

'We must avoid scandal,' asserted the Duchesse. 'I admit I have sinned with the King. But . . . should there not be special dispensations for Kings?'

Père Pérusseau was so embarrassed that he did not know what to say, and Richelieu took him by the arm. 'I have always been a good friend to you Jesuits,' he said coaxingly. 'You need good friends at Court, as you well know. I am asking you now to make up your mind whether the Duchesse should remain here or slip quietly away. If she is going, she must go without fuss.'

'I cannot help you,' cried the priest almost in tears, 'because I do not know what will be decided.'

The Duchesse exchanged a weary glance with Richelieu. It was useless to badger the man further. They could only wait and hope.

✤ ✤ ✤

Meanwhile Louis' condition had grown worse, and the Bishop told him that it was time he made his peace with God.

'And that, Sire,' he said, 'you cannot do while your mistress remains here. There is only one thing to be done. You must give the order for her to retire without delay that you may begin your repentance in time.'

The King agreed, and the word went through his apartments that at last his consent had been given. The gallery which connected his apartments with those of his mistress was knocked down, so that all might know that she was being sent away. Now was the time for the Duchesse and her sister to slip out of Metz as quickly and secretly as they could.

But they had many enemies. 'The King is dying,' said those Princes whom she had tried to keep from the King's bedside. 'There is no need now to placate the favourite.'

In the streets of Metz, in the taverns, the people were talking about the mistress's plight. They would drum her out of their town, they said; they would teach her to be somewhat less haughty than she had been when she had arrived.

The Duchesse was in turn furious and frightened; she dreaded falling into the hands of the mob – a fate which her enemies were hoping she would meet.

Maurepas was delighted at the turn of events and made no attempt to hide his pleasure. The Duc de Châtillon, who was the Dauphin's tutor, expressed the view that the dismissal of the favourite was the best thing that could befall the Royal House of France.

Richelieu found all his supporters melting away, and that there was a plan afoot to get him sent into exile. Meanwhile the Duchesse knew that her hours in Metz were numbered and she and her sister would have to face the hostile crowd on their way out of the town and across France.

While they were preparing themselves to leave, the Maréchal de Belle-Isle called upon them. He expressed his sympathy, for he said he did not care to see ladies in distress.

'You should know, Madame,' he said, 'that hostile crowds are waiting for your carriage.'

'I know it, Monsieur de Belle-Isle,' she told him, desperately trying to retain her courage.

'Then I hope you will allow me to place my carriage at your disposal,' said the Maréchal. 'It is big and, if the window blinds were drawn down, none would realise who travelled inside it.'

'How can I thank you?' cried the Duchesse.

'It is nothing,' said the Maréchal. 'I could not fail to help ladies in distress. Be ready to leave in my carriage. I will go away on foot. The carriage window-blinds are drawn. You will have left Metz behind you before the people discover that you have gone.'

Thus the Duchesse de Châteauroux fled ignobly from Metz.

The Bishop of Soissons and Père Pérusseau were in command, since the King was too ill to be anything but helpless in their hands. They gave their orders; the King must obey. It was their task to pilot him to Heaven, and he believed he would shortly leave this Earth.

Did he repent of his sins?

He repented with all his heart.

That was well, for only complete repentance would save his soul.

His repentance must be made public; he must confess his manifold sins; he must agree to banish the Duchesse de Châteauroux to a place a hundred and fifty miles from Versailles.

The King was drooping into unconsciousness; he was too ill to understand anything but that his soul was being saved.

Thus the enemies of Richelieu and the Duchesse were triumphant and already men and women were showing a new respect for the Dauphin.

The Bishop declared that the Queen should come at once to the King's bedside, and that all France should know that the concubine was being dismissed, and the husband and wife were amicably together again.

Louis consented to all this unaware of what he did.

And then suddenly the miracle happened. Louis woke up one morning to find that his fever had disappeared.

As the Duchesse drove away from the town of Metz, the Queen drove towards it. The latter was a most unhappy woman, because she believed that since the King had dismissed his mistress and sent for his wife he must be on the point of death. Moreover news had just reached her that her little Thérèse-Félicité had died.

There was a little comfort in the conduct of the people, who had gathered to see the carriages of the wife and the mistress going in their different directions, for they hurled abuse at the mistress, spat at her coach and threw stones at it; while they cheered the Queen on her way.

Louis was still very weak when the Queen arrived at Metz, and when she visited him and knelt by the bed he was moved to see her tears.

'I ask your forgiveness,' he said, 'for the humiliations I have made you suffer.'

Marie shook her head and smiled at him through her tears. 'You have my forgiveness,' she said. 'All you need do is ask for God's.'

It was an irritating comment and typical of his wife, but Louis was genuinely sorry for the distress he had caused her and eager now for peace. So he reached for her hand.

Paris went wild with joy. Louis had recovered, and had dismissed the Duchesse. He and the Queen were together again. He had conducted himself with valour among his soldiers. He was going to rule them nobly and well; and good times were coming back to France.

He was spoken of with the utmost affection. He was going to be the greatest King the French had ever known.

It was at this time that they did not speak merely of Louis our King. They called him 'Louis the Well-Beloved.'

As soon as he was well enough Louis was back in the army. Noailles had not been very successful during the King's illness, and Louis was beginning to understand that he had been mistaken in thinking this man was a great general.

Foolishly he had allowed Charles of Lorraine to cross the

Rhine unmolested on his way to help Bohemia against the attack which Frederick of Prussia was making. That Noailles should have allowed him to escape was disgraceful. The people cried out against him and, when he came to Metz to confer with the King, the old Maréchal found that he no longer had Louis' confidence; as for the new ally, Frederick of Prussia, he was furious at the lax behaviour of Noailles which, he said, amounted to treason.

Louis joined his armies at Freiburg which, on his arrival, fell to the French; but the winter was already upon them and it was impossible to continue the war.

Louis went to Paris where he was given a welcome such as Paris had rarely given its King. In spite of the bitter cold the people filled the streets to let him know how much they loved him.

Sitting back in his golden coach he looked as handsome as a god and, when the people recalled his valour in the field, they shouted themselves hoarse.

From the crowd one woman watched; she wore a shawl about her, and from this her face peeped out at the golden coach and its occupant.

He did not see her, but incautiously she allowed the shawl to fall back and disclose her features.

A man at her side noticed her and laughed aloud.

'Châteauroux,' he shouted, and immediately she was surrounded.

Desperately she fought to escape from the crowd. 'You are mistaken . . . You are mistaken . . .' she insisted.

But they knew they were not. They spat on her; they looked for stones and the rubbish of the streets to throw at her; they hurled insults at her.

Dishevelled, weeping with anger and humiliation, she ran as fast as she could; and when she had eluded them – for they did not want to miss the chance of seeing the King's procession for the sake of tormenting her – she leaned against the walls of an alley, panting and frightened.

In the distance she could hear the sound of the drums and the shouts of the crowd.

'Long live Louis! Louis is back. Long live Louis, the Well-beloved of his people.'

The Duc de Richelieu was back in attendance on the King in the Palace of Versailles. There were many to wonder what would happen next, and to tremble in their shoes.

The Duc de Châtillon and his Duchesse were terrified. They had been rather foolish. Although Louis had said that the Dauphin was not to be brought to his bedside at Metz when the Dauphin had begged to be taken there, the Duc had ignored the King's wishes and given way to those of his pupil. That was when he had believed that the King was dying and that he was obeying the wishes of the boy soon to be King.

He, like others, had made a mistake, and he believed he would be asked to pay for his mistakes.

Louis had shown no displeasure, had indeed been as affable as ever to the Châtillons, but they were beginning to know Louis' methods now.

Maurepas was wondering what was going to happen to him.

There were others who were anxiously contemplative; and in a house in the Rue du Bac where the Duchesse de Châteauroux was lodging with her sister, people called often, for it was said that messages from the King were being brought to the lady.

The people of Paris were aghast at these rumours. They had decided that their King was to be reconciled to the Queen, that the child-bearing would begin again; that there would be conjugal felicity between the royal pair, and the King would discard his mistress and give his mind to the government of France.

❖ ❖ ❖

The Duchesse was told that a gentleman of the Court had come to call upon her.

She received him eagerly, thinking that he brought a message from the King; but when he threw back his cloak she gave a cry of great pleasure, for it was Louis himself.

She flung herself into his arms and wept with joy.

'Louis . . . my Louis . . . I knew you would come or send for me.'

'You will come back to Versailles.'

'I have been so humiliated . . . so cruelly humiliated.'

'I know.'

She took his hands and kissed them, first tenderly and then passionately. She knew how to arouse his desire for her, a desire which obliterated everything else.

'I must come back,' she cried. 'I cannot bear this separation.'

'You *shall* come back.'

'I shall never be treated with respect again while my enemies remain. Louis, must they remain? Maurepas . . . he is the greatest of them. I have felt very ill at times since I left Metz. Louis, I believe that man tried to poison me.'

'Oh, no, he would not do that.'

'Would he not? He hates me because he knows I hate him. Châtillon, he is another. He and his wife have made the Dauphin hate me.'

'He shall be dismissed from Court – so shall his wife.'

The Duchesse nodded happily. 'The Bishop of Soissons and that fool of a confessor . . .'

'We will dismiss them all . . . if you feel you cannot return to Court unless we do.'

She held him to her; her eyes were unnaturally bright as though with fever. She felt that this was her most triumphant moment.

Louis spent the night with her at the Rue du Bac, and before he left he said: 'You must return at once to Versailles. We are too far apart.'

'I will return as soon as the Comte de Maurepas brings me a command from you to do so.'

Louis laughed. 'It shall be as you wish,' he said.

Her eyes narrowed. 'I would have Monsieur de Maurepas know that, clever as he thinks he is, he has acted rather foolishly in proclaiming himself *my* enemy.'

When Louis had gone she called her sister to her.

'Triumph!' she cried. 'Get ready. Soon we shall be back at Versailles. The humiliations of Metz shall be forgotten.'

'That is good news,' said her sister. 'When do we leave?' She stopped abruptly and gazed at her sister. 'Are you quite well? You look so strange.'

'Strange? I?'

'Your eyes are so brilliant. They look almost glassy . . . and how your cheeks burn!'

The Duchesse turned to her. 'I have suffered, have I not? Metz! Shall I ever forget it? But now others shall suffer as they made me suffer.'

'Was His Majesty very loving . . . very demanding?'

'Is he not always so?'

'Sister, I should lie down if I were you. You are too excited. I will bring you a cool and soothing drink.'

'Very well.' As the Duchesse took her sister's hand and pressed it, Madame de Lauraguais noticed how feverish she was, and anxiously hurried away for the drink. When she returned it was to find the Duchesse lying in her bed.

Madame de Lauraguais tried to make her drink, but she did not seem to understand; then she knelt by the bed.

'I am afraid . . .' murmured Madame de Châteauroux. 'They will stone me. Make sure the blinds are drawn . . .'

'The excitement has been too much for you,' murmured Madame de Lauraguais. 'Tomorrow you will be better.'

But next day the Duchesse was not better. She had a fever and it was clear that she was very ill indeed.

⚜ ⚜ ⚜

For two weeks she lay near to death. The people of Paris gathered in the market places and at the street corners to talk of her. All of them said it would be a good thing for France if she never recovered.

Many said that Maurepas had poisoned her.

At every hour of the day messengers went back and forth between the Rue du Bac and the Palace. The King, it was said, was suffering acute misery on account of the favourite.

Madame de Mailly came out of exile to visit her sister and to let her know that she bore her no ill will for her cruel conduct towards her; and the Duchesse was relieved to see her sister, to be able to receive her forgiveness in person.

'I am going to die,' she said, 'and there are so many actions of mine which I wish had never been performed.'

In early December she confessed her sins and was given

the last sacraments, and on the 8th of that month she died.

She was quietly buried a few days later in the chapel of Saint Michel in Saint-Sulpice at a very early hour in the morning, on the orders of the King who remembered the manner in which Madame de Vintimille's corpse had been treated, and wished to spare his beloved Duchesse this last humiliation.

Louis was heartbroken and nothing could arouse him from melancholy.

Even the Queen sent her sympathy, and the people of Paris, who wanted to form processions that they might proclaim their delight in the death of this woman whom they hated, refrained from doing so.

'She was arrogant and had an evil influence over the King,' they said, 'but for all that he loved her. To demonstrate against her cannot hurt her much now, but it would bring great pain to him.'

Hurt Louis! How could they? Was he not their adored young King, Louis *le Bien-Aimé*?

✤ Chapter IX ✤

MADEMOISELLE POISSON

There was one woman in France who received the news of the death of Madame de Châteauroux with a fatalistic calm. Something had to happen to sever the relationship between the King and Duchesse, she told herself and, although she had not expected this would be brought about by the death of the Duchesse, the cause of the severance was unimportant; it only mattered that the King was free.

When the news was brought to her at the Château d'Etioles she began making her plans. Her life's ambition was about to come to fruition. It was quite certain that this would happen, but naturally she herself must do all in her power to bring it about.

Madame d'Etioles had been born Jeanne-Antoinette Poisson. Not a very elegant name; but then, her family had been clever rather than elegant.

Her father, François Poisson, had been a man of ideas, determined to make his fortune. There were many ways of making a fortune in Paris if one were not too particular. François was not particular.

He was a butcher – a very successful one – with a genius for getting himself contracts. He very quickly obtained one for supplying the Hôpital des Invalides with meat, but in spite of his prosperity he was not content. Bad harvests had meant a shortage of grain, and a man such as François could discover ways of exploiting situations like that.

Unfortunately when a man kept only just on the right side of the law, one false step could send him tottering onto the wrong side.

François was caught in a grain scandal and there was none who infuriated the hungry people of Paris more than those men who made themselves rich out of the citizens' miseries. Found guilty it was necessary for him to leave the capital in a hurry before the mob laid hands on him.

This he did, leaving Madame Poisson to fend for herself and the two children – Jeanne-Antoinette and Abel.

Madame Poisson was certainly able to do this. She was a very handsome woman, a little above François socially since she had developed grand ideas from the male friends she continued to entertain after her marriage.

One of these friends was the rich farmer-general Lenormant de Tourneheim; this man was still enamoured of the handsome Madame Poisson and had been her lover for several years. Some people said that he was the father of Jeanne-Antoinette, for he showed he was very fond of the girl; however none but Madame Poisson could be sure about that – and perhaps even she could not be absolutely certain. However it was wise perhaps to let the rich financier believe the charming little creature was his – particularly when, with the flight of François, the family was left to look after itself.

François' effects had been disposed of to settle debts, and the family would have found themselves destitute but for the kindness of Monsieur de Tourneheim.

Monsieur de Tourneheim was indeed a worthy protector; not only was he rich but was related to the Pâris-Duverneys who could exercise some influence in very high quarters.

Therefore when François disappeared, Monsieur de Tourneheim took charge.

Her daughter, said Madame Poisson, was clearly going to be a beauty, and she wanted the best possible education for her. As for Abel, he was going to be the brother of a celebrated beauty and must not therefore disgrace her with his lack of education.

'What future do you plan for the child?' asked Monsieur de Tourneheim amused.

'The greatest that her beauty and education will bring to her,' was the prompt answer.

The family moved into the large house which belonged to the farmer-general, the Hôtel de Gesvres; Jeanne-Antoinette was sent to a convent in Poissy, and Abel to a school for gentlefolk.

It was a happy household, for Madame Poisson was genial and good-natured as well as attractive; she was very content with her life, and having all that she wanted she gave herself up to contemplating her daughter's future. It was after a visit to a fair that those ambitions took a definite turn.

This was a treat which she had promised the children, and Madame Poisson, setting out with one on either arm – her handsome son and her ravishingly lovely daughter – was so proud and happy on that day, particularly when people turned to stare at Jeanne-Antoinette and pass comments on her loveliness.

Jeanne-Antoinette begged to be allowed to visit the fortune-teller and, as she herself was eager to learn what great future awaited the girl, Madame Poisson did not need a great deal of persuading.

The old gipsy caught her breath at the sight of the lovely girl. Her complexion was fair, her skin seeming almost transparent; her eyes were large and alight with intelligence and vitality; she was extremely feminine and even at nine years of age she wore her gown with a grace and dignity which belonged rather to the Court than to a fairground.

'Sit down, my beauty,' said the old woman. She looked at the proud mother and added: 'It is not often that I have the pleasure of looking into such a future as this one's.'

She studied the small palm, the long tapering fingers, the delicate skin, and she sought to endow this fair young girl with the finest future she could imagine.

Why did she think of the King at that moment? Was it because she had seen him recently riding through Paris? – oh, such a handsome young man. He had been on his way to Notre Dame to give thanks for the birth of the Dauphin.

He had a Queen unworthy of him, it was said, one who looked more like a woman of the people than a Queen. The people said that with such a Queen such a King would have his mistresses, as his great-grandfather had before him.

Then the gipsy spoke: 'There'll be a great fortune for you, my pretty one.' She brought her brown old face close to the dazzlingly fair one. 'I see your hand in that of a King ... a great King ... the greatest of Kings. He is handsome. He loves you, my dear; he loves you dearly . . . and he puts you above all others.'

Madame Poisson doubled the gipsy's fee. She could scarcely

wait to get back to the Hôtel de Gesvres, to tell her lover of the gipsy's prediction.

Monsieur de Tourneheim was amused, but so great was Madame Poisson's belief in the gipsy's prophecy that she thought of little else.

'She must have the very best possible education now,' she declared. 'Only then can she be received at Court. She must be taught to dance and sing . . . everything that a Court lady should know. She must be clever as well as beautiful. How will she keep her place among all those jealous men and women if she is not equipped to do so?'

Monsieur de Tourneheim could not help being carried away by Madame Poisson's enthusiasm. Jeanne-Antoinette should have the very best education his money could provide.

Madame Poisson was delighted. She would watch her daughter in great contentment.

'That,' she would cry, 'that is *un morceau du roi!*'

❖ ❖ ❖

Jeanne-Antoinette was not kept in ignorance of the destiny which her mother and Monsieur de Tourneheim planned for her.

From the age of nine she gave herself up to preparations for the part she must play. She learned to dance and sing; she had a delightful voice; she was fond of the theatre and wanted to act. This she did with grace and charm during the little entertainments which were given for friends at the Hôtel de Gesvres.

'She would be a fine actress,' declared Madame Poisson, 'if a greater destiny did not await her.'

She painted with talent and played several musical instruments equally well. She was clearly very gifted and, marvelling at her beauty which became more enchanting every day, Monsieur de Tourneheim began to believe that Madame Poisson's aspirations for her daughter were not so absurd after all.

Meanwhile Jeanne-Antoinette took every opportunity of seeing the King. There were not many, as Louis refrained as far as possible from appearing in public, but when the girl saw the handsome man in his robes of state she thought him god-like and fell in love with him.

When she was nearing the end of her teens Madame Poisson decided that it was time she married. Who would make a suitable husband for this woman of destiny? A Comte? A Duc? Either was impossible. No Comte or Duc would be allowed to marry a girl whose father had been little more than a trades-man. Madame Poisson was worried. Jeanne-Antoinette could not become the King's mistress until she was married, and she must have a husband. What a wonderful thing it would be if someone, say from the Orléans or the Condé families, became so enamoured of Jeanne-Antoinette that in spite of family opposition he determined on marrying her!

She turned to her benefactor, Lenormant de Tourneheim, for help.

Monsieur Poisson had returned to Paris; the influential Lenormant had arranged for the charges against him to be quashed, for, said Madame Poisson, now that Jeanne-Antoinette was growing up it would not do for her to have a father who was still under a cloud. François settled in quite happily at the Hôtel de Gesvres, and Madame Poisson was able to keep the two men contented.

Now Monsieur de Tourneheim had a prospective husband for Jeanne-Antoinette. The heir to his fortune was his nephew,

Charles-Guillaume Lenormant d'Etioles; this young man should be Jeanne-Antoinette's bridegroom.

When the young man heard that he was to marry the daughter of François Poisson, the man who had been involved in a grain scandal, he was indignant.

'I refuse,' he told his uncle.

'My boy,' said Monsieur de Tourneheim, 'if you do, you forfeit my fortune.'

That was a shock to the young man who hesitated for a while and then ungraciously gave way.

They were married in March of the year 1741. Jeanne-Antoinette, just past twenty, was a beautiful bride and the young man found his excitement and interest in her growing with every minute.

After the wedding night he was deeply in love with her, and Jeanne-Antoinette, who had accepted the marriage as a necessary step on the road to her destiny, was astonished by his passion. However she resigned herself to accepting it.

'Swear,' said the young husband on one occasion, 'that you will always be true to me.'

'I will be a faithful wife,' she answered gravely, 'except, of course, in the case of the King.'

Charles-Guillaume was bewildered, but believing this was some sort of joke, thought no more of it.

Jeanne-Antoinette was discovering that it was very different to be the wife of a rich young man, heir to a great fortune, from being merely the daughter of a rich man's mistress. Charles-Guillaume was ready and able to give her all she wanted, and she had her chance of displaying those talents which since she was nine years old she had been busily cultivating.

In the Hôtel de Gesvres she set up her *salon*, and here she welcomed the intellectuals of Paris. Writers and musicians flocked to her parties, and always in the centre of these gatherings was the exquisite Jeanne-Antoinette, charming them all with her appearance and her conversation.

Two children were born to her, a girl and a boy; and, although she loved them devotedly, she never lost sight of what she had come to think of as her destiny.

Voltaire, who was a frequent visitor to the gatherings in the Hôtel de Gesvres, was very attracted by her, for she delighted him by discussing his work with great intelligence and by encouraging him to visit her and give that *éclat* to her gathering which, she said, radiated from his genius.

One day she said to him: 'If it should ever be in my power to help you, you may rely upon me to do so.'

Voltaire kissed her hand and, because she felt that he had not completely understood, she added: 'I have a presentiment that one day – very soon now – the King is going to fall in love with me.'

'He would but have to look at you,' was the answer, '– that would suffice.'

She smiled at him. 'He is surrounded by beautiful and accomplished women, women who have been born to the Court life, and who therefore fit perfectly into Versailles and all it stands for. But I know. Something within me tells me. As for myself I loved him from the moment I saw him. Indeed, I think I began to love him *before* I saw him.'

She could see that the writer did not take this conversation very seriously, and she was amused. One day he will remember, she told herself.

235

She began to feel a certain disquiet. Time was passing, and if she were going to captivate the King she must not delay too long. Already she was past twenty and the mother of two children.

Then she heard that Louis occasionally hunted in the forest of Sénart, and she remembered the ramshackle old château which was close to the forest and in the possession of the Tourneheim family.

'Why should we not have a place in the country?' she demanded. 'Let us go and inspect that old château.'

So she and Charles-Guillaume went. It could be made into something quite attractive; even Charles-Guillaume agreed to what Jeanne-Antoinette planned with enthusiasm; she herself designed the alterations; the architects and builders were put to work, and very soon she had her château in the country.

Jeanne-Antoinette planned an exquisite wardrobe, and ordered two or three carriages to be made for her – they must be different from other carriages, light and dainty, merely designed to take her for little drives about the château. They were made in colours which suited her – those delicate shades of rose and blue.

Thus it was that she brought herself to the notice of the King when he was hunting in the forest. That might have been the great moment, she believed, but for the fact that the King was already under the spell of that strong-minded woman, Madame de Châteauroux.

The day when the King's party sheltered in the château during a rain-storm seemed like a heaven-sent opportunity. But again Madame de Châteauroux was there to prevent the long-laid plans coming to fruition; and alas, the King had not been sufficiently aware of his destiny to help matters along by insisting on the beautiful Madame d'Etioles being brought to one of his supper parties.

Worse still, Madame de Châteauroux had begun to suspect that she had a rival in the pretty lady of the forest château, and from then on had made it quite impossible for Jeanne-Antoinette to put herself in the way of the King.

That had been most depressing. But now Madame de Châteauroux was dead.

✢ ✣ ✢

Towards the end of the year 1744 it was decided that, as the Dauphin was now fifteen and the King had been a husband at that age, it was time that a wife was found for him.

The Dauphin had changed a great deal from that spirited boy who had charmed the King with his clever sayings. He was growing fat and had become very interested in religion.

He did not share the Bourbon love of hunting; indeed he shrank from sport. This may have been due to the fact that on his first shooting expedition he had accidentally killed a man. He was so upset that he could not forget it and, when urged to go on a similar expedition and one of his shots injured a woman, he declared that he could no longer find pleasure in sport.

He and Louis were growing away from each other; in fact Louis' interest was in his daughters and he was often seen in the company of Anne-Henriette and Adelaide. Adelaide's high spirits amused him but his tenderness towards Anne-Henriette was most marked; and it seemed as though he could not give her enough affection to make up for having denied her marriage with the Duc de Chartres.

The Dauphin was excited at the prospect of having a bride

and, when the Infanta Marie-Thérèse-Raphaëlle arrived, he was determined to love her.

She was the sister of the little Infanta who had years before been sent to France as Louis' bride and who, on account of her youth, had been hastily sent home by the Duc de Bourbon and the domineering Madame de Prie.

Marie-Thérèse-Raphaëlle was four years older than the Dauphin; she had abundant red hair, but with this went a very pale skin and a not very pleasant cast of features. She came to France warily; remembering French treatment of her sister, she was determined that such conduct should not be meted out to her, and consequently she was haughty in the extreme. She possessed the solemnity which was typical of the Spanish Court and in complete contrast with the gay yet dignified splendour and grace which was the very essence of Versailles.

Only the Dauphin continued to be pleased with the Infanta and, as he made this clear to her, she began to unbend a little but to him only.

The King, smiling at the young pair, recalled the days when Marie Leczinska had arrived in France and he had thought her the most beautiful woman at Court.

Blind, he told himself. Absolutely blind! But how charming it is to be blind on certain occasions. Let us hope the Dauphin will be similarly afflicted.

The wedding of the Dauphin must be attended by a round of festivities, and the crowning event was to be the masked ball held in the Château of Versailles itself.

Throughout the Palace there was great excitement, not only because there was to be a ball at which, disguised behind masks, men and women could allow themselves to cast aside decorum and restraint for an evening, but because with the festivities following the Dauphin's wedding the King had appeared to come out of mourning for Madame de Châteauroux. He was not the man to exist long without feminine friendship, and sooner or later someone would step into the place vacated by the dead woman.

Thus many women, as they prepared for the ball, hoped that this night might see the beginning of a life of prestige and power; and friends of beauties primed them on the best mode of attack.

It was a brilliant occasion. The Salon d'Hercule and the Galerie des Glaces, with the six reception rooms between them, were put at the disposal of the guests, and even so there seemed scarcely enough space to accommodate all who came. Costumes, beautiful and bizarre, daring and glittering, made a sight to be remembered. Under the carved and gilded cornice of the Salon d'Hercule the guests gathered; they sat at the exquisite *guéridons* of silver in the Galerie des Glaces; the light from the seventeen crystal chandeliers and the smaller candelabra picked out the colours in the galaxy of jewels; it was one of the most dazzling balls which had ever taken place even in the Palace of Versailles.

And to all the colour, brilliance and splendour was added that tension which had its roots in the exciting question: Will the King choose a new mistress tonight?

Anne-Henriette was one who had come to the ball without any great pleasure. Every time such an occasion presented itself and she witnessed the excitement of others, she would feel sad.

She was but eighteen and yet she felt that all hope of happiness was lost to her.

She believed that the Duc de Chartres had become resigned. He had a wife now; sometimes he looked at her with regret, but was that because he had been forced to make a less brilliant marriage than he had hoped? He could go to war and make a new life for himself in the army. When he had been wounded in that campaign in which her father had been with his armies, she had heard that the Duchesse de Chartres was going to the front to be with the Duc.

I should have been the one, she thought.

He had offended Madame de Châteauroux when that woman had been dismissed from the King's bedside at Metz. And when the King had recovered, and Madame de Châteauroux had been taken back into favour, the young Duc had been alarmed for his future.

That was all over now, but such alarms and excitements would help one to forget. Yet what could a young Princesse do but sit at her embroidery, go through all the ceremonies which were demanded of her and continue to mourn for her lost lover?

Anne-Henriette adjusted her mask and stood close to the white and gold brocade hangings which decorated the Galerie. This was one of the rare occasions when a Princesse could mingle with the people as one of them, and she had heard that not only the nobility had been admitted to tonight's ball.

As she looked at that whirling mass of people she felt someone touch her hand lightly, and turning startled, she saw a masked face near her own.

'Have you ever seen so many people in the Galerie before?'

asked a voice which was different from the voices she usually heard and set her wondering why.

'I . . . I do not think there have ever been so many people in the Galerie.'

'Do you not find it a little . . . overpowering?'

'Why yes. I could wish there were fewer.'

'People here tonight have never seen anything so wonderful as this Galerie of yours.'

Of yours? It sounded as though he were not a Frenchman. Of course he was not. His accent was not of France.

'You are wondering who I am,' he went on. 'Shall we dance awhile?'

'I am ready to,' answered Anne-Henriette.

They moved among the whirling people.

'So much noise,' he said, 'one can scarcely hear the music. It is not easy to talk, is it?'

'Do we need to talk?'

'Perhaps not yet. But later.'

She found that she had stopped wondering whether she would meet the Duc de Chartres on this night, and if she did, what they would say to each other.

It was long since she had danced like this. She was conscious of a great pleasure, not only because she felt that the future need not be all melancholy, but because she was suddenly aware that it might be possible to escape from the past.

He had danced with her out of the Galerie and through several of the reception rooms; she did not know how long they danced or where he led her, but she found herself alone with him in a small ante-room, and there they stopped breathlessly to look at each other.

'You are fatigued?' he asked gently.

'No . . . no,' she answered quickly and marvelled that she was not, for she had grown frail lately and was easily tired.

'I must confess,' he said. 'I know you to be Madame Seconde. Do you know who I am?'

'I know that you are not French,' she answered.

'Then you have guessed half the truth. The rest is simple. Or shall I remove my mask?'

'No . . . I pray you, do not. I will guess.'

'Shall I give you a clue? I am a Prince, as Royal as yourself. If I had not been I would not have approached you as I did. I am also a beggar, an exile, come to France for the help I hope your father will give me.'

'I know you now,' she cried. 'You are the young Chevalier de St. Georges.'

He took her hand and kissed it. 'Charles Edward Stuart, at your service.'

'I am glad to have an opportunity to wish you Godspeed in your adventure.'

'May God bless you for that. I shall succeed, of course I shall succeed. When I have driven the German from the throne of England, when my father is restored and the Stuarts regain what is theirs by right . . . ah, then . . .'

'Yes,' she said, 'what then?'

'Then,' he said, 'I shall not come as a beggar to France. I shall not come to plead for money . . . men . . . ships.' He laughed suddenly and his eyes glittered through his mask. 'But,' he added, 'I shall never forget a February night in 1745 when I danced with a Princesse at a masked ball. And perhaps, because I cannot forget, I shall come back and plead once more with the King of France.'

'That,' she said, 'was a charming speech. Shall we dance again?'

'You are tired?'

'No . . . I am not tired. That is strange, for I should be. I want to mingle with the crowds in the ballrooms. I want to dance. I feel as though I could go on dancing all night.'

'Is that because your heart, which was heavy, has become light?'

'You say such strange things.'

'Come,' he said. 'You are right. It is well that we join the other revellers. There is much I have to do. In the summer I shall return to England . . . to Scotland . . . You will think of me while I am away?'

'I shall think of you constantly, and I shall pray for your success.'

'Pray, my Princesse, pray with all your heart. For what happens to me over there this summer could be of great importance to us both.'

So back to the dancers they went, and under that ceiling with its magnificent allegorical carvings the Princess Anne-Henriette began to be happy again. The Chevalier de St Georges had made her aware of him, and a pressure of the hand, a tenderness of the voice had brought her out of the melancholy past so that she could now look towards a future which held a certain elusive promise.

Marie the Queen watched the dancers. She recognised Louis in spite of his incongruous disguise. Even though several of his friends had come in similar costumes she knew which of them was the King. He and his friends had attempted to dress like yew trees clipped to various bizarre shapes; it was very effective and caused a great deal of amusement and applause – which made it clear that many knew Louis was in that group.

She felt sentimental tonight. Occasions such as this reminded her of the festivities which had followed her own marriage. Then they had been together, she and Louis – Louis a boy the same age as today's bridegroom. Did Louis remember, when he had seen their son with his bride, so happy to have her with him?

This wedding is so like ours, she thought. Poor Marie-Thérèse-Raphaëlle! I hope she will be happier than I have been.

But a King must have his mistresses, it seemed. Her dear father, Stanislas, was far from guiltless in that respect; and it was the lot of Queens to look on with resignation at the women their husbands loved.

Now Louis was dancing with a woman who was dressed in a flowing gown, and who was evidently meant to represent a huntress, because she carried a bow and arrow slung over her shoulder.

A creature, thought the Queen, of infinite grace; and she was deeply conscious of her own ungainly figure.

She sighed and allowed the Duc de Richelieu to sit beside her and entertain her with his dry comments on the company.

She decided to leave the ball early.

'Such entertainments,' she said, 'are not for me. I prefer the quiet of my apartments.'

She was relieved that, as this was a masked ball, she could leave without fuss. As she went she noticed that the King was talking animatedly with the masked huntress.

* * *

The huntress was saying: 'Sire, you could not hide your identity from me. I will confess I knew who you were as soon as you spoke to me.'

'You did not appear to be addressing the King.'

'It is a masque, Sire.'

'And now that I am exposed, you must tell me where I have met you before.'

'Your Majesty cannot remember?'

Louis desperately sought for the right answer. She was enchanting, this woman; he was sure that she was beautiful. Her body was fragrant, supple and yielding; and no mask could hide her charms. Vaguely he knew her, and yet he could not recall where they had met before. Surely he should have remembered. He was calling to mind all the women of the Court.

'I must remind you, Sire. Do you remember a certain rainy day in the forest of Sénart?'

'Ah!' cried Louis. 'I have it now. You were my charming hostess.' He was melancholy for a moment, remembering that then Madame de Châteauroux had been with him; but she had been rather tiresome, and he had wanted to know more of the châtelaine of the house near the forest. He was trying now to recall her name. 'It was so good of you,' he went on, 'to give us shelter.'

'Sire, it was the happiest day of my life.'

He could see her gleaming eyes through the mask. She flattered, but in a charming, innocent way. He was delighted with her and now, remembering her, he need not fear that when the mask was removed it would disclose some flaw. The young woman of the woods had been one of the prettiest he had ever seen.

'I admired your carriages so much,' he told her.

'So Your Majesty noticed them!'

'How could I fail to do so?'

'Had I known . . .'

'That would have been the happiest day of your life,' he said lightly and mockingly. Then he saw the faint flush on her neck and added: 'Forgive me. I . . . but meant to joke.'

'Your Majesty would ask pardon of *me*!'

She was certainly enchanting. How different she would be from dear Madame de Châteauroux or Madame de Vintimille! More of the nature of Madame de Mailly, but a thousand times prettier.

He said: 'Tell me, how is it you are here tonight?'

'Monsieur Lenormant de Tourneheim procured the invitation for me.'

'I feel very pleased with Monsieur Lenormant de Tourneheim.'

'Oh . . .' she paused and her body seemed to droop into sadness.

'Well?' he asked.

'I was remembering that Your Majesty is the most courteous man in France. I was foolish enough to think that the kind things you have said to me were for me . . . only for me.'

He touched her hand lightly. 'If you thought that they were for you only . . . tell me, would this be? . . .'

She burst out laughing; it was delightful, spontaneous laughter and it showed her perfect, white teeth.

She lifted her head suddenly and he saw the beautiful neck,

white as milk, strong yet graceful. She said boldly: 'Yes, it *would* be the happiest night of my life.'

Others had heard the laughter and Louis became aware that many were watching them. He was reluctant to commit himself. He knew who she was. Their adventure could go no farther tonight, as he must remain at the ball until the end, which would not be until morning.

He said: 'The time has come for me to remove my mask and go among the guests.'

Then he left her.

He took off his mask, and the company remained silent for a few seconds before the bowing and curtseying began.

'I give the order to unmask,' said Louis.

Everyone obeyed and the dancers turned to look at each other with cries of astonishment, both feigned and real.

'I pray you, carry on with your pleasure,' continued Louis as, waving his hand and smiling, he turned to speak to a lovely woman whom he complimented on her costume.

Then he strolled among the guests, stopping to talk here and there, but usually with the women, the most charming or the most beautiful.

She saw him coming towards her, and held her breath with trepidation. It was so much easier to talk to him wearing a mask, now she was afraid, afraid of taking one false step which might be an end of the dream.

He was smiling when he saw her as though he was seeking her alone in the vast crowd. Yet she was wise enough to know that was the secret of his charm – whether it was exerted for the benefit of the humblest soldier on the battlefield or the most ambitious woman at Versailles.

'Madame,' he said, 'your costume too . . . it is charming.'

Her legs trembled as she curtsied to the ground. Was it too deep a curtsey? Was it the way women curtsied at Versailles? Versailles was full of pitfalls for those who had never learned its etiquette. She must take care.

'You are a dangerous huntress,' he said lightly. 'I believe your arrows could wound . . . mortally.'

Those standing near laughed lightly, and she, wondering afterwards whether she did it on purpose or whether it was an accident, dropped her little lace handkerchief to the floor. It fell at the King's feet.

Louis looked at it and stooping picked it up. He smiled and tossed it to her. Then he passed on.

Those close by exchanged glances. Was it a gesture? Did it mean something? The King to pick up the woman's handkerchief . . . and to throw it to her in that manner! It was like an invitation . . . given and accepted.

✦ ✦ ✦

Could it be that the King this night had really chosen his new mistress?

She could scarcely wait for her carriage to take her home. Madame Poisson had not gone to bed. How could she on such an occasion? She was anxiously waiting to hear what had occurred.

She embraced her daughter. 'Oh, but you are lovely . . . lovely! I'll swear there was not any lady at the ball half as beautiful.' She looked into her daughter's shining eyes. 'Well, my love?'

'He danced with me. He talked to me. He seemed as though he liked me.'

'And he suggested that you should go to the Palace?'

Jeanne-Antoinette shook her head dolefully.

'That's how it is done,' said Madame Poisson. 'There is a supper party in one of the little rooms. Just one or two guests and then, after the party, he waves his hand and they disappear. The two of you are left alone together. Are you sure he didn't say anything about a supper party?'

'Yes, *Maman*.'

Madame Poisson lifted her shoulders. 'Well, the fortress wasn't captured in a day.'

'In a day! We have been fifteen years preparing for the capture.'

'But he liked you, did he not?'

'I swear he did.'

'Come, let me comb your hair. You must see him again soon. He is a man who would acquire the habit of seeing a woman and want to go on seeing her.'

She helped her daughter to bed, and there she lay, her eyes brilliant with reminiscence, her lovely hair spread out on the pillow.

If he could only see her now, thought Madame de Poisson. *Morceau du roi!* There never was a better.

It only showed, said Madame Poisson, that it was foolish to despair, for next morning, a carriage drew up outside the Hôtel de Gesvres and a man alighted.

He asked for Madame d'Etioles, and when, in the company of her mother, Jeanne-Antoinette received him, he told her that his name was Le Bel and that he was one of the King's principal *valets de chambre*.

'You are invited, Madame,' he said, 'to join a supper party which His Majesty is giving after the ball at the Hôtel-de-Ville. It is a small party.'

'I am honoured,' said Jeanne-Antoinette.

And when the King's messenger had gone, she and Madame Poisson looked at each other for a second in silence; then they put their arms about each other in a tight hug.

Their laughter verged on the hysterical. This was the dream, which had begun in the fortune-teller's tent, come true.

'There is no doubt what this means!' cried Madame Poisson at length, extricating herself. 'And there is much to do. You must have a new gown. Rose-coloured, I think. We must get to work at once. What a blessing Charles-Guillaume is away on business.'

Jeanne-Antoinette paused in her joy, which seemed to be touched with something like delirium; she had forgotten Charles-Guillaume who loved her with a passion which his uncle had likened to madness.

But she had always told him that she could only be a faithful wife until the King claimed her. There was no avoiding her destiny.

⚜ ⚜ ⚜

The ball at the Hôtel-de-Ville was very different from that which had taken place at Versailles. The people of Paris had determined to take a more active part in the celebrations, and they stormed the building and danced among the nobility.

Jeanne-Antoinette, accompanied by Lenormant and her mother, was alarmed. The Dauphin and his bride were present but they decided to leave as early as possible, and so rowdy had the company grown that no one noticed their departure.

On the road to Versailles the two royal carriages met. The Dauphin called a halt and, getting out of his, went to that in which the King sat.

'Sire,' he said, 'I advise you not to go on to the Hôtel-de-Ville. The people have broken in. It is like a madhouse.'

The King smiled. 'Where is the Dauphine?'

'In her carriage.'

'Then take her back to Versailles. I shall go on. For, my son, you have your business at Versailles to attend to; mine tonight takes me into Paris.'

The King, unrecognised and accompanied by Richelieu, pushed his way through the crowd. Eventually he saw her sitting with her mother and Lenormant. He sent Richelieu to them.

Richelieu went to their table and bowed.

'Madame,' said the Duc, 'I believe you await a friend.'

'It is so,' began Jeanne-Antoinette.

Richelieu swept his eyes over Madame Poisson's ample but still attractive form.

'His Majesty eagerly awaits you. Pray consider his impatience and come at once.'

'Go along now,' said Madame Poisson. 'We will go home. May good fortune attend you.'

'Good fortune already awaits the lady,' murmured Richelieu.

Louis caught her arm as she approached. 'Let us leave here quickly. We sup near this place.'

Richelieu accompanied them to their private room, and then Louis said: 'Your presence, my friend, is no longer needed.'

Thus it was that Jeanne-Antoinette found that the fortune promised her by the gipsy was at last beginning to materialise.

At dawn she was taken back to the Hôtel de Gesvres in the

royal carriage and, after a tender farewell, the King left her and returned to Versailles.

So far, so good, but what now?

✦ ✦ ✦

She need not have worried. Monsieur Le Bel called later that day to bring her an invitation for Madame d'Etioles to sup in the *petits appartements* at the Palace of Versailles.

Madame Poisson was gleeful. 'You must keep Charles-Guillaume in the provinces for a while,' she told Lenormant. 'He is a very jealous husband. Who knows what indiscretion he might commit if he discovered what was happening!'

So Lenormant and Madame Poisson conspired to further the romance between the King and Jeanne-Antoinette.

Every time he saw Jeanne-Antoinette Louis became a little more enamoured of her. Not since the days of Madame de Mailly had he been so loved for himself.

Jeanne-Antoinette was aware that his friends, and in particular the Duc de Richelieu who did not seem to like her, perhaps because he had not had a part in introducing her to the King, did not pay the respect which she felt was her due. She was not of the Court. She could not appear at any important function because she had never been presented. His friends saw her as one of the King's light-o'-loves who made the journey to his apartments by way of the back stairs.

If this procedure continued, the King himself would soon be accepting her as such; and that was not part of the destiny of which she had dreamed.

She must be of the Court, accepted as the King's mistress. Only then could her dream come true.

One day she said to him: 'Sire, my husband will soon be

returning. He is passionately jealous. I cannot come to the supper parties when he returns.'

Louis was astonished. It was not in the nature of husbands, he knew, to debar their wives from administering to the King's pleasure. But she was astonishing, this little *bourgeoise*. Dainty as she was, and so sharp-witted, occasionally she amused because she was so different from others.

'You must leave your husband for me,' he said.

Now he was aware of her dignity. 'But, Sire, should I give up my home, my standing for . . . for . . . a few weeks of pleasure such as this?'

The King was surprised. She was so humbly in love with him, so utterly adoring, that he could not believe he had heard aright. Then he thought he understood. In her *bourgeois* way she had set her standards, as the Court had at Versailles. To be presented at Court, accepted as the King's mistress, would give her every reason to leave her husband; but not if she were treated like a woman who might be smuggled up the back stairs for an hour or so.

Louis saw her point. There was an etiquette of every stratum of society and he, who had accepted it at Versailles, must respect it in other walks of life.

He looked at her. She was very pretty indeed; she was very fond of him he believed, and not only because he was the King. He in his turn was delighted with her. She was well educated. He thought of Adelaide and Anne-Henriette, and those girls of his who were still at Fontevrault. This pretty little *bourgeoise* had received a far better education than any of his daughters. She was more clever than they. The only thing she lacked was an understanding of Palace manners, which could be taught her in a week or two. And then . . . what an enchantress she would be! He would defy any woman at Court to compete with her then.

Why should not her education be undertaken? He could do a great deal towards it himself.

A presentation! A worthy title! Then he could have the delightful woman with him on all occasions.

He made up his mind.

'My dear,' he said, 'you must not go back to your husband. We will make you into a lady of the Court.'

'And then . . . I may be with you . . . always?'

He took her hand and kissed it.

She knew what this meant. She was to be brought to Court; many honours would be hers. She would be the acknowledged mistress of the King.

Her eyes were gleaming with emotion. Her lips moved.

'I will say it for you,' said Louis. 'This is the happiest night of *our* lives!'

✦ ✦ ✦

Charles-Guillaume came to the Hôtel de Gesvres in high spirits. He had been long away, and was longing to be with his wife and two children – but most of all with Jeanne-Antoinette.

When he entered the house he was greeted by his uncle, who looked at him solemnly.

'Is anything wrong?' he asked.

'Come along in,' said Monsieur de Tourneheim. 'There is something we have to say to you.'

'Jeanne-Antoinette . . . she is well?'

His uncle nodded.

'The children then?'

'They are also well.'

He led him into a small parlour where the Poissons were waiting for him.

It was Madame Poisson who explained. 'Jeanne-Antoinette has gone away,' she said.

'Gone away! But where?'

'She is at Versailles.'

'Versailles!'

'With the King.'

'But I don't understand.'

'She always explained, did she not?' cried Madame Poisson fiercely. 'It is no fault of hers. It is her destiny. She is to stay at Versailles with the King.'

'But this is fantastic. It cannot be true.'

'It is quite true,' said François. 'Our Jeanne-Antoinette has become the King's whore.'

His wife turned on him. 'Don't say such things. She is to be acknowledged as his mistress.'

'I'm a plain man with a plain way of saying what I mean,' said François.

'She must come back,' cried Charles-Guillaume. 'She must come back at once. What of me . . . what of the children? . . .'

'This was bound to happen,' said Madame Poisson. 'She always told you.'

'That! It was a joke.'

'There is nothing you can do about it,' said François. He jerked his finger at his wife and Lenormant. 'They arranged it. They always meant to.'

Madame Poisson folded her arms across her breasts. 'What has to be will be,' she said. 'There's no saying nay to it.'

'My Jeanne-Antoinette . . .' murmured the anguished husband.

Then he shut himself into the bedroom he had shared with her, and he would not come out when they sought to comfort him.

He wrote to her: 'Jeanne-Antoinette, come back. This is your home. I am your husband. Your children are here . . . Come back to us.'

Distracted he waited for her reply. She was kind, he knew. She would not ignore that anguished appeal.

And she did reply.

For the rest of her life, she said, she would be with the King. Neither of them could have prevented this thing which had happened to them. It had been ordained. When she had been only nine years old she had known that it would come to pass. Never, never would she leave the King.

With the coming of the spring it was necessary for Louis to return to his armies, and while he was away he wished Jeanne-Antoinette to learn the intricacies of Court Etiquette, so that when he came back again she should join him at the Court, be presented, and henceforth be known throughout France as the woman with whom he had chosen to share his life.

Her mother and Monsieur de Tourneheim made the arrangements, while poor broken-hearted Charles-Guillaume was dispatched to the South of France on business, that he might not distress them with his misery.

It was inadvisable to remain in Paris because the people had become aware of the existence of Madame d'Etioles, and they were not very kind to the King's mistresses when he was not at hand to protect them. Therefore to the Château d'Etioles went Jeanne-Antoinette.

But how different was life there now from what it had been in those days when she had sought to attract the King's attention by her sorties into the forest.

Now courtiers flocked to the château to cement their friendship with a lady who was clearly going to be a power in the land.

On the King's orders the Abbé de Bernis arrived. He was to teach her the family histories of the most noble families at Court. The Marquis de Gontaut must teach her the manners of the Court. It was very important to bow to some people and only nod at others, for a bow given to one who was only worthy of a nod could create a scandal at Versailles. Certain terms of speech were used at Versailles which would not be understood or indeed might have a different meaning outside. It was very necessary for a King's mistress to be aware of matters embodied in that all-important Etiquette, which, it was said, ruled the Court even more sternly than did the King.

She worked hard and with passionate desire to succeed. She swept about the lawns at the Château d'Etioles as though they were the gardens of Versailles. She grew in dignity and beauty.

Madame Poisson almost wept with joy every time she looked at her. There were few, she said, who were so blessed as to see that, which they had hoped and longed and worked for, come true.

The King wrote regularly to her that she might never doubt his devotion.

He was longing, as she was, for the time when they could be together at Versailles – openly together.

And one day a further example of his esteem arrived at the Château d'Etioles in the form of documents which assured her that she was no longer Madame d'Etioles; she was the Marquise de Pompadour.

✤ Chapter X ✤

MARQUISE DE POMPADOUR

The war of the Austrian Succession had taken a new turn for Charles of Bavaria, the candidate whom the French had supported, had died, leaving as Elector, a son who was too young to govern Bavaria, let alone wear the Imperial crown.

Here was a chance for peace, but Frederick of Prussia had no wish for peace and wanted his allies to keep Austria engaged on one side while he attacked on the other. Maria Theresa was however ready to make peace on condition that her husband François, Grand Duke of Tuscany, be proclaimed Emperor of Austria; and France, suffering under heavy taxation, could have seized this opportunity; but the Minister for Foreign Affairs, the Marquis d'Argenson, was not far-sighted enough to understand what loss and misery he could have saved his country, and, trusting Frederick of Prussia, he decided that the war must go on.

Meanwhile the new Elector of Bavaria made peace with Maria Theresa on terms very favourable to her. The Elector was to renounce all claims to the throne, to support Maria Theresa's husband, the Grand Duke, as claimant to the

Imperial throne and to sever his alliances with Prussia and France.

This decided d'Argenson to increase his activity against the Austrians, and as all through the winter, preparations had been going on to make war on the Flanders front, it was decided with the coming of spring to launch an attack.

The great Comte de Saxe had been in charge of operations for the French, and he was reckoned to be one of the greatest soldiers in Europe.

An extraordinary man of amazing energy, noted for his outstanding bravery, he claimed to be a bastard of Augustus II of Poland and Saxony – Augustus was reputed to have had three or four hundred illegitimate children – and his mother was the Swedish Countess of Konigsmarck.

It was said that Maurice de Saxe was hoping to oust Frederick of Prussia, and it was for this reason that he showed such stalwart courage in the service of France.

Louis travelled to Flanders in the company of the Dauphin who was to have his first taste of war. Arriving at Tournai, Louis found that a formidable force of Hanoverians, Dutch and English were drawn up against him and that one of the sons of George II of England, the Duke of Cumberland, was in charge of operations. Comte Maurice de Saxe was suffering from dropsy so acutely that to ride horseback was agony for him; he refused however to give up command and had a wicker chair on wheels made so that he could sit in comparative comfort and direct his men.

Louis was alarmed at the sight of him. 'You are risking your life,' he said, 'by going into battle in such a state.'

'Sire,' said the Comte fiercely, 'what matters if I die, so long as we win this battle? The English are boasting that they will have an easy victory. Cumberland says he will be in Paris in a week or so, or eat his boots. Well, Sire, as he must eat his boots, I will prepare a good sauce to go with them.'

The armies met before Fontenoy, and the battle began with the utmost politeness on both sides. The Captain of the English Guards approached the French Captain of Grenadiers.

'Monsieur,' said the Englishman, bowing to his adversary, 'I pray you, let your men fire first.'

'But certainly not,' replied the Frenchman. 'That honour shall be yours.'

Then the battle began and, in spite of the opening words of the two captains, was one of the fiercest ever fought on the soil of Flanders. Groaning and cursing, in acute pain, Maurice de Saxe roared his orders. The Dauphin had to be restrained from throwing himself into the midst of the battle; and the King's presence among his men gave them the determination to fight to the death for France.

For hours the battle raged. The numbers of dead were vast and it seemed that the French could not hold out much longer.

The King was told that he should leave the battlefield before it was too late and he fell into the hands of the advancing enemy; but Louis refused to go. His place was with his soldiers, he said; he would not turn and run at the first reverse.

Saxe however was at hand. The battle was far from lost, he roared, and he called down a plague on any who said it was. But he was undoubtedly alarmed, for ammunition was running short and he was in great fear of Cumberland's cavalry.

Yet if the battle were going badly for France, the other side was faced with terrible difficulties. The Austrians and the Dutch had been overcome and retired in disorder while only the Hanoverians and the English stood firm. Success was within their grasp but, whereas the French had Saxe to command them – a born soldier and a wily strategist – the English had only Cumberland who owed his command to the fact that he was the King's son rather than to his abilities.

The battle was in his hands; he could now bring up his cavalry and cut down the French from right and left, but he had not foreseen this possibility and had neglected his cavalry so that the horses were unfit for action; moreover the infantry could not have consolidated any gains made by the cavalry because they had been fighting for many weary hours and many of them lay bleeding in the battlefield.

Saxe saw his opportunity. Lashing his men to action with his tongue, himself swearing with pain in his wicker chair, setting such an example to them all that none dared complain, he ordered the artillery into action against Cumberland's cavalry.

In a short time Saxe's military genius had turned defeat into victory.

✤ ✤ ✤

Louis walked sadly over the field of battle, the Dauphin by his side. Wildly he was cheered by his loyal soldiers.

But Louis was silent. He looked at the dead bodies which were scattered over the field and, turning to the Dauphin, he said: 'Never forget this sight, and let it be a lesson to you. You see what is demanded to pay for a victory. When you are King of France, my son, remember this day and think twice before you allow the blood of your subjects to be shed.'

Saxe was brought to him in his wicker chair and Louis embraced the gallant old commander.

'To you,' he said, 'do we owe this victory, you . . . who are so ill. It is a miracle that you have lived through it all.'

'Sire,' said Maurice de Saxe, 'I am happy to have lived through such a day, in which I have seen Your Majesty victorious. Death will be nothing now.'

The King was visibly moved, and the old General went on: 'The wounded need our care. We are having them sent to Lille, where the ladies are eagerly waiting to succour them. But there are many English among the wounded. What should we do with them?'

'Send them with our own men,' said the King. 'They are no longer enemies – only men in need of help.'

Then he turned away. He could not contemplate such carnage without horror; he could only feel sickened that there must be so much slaughter for the sake of victory.

When the King returned to Paris after the victory of Fontenoy the people were wild in their enthusiasm. They believed that as he had distinguished himself in the field of battle with Saxe, so would he at home with the aid of his government.

But Louis had come to an important turning point in his life without realising it. He had been brought up with an unswerving faith in the old régime; it did not occur to him that modern ideas were impinging on the old feudal system and that the tide of changing opinion which was sweeping over France must either take him with it or he – and the monarchy itself – be destroyed.

So slight yet was that tide of opinion that it was not noticeable on his return from Flanders. When the people applauded him, when they showed so clearly their faith in him, it did not occur to him that the philosophers and thinkers were beginning to sow discord in the very heart of the nation.

Louis could have sensed this as quickly as anyone, but he did not want to exert himself. He wanted to return to pleasure, particularly now that he had a new companion to share it with him.

He did not hear the faint rumbling beneath the applause of the crowd. He would not recognise that the people were beginning to wonder why the nobility should not only hold the highly remunerative posts of state but be exempt from taxes. The rigid and foolish Etiquette which existed at Versailles was an outward sign of an unhealthy state. There were too many different classes in France, so that even among the lowliest there was envy and complaint. In such a society the continual cry from the lower strata was to replace it by one in which social distinctions had no place.

Food was being so heavily taxed that many went hungry. There was a growing complaint that the taxes were paid by the poor. Reforms were urgentiy needed. Louis was wise enough to realise that none of his ministers could supply what was needed. A new régime was clamouring to be born. Wise reforms might have brought about a bloodless revolution. The people were solidly behind the King, but the King had no belief in his ability to govern his people.

Always he had shrunk from responsibility. Now he left the solution of the nation's problems to his ministers while he set about the pleasant task of raising the Marquise de Pompadour to the place at Court he had chosen for her.

✢ ✢ ✢

The Marquise swept along the *Oeil-de-Boeuf*. In her delicately tinted gown, glittering with diamonds, she looked like a porcelain figure, so graceful, so slender, her colouring exquisite.

Lotus received her in the Galerie des Glaces; and never, he thought, had any looked so lovely as his little *bourgeoise*. Not a fault in the curtsey, no sign of trepidation. She might have lived all her life at Court.

She made her curtsey and, as he bent his head to speak to her, she was smiling. She knew he was thinking: This is another of our happiest days.

It was more of an ordeal to be presented to the Queen. Jeanne-Antoinette knew that every movement she made, every expression was noted and commented on by those who had assembled to watch her presentation.

They were wondering now how the Queen would deal with this young nobody who had captured the King and who was to be the chief lady at Court.

The Queen, herself agleam with diamonds though she was, could not have made a greater contrast to this dazzling young beauty. Her cold eyes surveyed the woman while Jeanne-Antoinette raised hers timidly.

But she is humble, thought Marie. It is more than Châteauroux and Vintimille were. She has a sweet face and gives herself no airs, and as there has to be a mistress, why not this woman?

When the Queen spoke graciously to her, Jeanne-Antoinette was unprepared.

'Your . . . Your Majesty is most gracious to me,' she stammered.

'I welcome you to Court,' said the Queen. 'I have heard you are very talented. You play, sing and act, I hear. That is interesting. One day you shall perform for me.'

Those watching were astonished. Not only the King but the Queen was accepting this low-born woman.

'It would be a great honour to . . . to do so . . . before Your Majesty,' said Jeanne-Antoinette; and although others might titter at the stammer, the Queen liked to hear it. It showed that the woman had not too exalted an idea of her own importance . . . yet.

She bowed her head and made to turn away.

Jeanne-Antoinette took her cue; she knew what was expected of her. She sank to her knees and slightly lifting the Queen's skirt kissed its hem.

The presentation was over. Jeanne-Antoinette, Marquise de Pompadour, was free to come to Court.

❧ ❧ ❧

The carriage drew up outside the Hôtel de Gesvres, and Jeanne-Antoinette alighted and hurried into the house.

'*Maman,*' she called. '*Maman,* where are you?'

Madame Poisson rose hastily from her bed.

She called to the servants: 'Bring the Marquise to me.'

The Marquise! Now she always referred to her daughter thus, enjoying a thrill of delight every time she did so.

Now she is there, she would tell herself many times a day, nothing else matters. I am content to go.

As Jeanne-Antoinette ran into the room, her mother thought: The loveliest creature I ever set eyes on! And she is mine . . . my own little girl. My own little Marquise.

'Well, little love?' she cried, embracing her daughter. 'Tell me all about it.'

'Were you resting, *Maman?*'

'Oh . . . just a little nap, you know. I'm not so young as Madame la Marquise.'

Jeanne-Antoinette laughed. 'The first part was easy,' she

said. 'One has to walk carefully though. One step out of place, and that would be a scandal.'

'Show me how you do it, little love,' said Madame Poisson. Jeanne began walking across the room. Her mother put her hand to her side. She could not tell her now. Her dear affectionate little Marquise . . . it would break her heart.

'What is it, *Maman*?'

'Nothing . . . I'm watching. So that's how you did it, is it? And what did His Majesty say?'

'Oh, he was kind enough. But the Queen . . .'

Madame Poisson was struggling to appear attentive, but the pain, which had been growing worse during the last weeks, would intrude.

I shall have to tell her sometime, she thought. But not now . . . Not on a day such as this.

As the months passed Jeanne-Antoinette gave herself up to the life in which she knew she must excel because it was her destiny to do so. That did not mean that she did not make every effort to fulfil her task to perfection. She had loved the King before she saw him, and to know him meant the strengthening of that love. His charm was irresistible; his gentle courtesy never failed to enchant her, but his continued sensuality, after the first weeks, was a little alarming. She would not confess to any – not even herself – that she found the tempo exhausting and that it had begun to make her uneasy.

She had determined that there should always be complete harmony between them. She would never speak harshly as had Madame de Vintimille, never domineer as had Madame de Châteauroux, and never bore him as had Madame de Mailly.

She had discovered something of the man beneath that shell of courtesy and charm. The fatalistic streak in the King had made itself apparent. He believed that what was to be would be; he could do nothing about it. She had discovered too, in spite of that air of almost sacred royalty, that he had little belief in himself as a ruler. His confidence was tragically lacking, and for these reasons he was not the man to bestir himself to avoid any calamity. Thus it was that he was ever ready to give way to his ministers. Such traits were not those which went to the making of a great ruler.

But Madame de Pompadour would never try to change his nature as her predecessors had done. She gave herself to the great task of pleasing him, and providing continual entertainment so that the bogy of melancholy and boredom might be kept at bay. Only thus, she believed, could she keep her place. She must make every possible effort to become his friend, the companion who could always offer him diversion; and, when he asked for it, advice. She wished to make herself an amalgam of all the women whom he had loved. She must be mistress, wife, mother, companion, serious and lighthearted; she must learn to fulfil the need of the moment.

Because she felt herself to have been chosen from her birth to fill this role, she had no doubt that providing she gave herself completely to it, she could succeed. There was only one of many duties in which she feared she might fail. Oddly enough this was in her role as mistress.

Louis had perhaps been slow in reaching manhood; but he was now near the climax of full vigour. Jeanne-Antoinette began to wonder how, after succumbing to those onslaughts of passion, she would be able to rise from her bed full of energy to plan entertainments for the King, when her inclination was to rest for half the next day.

She had an uneasy feeling within her that Louis could not be satisfied with one woman. And then? . . .

But she would wait and face that problem when it was nearer. In the meantime she must consolidate her position at Versailles; she must make herself indispensable to the King.

She was now taking charge of those parties in the *petits appartements*. Instead of allowing the Comédie Française to bring its shows to Versailles, she organised theatrical entertainments in which members of the Court took part, thus giving an added pleasure not only to those who performed but also to those who watched. She herself always took a prominent part, so that she might display to the King this further talent of hers.

There was no doubt that Louis was becoming more and more enamoured of the Marquise de Pompadour.

On one occasion when she played the chief part in a play and was taking the curtain call at the end, Louis went onto the stage and there, before the audience, kissed her tenderly.

The Court began to say that Madame la Marquise was firmly established; that never yet had Louis been so enamoured of any woman as he was of La Pompadour.

It would not have been in the nature of Jeanne-Antoinette to forget her family, and she was determined that they should all profit from her good fortune.

She wished there was something she could do for Charles-Guillaume, but she knew there was nothing short of returning to him, and that of course was out of the question. But there were the others.

They might sneer at her at Court and call her 'Miss Fish'. Let them! They could only do it secretly. Louis was ready to show acute displeasure to any who did not treat her with the utmost respect. She was eager not to make enemies.

She said to the King one day: 'But for Monsieur de Tourneheim we should never have met. I should probably have starved to death if he had not given my mother help when she needed it.'

'Do not even speak of such a calamity,' murmured the King.

'I would like to show him my gratitude.'

'Show him *our* gratitude,' was the answer.

'He has said that he would like to be the Director of Public Works. I wonder if . . .'

'From this moment he *is* the Director of Public Works.'

'I do not know how to thank you for all you have done for me.'

'It is I, my dear, who owe thanks to you.'

It was as simple as that.

'My father should have an estate in the country.'

'And so he shall.'

'As for my brother . . . if he came to Court, opportunities would occur for him.'

So it was arranged; a country estate for François Poisson, the Directorate of Public Works for Monsieur de Tourneheim, a place at Court for Abel.

Her two children should have their share of glory when the time came. In the meantime they were being well looked after by Madame Poisson. Perhaps they should be put into the hands of someone who could teach them the ways of the nobility to which before long they should be elevated. But not yet, thought Jeanne-Antoinette. They should not be taken from their grandmother yet, although she of course would see, as clearly as her daughter, that one day they must be.

And Madame Poisson, who had for so long shared her daughter's dreams and, as no other, shared her triumph, what should she be given?

The Marquise smiled tenderly. She already had her reward, for every triumph which came to her daughter was *hers*. She asked nothing more than to see her firm in the place which, for so many years, they had believed she was destined to occupy.

❖ ❖ ❖

Jeanne-Antoinette called at the Hôtel de Gesvres. This was going to be one of the happiest events of the last months. She was going to tell them of the good fortune which was about to spread before them.

But when she arrived at the house she was surprised that there was none of the family to greet her. She was immediately aware of the unusual quiet.

'Tell Madame Poisson that I am here,' she commanded the servant.

She noticed that the servant – who usually seemed overcome by embarrassment when she appeared, as though she were a stranger and not Mademoiselle Jeanne-Antoinette who had once been a member of the household – no longer seemed aware of the importance of the Marquise.

François Poisson appeared. He looked at his daughter in dismay, and said gruffly: 'We had not thought you would come today.'

'What has happened? What are you trying to keep from me?'

'It was her wish. "Don't tell the Marquise", she said.' He laughed without mirth. 'It was always "the Marquise this" and "the Marquise that". I said to her "She's only our Jeanne-Antoinette, and she ought to know the truth – she will have to one day."'

'The truth!'

'Ah, she puts on a very fine show when you come here, does she not? She pays for it after. I don't know how she managed to keep it from you. The pain . . . it is getting too much for her.'

Jeanne-Antoinette could listen to no more; she dashed past François, and was in her mother's bedroom.

Madame Poisson was lying in bed; her face was a dull yellow colour, her hair lustreless.

'*Maman* . . . *Maman* . . .' cried Jeanne-Antoinette. 'What is this? . . . What *is* this? . . .'

'There there,' murmured Madame Poisson, stroking her daughter's hair. 'Don't grieve, my lovely. It had to be. You should have let me know you were coming. I would have been up to greet you.'

Jeanne-Antoinette lifted her head and her mother saw the tears running down her cheeks.

'Don't . . . don't . . . my little beauty. Must not spoil your lovely face with tears for your old mother. Nothing to be sad about. I am not, dear one. I am happy . . . so proud. Dearest little Marquise . . .' She chuckled. 'We did it, did we not! You are there . . . just as we always said you would be.'

'*Maman* . . . I had come with such good news for you all. And this . . . and this . . .'

'It is nothing. I should not have let you see me thus. Had I known . . .'

'Do not say that. You should have let me know . . . Something could have been done.'

Madame Poisson shook her head. 'No, dearest Marquise, not all the King's power, nor his riches could save old Maman Poisson. It is the end for her. It had to come, you see. But do not grieve, sweet Marquise. It was such a happy life. And see what its end has brought me . . . all that I asked. How many can say that, dearest, eh, tell me that.'

She gripped a hand of the Marquise and it seemed as though she drew new life from her lovely daughter.

'Nothing to be sad for . . . nothing. My dearest, the beloved of the King . . . the first woman of France! How many women die as I die? I am one of Fortune's favourites, my dearest. I lived happy and I die happy. Remember that, and give me the last thing I shall ask of you.'

'Oh, *Maman*, dearest . . . I would give everything . . . to see you well again.'

'Bah! Life must end for us all. Those who die happy can ask no greater bliss than that. But this one request. You have promised.' Jeanne-Antoinette nodded. 'Shed no more tears for me. That is what I ask. When you think of me say this : "That which she asked from life was given to her, and she died happy".'

Everyone had noticed the change in Anne-Henriette during the last year. They knew that the difference was due to the Chevalier de St Georges. The Court was tolerant towards Madame Seconde, but at the same time it was deplorable that the poor child should have shown her feelings so blatantly; such conduct hardly accorded with the sacred Etiquette of Versailles.

Anne-Henriette was so gentle, so affectionate; scarcely like a royal princesse. The family loved her, they could not help it; but since her friendship with Charles Edward Stuart it had been a great joy to see her taking more interest in life.

A marriage between the Stuart and the Princesse of France? Why not? If the Stuart cause were successful, Charles Edward would be his father's heir and King of Britain. Therefore Anne-Henriette would have more chance of forming an alliance with the young Prince than she had had with the Orléans family.

Anne-Henriette herself believed this was so. Her father had implied that a British marriage would be welcome. One could not have too many allies, and the best way of cementing friendship between two countries was by such marriages. But of course Charles Edward must win his crown before he could aspire to the hand of a Princesse of France.

So she followed his adventures with exultation; she was certain that before long he would be victorious, and then he would come back for her, and that happiness, which she had once thought had passed her by for ever, would be hers.

Dear Papa! thought Anne-Henriette. He wanted Charles Edward to succeed if only for the sake of his daughter. He had lent ships and would have done more but, as he had explained to her, it would not be good politics to offend the existing British King.

So Charles Edward had landed in Scotland, and she had heard that Scotland was for him, that he was in England and had taken Carlisle and Derby, that he was within ninety-four miles of London itself, and that the people were lethargic and not anxious to take up arms in defence of the German or in support of the Stuart.

He will win his crown, Anne-Henriette told herself; and when he has done so, he will return to France. She remembered his words to her: 'Not to plead for a refuge, not to plead for arms and money. But still to plead with the King, your Father.'

Soon, prayed Anne-Henriette. And she dreamed that she saw him with the crown on his head and his Queen beside him – Anne-Henriette, Queen of Britain.

There was all that excitement at Versailles which attended a royal birth. This was a very important one. The birth of an heir to the Dauphin.

The Dauphin was beside himself with delight. This, he told himself, was all he needed to make his happiness complete. A child for himself and Marie-Thérèse Raphaëlle. If it were a boy, that would indeed be perfection, but they would be happy with a girl.

There was only one anxiety, and that was for his beloved wife. He suffered as acutely as she did. Thus it was when one loved.

The rest of the Court might not appreciate his wife. What cared she for that – or what cared he? She had been chosen for him, he for her, and he could laugh now to remember their suspicions of each other. How odd that seemed now!

In two years they had grown to love each other, and so deep was this love that they cared nothing for the opinion of anyone else. Let them smile at his serious ways; let them insist that he was only a boy. Let them say she was plain, dull, lacking the grace which would commend her at Versailles. For him she had perfect beauty, perfect grace. Let the rakes and the roués laugh at the love between two young people. There could only be jealousy of such love because they had either missed it or forgotten what it meant.

And now . . . a child to share this bliss. But she must suffer first and her suffering was his.

But it could not be long now.

Up and down his apartment he paced. They could smile at the young husband's anxiety, but they could not understand it. Nor would he mask it from them lest that should seem a disloyalty to her.

To love like this was to suffer. This anguish was the price which was asked for so much happiness.

It shall be the last, he told himself. Never again shall she suffer thus, shall I suffer thus. What do we care for heirs? What do we care for France? With love such as ours we can only care for each other.

Afterwards he would tell her this. Never again, he would say. Never, never.

He heard the cry of a child, and he exulted. He heard the words: 'A girl. A daughter for the Dauphin.'

What did it matter that she had not borne a son? It was over and never, never, vowed the Dauphin, would they have another child, since it meant suffering such as this.

He was right. She bore him no more children, for a few days later she was dead.

A broken-hearted Dauphin was seen at Versailles, dazed by his wretchedness. He had lost her who had meant everything to him; he kept asking himself how life could be so cruel? She to die giving him a daughter who, it was clear, could not long survive her.

There was Anne-Henriette to comfort him, his gentle sister who had herself suffered. He could talk to her, and her only, of all that Marie-Thérèse-Raphaëlle had meant to him, because she understood.

And in a little while it was his turn to comfort her because the man she loved had met cruel defeat at the hands of the Duke of Cumberland on Culloden Moor, and Bonnie Prince Charlie, although he had escaped, was a wandering exile of whose whereabouts none could be sure. But there was one point about which everyone seemed certain.

Even if he lived, even if one day he returned to France, he would never win the throne which had once been the proud possession of his ancestors.

❋ ❋ ❋

The Marquise de Pompadour flitted about the Court, always in the centre of activity. Those who wished to find favour with the King paid homage to the Marquise. She showed no signs of the great anxiety which had begun to beset her.

At the end of the day she would feel exhausted. She could not understand these attacks of fatigue. She longed to bear children for the King, for he was a man who loved children and she believed that they would bind him closely to her.

She had had a miscarriage – a great misfortune to her, but a delight to her enemies. There was no time to lie abed and recover her strength, for she knew that her enemies were all about her waiting to put another in her place. Comte Phélippeaux de Maurepas, who had been in decline after his fracas with Madame de Châteauroux but who had crept back to Court, was one of her greatest enemies, and she believed that many of the lampoons and the songs about her, which were being sung in Paris, originated from this man. He should be dismissed; but she was eager not to make more enemies. Another who did not look on her with favour was Richelieu, that old friend of the King's; Richelieu liked to provide the King with mistresses – women who would use their influence on his behalf; he was piqued because the King had chosen a mistress without his help.

But she would try to make friends before she attempted to have anyone dismissed.

The King was still deeply in love with her. More than that, he showed a steady friendship towards her. It was this quality in their relationship which pleased her more than any. He could never have known a woman who studied his needs every minute of the day as she did. He had never yet been bored in her company. There was only one respect in which he found her lacking, and he had made a significant remark one night when, try as she might, she could not give a ready enough response to his passion. 'Why, my dear,' he said, 'you are as cold as your name.'

That reference to Mademoiselle Poisson had frightened her. She knew that at some time in the future there would have to be another woman. Oh, not another woman, other women. That would be the only safe way. His little *affaires* must not last more than a few days. And if they were with women far far below his rank they could never hope to replace her as his companion.

But she pushed these thoughts into the background. They were for the future.

In the meantime she was young, and she forced herself to keep up with the furious pace which was demanded of her.

She consulted experts on a diet which would have an

aphrodisiac effect, and she was eating a great many truffles. She was ready to face any discomfort for the sake of satisfying the King.

She brought Voltaire to Court. He was her ardent admirer, and she hoped that his plays might amuse the King, and that she might at the same time improve that writer's fortunes.

Voltaire however was unaccustomed to the rigid Etiquette of the Court and almost spoilt his chances of recognition.

The Marquise was to remember that night. They had put on *Le Temple de la Gloire* and she had arranged that it should be performed in the *petits appartements* to a very small audience.

This was a great honour for Voltaire, especially as he was invited.

The Marquise told the writer that she thought the play would please the King because one of the parts in it – Trajan – was meant to represent His Majesty.

Jeanne-Antoinette herself must play one of the goddesses – the principal goddess – because, tired as she was, she felt that she dared not let another woman parade her charm and talent before Louis.

In the excitement of the evening she forgot her tiredness, and her obvious talents for this sort of entertainment delighted the King. He was astonished by her versatility and did not hesitate to show his pleasure.

Unfortunately Voltaire – carried away by the success of his play and the lack of formality which was the custom in the *petits appartements* – went to the King and took his arm. 'Did you see yourself up there on the stage, Trajan?' he asked.

There was silence in the room while the Marquise felt her heart sink with dismay. Lack of formality there might be in the *petits appartements,* but that did not mean that guests forgot the identity of the King. The upstart writer had made a *faux pas* which would not be forgotten. Louis was embarrassed. He gently disengaged his arm and turned away without replying.

The evening had ceased to be a success.

Later, when they were alone, Louis said: 'We should never allow that man to come to Court again.'

Jeanne-Antoinette was filled with disappointment. She believed in the talent of Voltaire and had been hoping to do her old friend much good.

'He forgot his manners,' she said. 'But I trust, Louis, you will not hold that against him. He knows how to write, so could he not be forgiven for not knowing yet how to behave?'

'It was somewhat embarrassing,' murmured the King. Then he smiled at her. 'Madame la Marquise,' he went on, 'you have the best heart in the world. Let us say this: for a time we will have the plays at Court, not the man.' Then, seeing that she was still unhappy, he added: 'For a little time.'

'You are so good to me, Sire,' she murmured.

He left her in the early morning; and she lay alone in her bed feeling too tired even for sleep, yet enjoying the luxury of relaxing mind and body.

She began to cough. There had been attacks of coughing lately, although she had endeavoured to repress them in the presence of the King.

She put her flimsy white handkerchief to her lips, and when she withdrew it was horrified to see that it was flecked with blood.

The melancholy of the Dauphin was becoming a source of irritation at the Court. Moreover it was now considered necessary that he should provide an heir.

Louis sent for his son one day and reminded him of this.

The Dauphin shook his head. 'I want no other wife.'

'This is folly,' said the King. 'You talk like a shepherd. Of course you must have a wife, and we have one for you.'

The Dauphin showed no sign of curiosity, and the King went on: 'It is Marie-Josephe, daughter of Elector Frederick Augustus of Saxony. The Queen is not very pleased because, as you know, the father of this girl took the crown of Poland from your grandfather, Stanislas. Oh, come, show a little interest.'

'Father, I cannot show what I do not feel.'

The King lifted his shoulders in exasperation. 'The Duc de Richelieu has already left for Dresden,' he said. 'He will make the arrangements for your marriage, which will not be long delayed.'

Then with his irresistible charm Louis ceased to be the King and became the father. He laid his hand on the Dauphin's shoulder. 'Be of good cheer, my son,' he said. 'And remember this: every sorrow, no matter how great, must pass.'

Then the Dauphin only looked at him with disbelief in his melancholy eyes.

It was a frightened little girl of fifteen who was married to the Dauphin a few months later.

It was a terrifying ordeal to say goodbye to your home and come to a new country, particularly when the Queen of that country might not be friendly disposed because she remembered that your father had displaced hers.

But solemn little Marie-Josèphe was determined to be a good wife. She knew she was not beautiful, but neither had her predecessor been, and in two years *she* had succeeded in winning the love of the Dauphin. She herself was determined to do the same.

The Queen's coldness was apparent, but that was made up for by the warmth of the King's greeting. He seemed to understand exactly how a young girl would feel on leaving her home and her family. He implied that he would be a father to her and that he was very glad to have her with them.

There was another whom she noticed when she first made the acquaintance of the royal family – a sad-eyed girl in her late teens who embraced her warmly and with sympathy such as she had rarely encountered.

This was the Princesse Anne-Henriette, the Dauphin's sister, who came to her on the day of the wedding celebrations and told her how the Dauphin had loved his first wife and how bitterly he still mourned her.

'You must not be hurt,' said the Princesse, 'if he does not appear to be interested in you. If he were it would merely show his fickle nature. Be patient for a while and then, I know, one day he will love you as he loved her.'

'You are so kind to me,' said the frightened little bride. 'I cannot tell you what the friendship, which you and His Majesty have shown me, can mean when one is a long way from home.'

'To be sent from home,' murmured Anne-Henriette. 'It is something we Princesses all have to fear. It hangs over us like a shadow, does it not?'

And she was thinking that, had she been called upon to

leave home for England, to be the wife of Charles Edward, she would have been completely happy. Where was he now? A fugitive . . . hiding from the Hanoverian forces. One day though he would drive the German usurper from the throne; the real Kings, the noble Stuarts, would reign again in England; and when that happened he would not forget the French Princesse whom he had promised to make his Queen.

The little Dauphine was watching her. 'I am sorry,' said Anne-Henriette. 'My thoughts were far away.'

And the young bride put her hands in those of her sister-in-law and smiled at her. It is strange, thought Anne-Henriette, that because we are both afraid of the future we can give courage to each other.

✤ ✤ ✤

The ceremony of putting the newly married couple to bed was over. The Dauphine trembled, for as yet the Dauphin had scarcely spoken to her.

He hates me, she thought; and fervently she wished that she were home at the court of her father.

The Dauphin was lying at one side of the bed; she was at the other. It seemed as though he wanted to put as great a distance between them as possible.

Neither of them spoke, but at last she could endure the silence no longer and she said: 'I am sorry. I did not want to marry any more than you did. I did not want to come to France. I cannot help it. It was not my wish.'

Still he said nothing. Then she saw that the tears were quietly falling down his cheeks.

To see him cry like that made her feel that he was younger

than she was, in more need of comfort, and she forgot the greater part of her fears.

She stretched out a hand and timidly touched his arm.

'I am sorry,' she said. 'I know how you feel.'

He turned slightly towards her then. 'How can you know?'

'Perhaps,' she said, 'because I love my family. I know what it is to love people and to lose them.'

'You cannot know what it is to lose Marie-Therese.'

'I do know. You loved her dearly, and she died. You feel you will never be happy again.'

He nodded, and suddenly he threw himself down upon his pillow and began to sob. 'No one understands . . . no one . . . no one!'

'I understand,' she said, and stroked the hair back from his forehead. 'Poor little Dauphin, I understand.'

He did not reject her caress and she continued to stroke his hair.

'You . . . you will despise me,' he said.

Then it seemed to the young girl that she had acquired new wisdom. 'No,' she told him, 'I shall not. I respect you for loving her so much. It shows me that you are a good person . . . that . . . that if I am a good wife to you I shall have nothing to fear. You might in time love me like this. That makes me happy, for when *she* first came you did not love her any more than you love me.'

The Dauphin turned his face away from her, and every now and then his body heaved with his sobs.

She bent over him. 'Please . . . you must not try to suppress your grief. It does not matter if you show it to me. I understand. It makes me happy that you loved her so much.'

The Dauphin did not answer. But he took her hand and held it to his hot, damp cheek.

And that night the Dauphin, mourning his first wife, cried himself to sleep in the arms of the second.

✤ ✤ ✤

So necessary had the Marquise de Pompadour become to the King's comfort that she found herself rich, courted and almost first minister of France. In every château she had her special apartments, and she had already acquired the châteaux of Selle and Crécy and had spent a great deal of money in embellishing them.

She became noted for her extravagance, for the desire to possess beautiful things had always been with her, and in the past she had often dreamed of what she would do when she was in that position which was now hers.

Abel was now at Court and had been given the title of Marquis de Vandières; but he was uneasy.

'I find it embarrassing,' he told his sister, 'to be treated as such an important person, not because I have done anything to make me so, but because of my relationship with you.'

'You *are* important,' she told him gaily. 'If anyone shows disrespect to you, I shall be very angry with them.'

'That is the point,' he told her sadly. 'They do not show their contempt, but I feel they despise me all the same.'

Poor Abel! He lacked the ambition of herself and her mother.

'I should be content,' he told her, 'if I might become Director of Public Works when Lenormant gives up. That would be enough for me.'

'I am angry with my family,' she told him. 'I want to help them so much, and they will not let me.' She was sad thinking of the loss of her mother and her little son, who had died recently. She would have insisted on their joining in her good fortune. There was her little daughter Alexandrine; a good marriage should be made for her.

As for François Poisson, he could have had a title had he wished.

He had laughed when she had suggested this to him; he told her he was happy enough on his country estates, and asked for nothing more.

'The Marquis of this . . . the Comte of that! Oh, that's not for me. I'll stay plain Poisson. Don't worry about old François. You get on with your whoring at the Palace. I'll keep out of the way, but I'll remain old Poisson.'

Surely, she thought, a woman in my coveted position had never had a family which demanded less!

Meanwhile she continued to reign at Court, and how happy she was when she and the King could escape from the wearying Etiquette of Versailles. What pleasure to sit down to a meal in the *petits appartements* without the presence of the *officiers de la bouche* – those five servants who must taste every dish before it was served to the King – or of the *officiers du goblet,* five others whose duty it was to taste the wine.

The poor Queen had not the opportunity of escaping from Etiquette as had the King. Perhaps she was more patient and accepted it more readily. She had not been at Trianon for many months because a dispute was in progress, between her governor there and her fruit-woman, as to who should supply the candles for the house. It was a fine point of Etiquette, as candles must not be supplied by the wrong person; and until the dispute was settled there could be no candles for Trianon.

The whole Court had heard of the affair of the Queen's counterpane on her official bed, and no one thought it extraordinary. She had noticed that the counterpane was dusty and pointed this out to one of her ladies. The complaint was passed on to the *valet de chambre tapissier* who declared that it was not his duty to remove such dust, as the counterpane was not *tapisserie* but *meuble,* and must therefore be removed by a *garde meuble*. A controversy then ensued, between the guards of the furniture, to discover whose duty it was to dust the counterpane; for, if a servant had performed this duty when it was another's, it would have been considered a breach of Etiquette, and it was the constant desire of the lower stratum at Versailles punctiliously to ape the upper.

Thus again and again ridiculous situations ensued; but Etiquette was sacred and no one did anything about reforming such silly rules.

There was one occasion when the Marquise feared that she and the King would find themselves in a very difficult situation and that they might be guilty of one of the worst breaches of Etiquette it was possible to make.

They had supped in the *petits appartements;* the King had eaten well and drunk even better. It was one of those delightful occasions when, as far as possible, Etiquette was ignored at the feast.

The Marquise had been at her most vivacious and delightful, and the King had early given the order '*Allons nous coucher*' that he might be alone with her.

The formal *coucher* in his state bedroom had been completed and the King joined Madame de Pompadour in her own apartment.

'Ah,' he cried, stretching himself out on the bed, 'what pleasure it is to escape! My dearest Marquise, I grow more and more weary of the formality of Versailles. I love my château beyond all, but always there is the unbidden tutor at my elbow: Etiquette.'

'Your Majesty should dispense with it.'

'I do on every possible occasion.'

'On all occasions, perhaps,' she told him.

'The people would never allow it. They think of us as puppets . . . always clad in brocade and velvet, continually receiving the bows, curtsies and homage of those about us, and that is what we are doing.' He yawned. 'The wine was good tonight.'

'And Your Majesty showed his approval of it.'

'Was I somewhat intoxicated?'

She knelt by the bed and looked at him with that adoring expression which gave him such delight.

'As usual your manners were perfect. It would be impossible for them to be otherwise.'

'My dear,' he said, 'how beautiful you look! Why do you kneel there? I would have you come nearer.'

She smiled and rose.

While she removed her gown she said: 'One day I shall show you my little Alexandrine.'

'You love this daughter of yours dearly,' he said. 'Is she as beautiful as you are? But that is impossible.'

'Alexandrine is remarkably ugly. I am not sorry. I do not wish her to be a great beauty.'

'That is a strange thing for a fond mother to say.'

'No,' said the Marquise, half closing her eyes. 'Great beauties have many enemies. I should like Alexandrine to live quietly and peacefully. My mother had ambitions for me, and I achieved them. Mine for my daughter are quite different. I hope I shall achieve them too.'

'I suppose,' said the King, 'you want a noble husband for her.'

'I shall want to choose him with care,' she said. 'He must be worthy of her.'

'Rich, noble . . . powerful,' murmured the King.

'And kind,' she added. 'I would have her husband as kind to her as my King has been to me.'

Now the King's eyes glistened, for there was nothing but her abundant hair to cover her exquisite form, and charmingly it failed to do so.

The King held out his hand and she went to him.

It was an hour later when she discovered that all was not well with Louis. He was gasping for breath, and hastily lighting a candle she saw his face was purple.

She cried: 'Louis . . . Louis . . . what is wrong?'

He managed to stammer: 'Hurry . . . Send for a doctor.' But immediately he remembered Etiquette was intruding upon them. 'Say it is *you* who are ill,' he added urgently.

She nodded, understanding, and called to one of her women. 'Bring Dr Quesnay at once,' she told her. 'Do not say that the King is ill. Say that I am.'

The doctor arrived and was astonished to be greeted by the Marquise. 'Madame,' he stammered, 'what is this illness of yours?'

'Hush, I pray you. It is His Majesty.'

Quesnay went to the bed and examined the King. He gave

Louis a pill and asked for cold water with which to bathe his face.

The Marquise stood trembling by the bed.

'Monsieur,' she cried, 'I pray you tell me . . . how bad is he?'

The doctor looked grim. 'Too much indulgence must be paid for. The King takes too much pleasure.' He lifted his shoulders. 'He is still a young man, and that is fortunate. If he were sixty you would have had a dead man in your bed this night, Madame.'

Louis called to the doctor. 'Help me to rise,' he said. 'I must go back to my own bedchamber. If I am going to be ill it must not be here.'

When he had drunk several cups of tea which the Marquise's woman had prepared on the doctor's orders, Louis was taken back to his bedchamber by Quesnay. The Marquise, anxious as she was about the King's health, could not help shuddering to contemplate the awful calamity which the scandal of the King's dying in his mistress's bed would have caused, for Etiquette would be outraged if any king of France died elsewhere than in the state bed. All that night Quesnay was with the King, and in the morning the Marquise received a tender note from her lover.

'My dearest,' wrote Louis, 'what a fright we both had! But I send this note to you by the doctor so that he may assure you that all is well . . .'

It seemed strange that Etiquette could have seemed so important to them both at such a time; yet such was its hold over the Court that it could dominate all occasions.

It was no small part of the life at Versailles. None would have been surprised to hear that the King and the Marquise had spent the night together; indeed had they not done so the Court would have been buzzing with the news. Yet one of the greatest scandals possible would have been for the King to die in his mistress's bed.

Remove such unreasonable conventions? As easy to take away the foundations of the magnificent honey-coloured château itself.

♣ Chapter XI ♣

PRINCE CHARLES EDWARD STUART

There was news at last of the Chevalier de St Georges. He had arrived on French soil, and the Court prepared itself to receive him. Because Britain was an enemy of France at this time a brilliant reception should be given to the young man whom the Hanoverian King in London feared more than any other.

Anne-Henriette's feelings were a mixture of joy and apprehension. It was so long since she had seen him, and she had imagined his return would be so different from this. She had dreamed of his coming to France as the heir to the throne of Britain to ask the French King for the hand of his daughter.

This was quite another matter and she was unsure of her father's real feelings towards the young Prince. This welcome was extended, it was true, but was it because he was fond of Charles Edward, or as a snub to his enemy across the water?

Politically it was an advantage to shelter one who laid claim to an enemy's crown. Was that why her father had ordered that a grand welcome should be given the young man?

She had not dared speak to her father of possible marriage. He did not like to think of the marriage of his daughters. If the subject were raised he would frown and say: 'They are young yet.' He often talked of Louise-Elisabeth in Spain. 'What good has that marriage brought her?' he demanded. 'We might have kept her at home with us. I like to have my daughters around me.'

Adelaide came to her sister. She wanted to talk secrets, so in her imperious way she ordered the attendants out of the room.

Adelaide was very pretty. People were right when they said she was the prettiest of the Princesses. But sometimes there was a wildness in her expression which seemed a little alarming to gentle Anne-Henriette.

She retained much of the waywardness of her early childhood when, after she had been allowed to stay at Versailles while her younger sisters had been sent to Fontevrault, she had been rather spoiled by her father and the rest of the Court who thought they could seek Louis' favours through his favourite daughter.

Anne-Henriette had seen Adelaide lie on the floor and kick when she could not get her own way, which was very distressing to the servants, who were afraid of offending her. When Anne-Henriette had pointed this out to her, Adelaide had looked astonished. 'How else should I get what I wanted?' she demanded.

One could never be quite sure what Adelaide would do next. She had the maddest ideas and never paused to consider them very seriously before trying to put them into action.

Anne-Henriette, contemplating that occasion a few years ago when her young sister had really intended to run away from Versailles and join the army, trembled for her future. Only Adelaide could be so brave and so innocent, so wildly imaginative and so utterly ignorant.

Adelaide had heard much talk of the English who, although the Austrians were the most detested of France's enemies, were the most feared.

'I hate the English,' she declared to her *gouvernante*. 'I hate them more than anyone in the world, because they make my Papa anxious.'

She had sat intent while with her *gouvernante* she read the story of Judith, the beautiful daughter of Merari who, fascinating Holofernes, lured him to her bed and when he slept killed him.

After reading that she went about for some days, obviously brooding, so that everyone asked: 'What is wrong with Madame Adelaide?'

But she told no one what was going on in her turbulent brain, and a few days later Adelaide was missing.

There had been great consternation at Court. All sorts of theories had been brought forward. One was that Adelaide had been kidnapped. The King's daughter, stolen from Versailles under the very eyes of the Court!

All Paris was angry. This child, this beautiful Princess, to be lured from her home. For what purpose? It was said that she had been stolen by France's enemies, that she would be held for a ransom. The distracted King sent out search parties and himself joined in the search.

And then . . . Adelaide was discovered on the road not far from Versailles itself.

She was brought back, to the joy of the family and France, but much to her disgust.

She had tried to elude her captors, commanding them to leave her, declaring that she had work to do and ordering them to stand aside.

But on such an occasion even the imperious Adelaide could not have her way, and she was taken back to the Palace.

The King embraced her; she clung to him because he was the one person whom she could not resist. In her eyes he was perfect, and she made no secret of her love for him.

'But why did you cause us this anxiety?' asked Louis. 'How could you? My child, did you not consider how anxious we were?'

'It was to be a secret until it was done,' she told him. 'I was going to bring the King of England to you . . . in chains, Papa.'

Her eyes flashed, and it did occur to those watching that perhaps Madame Adelaide was a little unbalanced.

'But, my dear, how could you, a little girl, do that?'

'I was going to be like Judith. She did it. Why should not I? She did it with Holofernes, but I would have done it with all the English lords except the King, for then he would have been alone without anyone to help him, so I should have had him put in chains and brought to Your Majesty. You would not have been annoyed with me then, Papa, would you?' she turned to scowl at those who had brought her to the King. 'But these people brought me back. They should be put into dungeons, Papa, because it is due to them that the English are not beaten.'

The King shook his head and looked at her, half amused, half exasperated.

'But how did you propose to conquer the English?' he asked.

'It is easy. I should invite all the lords to sleep with me . . . not together of course, that would have been folly.'

'I . . . I should hope so,' said the King weakly.

'One by one,' she confided, 'and then . . . when they were asleep I should simply have cut off their heads.'

There was a titter from the courtiers. 'My dear child,' said the King, 'it would perhaps have been more seemly to challenge each in turn to a duel.'

She considered this, smiling to see herself, sword in hand cutting off English head after English head. 'But no, Papa,' she said at length. 'You know you have forbidden duelling; therefore it would be sinful to fight *duels.*'

The King looked at his daughter helplessly. He wondered then whether her education had been in the best possible hands. Perhaps it had been unwise to allow her to stay at Versailles when her sisters were in the care of the nuns, and to have given way to her on so many occasions.

She was twelve years old when she had planned to lure the English to her tent and cut off their heads one by one. Perhaps, thought Anne-Henriette, at twelve she should have had a more practical outlook, a more balanced knowledge of the world.

That had happened a few years ago, and now Adelaide was considering what the return of Charles Edward Stuart was going to mean to Anne-Henriette.

Adelaide stood before her sister in her rose-tinted dress which was embroidered with gold-coloured stars.

'What is going to happen when he comes to Versailles?' asked Adelaide.

'I do not know,' Anne-Henriette replied.

'I wonder whether you will be allowed to marry him.'

'I do not know.'

Adelaide murmured. 'I do not think you will be, Anne-Henriette.'

The elder Princesse shook her head. 'I have come to believe that in love I am ill-fated.'

'First Chartres, and now Prince Charles Edward. Why, sister, you are indeed unfortunate. I tell you what I would do, were I in your place. I would sell all my jewels and lay my hands on other people's, and one night I would leave the Palace and go with him to England.'

'And invite all the great captains to my couch, that I might cut off their heads?' said Anne-Henriette with a smile.

'Well,' Adelaide defended herself, 'it would be better than staying here to mourn. I will tell you something, sister. Even if the Prince came back as heir to the throne of Britain, Papa would not consent to your marriage.'

'Oh, but then everything would be so different. Then all our troubles would be over.'

Adelaide looked grave. 'No, Anne-Henriette. Even then Papa would not agree to your marriage. He will never agree to any of us marrying.'

'That's nonsense. We have to marry one day. Louise-Elisabeth married.'

'And Papa is continually regretting it.'

'That is because she has not yet had all the honours he wished for her.'

Adelaide shook her head and her wild eyes looked cunning. 'Oh, no.' She laughed suddenly. 'Our sister is very beautiful, they say. And, do you know, Papa is very pleased when he hears of her beauty. He was furious though when he was told of a certain scandal in which our sister was involved.'

'Adelaide . . . Adelaide . . . what's going on in your head?'

'You need not look at me like that. I know more about affairs than you do. I know more about Papa. I know more about him than anyone else in the world. I'll tell you why. It is because I love him. Nobody loves him as I do. He is the most handsome man in the world. There is nobody I would want to marry but Papa.'

'You talk like a baby, Adelaide. Only children want to marry their parents.'

'And you . . . you,' cried Adelaide, 'you think as you have been taught to think. Why should not parents love their children more than anyone in the world? They belong to each other. I love the King. I will never love anyone as I love him. And he loves me . . . and you, and Louise-Elisabeth too. That was why he was so angry when he heard that she had a love affair with the Ambassador, Monsieur de Vaureal.'

'Naturally he was angry. He would be sorry if scandal touched any of us.'

'But Papa's anger is different from that of our mother. Do you not know?'

'Adelaide, what nonsense is in your head now?'

Adelaide had become haughty, full of dignity, as she could without a moment's warning.

'If you will not listen, then do not do so. I will say this: Papa will never agree to your marriage with Charles Edward . . . nor to anyone else. Nor my marriage either.'

With that Adelaide inclined her head and walked with the utmost dignity from the room.

⚜ ⚜ ⚜

They danced — Anne-Henriette and Charles Edward Stuart — at the ball given at Versailles in his honour.

He looked older, but he was still very attractive and, in scarlet velvet and gold brocade, his person dazzling with jewels, he looked more like a powerful visiting prince than an exile.

In attendance were a few – a very few – Scottish noblemen who behaved as though they were his pathetic little court. He had his servants attired in the royal livery of Britain and he wore the Order of St George.

As their hands touched in the dance, Anne-Henriette's anguished eyes met his; he had changed, she knew. This was not the idealistic Prince whom she had loved in the early part of 1745. Even the way he looked at her had changed. Was there a certain speculation in his eyes?

Was he thinking: What hope of marrying the girl? How much help would the King of France be prepared to give to his daughter?

Anne-Henriette was gentle, but that did not mean she was lacking in perception. She saw those looks.

She said: 'I hear my father has put a house in Paris at your disposal.'

'In the Faubourg St Antoine,' he said. 'His Majesty is generous. There is an allowance to go with the house. So you see, Madame Anne-Henriette, I shall have time to make further plans.'

'You are making those plans?' she asked eagerly.

'One always makes plans.'

'In your position . . . yes.'

'It is the greatest regret to me that I have to return thus.'

'I had such high hopes. You were so near London.'

He shook his head sadly and she thought of the romantic stories she had heard of his adventures in the Island of Skye.

'News was brought to us from time to time,' she told him. 'Your friend Flora MacDonald . . . she . . . she was very good to you.'

'I owe her my life,' he said, and for a moment it seemed as

though the young Prince had taken the place of this dis-illusioned man.

He was thinking of Flora, the bravery, the resource of Flora; he was thinking of himself, almost suffocated by the garments of a serving maid – Plump Betty Bourke, maid to Flora MacDonald. And thus they had come through dangers together.

When he thought of those days, this young Princesse seemed like a child to him. One could not live as he had lived, suffer as he had suffered, and remain idealistic, believing in simple love as this girl did.

He had left something of the charming and romantic Prince on Culloden Moor, with those brave men who now lay buried there, victims of the Butcher Cumberland.

He could only look at this young girl and think: If her father would permit the marriage he could not fail to do everything within his power to help me regain the throne.

He let a mask slip over his face. 'What joy,' he said, 'it is to be back at Versailles. I do not believe I could know greater joy than this. A throne . . . my rightful throne . . . if it were now mine – it could not bring me the joy I now experience with your hand in mine.'

The ecstasy which had touched her face was very fleeting; then, although she smiled at him, there was a certain sadness in that smile.

✤ ✤ ✤

The King received his guest with accustomed charm.

'I trust,' he said, 'that you are comfortable in the Faubourg St Antoine.'

'Very much so, Sire.'

300

'I am glad to hear it.'

'I owe so much to Your Majesty's munificence, and having tasted your generosity, Sire, there is one other matter about which I dare approach you.'

Louis looked embarrassed. He guessed the nature of this request, and it was going to be unpleasant to refuse it. He thought too of Anne-Henriette, his dear daughter who, when her friendship with this young man began to blossom, had ceased to mourn the loss of the Duc de Chartres.

'It concerns the Princesse, Sire,' went on Charles Edward.

Louis looked at him steadily. 'I hope soon to receive a visit from my eldest daughter,' he said. 'That will give me great pleasure. I often regret having given my consent to her marriage. It was not a brilliant one, and I have promised myself that I will not part with any of the other girls – unless of course it is a match so important to the state that I am forced to accept it. France would have to derive great benefit before I would lose another of my daughters.'

'Then only for an alliance which would make her a Queen . . .'

'No less, no less,' said Louis. 'I am a King, but I am also a father. I like to have my family about me. And you . . . I hear you are causing a great flutter in the hearts of some of our ladies.' Louis laughed. 'Take my advice. Enjoy life while you have a chance. You are young, and youth passes, you know . . . so quickly.'

Louis' eyes were friendly, but they held a warning. You are here as my pensioner, they told the young Prince. You failed to regain your throne in '45 as your father failed in '15. We have to make up our minds to accept these Germans as Kings of Britain. In the circumstances you are no fit husband for a

Princesse of France, and of course in no other circumstances could you become my daughter's lover.

The Prince read those thoughts.

The King, he knew, frowned on any who approached his daughters. He himself could take a mistress; he was amused by the *amours* of such as Richelieu and Clermont. But his daughters were sacred. Woe betide the man who attempted to seduce one of them.

An exile must constantly bear these matters in mind.

The King smiled suddenly. 'I hear the Princesse de Talmond has declared that she thinks you the most charming man at Court. She is forty, I hear, but I should think she would be interesting . . . very interesting.'

'Thank you, Sire,' said the Prince.

And when he left the King's presence he knew that all was over between him and Anne-Henriette, unless by some miracle King George abdicated and the people restored the Stuarts to the throne, as they had in that glorious year, 1660 – nearly a hundred years ago – when another Stuart had come back in triumph to the land he was to rule.

❧ ❧ ❧

Louis was sorry for Anne-Henriette. The poor creature had become very melancholy once more. He decided that, as he had on two occasions been obliged to deny her the man she wished to marry, he would make a great effort to bring her back to happiness.

He often summoned her to his apartments where they would drink coffee, which he prepared himself. He would take her round his workshop and show her his ivories, then to the still-rooms that she might taste his concoctions.

'You are growing up fast,' he told her. 'You shall have your own household.'

Since he exerted all his charm, Anne-Henriette quickly succumbed to it, and father and daughter were so much together that it began to be said that the King cared more for his daughter than for Madame de Pompadour.

For many years there had been in France a conflict between the Jansenites and the Jesuits. The Jansenites took their name from their founder, Cornelius Jansen, the Dutch theologian who had protested vehemently against the love of comfort which was prevalent among high officials of the Catholic Church. The followers of this creed were stern men who sought to bring austerity back to religion; but under cover of Jansenism certain groups in France had made an effort to strike at the Church. These men did not concern themselves with Augustinian theories; they were anxious to make France independent of Rome. It was another phase of the struggle for supremacy between the State and the Papacy; thus the dispute lay between the Jesuits and Rome on one side, and the *Parlements* and those who wished to see the state supreme on the other.

As long ago as 1713, Clement XI had denounced Jansenism in his Bull *Unigenitus;* and there was now a party in France which sought to maintain the power of the Jesuits.

To this party the Dauphin had given his support; he had become very devout and in this was joined by the Dauphine, for whom he was beginning to have an affection which almost equalled that which he had felt for his first wife. The Queen also supported the Jesuits.

Louis himself was not very pleased with the clergy. Quite recently the Bishop of Soissons had taken it upon himself to reproach him for his association with Madame de Pompadour.

He had dared to write to Louis deploring the fact that the nation expressed no horror when the sin of adultery was committed. 'If,' wrote the Bishop, 'Your Majesty were a private person in my diocese I should feel it my duty to deliver a public rebuke. I now ask Your Majesty to remember your repentance when you believed yourself to be on your deathbed at Metz. Then you swore to mend your ways. But God gave you back your life, and what has happened? You have taken as mistress the wife of one of your subjects.'

Louis, reminded of the nearness of death which he believed he had faced many times, might have been impressed, but the Bishop had spoilt the effect of his little homily by his next words.

'Now we see at Court in the highest of all ranks, a person of the lower class, a woman without breeding or birth, who has been elevated in the name of debauchery.'

Louis was angry with the Bishop then, and when he compared his Marquise with any of the Court ladies he could assure himself that the Bishop talked nonsense. No, the King was definitely not pleased with the clergy.

As for Madame de Pompadour, she was terrified of that body. Those men who were always exhorting kings to repent were a menace to the kings' mistresses. Repentance meant returning to the pious life, and that could only mean dismissal from Court for such as she was.

Therefore the Jesuits could expect no friendship from her. And as her ascendancy over the King was becoming more and more apparent, a party began to gather about the Dauphin, the object being to strengthen the clergy and the Jesuits, and eventually to oust the mistress from the Court.

And since Anne-Henriette was so favoured by the King, she found that she was invited to the Dauphin's apartments and there courted and honoured by his friends.

Anne-Henriette was a little bewildered; but these attentions did prevent her brooding on the scandalous behaviour of Charles Edward, who was now deep in a tempestuous love affair with the forty-year-old Princesse de Talmond.

✢ ✤ ✢

Madame de Pompadour was perpetually watchful. Life was exhausting but highly enjoyable. Louis was delighted to find that she shared his interest in architecture, and many a happy hour was spent discussing plans for embellishing and altering existing buildings or acquiring new ones.

She had made Crécy an enchanting place, the King told her, and he promised to build a house especially for her.

It would be so interesting not to buy something which was already in existence but to construct it together from the beginning. She had already bought the Hôtel d'Evreux in Paris, and she and the King, driving together one day, discovered the ideal spot overlooking the Seine between Meudon and Sèvres.

'This is the place,' declared Louis. 'What a beautiful view you will have from your windows!'

'Your Majesty has given the name to my house: "Bellevue".'

'Bellevue let it be.'

It was wonderful to shut themselves away from everyone and draw up plans for the house. It brought them so close together.

'We will use Lassurance as architect,' said Louis. 'I cannot think of a better.'

'I also want Verberckt.'

'His work is exquisite.'

'I think we ought to call in Boucher for the ceilings.'

'A great artist.'

And the cost? It never occurred to either of them to think of it. Louis had been accustomed to decide something should be done and the treasury provided the means to do it. As for the Marquise, although she kept her accounts with accuracy, she had always believed that the wealth of Kings was limitless.

While they planned the house and often drove out to Bellevue to see how the workmen were progressing, she thought a great deal about the King's new friendship with Anne-Henriette. She was aware, for her friends had pointed this out to her, that the Princesse was being drawn into politics by her brother and the Jesuit party.

It had always been the policy of Madame de Pompadour to persuade Louis, never to cajole or threaten as Mesdames Vintimille and Châteauroux had done. Her plan always was to soothe the King, to be the person to whom he came for comfort of any sort. She believed – and rightly so – that the way to hold her position was never to place Louis in embarrassing situations.

Never had she reproached him for neglecting her for Anne-Henriette. She would not draw attention to the subversive nature of those gatherings in the apartments of the Dauphin and Dauphine.

It occurred to her however that, if one of the other daughters were brought to Versailles, Louis' attention might be diverted from Anne-Henriette.

She had made inquiries as to the character and appearance of the next daughter, Victoire, who was now about fifteen or sixteen. She was pretty, but hardly of a nature to charm the King to any great extent.

So the Marquise said to the King: 'Louis, it must be a long time since you saw your little daughters.'

'A very long time.'

'Are you going to leave them in that convent for ever?'

'They have not yet completed their education.'

'But Madame Victoire is only a year younger than Madame Adelaide. I know how delightful it is to have daughters. I have my own little Alexandrine, you remember.'

'That dear child,' said Louis. 'The-not-so-pretty one. We must make a match for her one day. But what are you saying of Victoire?'

'I was wondering whether you would not like to have her join her sisters here at Versailles.'

Louis was thoughtful for a moment. It would be rather pleasant to have another adoring daughter at Court.

So Victoire returned to Versailles.

Grand apartments were prepared for her, and the King was at first delighted with his daughter.

Victoire however was not gay by nature and, as soon as she arrived at Versailles, Adelaide decided that she would look after her.

She went to her apartments and when she found they were so grand she was jealous. She studied her sister, who was inclined to be, Adelaide quickly discovered, of an extremely lethargic disposition.

'We shall go for a walk in the gardens,' Adelaide declared.

'I like it here,' said Victoire.

'I like it in the gardens. Come, we do not sit about all day at Versailles.'

'Why do you not? It is very pleasant.'

Adelaide smiled at her sister. There was really no need to be jealous of *her*. The King was merely interested in her because she was the latest arrival. Adelaide was amused to remember that this sister of hers had been for ten years in Fontevrault, as she herself might have been but for her own resourcefulness. She derived great pleasure from Victoire's society because she could constantly remind herself of what she had escaped.

'Come,' commanded Adelaide, and already such power had she over the lazy Victoire that the young girl obeyed.

As they walked together, Victoire was commanded to tell Adelaide about the convent. What were the nuns like? What clothes did they wear? Was it hideously boring, and was she not beside herself with delight to be back at Versailles?

Victoire explained and agreed.

'You need to be looked after. There are pitfalls at Versailles. It would be a scandal if you offended against Etiquette.'

'What would happen?' asked Victoire idly.

'You would no doubt be sent back to Fontevrault. But do not be afraid. I will always help you. What are Sophie and Louise-Marie like?'

'Sophie never says anything if she can help it. She is always afraid to.'

'Afraid? Of what?'

'Oh life, I suppose.'

'When Sophie comes home I shall look after her.'

'But you are going to look after *me*.'

'I shall look after you both. I will tell you something. *I* am the most important person at Versailles.'

'You . . . but what of our father? What of the Queen? What of the Marquise?'

'The Queen counts for nothing. The Marquise is always afraid of losing her position. As for our father, he loves me so dearly that he will do all I say. Now you are here I shall let you join in my plan.'

'What plan?'

'Having the Marquise dismissed from Court.'

'But the King would never allow that.'

Adelaide laughed and looked wise. 'You will see. There are many plots at Versailles, but mine is the best. Anne-Henriette and the Dauphin and the Dauphine have a plot too. It is not as good as mine.'

'What is yours?'

Adelaide put her fingers to her lips. 'When you have proved yourself worthy, I may let you into my secrets. If Sophie is so stupid, there is no point in my pleading for her to be brought back, is there?'

Victoire nodded her agreement.

'What of our younger sister?'

'She is not stupid. She talks a great deal and always wants her own way. She says that as she has a hump on her back she must have some compensation. So she is going to live exactly as she wants to.'

'Oh,' said Adelaide. She did not add that she was even less inclined to plead for the return of Louise-Marie than she was for that of Sophie. She took Victoire by the arm and put her face close to hers.

'Have no fear. I am at hand to look after you.'

Victoire nodded; she was thinking of being alone in her apartment, lying down on her bed and going to sleep.

After dinner of course. She wanted her dinner badly.

'You and I are allies,' Adelaide told her. 'You understand?'

Victoire did understand. She began to follow Adelaide about the Palace in a respectful silence.

The Court was amused by the lazy, docile Victoire, who had become like a slave to domineering Adelaide.

As for the King, he was no longer enamoured of this newly arrived daughter whose education seemed to have been somewhat neglected at Fontevrault.

He was disturbed by the Dauphin's attempt to dabble in politics, and in order to avoid the unpleasant, avoided his son. He began to see that it was far more interesting to spend his time with the vivacious and intelligent Marquise than with the members of his family.

Moreover this growing interest in architecture, which they so enthusiastically shared, was becoming more and more absorbing. There were eight new buildings now in the course of construction or reconstruction. A delightful occupation.

The citizens of Paris looked on in bewilderment at this extravagance. They occasionally saw the Marquise adorned at the cost of thousands of livres.

It seemed incredible that Louis, the Well-Beloved, knowing the condition of the people, suffering as they were under cruel taxation, could allow the woman to spend so much of the country's money.

As usual there were many to blame the woman and spare Louis. But there were some who said: 'But the King is no longer a child. He *must* understand the state in which thousands of French families are living. Yet what can he care for the suffering of his people if he encourages the extravagance of the Pompadour?'

The course of the war had changed again. Frederick had made peace with Austria, and his rights in Silesia had been recognised. Philip V of Spain had died, and his son, Ferdinand VI, no longer wished to take the offensive. France stood alone, fighting a war in which she had lost all interest.

Thus the peace which might have been made two years before on the same terms was, after so much fighting and the loss of many French lives, eventually concluded.

Looking back Frenchmen began to ask each other why they had been involved in the war at all. It was true they had supported the claim of Charles Albert to the Imperial crown, but when he had died and his young son had shown no inclination to fight, France no longer had any interest and should, but for the mismanagement of the Marquis d'Argenson, Minister for Foreign Affairs, have retired. Now, Maria Theresa's husband, Francis of Lorraine, was elected to the Imperial throne; Frederick had his interest in Silesia, and because Louis, as he said, did not wish to act as a tradesman, he gave back all that he had won in Flanders. He did however secure Parma and Placentia for his daughter, Louise-Elisabeth, and Guastalla for her husband, Don Philip, and Louisberg and Cape Breton in America came into French possession.

This was the result of the peace of Aix-la-Chapelle.

The English, who had been far from victorious, were wily enough to secure the best terms for themselves. Always alert for the expansion of trade, England secured rights for importing slaves and trading with Spanish colonies. There was one demand which the ministers of Hanoverian George made, and that was that Louis should cease to offer a refuge to members of the Stuart family.

The people in the streets of Paris discussed the peace in bewilderment.

What was it all for? they asked, recalling the privations of the past years. Continual taxation, to pay for . . . what?

And the King had not wished to act like a tradesman!

The women of Les Halles, who were very influential in forming mass opinion, declared that Louis carried his good manners too far. Was it not a pity that he, who was so anxious to play the gentleman with his enemies, should not have thought a little more of playing the good father to his poor subjects?

✦ ✦ ✦

The loyalties of the people were shifting. Charles Edward had always had the power to charm and, because he realised that he was in danger of being expelled from France, he was determined to exert all his powers to remain.

He was in love with Paris which had provided such a happy consolation for his failures. The brilliance of the balls and the opera, the wit of the people, the elegance of the society in which he moved, afforded the utmost pleasure to him. With his superficial charm and his love of flattery, he could contemplate, without much regret, the rest of his life spent in these congenial surroundings.

And now came the peace and the demands for his expulsion from France by Hanoverian George.

Louis found himself in one of those situations which all his life he had done his best to avoid. He had to ask a guest to leave. It was most unpleasant and, because of this, he tried to shelve the matter until the last possible minute.

Meanwhile Charles Edward was seen more and more in public, and he never failed to ingratiate himself with the people. He made regular appearances at the Opéra, and there he was treated as a royal Prince. The audience rose when he entered his box, and he would stand smiling, glittering with jewels, as he accepted the acknowledgement of royalty and popularity.

He was quick to sense the changing attitude towards the King, and smiled a little sadly at the peace celebrations.

'I cannot help feeling this melancholy,' he told his friends. 'I love France. I look upon Frenchmen as I would my own people; and I think of the blood they have shed in this war which now they delude themselves into thinking they have won. The peace! What has it brought France? Tell me that. A little gewgaw for the King's daughter. Is it such a matter of glory that the eldest daughter of the King of France has become the Duchesse of Parma? A few miserable possessions in America! And of course you rid yourselves of one unwelcome guest; that is if you are going to allow sly George to dictate to you.'

His friends talked of this. Their lackeys heard them, and in the cafés and barbers' shops, and the streets and markets, the cry was taken up: 'Are we going to take orders from German George?'

The Princesse de Talmond, who doted on her young lover, was determined to keep him in Paris. She added her by no means insignificant voice to his protests.

Louis meanwhile procrastinated.

'I think it would be advisable, in view of the peace terms,' he told Charles Edward, 'for you to begin to think about leaving France.'

'Sire,' answered the Prince, 'I have already *thought* about that catastrophe.'

'Alas that it should be thus,' murmured Louis. 'One is in the hands of one's ministers. There had to be peace, and terms . . .'

With that he changed the subject. He had asked the Prince to think about leaving, and if it were necessary to force him to do so, that would be the duty of others. For the time being he was prepared to let matters stay as they were. Who knew, the affair might blow over. George might forget the young man was in Paris. That would be so much more pleasant.

Louis had other matters to think of. Bellevue was nearing completion. What a delightful château! The Marquise was indeed a remarkable woman. He was fortunate . . . fortunate indeed to have found her.

But George II was not going to allow the young man, who was the greatest menace to his security, to continue at the Court of France where, it was very likely, he would soon be hatching another plot to bring the Stuarts back to the throne; and orders were given that the British Ambassador should drop gentle hints to Louis that there was surprise and indignation across the water because, in spite of the peace terms, the young Stuart Prince still remained in Paris.

The Prince de Talmond was eager for the exile of Charles Edward, as he did not like the scandal which he was causing with the Princesse; and even if Louis was dilatory in sending his exile from France, the Prince de Talmond was ready to make a stand.

He forbade Charles Edward to enter his house, but the young Stuart, so certain that he had the Parisians on his side, continued to call on the Princesse.

When Charles Edward next presented himself at the house of his mistress he was told that she was not at home.

'That is a lie,' cried Charles Edward, who felt that as he had succeeded in evading the wishes of the King of France he was not going to submit to those of the Prince de Talmond.

The door was shut and he, suddenly wild with rage and sensing that a defeat in this quarter could be the preliminary to a greater one, began to hammer madly on the door.

A crowd collected to watch the furious Prince, but he was warned by some of his Scottish friends who were with him that it would be foolish to cause such a disturbance, as it might make it easier for the King to insist on his departure.

Charles Edward saw the point, and left. As he walked away he smiled in an easy, friendly way at the crowd, shrugging his shoulders.

'You see,' he said, 'I am not allowed to call on my friends. You know why? It is the wish of German George. My good people, my dear friends, how much longer will you allow yourselves to be ruled by the usurper of the British crown?'

His gallant smiles for the women, his *camaraderie* with the men, had their effect on the crowd.

'He is right,' murmured the people. 'We won the war, and the British take the spoils.'

That day two women, fighting in Les Halles, collected a huge crowd to watch and jeer, spurring them on to greater efforts.

One, a vegetable vendor, had the other, a coffee-seller, by the hair, so that the tin urn on her back went clattering onto the cobbles and both women lay in a pool of coffee.

'Idiot!' cried the vegetable woman. 'Pig! Let me tell you this: You are as stupid as . . . as the peace.'

The crowd roared its approval. A new catch phrase was born: 'As stupid as the peace.'

✦ ✦ ✦

The King summoned Comte Phélippeaux de Maurepas to his presence. He liked Maurepas. The man was so amusing; he never made heavy going of state affairs and treated everything as though it were a joke. He was so witty that it was always a pleasure to be with him. It was said by his enemies that he was more interested in writing a witty satire or epigram than in considering affairs of state.

He had suffered from the withdrawal of royal favour on the insistence of Madame de Châteauroux after her humiliation at Metz, and now Louis feared that Maurepas was not attempting to please Madame de Pompadour. This impish man was ready to snap his fingers at the King's mistresses – which was foolish of him; but Louis could not help liking him.

Now he called in his help in this matter of Charles Edward Stuart.

'There can be no longer delay,' he told Maurepas. 'There will be trouble with Great Britain if he remains here. It is a part of the peace treaty, and we must carry out our obligations.'

'Sire, it is a delicate matter. The Prince declares that he holds letters from you, offering him refuge as long as he desires it.'

Louis shrugged his shoulders. 'One cannot look into the future. Such offers were made years ago when there seemed a fair prospect of his gaining his kingdom.'

'Sire,' replied the minister, 'public opinion is strong in favour of this Prince. He has a certain charm, and he has used this to the full. The people are saying that asylum was offered him and France should honour her pledges.'

The King turned away testily. 'It is precisely because we must honour our pledges that he must go.'

'It being more important, Sire, to honour pledges given to a powerful nation than to an exile.'

'That is true,' said the King.

'And our people, who ask us to snap our fingers at German George and keep the pretty Stuart with us to charm our theatre audiences and seduce our ladies?'

'This is a matter of diplomacy.'

'They may murmur instead of cheer, Sire. They may sympathise with the pretty Prince against their handsome King?'

'The people!' cried Louis contemptuously.

'They will say our King promised to befriend this romantic young man.'

'It is impossible for a king to be a true friend on all occasions.'

'And indeed this is one of them, Sire.'

Louis wondered why he allowed Maurepas to delay him in this contradictory manner. Yet he knew why; the man amused him. He was too careless of his future – or perhaps too sure of it – to ponder before he spoke. No doubt that was why the King enjoyed his company more than that of many of his courtiers.

He said almost curtly: 'If the Prince will not go of his own accord, he must be arrested and ejected.'

'There would be a scandal, Sire. The people might prevent his arrest.'

Louis shuddered. He could see an unpleasant incident growing out of a situation which was really of no great importance. Charles Edward, a wandering exile, was an insignificant person. It seemed absurd that the peace of Paris and of the King should be disturbed on his account.

'That is why I wish you to deal with this matter. Go now to the Prince. Warn him to leave Paris without delay. Tell him that if he does not, tonight he is to be arrested. Stress that we have delayed too long and do not intend to wait any longer. He should be gone by nightfall.'

Maurepas bowed.

❧ ❧ ❧

In the company of the Duc de Gesvres, Maurepas called on Charles Edward in a house which he had rented in the Quai des Theatins.

Charles Edward received them with that air of bonhomie which he extended to all.

'This is a delight,' he declared. 'Welcome to my exiled dwelling.'

'Sir,' said Maurepas, 'before Your Highness welcomes us so wholeheartedly, I pray you listen to what we have to say, for when you have heard it you may wish to moderate that welcome or perhaps not give it at all.'

'This sounds ominous,' said Charles Edward.

'Alas that we should be the bearers of such news,' murmured de Gesvres.

'In point of fact,' went on Maurepas, 'we come on a mission from His Majesty. He asks you to leave this country before nightfall. If you do so he will continue with your allowance.'

Charles Edward gave them a look of disdain. 'Is this how the King of France honours his pledges?' he demanded.

'It is how he honours the pledge made to the King of England,' said Maurepas.

'I am not prepared to discuss my future with the King's ministers,' said Charles Edward. 'If he wishes to break his promises to me, then let him tell me so personally.'

'His Majesty wishes to make your going as comfortable as possible.'

'So he tells his servants to order me out, eh?' cried Charles Edward flushing scarlet.

'Sir, you would be wise to leave before nightfall.'

'Impossible,' cried Charles Edward arrogantly. 'I have arranged to attend the Opéra.'

That night at the Opéra was a glittering state occasion. Charles Edward arrived, a handsome figure, in a red velvet coat and a waistcoat of gold brocade. He wore not only the Order of St Andrew but that of St George, and when he entered the theatre, affably gracious and very charming, the audience rose to pay homage to him. He was exultant. He was more popular than he had been before his failure at Culloden. The people's dissatisfaction with the peace – and with their King – had enhanced that popularity. It was most agreeable to the young Prince.

Suddenly a wild cheering rang through the Opéra house. This was beyond even his expectations. It meant that if the King and his immediate circle deplored his presence in Paris, the people did not.

What joy to see that in one of the boxes was George's ambassador and his *entourage*! They looked stupid, gloated Charles Edward, in their astonishment.

He took his seat and the performance began.

He was so delighted with his reception that he did not notice that as the evening wore on there was a certain tension in the atmosphere. People whispered to one another, for the news had seeped into the Opéra House that over a thousand soldiers were stationed outside, and that they were posted at all the doors so that no one would be able to leave without permission.

Charles Edward, unaware of what was happening, passed out of the Opéra House, and as he was about to step into his carriage, he found his way barred by the Colonel of the Guards.

'You would speak to me?' asked the Prince haughtily.

'I have a warrant for Your Highness's arrest,' was the answer.

The Prince looked about him helplessly, but immediately other armed men had come forward to join the Colonel.

'I must ask your Royal Highness for his sword.' The Prince's face flushed with anger, but he was aware of the warning looks in the eyes of the Scottish lords who were his companions.

He hesitated for a moment, but he knew that a few cheers from the people could not save him from his fate.

He unbuckled his sword and handed it to the Colonel of the Guards.

'This is a monstrous thing,' he said. 'I was offered refuge in France. If I had the smallest patch of ground I would not hesitate to share it with my friends. The French nation will be ashamed of this action.'

'I must ask your Royal Highness to step into the carriage.'

Charles Edward shrugged his shoulders and obeyed.

They bound his arms and legs with a silk cord, and the carriage left the Opéra House for Vincennes.

The people stood about in the streets and talked of the affair.

'Such a handsome Prince,' they said. 'We shall miss him in Paris. A pity. Why should he be banished? Oh, I'll tell you why. It is because German George says we must not entertain him here. German George? Oh, did you not know? It is not French Louis who rules this country. He stands aside for German George. That is, since we won the war, you know. It is all in the peace terms.'

Louis sent for Anne-Henriette and embraced her tenderly.

'I thought, my dear,' he said, 'that you would like to see this.' He handed her a letter which she saw was from Charles Edward.

'Monsieur, brother and cousin,

I have felt much uneasiness because I was unable to communicate with you directly and found it impossible to reveal my true sentiments to your ministers. I hope that you will never doubt my affection for you, and as you desire me to leave France I am ready to do so at once . . .'

Anne-Henriette did not look at her father. She continued to stare at the letter.

This was the end of her hopes. It was the same heart-breaking conclusion which she had known before.

In that moment a great melancholy enveloped her, and she told herself that never again would she love anyone; she was twenty-two years of age and she believed that her life was over.

'He has already left,' said Louis gently. 'He is on his way to the Papal city of Avignon. There doubtless he will stay until he has made his plans.'

She did not answer, and Louis, putting his arm about her, led her to a window. Together they looked out on the Avenue de Paris.

'My little daughter,' he said, 'I understand your grief. But we cannot choose our husbands or wives. We have to learn to accept what is provided for us. And then we make the best of what we have.'

She thought how different it was for a king such as himself to make the best of his life. He had a very happy existence. He had his hunting, his gambling, his architecture and, when he fell in love, the woman of his choice was delighted to share his life.

There was one law for the King, another for his daughters.

But she did not tell him this. She allowed him to think that she was comforted.

♣ Chapter XII ♣

THE ROAD OF THE REVOLT

All the Court wondered how long the reign of the Marquise would last. She was clever, they were ready to admit that, but could she continue to hold the King?

They did not doubt her wisdom. She gave herself slavishly to amusing her lover. She must do everything that he demanded, and do it superlatively well. The King's interests were hers; if he wanted to hunt, so did she. Was it cards? There was the Marquise, scintillating, cautious or gay, whichever mood suited the King's. Was he melancholy? The Marquise could be trusted to remember some spicy bit of scandal to make him laugh.

All she wanted was to please him. It would be difficult for a man of Louis' temperament to find fault with that.

But there was one flaw which prevented her from being the perfect mistress.

Sexually Louis seemed insatiable. His courtiers discussed him freely. Being men of great experience in this direction they understood him well. Louis was not yet awakened to sexual maturity, which seemed strange in a man of his nature. He was deeply sensual but there had been ingrained in his character a sentimentality which was incompatible with that deep physical need. It may have been due to his upbringing. He had been kept innocent under the alert eyes of Villeroi and Fleury, and he was taking a long time to throw off their influence.

In the midst of his highly immoral Court he had remained a faithful husband, and only the lack of response from the Queen had sent him to Madame de Mailly. To Madame de Mailly he had for long remained faithful, as he had to her sisters whom he had mourned sincerely and deeply for some time after their deaths, when he had abstained from love-making altogether.

And now with the Pompadour he was the faithful lover. There had been temptations of course. It was remembered that at a recent ball he had shown some attention to a beautiful young woman. But the Pompadour's spies had quickly warned her what was happening and, in her graceful way, she had the young woman hurried out to her carriage and driven away from Court; and Louis had not been sufficiently interested to prevent this happening.

But could Madame de Pompadour continue to hold the King as her lover?

The truth was that Madame de Pompadour was not a healthy woman, and the exhausting life she was living was beginning to make its mark upon her.

It was said that she owed a great deal to her cosmetics, and without them could not at times hide the fact that she was weary and not in the best of health.

She had a cough which only her enormous will-power suppressed on important occasions. And she was tired.

Could a tired woman keep up with the constant demands of the King? She must plan his entertainments, hunt, play cards, act, sing, dance far into the night. This she did with a grace and charm which could not be rivalled.

But how did she fare later during those nights when it was even more important that she please the King?

The Court was alert.

Was Louis changing? was the eternal question. For how long would the faithful attitude continue? He would not of his own accord turn her out; he was too easy-going, too anxious to avoid embarrassment.

But a new mistress might do what Louis shrank from doing. They had seen what had happened in the case of Madame de Mailly.

How long then would Madame de Pompadour continue to hold her position at Court?

♣ ♣ ♣

There were two men who were eager for her dismissal: Richelieu and Maurepas.

Richelieu, as First Gentleman of the Bedchamber, considered himself the King's counsellor in the choice of mistresses, and he had not chosen Madame de Pompadour. From the first moment, when she had seen the King in the Forest of Sénart, she had worked entirely without help. He wanted to replace her by a mistress of his own choosing.

Maurepas had made no attempt to ingratiate himself with her. He had continued to amuse with his satires and epigrams concerning the most interesting topics at Court, and naturally the King's mistress must be one of these. He had taken a mischievous delight in discovering the truth about her origins, and had attacked her on this. At least he had done so with a certain amount of anonymity, but the spate of songs and verses which were quoted in the streets were in his style, and few were in any doubt as to where they originated.

He made great play on her name of Poisson, and consequently she was known throughout Paris as The Fish or Miss Fish.

The songs and satires were called *poissonades* and eagerly the Parisians waited for the next to appear; the songs could be heard in the cafés and markets; moreover they were instrumental in working up public hatred against the mistress, for even now the people were disinclined to blame the King for their misfortunes, and Mademoiselle Poisson made a useful scapegoat.

Through the verses of Maurepas the people knew exactly how much was being spent on the various building projects. It was said that Bellevue had already cost six million livres although it was by no means finished, and that fortunes were spent on the entertainments of a few days. One dress, worn by the Pompadour for one occasion, it was pointed out, would keep a French family in luxury for a year.

The Marquise was aware that Maurepas was doing her a great deal of harm, and she knew that she should bring about his dismissal. She would not presume to ask the King for this, particularly as she knew that Louis had a certain fondness for this minister who had been of the Court for so long and had the power to make him laugh. Louis would always forgive people who made him laugh a good deal.

Still she would not ask Louis to dismiss him, and meanwhile the damaging *poissonades* were being circulated throughout Paris.

Richelieu planned to bring about two desirable objectives at one stroke.

He wished to see Maurepas dismissed because the minister had too much influence with the King. He believed that if he could sufficiently alarm the Marquise that she asked Louis for the minister's dismissal, she might bring about her own at the same time.

It was a scheme which appealed wholeheartedly to the mischievous Richelieu, and he began by asking for a private audience with the Marquise.

This she granted; she was always gracious to ministers, following her policy of making as few enemies as possible.

Richelieu bowed low and kissed her hand.

'Madame la Marquise,' he began, 'it is so good of you to grant me this private audience! I will not delay by telling you that you are the most beautiful woman in France, for that you already know. I will not waste time by telling you that you are the most admired and envied . . .'

'No,' she interrupted with a smile, 'pray do not. Tell me your business instead.'

'Madame,' Richelieu took a step nearer and looked full into her face. 'I am disconcerted to see that you are not looking as full of health as could be wished.'

Her expression hardened a little. Was he right? Did he see a look of fear? She was mistress of herself immediately. He admired her very much. There was not a lady in Versailles who had more graces and poise than the Marquise de Pompadour.

'I feel well,' she said, 'very well.'

'How relieved I am, although I have come here to ask you to take the utmost care.'

'I do take care of my health, Monsieur le Duc. But it is so good of you to be so considerate on my account.'

He took a step even nearer. 'Madame la Marquise, you have your enemies in this Court. It would be impossible not to. You ... so charming, so courted, so loved ... so powerful.'

'I think, Monsieur le Duc, that I can take note of my enemies as I do of my health – and with the same assiduous care.'

'But I would tell you of my suspicions. Madame, has it occurred to you that your health may have been impaired by your enemies?'

'I do not understand you.'

'You are too trusting, Madame. What if your enemies should seek not only to poison the public mind against you, but to poison *you*?'

She put her hand to her throat in sudden forgetfulness of her dignity.

'Poison ... me!'

'You are young. You have everything you desire. But you are suddenly ill. There could be an explanation. Do you think that one who can say such venomous things about you would hesitate to harm you in other ways?'

She laughed lightly. 'I think you are mistaken,' she said.

'I trust I am,' said the Duc. 'I trust I am.'

And when he left he knew that he had frightened her. He believed that now she would take steps to have Maurepas sent away – and the King liked Maurepas.

It would be a test. It would be possible to see how deep was the King's regard for this woman. If he would be prepared to dismiss Maurepas on her account, it would be certain that he was determined to be as faithful to the Marquise now as when he had first made her his mistress.

Richelieu waited impatiently to learn the results of his little manoeuvre.

* ❖ ❖

Maurepas poisoning her!

It was a ridiculous suggestion. She knew that her fits of exhaustion were not due to poison.

Richelieu was a fool if he thought she did not see through his schemes. He wanted her to take that ridiculous tale to the King. It was just the kind of story which would irritate Louis.

An accusation such as that would have to be considered, and an unpleasant scene would ensue. Maurepas would prove his innocence and she would be blamed.

She was not such a fool as Richelieu thought her.

But it was true that the odious man was poisoning the minds of the people against her. Every one of her actions was spied on, exaggerated and reported to the people. Greatly she wished that she could bring about his dismissal.

She broached the subject of the lampoons to Louis one night when he came to her bedchamber.

'They are growing more scurrilous,' she said.

The King nodded.

'There is no doubt that Maurepas is the author of most of them. He has his imitators, but somehow he always sets his mark on what he writes.'

'The others are poor imitations,' said the King.

'They are not doing us much good with the people,' she suggested tentatively.

'Oh, there have always been these rhymes,' said the King lightly. 'I myself do not escape them, for everything they say about you reflects on me.' He was impatient to end all conversation, and she, ever watchful that he should not suffer the slightest tedium, ceased to speak of the matter.

* * *

Richelieu conveyed to Maurepas his belief that the Marquise was trying to have him sent from Court if he did not refrain from circulating his wicked rhymes through Paris.

The result of this was exactly what Richelieu had expected.

That very night there was an intimate supper party in the *petits appartements*. The Marquise sat on the right hand of the King, and both Maurepas and Richelieu were of the party.

As the Marquise took her place she noticed a paper protruding from her table napkin, and glancing hurriedly at it saw that it was a verse of a particularly offensive nature, suggesting that she suffered from leucorrhea.

With great presence of mind she hid the paper, and the King did not even notice that it had been there.

She was conscious of Maurepas' disappointment. He had hoped that she would read the verse, and accuse him of having written it. He would then have used his wit to anger her to such an extent that the King would surely be annoyed at the scene which would inevitably ensue, and for which – Maurepas could trust his own wit and ingenuity to accomplish this – he would blame the Marquise.

She however did nothing of the sort.

Maurepas had to watch her with grudging admiration. So did Richelieu, who had seen her pick up the paper and guessed its nature from the way she so quickly disposed of it.

Mischievously Richelieu looked from France's wittiest minister to one who might well be France's cleverest woman.

One of them would have to go sooner or later, he was sure.

He found great pleasure in watching this duel, for he would be delighted to see the dismissal of either, if he could not hope for both.

✤ ✤ ✤

Madame de Pompadour had so far said nothing to the King about the verse she had found on the table. She did not want to call his attention to her ill health, and she did not want to make a scene.

But she knew that she could not ignore such an insult. To allow without protest such a verse to be presented to her at the table in the *petits appartements* would be an admission of her own uncertainty.

Before approaching the King however she would try to make peace with Maurepas. If he would stop circulating these vile verses about her she would be ready to forget all that had gone before, and there should be a truce between them.

She called on Maurepas the next day.

Maurepas could scarcely contain his mirth as he greeted her. He would exaggerate everything that was said and have an amusing tale to tell his cronies later.

'Madame le Marquise,' he cried; and there was irony even in his bow. 'I am overwhelmed by this honour.'

'I wish to speak to you on a matter of urgency,' she told him.

'And Madame did not send for me?'

'I do not send for Ministers,' she answered promptly. 'That would be presumption on my part. If I have anything to say to them I call upon them.'

'You are gracious, Madame.'

'You know, Monsieur de Maurepas, that unpleasant verses are being circulated about me.'

'It is deeply regrettable.'

'The King has instructed the Administration to discover who is responsible for them.'

'And they have not?'

'*You* have not, Monsieur, because you, I understand, are responsible for the Administration of Paris.'

'Madame, your reproaches are more than I can endure. Efforts shall be doubled and, when the culprit is discovered, I assure you that no time will be lost in bringing the scoundrel before the King.'

She looked at him intently. Then she said slowly: 'I believe, Monsieur, that you and Madame de Châteauroux were not good friends.'

He raised his shoulders and eyebrows simultaneously, in an expression of mock regret.

'I see, Monsieur, that you do not feel very friendly towards the King's mistresses.'

'But, Madame, they have my deep respect . . .' His cynical eyes surveyed her . . . 'no matter whence they come,' he added.

'I am glad to hear it,' she told him crisply. 'I felt sure that you were too wise to make enemies of them intentionally.'

'It is you who have the wisdom, Madame,' he said. 'Wisdom which matches your youthful beauty.'

There was no mistaking the mockery and the meaning behind his reply.

She knew that he intended to go on writing verses about her, and the particularly obnoxious one she had received last night was an example of what they would be like in the future.

So much depended on this, but she knew she could not put off showing that verse to Louis.

He wanted to make love. Did he not always? She must not appear tired or jaded in the least. She had ridden with him, and he could be in the saddle all day without fatigue; she had taken part in a little play which she had staged for his entertainment.

'Madame,' he said at the end of the evening, 'you are the most remarkable woman in France. All the best qualities of womanhood rest within your perfect form.'

That was good; but there was still the night before them; and it was the nights which she feared were beyond her talents.

But she was determined to bring this matter of the verses to a head. She knew that both Richelieu and Maurepas were waiting to see what she would do, so action was imperative, and it must not be delayed action.

'Louis,' she said, 'I am sorry to bother you with this matter, but I have suffered a great deal from these cruel verses of Maurepas. This one was on the table in my place last night. I think that it is too crude to be accepted without demur, and I am going to ask you to dismiss him from Court.'

Louis frowned and took the verses. He read them through and flushed.

Then he held the paper in the flame of a candle.

He took her hand and repeated the words with which he had dismissed the guests of that night's party: *'Allons nous coucher.'*

It was the hour of the *lever,* and Maurepas was in attendance.

The Comte was alert for some change in the King's attitude towards him for he did not see how the Marquise could retain her dignity and do otherwise than show him that verse. Her manner when she had called on him had, he believed, held a threat in it. A weaker man, he told himself, would have been afraid, would have sworn he would discover the culprit and put an end to the scandal sheets.

Not he! Not Maurepas! Afraid of the King's mistress? He had not been afraid of Châteauroux, so why should he be of Pompadour?

Châteauroux had sent him into exile for a while, and what had happened? She had died, and back he came. He was the one who could laugh at that little battle now.

Mistresses should learn that their period of glory must necessarily be brief, whereas ministers could retain office as long as they were clever enough to do so.

The King was unusually jocular on that morning. 'Why, Comte,' he said, his eyes scrutinising Maurepas, 'you look dazzling this morning.'

'Sire, I am to attend a wedding.'

'Ah! It suits him, does it not, attending weddings? Did you ever see a man more pleased with himself?'

'Sire, my pleasure is great because it is someone else's wedding and not my own.'

The King laughed with the rest, and Maurepas felt gratified. 'Well, make the most of your pleasure,' said the King. 'I shall expect to see you at Marly.'

'Thank you, Sire,' said Maurepas, his spirits rising still further.

He was exultant. She has shown him, he thought; and this is his answer. Madame la Marquise, there can be no doubt that your days at Versailles are numbered. Silly woman, you should have accepted my insults. You should have learned that I am a man whom no mistress dares flout. I bring bad luck to the mistresses of Kings.

He obeyed the King inasmuch as he enjoyed the festivities at the wedding of Mademoiselle Maupeou, and when he returned to his apartments he was met by a gentleman of the King's household.

'Monsieur de Maurepas,' said that gentleman, 'I bring a message from His Majesty.'

Maurepas tried not to look concerned as he read:

'Monsieur,
    I told you that I should let you know when I no longer required your services. That moment has come. I order you to hand in your resignation to M. de Saint Florentin. You will go to Bourges. Pontchartrain is too near . . .'

He tried not to show his anger and despair. In what he believed was his moment of victory he had been brought face to face with defeat.

The news spread through the Court.

'Maurepas has had his *lettre de cachet*. He leaves at once for Bourges.'

Richelieu could not hide his pleasure. The Queen, whose support Maurepas had received, was deeply distressed.

But the whole Court now knew the depth of the King's regard for the Marquise de Pompadour.

Madame de Pompadour had taken to using the significant word *'nous'* to ministers and ambassadors. She was always at the King's side, and he delighted in showering gifts on her. She was fascinated by beautiful china and took a great interest in the works at Vincennes and, when the King bestowed upon her the village of Sèvres, she began to make plans for bringing the china works to that neighbourhood that she might give them her personal supervision.

But every interest was the King's interest; and only rarely, as in the case of Maurepas – where there was no alternative – did she seek to impose her will upon him.

It was clear that not even Mesdames de Vintimille or Châteauroux had held such sway over him.

Homage was paid to her throughout the Court, but the people continued to hate her. The *poissonades* had done their work well. The fact that the mistress was not of the nobility only made the people hate her more. 'Who is *she*?' they demanded of each other. 'Why, it might have been one of us!' Such conclusions made envy doubly acute.

The peace was still derided throughout Paris. There were bitter complaints because that tax, the *vingtième*, which had come into existence in 1741 and which, they had been assured, had been imposed only for a short time, was continued. Many refused to pay it and in the affray between tax collectors and the taxed there were a number of deaths.

The people in the country were no less disgruntled than those in the towns, and there was murmuring against the administration in Paris when the tax collectors came to assess the crops. A good harvest meant increased taxation. There was no incentive to work.

There was a new and subtler element creeping into the discontent. Previously there had been religious quarrels between the Jansenites and the Jesuits; now new enemies to religion had appeared. These were the sceptics.

In her love of art, the Marquise had sought to help writers and philosophers as well as artists and musicians, and thus she had assisted in opening up a new and intellectual field.

Toussaint brought out his book *Les Moeurs* which was judged to be impious and was consequently burned in public. Diderot wrote his *Letter on Blindness for the use of those who see*. For this he was sent to Vincennes. Voltaire, fearing persecution for freedom of expression, left Court and went to Berlin.

The writers and philosophers might be penalised, their books might be suppressed, but already certain of their ideas had escaped into circulation and were being considered.

People were beginning to wonder whether there were not many evils in the old régime.

In the cafés men and women would sit talking or listening to some enthusiast who had ideas for destroying the old way of life and substituting a new one.

The fabric of the old régime was not yet torn but it was wearing thin. It needed careful patching, but the King and his ministers did not notice this. For so long had it lasted, that no doubts occurred to them that it would endure for ever.

So the entertainments continued, the endless rounds of pleasure. The King and his mistress must visit the many châteaux in which they delighted; there must be the intimate little supper parties, the plays and entertainment.

Bellevue was on the point of completion, and Madame de Pompadour was excitedly planning a grand banquet and ball which she would give there – the first in this new and magnificent house.

There was a danger at Bellevue for the reason that, situated as it was, so near the capital, many Parisians had walked there to watch its progress; and the construction of Bellevue and its many extravagancies became one of the main topics of conversation in the cafés and on street corners.

'Have you seen it recently? They say that already six million livres have been spent on that house!'

Six million livres, and in Paris many people could not afford to buy bread at two sous.

⚜ ⚜ ⚜

The Marquise was at Bellevue supervising the decorations.

She was supremely happy, for ever since the dismissal of Maurepas she had felt great confidence. She loved the King dearly and she knew that the affection he had for her went very deep, so deep that she did not believe he would ever desert her.

If the time came when she was unable to satisfy him she would not reproach *him*. She would give herself entirely to contributing to his pleasure. She already had a plan. She would find others to supply what she could not – not clever women, but pretty little girls, young girls preferably, with perfect bodies and blank minds.

It was a plan for the future – not to be acted on until the need arose – but she would be watchful and prepared for the moment when it came.

She would be the King's dearest friend and companion, his confidante, the person at Court in whom he knew he could place absolute trust – never complaining, never demanding, always charming, always ready to sacrifice herself to administer to his pleasure.

Thus she would hold her place; and, if Madame de Pompadour was not known as the First Lady of France, what did it matter as long as her power was complete?

Now for the entertainment.

How proud she was of this delightful château, and how interested he would be. They would sit side by side at this brilliant table decorated with flowers and candlesticks of gold and silver. Between them there would be that intimacy which all others envied and marvelled at.

One of her women came to her as she stood inspecting the table. The woman appeared agitated.

'What is it?' asked the Marquise with a smile, for she was rarely anything but charming, even to the most humble.

'Madame,' said the woman, her teeth chattering, 'the people are gathering in Paris. They are talking about Bellevue and the money that was spent on it; and they are comparing it with the price of bread. It is said that they mean trouble.'

'Trouble? Oh, not tonight. The King will be here. You know how they love the King. The fact that he is here will please them.'

'Madame, they say the crowd is very ugly.'

'Oh, these Parisians! So excitable!'

Madame de Pompadour leaned forward and re-arranged a bowl of flowers.

✤ ✤ ✤

'Sire,' said Richelieu, 'they say the people of Paris are restive tonight.'

'Why so?' asked Louis languidly.

'They have been growing more and more angry as Bellevue was being built.'

'What concern of theirs is Bellevue?'

'They think it has some connexion with the price of bread. It is these ideas that have been circulating in the cafés.'

'We will take no notice of them.'

'But Sire, it would seem that tonight they plan to take notice of us. They are massing in the squares. I have just heard that their leaders are planning a march to Bellevue,' Richelieu found it difficult to hide the malicious glee in his voice. 'Sire, might it not be wise for you to remain at Versailles tonight? Let the Marquise have her entertainment without you.'

Louis looked surprised. 'The Marquise expects me.'

'Sire, the people love you, but they do not love ... Bellevue. Do you not think, in the circumstances, you should remain at Versailles? The people can be wild when they are in a mass.'

'But you would seem to forget,' said Louis, 'that I have promised the Marquise.'

When the King's carriage arrived at Bellevue the shouts of the people could be heard in the distance. They sounded angry and ominous. It was true. The mob was on the march and its objective was the château of Bellevue.

The Marquise was suddenly frightened, not for her safety that night – and she knew that the people hated her beyond anyone else in the Kingdom – but because it was the construction of Bellevue which had infuriated them, and Bellevue was her creation. So if anything happened tonight she would be blamed.

Nothing must happen.

Louis had come because he had promised. But there must be no regrets in their relationship. Everything that she brought to him must be desirable in his eyes. She must never plunge him into unpleasantness. Unpleasant! The mob could be dangerous. And who knew, in the horror of an attack on Bellevue, they might forget that Louis was their well-beloved King.

She turned to Louis. 'I am afraid for your safety,' she said, 'so I am going to cancel everything I have arranged. I pray you put no obstacle in my way. If you should suffer the slightest pain tonight through the disaffection of these wild people of Paris, I should never forgive myself.'

Louis pressed her hand. He was grieved to see her so upset. Moreover he was extremely anxious to avoid an unpleasant scene.

'You must do as you wish, my dear,' he said.

She gave the order.

'We are leaving the château,' she told her guests. 'We shall take supper in a cottage which is at the end of the gardens. All lights will be extinguished in the château so the mob will realise that no one is there. Now . . . there is no time to lose.'

Thus it was that the grand entertainment at Bellevue was cancelled; there was no play, no fireworks, no ball.

The guests crowded into the little house, where a picnic supper was served instead of the grand banquet, with guests sitting on the floor and crowding every room.

The King was charming as he always was during these more intimate parties and did not seem to mind in the least that the grand affair at the château had been cancelled.

Here again, said the Court, this showed his deep regard for the Marquise. They seemed as happy together in the modest cottage as they did in the state apartments of Versailles.

Meanwhile the angry mob had marched to the château only to find it in darkness.

They had been misled, they grumbled. There was no banquet tonight. They would not have the pleasure of storming the place and helping themselves to the food which had been prepared for the noble guests.

Many of them were wishing they had not made the journey from Paris. They were not yet ready to hate the King. For the moment they still saw him as a young man misled by favourites, extravagant because he had never been taught to be otherwise. The legend of the well-beloved took a long time to die.

So while the intimate supper party went on in the little house in the grounds, the people straggled back to Paris, as disgruntled with the leaders of the march as they were with the châtelaine of Bellevue.

❧ ❧ ❧

Discontent rumbled throughout the capital, and one summer's day serious riots broke out.

The child of a working woman, who lived in the Faubourg St Antoine, went out into the streets to buy bread for his mother and he never returned.

The frantic mother ran into the streets, searching for him, and when he was not to be found she continued to run through the streets calling out her misfortune, tearing at her hair and her clothes, and shouting that her child had been kidnapped.

The people gathered. What was this story of a missing boy? Taxes. Starvation. And now were their children to be taken from them!

The Comte d'Argenson had put forward a plan to clean up the city and remove the many beggars and vagabonds who infested it. These people were homeless and destitute and, as colonists were needed in the Empire, it was decided that they should be shipped either to Louisiana or to Canada to work on the silkworm farms which French colonists were setting up there.

The beggars grumbled. There was no liberty in France any longer, they declared; but as the people were glad to see their city rid of these wandering beggars, no significant protest was made.

It was a different matter when a child belonging to a decent woman was stolen.

The people gathered about the stricken mother offering sympathy, some declaring that they had heard stories of missing children – little boys and girls who were sent out to shop for their parents and never returned.

Rumour grew and the stories became fantastic.

'The police kidnap the children and then ask payment for them. There was a woman in the Faubourg Saint-Marcel who was forced to work for weeks in order to pay the ransom demanded for her child!'

'They are taking our children to ship them to the Colonies.'

'They are robbing the people, not only of their food, but of their children!'

Wilder grew the rumours, and the wildest of all was born in the St Antoine district and quickly swept through Paris.

'Ship them to the colonies? Not they! There is a person . . . let us not mention the name. A very highly placed person. He – or she, shall we say – suffers from a dreadful disease, and it is only possible to preserve life by bathing in the blood of children.'

So that was what was happening to their children! They were being slaughtered that some highly placed person of the Court might take daily baths in their blood!

'A hundred children are missing,' they said in the cafés.

'A thousand children have been stolen!' was the cry in Les Halles.

'People of Paris, guard your children,' was the admonition of the agitators on the street corners. 'Those selfish monsters who have priced our grain so high that we cannot afford our bread, those who demand the *vingtième,* now ask for the blood of your children.'

The mob was on the march.

Several gendarmes were killed in the streets when the crowd fell upon them with clubs because someone had said they had seen them talking to children. One policeman ran for shelter into a house in the Rue de Clichy, and in a very short time that house was wrecked. In the Croix-Rouge a restaurant keeper had been said to be on very friendly terms with the police who often drank wine in his shop. His restaurant was mobbed and destroyed.

It was necessary to call in the Guards and musketeers to restore order. Proclamations were read in the streets. There had never been orders to arrest children. If the police were guilty of kidnapping children, such cases would be investigated if the parents would come forward and make their accusations. Any who had suffered would receive compensation.

Those who had led the revolt were arrested, tried, found guilty of treason, and sentenced to public hanging in the Place de Grève.

Louis rode into his capital. The people watched him sullenly.

In the Place de Greve were the rotting bodies of those who had led the revolt; they were not the only guilty ones. There were thousands in Paris who had marched through the streets, who had destroyed the houses, who were responsible for the murders and who poured insults on the name of the King and his mistress.

They saw him differently now. He was not their innocent Louis. He was to blame. He squandered money on fine buildings and his mistress, while *they* were starving.

No one shouted Long live Louis, Louis *le Bien-aimé*.

They received him in silence which was broken only by one voice, which cried 'Herod!'

Several others took up the cry. They were determined to believe the worst of him. It was a ridiculous story that he should have had children kidnapped so that he, or his mistress, might bathe in their blood. But such was the mood of the people that they were ready to accept this even while he rode among them.

Louis gave no sign that he noticed their indifference. His dignity remained unimpaired. He looked neither to right nor left.

Thus for the first time the King rode unacclaimed through his city of Paris.

Had he been more in tune with his people, had he attempted to explain – even then they would have listened to him.

They were still prepared to say: he is young even yet. Let him dismiss his mistress, let him spend his time governing the people, finding means to alleviate their suffering instead of frittering away time and money on building fine palaces. They were still prepared to make up their differences, to take him back after this coolness, this little quarrel between them and their beloved King. Would he but make the right gesture, would he but assure them that he was ready to be their King, they in their turn would be ready to welcome him back to their esteem, to believe in him, to accept his rule, to continue to serve the Monarchy.

It was for him to say. Two roads stretched out clearly before him. If he followed the one his people asked him to, very soon in the streets they would be shouting again: Long live Louis, Louis the well-beloved.

Louis returned to Versailles.

He was hurt by his reception. 'Herod', they had called him, those sullen, glowering people.

He told the Marquise of his reception.

'I shall never again show myself to the people of Paris, never again shall I go to Paris for pleasure. I will only enter that city when state ceremonies demand it.'

'It will soon be necessary to go through Paris on our way to Compiègne,' she reminded him.

'There should be a road from Versailles to Compiègne which skirts Paris.' Louis paused. 'There *shall* be such a road,' he added.

The King and the Marquise smiled at each other. The prospect of building was always so attractive to them both.

'A road to Compiègne,' cried the King. 'It shall be made immediately.'

And when the new road was made it was lightly referred to by the people of Paris as *La Route de la Révolte*.

Louis had chosen. Never again would the streets of Paris echo with the cry of 'Louis the Well-Beloved'.

❧ Bibliography ❧

Pierre Gaxotte. Translated from the French by J. Lewis May. *Louis the Fifteenth and His Times*.

M. Guizot. Translated by Robert Black, MA. *The History of France*.

Lieut-Colonel Andrew C. P. Haggard, DSO. *The Real Louis the Fifteenth* (2 volumes).

G. P. Gooch. CH, D Litt, FBA. *Louis XV. The Monarchy in Decline*.

Iain D. B. Pilkington. *The King's Pleasure. The Story of Louis XV*.

Ian Dunlop. With a foreword by Sir Arthur Bryant. *Versailles*.

Casimir Stryienski. Translated by H. N. Dickinson. Edited by Fr. Funck-Brentano, with an Introduction by John Edward Courtenay Bodley. *The National History of France. The Eighteenth Century*.

Baron Ferdinand Rothschild, MP. *Personal Characters from French History*.

Lieut-Colonel Andrew C. P. Haggard, DSO. *Women of the Revolutionary Era*.

C. A. Sainte-Beuve. Translated by Katherine P. Wormeley,

with a critical introduction by Edmond Scherer. *Portraits of the Eighteenth Century, Historic and Literary*.

William Henry Hudson. *France*.

Louis Batiffol. Translated by Elsie Finnimore Buckley. *National History of France*.

Catherine Charlotte, Lady Jackson. *Old Paris, its Courts and Literary Salons*.

Louis Adolphe Thiers. Translated with notes by Frederick Shoberl. *The History of the French Revolution*.

An abridgement of Louis Sébastien Mercier's *Le Tableau de Paris*. Translated and edited with a preface and notes by Helen Simpson. *The Waiting City*.

The Road to Compiègne

No longer the well-beloved, Louis is growing ever more unpopular – the war and his mistresses having taken their toll. As the discontent grows, Louis seeks refuge from any unpleasantness in his extravagances and his mistress, the now powerful Marquise de Pompadour. Suspicions, plots and rivalry are rife as Louis's daughters and lovers jostle for his attention and standing at Court. Ignoring the unrest in Paris, Louis continues to indulge in his frivolities but how long will Paris stay silent when the death of the Marquise de Pompadour leads to yet another mistress influencing the King . . .

Flaunting, Extravagant Queen

At the age of fifteen, Marie Antoinette, beautiful and charming bride to the impotent Dauphin, is plunged into the intrigue of Versailles. Frivolous and reckless, she flouts the strict and demanding etiquette of the glittering court, and discovers the true nature of love, hate and jealousy.

But the clouds of revolution are overhead, and Marie Antoinette, who only wishes to enjoy life, learns too late that the price of her enjoyment is very high . . .

arrow books

Madame Serpent

Jean Plaidy

Sullen-eyed and broken-hearted, fourteen-year-old Catherine de' Medici arrives in Marseilles to marry Henry of Orléans, second son of the King of France. On the promise of a dowry fit for a king, Catherine has left her true love in Italy, forced into trading her future for a stake in the French crown.

Amid the glittering fêtes and banquets of the most immoral court in sixteenth-century Europe, the reluctant bride becomes a passionate but unwanted wife. Humiliated and unloved, Catherine spies on Henry and his lover, the infamous Diane de Poitiers. And, tortured by what she sees, Catherine becomes dangerously occuped by a ruthless ambition destined to make her the most despised woman in France: the dream that one day the French crown will be worn by a Medici heir . . .

arrow books

ALSO AVAILABLE IN ARROW: THE MEDICI TRILOGY

The Italian Woman

Jean Plaidy

When Catherine de' Medici was forced to marry Henry of Orleans, hers was not the only heart broken. Jeanne of Navarre once dreamed of marrying this same prince, but, like Catherine, she must comply with King Francis's political needs. And so both Catherine and Jeanne's lives were set on unwanted paths, destined to cross in affairs of state, love and faith, driving them to become deadly political rivals.

Whilst Jeanne is instead married to the dashing but politically inept Antoine de Bourbon, the widowed Catherine continues to be loved by few and feared by many – including her children. But Catherine is now the powerful mother of kings, who will do anything to see her beloved second son, Henry, rule France. As civil war ravages the country and Jeanne fights for the Huguenot cause, Catherine, a fickle Catholic, advances along her unholy road making enemies at every turn . . .

arrow books

ALSO AVAILABLE IN ARROW: THE MEDICI TRILOGY

Queen Jezebel

Jean Plaidy

The ageing Catherine de' Medici has arranged the marriage of her beautiful Catholic daughter, Margot, to the uncouth Huguenot King Henry of Navarre. Margot, still desperately in love with Henry de Guise, refuses to utter her vows. But even Catherine is unable to anticipate the carnage that this unholy union is to bring about . . .

In the midst of an August heatwave, tensions run high between the Catholic Parisians and the Huguenot wedding guests: Margot's marriage to Henry has not resulted in the peace that King Charles longed for. Realising her weakening power over her sickly son, Catherine sets about persuading Charles of a Huguenot plot against his life. Overcome by fear, he agrees to a massacre that will rid France of its 'pestilential Huguenots for ever'. And so the carnival of butchery begins, marking years of terror and upheaval that will end in the demise of kings, and finally expose Catherine's lifetime of depraved scheming . . .

arrow books

ALSO AVAILABLE IN ARROW BY JEAN PLAIDY;
THE PLANTAGENET SERIES

The Plantagenet Prelude

When William X dies, the duchy of Aquitaine is left to his fifteen-year-old daughter, Eleanor. On his deathbed William promised her hand in marriage to the future King of France. Eleanor is determined to rule Aquitaine using her husband's power as King of France and, in the years to follow, she is to become one of history's most scandalous queens.

The Revolt of the Eaglets

Henry Plantagenet bestrode the throne of England like an ageing eagle perching dangerously in the evening of his life. While his sons intrigue against him and each other, Henry's conscience leads him to make foolish political decisions. The old eagle is under constant attack from three of the eaglets he has nurtured, and a fourth waits in the wings for the moment of utter defeat to pluck out his eyes . . .

The Heart of the Lion

At the age of thirty-two, Richard the Lionheart has finally succeeded Henry II to the English throne. Now he must fulfil his vow to his country to win back Jerusalem for the Christian world. Leaving England to begin his crusade, Richard's kingdom is left in the hands of his brother, John, who casts covetous eyes on the crown.

arrow books

Uneasy Lies the Head

Jean Plaidy

In the aftermath of the bloody Wars of the Roses, Henry Tudor
has seized the English crown, finally uniting the warring Houses
of York and Lancaster through his marriage to Elizabeth of York.

But whilst Henry VII rules wisely and justly, he is haunted by
Elizabeth's missing brothers; the infamous two Princes, their fate
in the Tower for ever a shrouded secret. Then tragedy strikes at
the heart of Henry's family, and it is against his own son that the
widowed King must fight for a bride and his throne . . .

arrow books

Katharine, the Virgin Widow

Jean Plaidy

The young Spanish widow, Katharine of Aragon, has become the pawn between two powerful monarchies. After less than a year as the wife of the frail Prince Arthur, the question of whether the marriage was ever consummated will decide both her fate and England's.

But whilst England and Spain dispute her dowry, in the wings awaits her unexpected escape from poverty: Henry, Arthur's younger, more handsome brother – the future King of England. He alone has the power to restore her position, but at what sacrifice?

arrow books

The Shadow of the Pomegranate

Jean Plaidy

Whilst the young King Henry VIII basks in the pageants and games of his glittering court, his doting queen's health and fortunes fade. Henry's affection for his older wife soon strays, and the neglected Katharine decides to use her power as queen to dangerous foreign advantage.

Overseas battles play on Henry's volatile temper, and his defeat in France has changed the good-natured boy Katharine loved into an infamously callous ruler. With no legitimate heir yet born, Katharine once again begins to fear for her future . . .

arrow books

The King's Secret Matter

Jean Plaidy

After twelve years of marriage, the once fortuitous union of Henry VIII and Katherine of Aragon has declined into a loveless stalemate. Their only child, Mary, is disregarded as a suitable heir, and Henry's need for a legitimate son to protect the Tudor throne has turned him into a callous and greatly feared ruler.

When the young and intriguing Anne Boleyn arrives from the French court, Henry is easily captivated by her dark beauty and bold spirit. But his desire to possess the wily girl leads to a deadly struggle of power that promises to tear apart the lives of Katharine and Mary, and forever change England's faith . . .

arrow books

A Blunt Instrument

Ernest Fletcher, a man liked and respected. So when he is found
bludgeoned to death, no one can imagine who would want him
dead. Enter Superintendent Hannasyde, who slowly uncovers the
real Fletcher, anything but a gentleman, and a man with many
enemies. But the case takes a gruesome twist when another
body is found . . .

Behold, Here's Poison

Gregory Matthews, patriarch of the Poplars is found dead. Imperious
Aunt Harriet blames it on the roast duck he ate, but a post-mortem
determines it's a case of murder by poison. Suspicion falls
immediately on his quarrelsome family, and it is up to Hannasyde to
sift through their secrets and lies before the killer strikes again.

Death in the Stocks

When the body of Andrew Vereker is found locked in the stocks on
the village green, Hannasyde soon realises that this may be his
toughest case yet. Vereker was not a popular man, his corrupt
family are uncooperative, and the suspects are many.

They Found Him Dead

The morning after his sixtieth birthday party, Silas Kane is found
dead at the foot of a cliff. The coroner rules death by misadventure,
but when Kane's nephew and heir is found murdered, a new
and sinister case develops for Hannasyde to investigate.

arrow books

Order further titles by Jean Plaidy
from your local bookshop, or have them delivered
direct to your door by Bookpost

☐ Uneasy Lies the Head	9780099492481	£7.99
☐ Katharine, the Virgin Widow	9780099493143	£7.99
☐ The Shadow of the Pomegranate	9780099493150	£7.99
☐ The King's Secret Matter	9780099493167	£7.99
☐ Murder Most Royal	9780099493228	£7.99
☐ Saint Thomas's Eve	9780099493235	£7.99
☐ The Sixth Wife	9780099493242	£7.99
☐ The Thistle and the Rose	9780099493259	£7.99

Free post and packing
Overseas customers allow £2 per paperback

Phone: 01624 677237

Post: Random House Books
c/o Bookpost, PO Box 29, Douglas, Isle of Man IM99 1BQ

Fax: 01624 670923

email: bookshop@enterprise.net

Cheques (payable to Bookpost) and credit cards accepted

Prices and availability subject to change without notice.
Allow 28 days for delivery.
When placing your order, please state if you do not wish to receive any
additional information.